THE
SEVEN
WHO
FLED

by the same author

★

THE ASIATICS, *a novel*

THE ASSASSINS, *poems*

★

FREDERIC PROKOSCH

THE SEVEN WHO FLED

HARPER & BROTHERS PUBLISHERS
NEW YORK AND LONDON
1937

THE SEVEN WHO FLED

Copyright, 1937, by Harper & Brothers
Printed in the United States of America

8/7

FIRST EDITION

G-M

To my father

CONTENTS

*

PROLOGUE

1

Prologue: The Flight from Kashgar

VERY LATE ONE WINDLESS SEPTEMBER NIGHT twenty-two men and a beautiful woman were crossing a dried river bed on the caravan road that led from Kashgar eastward toward Aqsu. Painstakingly the fifteen porters threaded their way between the rocks, guiding the mules and camels with their stained, weather-beaten cases.

The river basin was almost a mile wide. It was as dry as bone: cloudlets of dust sprang into being behind each fresh footprint. Yet there was something deceivingly soft and liquid about the landscape. The shore on both sides was covered with small black pebbles—chips of basalt and obsidian. These caught the starlight and cast forth countless different colors—dark green, dark purple, copper, pearl gray.

Dry as bone, the earth was. The dust crumbled away like ashes—equally warm, though it was long after midnight, and equally insubstantial. The tread of their feet was totally soundless. The only sound at all was the urgent and irregular whisper of their breath and the rustling of the straw-lined cases on the camels' backs.

Finally they reached the other shore. The camels whined irritably as they climbed the slope, the Turki porters whispered furtive curses.

They reached the crest of a small hill. Here, among a few straggling tamarisks, they paused for several minutes. The night was dazzlingly clear. Far away they could discern the edge of the desert: the darker line of poplars, the fluctuating thread of the road, the suggestion of a bluish town nestling among the trees and capturing the starlight on each little roof.

The gravel, as they turned around, now caught the light and glittered like a ripple-laden sea. And far away, the Tian Shan mountains cast up their foam-like shimmer from the horizon.

But as they watched, the mountains appeared to fade away, to grow more and more remote. The reason for this, they knew as soon as they once more turned eastward toward the road, was that the night was drawing to a close. A slender ribbon of gray was fluttering over the dunes in the east.

☆

What had happened was this.

There had recently been, all over Sinkiang, considerable disturbances. General Ma's army had swept bloodthirstily through the desert; the Tungans were still waging a truculent guerrilla warfare against the provincial government; the Soviet government in the north had sent down its agents to Urumchi and Kashgar to support the Governor's forces. The cities, the towns, the tent-sprinkled plains, all rustled with distrust and detestation.

One day the Amban at Kashgar, a timorous, sedentary man, had petulantly issued orders that all Europeans leave the city. Meaning by that, of course, all Europeans whose motives appeared to him uncertain or unfamiliar. The officials made inquiries; the soldiers behaved impudently; the Amban wearily explained that orders from the Governor at Urumchi had to be obeyed. The atmosphere in the city grew hostile, full of glances, full of suspicious little whispers.

And so early one morning seven Europeans gathered at the ill-smelling *serai* outside the poplar-lined walls of the old city and joined a small caravan that was starting eastward on a long journey toward Aqsu, An-hsi-chou, Suchow, and the Hwang-Ho. The caravan had been hired by a wealthy and cultured Chinese fur merchant, Dr. Liu; his eventual destination, he explained, was Lu-chow, in the province of Szechuan. But he would leave them when they reached the Hwang-Ho. From there they planned to go on to Shanghai, by bus or boat or train. It would be a desolate journey. The caravan was small and ill-equipped, the road was thoroughly bleak and hazardous. But there was no time to be lost. Sinkiang's was an ill-tempered climate. There was nothing else to be done,

[5]

and so the flight began, soon after dawn, through the gray morning airs into the desert toward Aqsu.

☆

They were standing in the very middle of Asia. Two thousand miles to the east lay shining the city of Pekin, two thousand miles to the west rose the pebbled shores of the Caucasus. The world, the whole rest of the world, was far, far away. Incalculably far away. For it was not the miles alone that intervened. There were the vastness of the desert, and the incorruptible snow of the ranges, and the swampy, salt-ridden plateaus. And more than that. There were, also, the manifold tribes to whom miles were but beads in an endless chain and to whom time was still as single as the blue dome of the sky; to whom the past intermingled melodiously with the future, and the years were only trivial notes in the subdued and melancholy tune of their eternity.

Miles to the north Sinkiang lay transfixed by the Mountains of Heaven, the Tian Shan, whose peaks, now that the sky was growing gray, were gently emerging from the cloudless horizon. Beyond these, westward, spread the Famine Steppes of the Turkestan, its lost rivers, its secret cities, the land of Tamerlane. And northward, beyond the summits of the Altai which lay cast across Mongolia like a string of pearls, lay Siberia's bleak, incessant slopes. Far, far into the northeast rippled the immensities of the Gobi, and eastward ran the uncountable rivers and hills and groves of China. Southward, the legendary deserts of Sinkiang—still red, so the people believed, with the blood

[6]

spilled by Genghis Khan; beyond these, the plateaus of
Tibet, white and secretive; beyond these, the very pinnacle
of the world, the Himalayas, which sloped still further
southward toward the hot plains of India and the Bay of
Bengal.

☆

Dr. Liu brought out his tin of tea and lit his little lamp.
A pale blue flame, tear-shaped, sprang up, and soon the
kettle was boiling. Layeville, the tall, handsome Englishman, knelt down beside him on the gravel. Dr. Liu turned
toward him and smiled.

"That," and he pointed his thin clawlike fingers toward
the distant group of bluish houses among the trees: the
morning's haze, or perhaps a cloud of smoke, was hanging
over it like a veil: "that is Aqsu." The little blue flame
flickered unsteadily in the pearly darkness. It shed a gentle,
wavering pallor upon Dr. Liu's features as he stooped over,
listening to the bubbling water. Ghostlike he looked to
Layeville, a creature of another world.

"I cannot promise," he added, in his tinkling, delicate,
exact English, "what will happen to us in Aqsu. It is a
lonely place, Aqsu. An outpost, as you say. No one is safe
there, in these days, no one. But," and he smiled, the dry
skin of his face melted into a hundred wrinkles, "we must
hope for the best. . . .

"Tell me," he murmured then, very softly, so that no
one else could hear; his eyes traveled absent-mindedly
across the distant horizon; "tell me, Mr. Layeville, who are
your European friends? Do you know them all? Do you

[7]

know them well? . . . Remember, all of you are strangers
to me." He spoke in a thin sing-song voice. He didn't appear to notice what he was saying, his mind seemed far
away. "Where have they come from? Where are they
going?"

But Layeville couldn't tell him very much. He glanced
at the other six as they scattered about, each one for his
private little matutinal ceremonies.

Serafimov, the Russian, was pouring water over his head
out of a red jar, drop by tentative drop. He looked like a
huge ape, bending over clumsily, his powerful legs spread
apart, the water trickling over his black hair, his beard, his
brown enormous neck, his shaggy arms. Gorilla-like, until
he opened his eyes once more: through those beautiful
pale gray eyes gazed the hesitant and innocent mind of
a child.

"An exile," explained Layeville, nodding in Serafimov's
direction. "A man without a home," he added, half to himself, "looking for a place where he can lose his identity."

"A fugitive from the Soviet?" murmured Dr. Liu.

But Layeville didn't know.

At Serafimov's side the little Belgian, Goupillière, was
kneeling on the ground, holding in his left hand a small
mirror of polished steel, shaving himself with his right.
Graceful and delicate as a cat. He balanced himself perfectly; each movement was sleek and efficient.

"That man," said Dr. Liu, "I find interesting. Look at
him closely. . . ."

Layeville sat and watched Goupillière. Yes, there was
something odd in that face. Ambiguous, yet intense. At
first he could not tell what it was.

Then he knew. It was quite obvious. There were, literally, two sides to the man. The right half of Goupillière's

face was as smooth and fresh as that of a girl, as sly as that of a harlot. But across his left cheek ran a huge scar, from mouth to ear. And this half of his face seemed contracted with a violent intensity, an obsession, a frightful, frightened squint. Layeville found suddenly that the man filled him with disgust. There was something profoundly alienating in the noiseless conflict between those two halves—the ironical and the ferocious, the stealthy and the twisted, the eavesdropper and the avenger.

"He traveled with M. and Mme. de la Scaze," said Dr. Liu, following Layeville's gaze. "That is so, isn't it?"

Layeville nodded.

"A relative? A friend? A cousin, perhaps?"

It couldn't be, thought Layeville, glancing at de la Scaze. Two more different men could hardly be imagined. They stood at opposite poles of experience—the one hungry, the other drugged; the one watchful, furtive, resilient, fiercely alive, and the other meditative, lazy, gentle, unhappy. He was standing quietly, running a green silken handkerchief across his high forehead and over his thinning hair with his right hand, holding his *pince-nez* in his left hand, which he was resting on his hip; gazing into the western distance over which the last uncertainties of the night were still hovering. His eyes were inflamed with weariness—or was it, wondered Layeville, something other than weariness? He seemed to tremble as he stood there silently; his pallid, over-sensitive face looked unnaturally flushed. The face of an agèd child, thought Layeville, a child reared among old women and shadows, with the thin silky hair hanging into his forehead, the eyes so dreamy, so passive, so estrangingly vulnerable.

"A very rich man," murmured Dr. Liu. "He moves to and fro across the world out of pure boredom. . . . Yes, I

[9]

have known others like him. The last of the real Europeans. They have no home." He turned down the flame and lifted the cover from the kettle. The steam came spiraling forth like a ghostly flower.

"And his wife, Mme. de la Scaze," he continued, reflectively, as he poured the steaming water into little tin cups, "she is a Spanish lady, I believe? Very beautiful," he said in a high, thin sing-song voice, wearily raising his wrinkled eyelids again. His voice was like a little frayed ribbon fluttering pointlessly in the air. Everything he said, even the most trivial phrase, created the curious double effect of complete naturalness and complete artificiality. "Very beautiful. . . . You agree?"

Yes, she was beautiful, thought Layeville, there was no doubting it. Much younger, surely, than her husband, hardly more than twenty. She was sitting quietly in the shade of a tamarisk, eyes half-closed, quite motionless, her two hands symmetrically clasped behind her black, shining head. Her face was olive-skinned, and yet seemed luminous, almost transparent. Her lips were parted; now and again she ran her tongue across them quickly. Long black lashes shaded her black eyes. Wholly sensuous, thought Layeville; there was a deep electrical nervousness behind that calm; a mystifying, feminine mingling of intensity and resignation. Something was lying in wait there. She was waiting for life to open out, she was still half-asleep.

He saw Dr. Liu glancing from her to her husband, and back again, his eyebrows moving ever so faintly. Yes. It was true. Utterly, hopelessly apart. A wall of glass seemed to rise between them.

At that moment the two young ones—the German and the Austrian, Wildenbruch and von Wald—came running back up the hill. Simultaneously the sunlight at last leapt

[10]

through the thinning clouds, and fell on the Austrian's blond curls as he paused for a moment to tie his boots. The whole landscape seemed to flash with light at that moment, it seemed to Layeville—so glowing, so alive were the posture and color of von Wald's young body. He was smiling with delight. He ran his big sunburnt hand through his golden hair and then over his chin where the first strands of a blond beard were beginning to show. His lips were parted, his blue eyes were sparkling with eagerness and joy. There was nothing subtle or inverted there; his heart was still a mirror, pure and simple.

They were members, these two, of a German geological expedition sent to Sinkiang a year ago, and like the others they had happened to be caught in Kashgar at an inopportune moment. All this Dr. Liu explained in his thin, weary voice.

"But it is the other one," he added, with an intelligent little smile, "who will be the great man, I think. The powerful man, the dangerous, modern man. . . ." He bent over and sipped at his tea, fastidious and cat-like.

Layeville glanced at Wildenbruch. He was walking along stiffly and without a word, swinging his arms to and fro in a regular rhythm. Very spruce, he looked, very military. His hair was clipped off his thin, pointed head. He looked as brown as an Indian, as hard as steel. There was no trace of a smile on those ascetic lips, no spark of gaiety in that gray, knife-like gaze. He seemed to see nothing as he walked along, nothing except some potent, thrilling, relentless vision in his own heart.

Layeville turned, and caught Dr. Liu's glance. He blushed. He had begun to like Dr. Liu. Indeed, he felt more at ease with him than with any of the others. And yet, he could not quite bring himself to trust him.

[11]

"And you?" said Dr. Liu, with a quizzical smile. "You are an explorer, I understand. But why are you here? Here in desolate Sinkiang?" He paused for a moment, and scratched his left ear thoughtfully. "Exile? Fear? Exhaustion? Languor? Adventurousness? Ambition?" He nodded at each of the other six in turn. "Any of those?"

Layeville lowered his eyes. He stared at his long thin legs, his shabby canvas shorts, the white cap beside him, his slim musical hands. Suddenly he perceived his body as something apart. A pale, slender island in the sea of humanity. A snow-flecked island surrounded by winds, an inaccessible and solitary island in an endless sea.

He raised his eyes and looked toward the peaks in the distance. The snow had now captured the rising sunlight. Beautiful it looked, pure, icy, incorruptible. The end of all things; all things ended there.

"No," he murmured, half to himself, "none of those."

☆

As they approached Aqsu, toward noon, they saw that something was wrong. The whole town seemed to be wrapped in dust; even from a distance they could see the white flicker of shapes scurrying to and fro.

Then, as they entered the town, three wolf-faced Turkis on horseback rode up to them. For a moment they stared sullenly at the party of Europeans. Then they began muttering to Dr. Liu.

He spoke to them calmly for several minutes, and then turned to the rest and said, in English:

"They have received orders to accompany us into Aqsu."

[12]

He nodded to the Frenchman and the little Belgian and repeated the words in a halting French.

So they followed the horsemen into the town. There they discovered what was wrong. At the very moment, apparently, that they themselves had been drinking their morning tea, a band of Tungans had swept through the blue, dawn-lit streets. They had looted the shops, broken the windows, set fire to three of the houses, and had murdered half a dozen men.

They had left again shortly after sunrise, but the town was still in an uproar. Mohammedans, tall stooping figures in colorful robes, hastened through the streets with apprehensive glances; others stood gesticulating in the poplar-shadowed courtyard of the *serai*. The women stood huddled with lowered eyes and veiled faces in the mulberry grove, among whose branches, now dappled with the ruddy hues of autumn, the doves were cooing and fluttering in sympathetic distress. There was a constant whimpering noise in the streets, a constant rustling and fluttering of garments—all of it quite subdued, rather plaintive, oddly pointless. Frightened beggars and lumbering tribesmen in black skullcaps and shaggy blue coats were moving about in the sweltering square. Their eyes, as the strangers passed, looked furtive and hostile.

The Europeans were led to the *serai*. There they waited for three days.

On the evening of the second day the Frenchman, de la Scaze, began to tremble and sweat with fever.

★

In the early afternoon of the third day at the *serai* a messenger arrived. He talked to Dr. Liu for an hour, casting covert glances toward the rest of the company now and again, looking carefully at all their papers.

Finally Dr. Liu explained. The two young geologists, he murmured, sadly, were under arrest. They would have to proceed to the prison with the guards. It would, of course, be only temporary, he explained. Two or three days, a week at the most.

Furthermore, two others would have to stay here in Aqsu as hostages. Temporarily, at least. The rest would be allowed to proceed toward An-hsi-chou and Kansu. He glanced solicitously at de la Scaze, red and prostrate at the other end of the room.

"Very sick," he murmured. "Very sick, poor man . . ."

☆

And so, on the following morning Wildenbruch and von Wald bade them all farewell. They looked quite calm; von Wald, in fact, was smiling. The prison was a shabby little building only a stone's-throw down the street from the *serai*. Layeville waved his hand after them, and they waved back, Wildenbruch stiffly and von Wald almost gaily, as they entered the dark, squatting doorway.

According to their original plans, de la Scaze and his wife were to accompany Dr. Liu and his caravan into China. But now it became clear that de la Scaze was too sick to undertake the journey. His face was dark as a plum, his *pince-nez* was clouded with sweat.

"Very sick," murmured Dr. Liu, regretfully. "He will

[14]

have to remain in Aqsu. He must recover before he can travel safely. There is nothing else to do. He can follow us in a week or two, when he is well again."

He accordingly made arrangements that de la Scaze be taken to a small private inn in the middle of the city, where he could have a room of his own, until he recovered.

The huge Russian and the little Belgian were chosen to stay on in the *serai* as "hostages." Serafimov didn't care; he was quite sleepy and indifferent; nothing seemed to matter to him. He lay down in a dark corner of the *serai* and instantly began to snore. And Goupillière, too, seemed quite willing to stay. He would wait here, he explained in a thin, officious voice, until de la Scaze had recovered. And, sooner or later, they would manage somehow to follow the others to Shanghai.

☆

At noon Dr. Liu's caravan departed from Aqsu. It pointed eastward into the desert, and with it went Layeville and Mme. de la Scaze.

It was a hot day. Dark clouds were hanging over the horizon: northward, southward, eastward, westward. But overhead the sky was cloudless, the air glistened like a diamond, as the caravan marched slowly into the empty land.

[15]

BOOK ONE

Layeville

2

Desert

FOR A WEEK THEY TRAVELED THROUGH GENTLE COUN-
try which charmed Layeville: undulating plains,
poplar-sprinkled regions, meadows of iris and yellow
roses, barley-fields, willow-edged streams. In the villages
the boys would greet them with melons, apricots, pears,
peaches, and little colored bundles of Turkestan tea.

There were seventeen camels in Dr. Liu's caravan. They
were patient and well-behaved until they reached the bad
lands. Then, for several days, they were plaintive and irritable. They screamed and spat and flung their legs about
on the slightest provocation. Finally they grew calm and
submissive again.

Then came a great plateau, and for a day or two they

followed the tracks to the northeast. They passed two or three wretched mud villages and a few straggling farms. Then they met the desert again.

The ground was soft here. The camels sank deep into the ground at every step. The sand turned into clay, and finally into gravel and rocks. They passed a forest of dead trees, and a ruined monastery, and a spectacular black gorge. The mornings now were blue and icy, but the air at midday was sweltering.

And presently the real desert began. Even peace, and even solitude itself, couldn't manage to survive in this landscape. Peace and solitude were in a sense human qualities, after all; impossible for them to exist above the blinding heat of the gravel, the blinding glare from the pebbles. Heat slid up from below and flowed down from above, twining itself about each weary arm, each aching forehead, each burning eye, like a vegetable, a great itching mossy tangle.

The camels began to lose huge tufts of hair as it grew steadily hotter. They developed sores for no evident reason, and thin black rivulets of blood ran down their sides. It was frightening to touch them: their bellies were hot as frying-pans. Their bells had been hushed for fear of attracting marauders; and they moved through the stifling silence like ghosts, with abject bloodshot eyes.

This heat was unnatural, observed Dr. Liu, irritably. There was no reason for it, the great heat should have been over at least a fortnight ago. Mme. de la Scaze had grown faint in the sun, and was now carried in an improvised litter. Oddly elegant and wicked she looked, lying there unsmiling, little sparks of irritation in her black eyes and a pout of disdain on her lips. She disliked him, Layeville was sure of that. And he disliked her too. Women had

always held little attraction for him. And it was the watchful, patient, female quality in her that estranged him.

Once there was a vicious little storm which stirred the
hot air into a frenzy. The sky grew black, but not a single
drop of rain fell. It passed quickly, only a whimsical dark
tumult in this enormous glaring sea.

They passed a red ruin on a hill: "A deserted robber
castle," said Dr. Liu. Skeletons of dogs lay all around it,
inscribing in their delicate hieroglyphics some degraded
and violent tale upon the sand.

Then came a region of huge boulders: porphyry, basalt,
iridescent blue rocks worn smooth as glass. Dazzlingly
beautiful this was, and surely the most desolate land in the
world. And then downhill again into a valley which had
once been a lake, centuries ago. Huge cracks rippled across
the earth. There were long strips of gravel as white as
snow, then mud as black as a cistern, and shimmering
crystalline ridges. And beyond these, a dry river bed full
of posturing stones molded by the sky and the prehistoric
torrents.

Very gently, after this, glimmered the wonder of an
oasis. The green streamlet flowing from nowhere, the tall
poplars, *populus euphratica,* the cool gorge, the hares, the
antelopes, the birds; and even a wolf, it seemed—a quick
gray shape disappearing in the darkening ravine. And at
the top, overlooking the greenery, a small broken temple.
"A refuge for robbers," said Dr. Liu, with a wistful pride,
as he stooped to wash his forehead at the singing brook.

The night was spent in the coolness of the gorge. The
stars peered through the foliage—ah, the very same stars,
reflected Layeville for the fiftieth time, that had glanced
and would presumably again glance down on Kew Gardens, on Savernake Forest, on King's Chapel, on all the

familiar spires, towers, gardens, bridges, and castellations which now seemed objects of another world, a lovable jewel of a world!

☆

But the soft rustling of the leaves, the whisper of the running water, and the cool green air gliding across their hot brows and hot bodies, all were forgotten the next day. The heat grew worse and worse and the landscape looked really cadaverous—a gigantic corpse with only a few teeth left in the skull, and a few desperate hairs curling above the bits of flesh.

They passed some ruins. A dead town. "Dead five thousand years!" said one of the porters. And then a dead forest. Trees that had been leafless for decades, all still standing desperately like cripples.

One of the porters, a bright old buffoon named Izakh, was bitten in the palm of the hand by a yellow scorpion. He groaned and gesticulated all day long; it seemed that he must be acting. But in the evening the hand was as large as a melon, soft and red.

At nightfall they met another caravan, Turkis from the north. They pitched camp beside Layeville's, and lay on their sheepskins, huge stupid grinning men, lecherous and filthy as bears, playing their whining indecisive flutes beside the fire in honor of the beautiful Spanish lady until the rest had fallen asleep.

The youngest of the porters, a slender, very dark boy from Maralbashi named Asis, told Layeville a bandit story.

[22]

He spoke a slow and halting Hindustani, and this gave to
the tale a queer deliberate tenderness—as if each murder
were a gentle act of love. His black eyes shone.

"We were going toward An-hsi then also. . . . It was
midnight, but two of us were still awake. We heard a noise
coming down from the hills. Horses!" His voice grew tense
and whispering. His eyes sparkled. "The men had old
Berdane rifles. All of us were killed, except one old lama
and four strong young men. The camels were taken away
and sold later. The lama was left to go where he pleased.
We four were driven to the fortress. We had to work, drag
stones, build walls. It was very hot and we had nothing to
eat except the flesh of the dead horses and of rats." His
voice had grown very casual and offhand. "One of us went
mad and cried all day long; he grew afraid of stones, of
food, even of water! He thought that everything was alive
—the stones, the food, and even the water. He died. Another died from torture." His voice was very suave now
and his eyes were soft as velvet. "We two fled. We met a
caravan near An-hsi. So I am still alive. But my friend died
in An-hsi, and I buried him on a hill, with the sad tears of
true friendship!"

Suddenly he smiled at Layeville, rather mischievously.
"It will happen to you too, perhaps! Perhaps they will kill
you too! You must not be surprised at anything, anything.
Remember, I have warned you!" His eyes twinkled, careless and amused. "You look so earnest, Sir Lord! No, no,
do not be afraid!"

★

Nor was he, really, afraid. It was something else that he felt, a kind of foreboding not connected with physical fear. Now and then he felt suddenly convinced that this would be his very last journey. And for that reason the passing miles, the passing days, the torrid passing landscapes, developed a quality of both abstraction and terrific concentration. For years life had been for him a sort of desiccated thing; a passionless, yellowish, perfunctory sort of thing. Now it was growing real again, day by thrilling day. Even when he lay dizzy and haggard with heat, he felt this accumulating thrill in his heart.

As for the heat, the next day was the worst of all. The stones were so hot, they looked as if they must burst and bleed away into the suffocating heat that surrounded each object like a bandage.

One thing was very strange. The sunlight was so fierce that the sky by contrast seemed almost black. The heat appeared to be flashing across an incandescent night. The land too looked black, gilded only by this vast flaming ball. And when night did arrive it was soft and silvery by contrast, and the landscape appeared actually to grow light; the stones, the hills, the sleeping camels gleamed in a tranquil, inverted dawn.

At one point a violent wind arose, but instead of cooling them it only hammered the heat more deeply into their bodies. Sweat seeped through everything till no moisture at all seemed to be left in their limbs. Their faces grew almost black with this wind, their eyes seemed to be driven inward and buried deep in the brain. Spasms of dizziness and intolerable itchings seized them, the younger ones particularly. All desire of any kind left the body, the skin grew limp, the blood hung heavy, and the intimate touch of another body seemed intolerable indeed.

Little green sores budded forth all over Layeville's arms, belly, thighs. For hours his skin felt as if it were aflame. He longed to tear off his clothes and claw at these moist burning crevices. But he derived a certain feeling of power, almost of ease, from controlling himself. This feeling remained with him. He realized with surprise, once or twice, that he was better off than the rest. Now and then he even felt an odd little wave of delight flowing over him. Delight with his own endurance, his power.

The trail led once more through the rocks of a river bed. For a mile or so a little black stream, slender and vicious as a cobra, crept amongst the discolored stones. The camels refused to drink from it. It smelled like a dead thing, or a dying one. After about a mile it darted under a rock and disappeared forever.

Toward evening the world began to resemble a star; spent, lifeless, purposeless. Nature lay there in front of them, quite hideous and exposed, all of her pointlessness and boundlessness at last unmistakably obvious. Any heat, any cold, any sort of sterile frightfulness seemed possible here. There existed no sort of mitigation.

The men that day became effigies, horrible dolls. Dr. Liu as well as Mme. de la Scaze rode all day beneath curtains, in a kind of impromptu howdah. The porters covered their heads and faces. They moved like dolls, as if their dark limbs were half unhinged. Their eyes peered through toward the east, embers half-dead glowing underneath the aching purple eyelids. They didn't speak. There was no motion, no gesture except the monotonous trudging, the swaying back and forth on the camel's backs, the limp and weary swaying of dark arms.

An empty world. No more hills, no insect, no life at all,

not even any colors now, no shapes except the accidental curves of the centuries, no sound, no smell. The utter desert this was indeed, far more lonely than a sea of pure sand, just as a limitless bog is more lonely than the Pacific. A yellow naked body, grotesque and charred; yet possessing, cuppled in its hollows, the unspeakable years; on intimate terms with the sun and nothing but the sun, giving its shrunken secrecies daily to the sun, smelling of nothing at all except the sun, each stone palpably adoring the sun and indifferent to everything except the sun.

Desert: a feeling for which no word could exist. Sensations were nameless, energy was uprooted. The land was measurable, yes: but it might as well have been boundless, and as far as the spirit could encompass it, it was indeed boundless! No mind, reflected Layeville, could stand it here except those who, like plants and animals cast into the wilderness, had thrust aside all recollections of home, of human faces and habits, and had at last grown totally new senses and new ways, having intuitively likened themselves to their scenery.

But the others felt fear. Layeville saw that day how a certain specialized sort of fear tore at them constantly. Fear of each passing mound, each curiously shaped rock, and most of all, of course, the sun. During that one day their faces grew hollow, hateful, really evil. Once there was almost a fight between two young porters who were inseparable friends. One man moaned all day. Another tried to flee. One night he was gone, but the next morning back again.

"Where do you wish to go?" asked Dr. Liu, wearily. But the poor wretch didn't know, of course.

And they all grew anxious lest they should be attacked, now that they were approaching An-hsi and the southern edge of the Gobi. They were shuddering with nervousness as dusk approached.

☆

The night was almost unendurable. They slept in a tiny oasis—a cluster of trees surrounding a pool no larger than a billiard-table. The porters threw off their clothes and lay down at the very edge of the water. They didn't move at first, for each tiniest gesture was of course exhausting. Layeville heard them breathing all night long, saw and smelled their brown bodies shining in the moonlight, could almost feel the slow and tedious rhythm of their blood. As the night wore on they grew restless, began to writhe gently and to reach incessantly into the foul water in order to cool their temples, their necks, their thighs. Then too they began to think of one another, so extreme and incalculable is human nature at these moments; but their urgent, necessary gestures were those of pain and terror really, not at all of love.

Layeville looked through the trunks toward the moon. The familiar moon. Only its face now seemed, instead of silvery and serene, full of an imbecilic torpor, staring down on this territory so immensely loathsome and majestic.

In the middle of the night he began to hear strange muffled sounds. It was as if a caravan were passing by. The hushed tinkle of little bells, the padded and rhythmical footfalls, the panting and murmuring, now distinct, now vague.

"Yes, we all hear those sounds," explained Dr. Liu in the morning. "We think we hear ghosts passing by, their prayers, incantations, ecstasies, and so on. I have heard men say that these are the sounds of the lonely ones who are doomed to an eternal existence without hope, unable to leave this world.

"But of course," he added wearily, "it is only the sound of our beating blood. Fancies created by the desert heat. Don't let them disturb you!"

3

An-hsi-chou

ON THE FOLLOWING AFTERNOON THEY ARRIVED AT
An-hsi-chou. Here they stayed two weeks and
waited for a caravan to arrive from Siningfu.
The great heat had ceased and the nights grew cooler--
each night, Layeville observed, a bit cooler than the one
before. Winter was still far away, but suddenly they were
reminded that the cold was slowly approaching. And also
that of the two enemies, heat and cold, the second was,
after all, the more dangerous.

*

Layeville would sit under the mulberry trees with Asis and watch the villagers. Asis would explain to him what the villagers were gossiping about. This calm, lonely bit of life in the middle of the wilderness gave rise to odd characters. There was the one who polished stones all day long, setting them out in rows in the sun so that they glittered like jewels. One stood by the pool, molding jars out of black clay. One squatted in the middle of the square, watching the sky all day long.

"He is mad," they explained; "he is watching the sky for omens."

"Good omens or bad omens?"

They smiled shyly.

"All omens are bad omens in this city!"

There were the girls, quite as strong and slender and carefree as the boys, collecting fuel and baking cakes. Lovely they looked, their arms raised as they carried the black loaves on their heads, their flawless, tremorous breasts drawn upward, the down in their armpits shining. Others were dyeing garments for an approaching festival, still others were painting on silk or on red earthenware.

The men, as always, were more variable and appeared more lonely and distracted than the women. Many of them seemed a little bit mad. Each one had something special about him, held in defiant and agonizing possession a quality of his own as if it were a treasure to be watched and eternally defended. Being totally unexceptional, thought Layeville, might all in all be a quality as rare as perfection of face, and perhaps a quality equally desolate and solitary.

One was strong; he was stripped to the waist, and the muscles of his chest stood out and shimmered metallically, like a coat of mail, but he did nothing all day long. One was chronically industrious and carried great sacks of barley in from the fields from dawn until dusk; he was the ugliest of all, and the happiest. One was proud and vain. He wore fine embroidered boots, smiled to himself, closed his thin eyes. He appeared to be wholly contemptible, but, hinted the villagers, "He is cruel and brave."

Others had gotten into strange ways. One was pious, prayed all day to the distant Nan Shan mountains until his devout eyes grew so vague that they seemed forever to be fastened on invisible and thoroughly fruitless territories. One was very stupid but full of love, and lay on the grass all afternoon in the shade of the dripping trees. One was building a pyramid of stones a mile outside the village. It was "an altar to the black spirits," and whenever he returned to the village he looked very light-hearted and relieved. He had suffered a great deal, they said: his three strong sons had died of the plague and no one was left in the world to love him, welcome him, or comfort him.

One was inordinately wise, so they said. He smiled as he listened to them gossiping, but never uttered a word himself. He was the laziest of all, and his face resembled that of a turtle. Another was obsessed by fear. He was building a new house, and was constantly reminding his neighbors of unsuspected dangers. He was detested by all of them. Another was extravagantly handsome; he was the coquette; he had learned that people thought of him as beautiful, and though he scorned them all and longed for the wealth and the exciting promiscuities of distant cities, still he could not resist flirting with everyone in the village, old or young. He was very spoiled, and a lonely future lay in store for him. Everyone hated him, but they all coveted his sparkling smile, and he more than suspected that all that most people really long for in their heart of hearts, is

[31]

the unattainable and fleeting glow of personal beauty. He was very stupid by nature, but that one instinct gave him an odd womanly wisdom.

They looked to Layeville like uncovered caricatures of the men he had known in the past. Odd influences were at work here, hidden, hypnotic. Men still believed in demons, for example, and incarnations. Nothing definite existed. Physical truths signified nothing at all in these enormous landscapes. A tale told in one village one day became another thing in the next village, five days away. There was no way of proving anything, nothing was definite, not even the quantities of time or place, and men existed by belief, fear, and prayer. They became, not unnaturally, impetuous and cruel. But in watching them, Layeville could see faintly yet unmistakably how much remained that was primitive, cruel, tribal, and forever unfathomable in even the most civilized men in the most civilized places, as he remembered them. He could detect in their European past likewise the idolatrous silks rippling in the wind, so to speak, the lizards on the ground, the expectant vultures, the skulls of camels, the remembrance of beautiful places, and beyond these the terrible and dangerous desolation full of yellow reeds and ancient principalities: objects and areas to be regarded with superstition, suspicion, fright. They were still nomads, survivals of prehistoric unrest and despair. They still could endure suffering by entering the realms of unreality; they still sought inspiration in chants, prophecies, and recollections of remote ancestors; they still were governed by migrations, by the stars, the moon, rain, and sunlight, by a love of death, and by the words of very old men. Each went his own way, according to what he most vividly remembered out of his own past: a voice, a caress, a fireside tale, a terrifying vision at noonday. A million different paths, all of them deeply touching and indeed full of a certain stylized beauty if contemplated from afar, like the figures in an elaborate ritual dance. To what sort of relief they led in the end there was of course no telling. But the thing that was notable was that they very obviously, though ever so calmly, ever so stealthily, all led away from the same thing, the tugging anguish of fear and futility. There was not one, however wise or idiotic, sulky or gay, of whom this was not plainly true. And it made them all appear at certain moments both fearful and singularly lovable.

Layeville felt profoundly thrilled as he watched these lonely people. Closer, closer to reality! Closer to the real secret that awaited him, he now felt sure, at the end of his journey.

4

The Black Rocks

AFTER THEY LEFT AN-HSI THE LAND CHANGED. SOON they came to the edge of the vast desert. For a day they traveled through resplendent valleys, past streams deep in their flowering banks, past radiant swamps and the tall sword grasses, regions filled with birds. Gulls, turpans, geese, herons, and the big grebes, *columbus cristatus*: the men would shoot them down at twilight and roast them beside the water. One place was full of hares, thousands of them. But their flesh was coarse and bitter.

The world seemed suddenly to have grown alive again. Asis climbed a tree and cried out that he could see the white peaks of the Nan Shan far off. The water in the streams was growing cooler, the nights were suddenly brisk,

and early one morning they were surprised to find a thin
sheet of ice in the water-bucket.

✩

Layeville grew more familiar with the porters, little by
little. They told him about themselves, their quarrels,
their escapades, their jokes, their tastes in love. He saw
with pleasure that they liked him; and he began to like
them too, they were so gay and simple. They enjoyed
squatting beside him after they had been eating and drinking at night. They would argue loudly and call each other
names, playfully. They particularly tried to amaze and
shock him, and would peer slyly at him from time to time
with a knowing grimace. They all spoke Hindustani, so
that he could understand.

"Asis, you scoundrel," one of them would say in a whining tone. "Asis is contemptuous. Oh, Asis, why are you so
contemptuous! Oh, oh!" He began to wail grotesquely.
"He thinks I'm a drunkard and a fool. Don't you, Asis?"
He leered like an old fox. He had a huge wart over his left
eye, which had the effect of giving a rather ferocious and
nonsensical air to everything he said. He seemed to realize
this, and played up to it gaily.

"No, Ibrahim." Asis sounded deeply hurt.

"You don't? Very well, then be kind to me. Say that you
forgive me."

"I do not forgive you, Ibrahim, nor indeed shall I ever!"

"Oh, Asis! Why not?"

"You are worse than a drunkard and a fool. You know
what you are. You are a ———"

But Ibrahim interrupted him with a cry of pretended dismay. "Oh, Asis, you cruel man! How can you be so cruel?" And they would all roar with laughter.

"Asis," he went on, in a high, disconsolate voice, "you are a most intolerant man. Salik, you must stop being kind to Asis; he is a cruel and cold-hearted man. Everyone must stop loving Asis until he has repented!"

"Stop saying such unkind things about Asis, Ibrahim," said an older one with sly and melancholy eyes. "Those are untrue and unloving words." Tears shone in his eyes, but they were tears of laughter and delight. "Come now, Ibrahim. Kiss Asis and forgive him. For shame! This is no time for quarreling!" And everyone howled with laughter all over again.

They were strong men, flexible and full of patience. They would sit in the cold evening wind, stripped to the waist, and gathered around the dung fire; forever happy except in times of real physical suffering—thirst or cold or fever. Their coarse masculine features never betrayed self-doubt or frustration. They thought of nothing. Nothing within themselves disturbed them, not a thing. Life for them was a tangible and simple affair—for most of them, at any rate.

There were Asis, the favorite of them all, and jolly Ibrahim, the old fox. These two were friends and were forever teasing each other and laughing together. Then there was Salik, the lazy one. There was a mystifying look in his big almond eyes, his high cheek bones, and his soft childish lips. He seemed very preoccupied and gentle, as if the burden of the world were on his small shoulders. He seemed to be the only virtuous one of the lot, if one could judge from appearance and deportment. But there was something odd about his brooding gaze, his shy modesty. One day Layeville asked Asis about him.

"Salik is a dangerous man," replied Asis, with unexpected precision. "He is a murderer. He has murdered three men."

Layeville was puzzled. "Why did he murder them? For money?"

Asis appeared not to understand. "Why? Because he is a murderer! That is the reason. A murderer," he repeated like a parent explaining a simple but very fundamental point to a backward child, "not a robber. A dangerous man, Sir Lord!"

Then there was Adilakesh, the old cynic, who came from Urumchi. He had great sores on his temples, being diseased like all the rest of them, and little beady eyes like a chipmunk's, rather surprised and timid. He had developed with the years various dingy habits of which nothing could cure him; he would merely look bewildered when they scolded or whipped him. "I am a wretched man," he would say, weakly. "I am contemptible, but I assure you it is because I have suffered too much." Or: "I am a very weak man. I cannot bear much. My body has grown frail and rebellious." Or again: "I am an untrustworthy and wicked man. O Allah, forgive this man who deserves nothing but scorn!" The men ended by laughing at him or ignoring him. He was like one of those tiresome beetles that give off a certain disconcerting odor when they are crushed. Punishing him for his nasty ways merely produced an additional whiff of squalor and furtiveness.

And then there was Akhejon, a Turki from Khotan, a great smiling fellow, but a real knave. And yet, full of charm and affection. He was still young, with only a bit of a beard, and huge black eyes glittering out of an unfor-

[37]

gettable face. He was the one of whom Layeville was fond-est. He loved to tell bloodthirsty tales—of how his sister was roasted to death over a camp fire because she had be-trayed a secret to the Russians; or how a notorious robber and his two sons were boiled to death in a caldron of oil on the road to Yarkand. Many of his stories had to do with boiling and burning. But most of all he loved to tell about himself. "Oh yes," he would say, rather insolently, eyes sparkling with boastfulness and pleasure, "I remem-ber . . ." And off he would go.

He told about a snowy evening in the north, when he and a young friend had been trapped in a ravine by a pack of wolves. "I could see their teeth flashing and their eyes shining through the falling snow. I knew they would at-tack us at sunset." So he tore off a great branch from a birch tree and with that desperately beat his way through them. His cowardly young friend stayed behind and was devoured shortly after sunset, limb by limb.

Once he had been imprisoned—for something very trivial, he explained, apologetically, for killing his sweet-heart's husband in a brawl. The prison was a wooden shack built on a wall and overhanging the river. "The place was full of rats. They would nibble at my ears and my toes when I lay asleep. Finally I could stand it no longer. So I plunged head first down into the river far below. It is a miracle that I am still alive!" But that wasn't the end of the tale. As he was swimming across to the other shore, four men were sent after him in a boat. Closer and closer they came, crying angrily and flourishing their rifles in a very threatening manner. They were about to seize him when, in a moment of incomparable brilliance and forti-tude, he dove under the boat and by an amazing maneuvre

contrived to upset it. Then, one after the other, he over-
powered his spluttering pursuers, seized them and dragged
them underwater until they were unconscious.

"Unconscious, that is, or dead. But I couldn't wait to
make sure. I was very tired, you see," he added, sadly and
rather reproachfully. "A man can do only so much. There
are limits to every man's strength. . . ."

☆

Once they passed a dead village. The walls had been
burned, the roofs had fallen in long, long ago. The only
creatures here were the scorpions who were lurking in the
dark crevices. A little temple was still standing, but the
old clay Buddhas within its walls had fallen apart; one of
them had been cruelly decapitated. All this had happened
years, perhaps decades, ago. But the hostility and hatred
were still visible there, the very last touches of humanity
to survive.

And once, at dusk, they passed a group of huts, still
standing, yet similarly lifeless. Lifeless, however, in a more
frightening, more modern, way. Dr. Liu explained that
these were no doubt the traces of General Ma's recent
march across the desert. A number of dead bodies were
lying about, two or three of them soldiers, the rest of them
villagers. One was squatting over his oven with his throat
torn open, one lay sprawled across a threshold, one sat
hidden in a corner. It was quite horrible, for they were
almost skeletons now, but not quite. Their clothes looked
queerly worn and filthy, mere ghostly rags. They still
looked just human enough, these raggedy shapes, to look

also a bit unhappy: not tragic, somehow, but simply, in a terribly touching and unforgettable way, unhappy.

☆

Now the hills began. Very gently at first, mere wavelets in the ocean. But beyond these were the red hills, strange and beautiful in the clear glow of twilight that lapped against them like the rippling of water against the shore. And beyond these, still harmless and remote, the actual ranges. It was these last that made Layeville's heart beat more quickly. The mountains! The infinite white mountains! Still far, far away, they were.

The porters grew less carefree and sketchy in their ways. The hours at noon were still glaringly hot, while the nights were growing colder and colder. But it was neither the cold nor the heat that really embarrassed them. It was the shimmering landscape that lay ahead. And the dreamlike ripple of white that rose still beyond.

"It is really too late for this route," they would mutter. "If we hadn't waited in An-hsi it would not be too late. But we waited two weeks. Two whole weeks. Two weeks is a long time when one is racing against the snow and ice."

Hour by hour the past ebbed away. Once or twice Layeville thought of the other five they had left behind in Aqsu; the fever-stricken de la Scaze, and the two young geologists, Wildenbruch and von Wald; and the furtive little Belgian, and the huge imponderable Russian. He asked Dr. Liu what he thought would happen to them. Dr.

[40]

Liu looked very vague. "One must not look too carefully into the future," he observed.

And presently he forgot about them.

☆

The land now became quite desolate again. First came an area of black waste. The multifoliate basalt crystals glimmered in the sunlight, and new and lovely colors— violet, red, gold, silver—flashed forth from the black. Feathery black mirages pirouetted across the horizon— strange vegetations of black and gold, golden cities, black seas.

Then came the cliffs. Up they rose from the stony slopes, fortresses, cathedrals, castles. And further on, the obscene shapes of stone, incredibly convincing and revolting. Even Asis thought them unpleasant, and refused to joke about them.

In this valley the heat once more became intense. But it wasn't the pure heat of the desert. It was a cloistered and sickening heaviness of the air, breath issuing from the mouth of a sick land. The camels cried with distress as they climbed the fœtid, swollen slopes; their eyes became dull again, the sores and swellings reappeared, the odors of disease hung about them, and their progress became funereally slow and cheerless.

There was actually something vicious in the air, it seemed to Layeville. For the men as well as the camels developed curious disorders. Each sudden gesture created pain, and the skin grew dry and inflamed. They all were insanely thirsty, of course. Their eyes grew hollow as before, but breath came more heavily, and Layeville knew that he would be sick if they didn't find water soon.

He rode up to Dr. Liu's litter. Dr. Liu was looking very badly. His face was green, literally green, with an unsavory, fungoid sort of moisture, a sort of slime, shimmering upon his skin. His eyes were tiny, feeble things, hiding behind a grayish veil.

"How much further is the well?" asked Layeville.

"An hour," replied Dr. Liu in a thin gray voice, but with evident conviction.

But they went on for two hours, three hours. And when they reached it it was dry! Layeville lay down beside it and closed his eyes with weariness and distress.

"Only one hour to the next one," announced Ibrahim, bravely.

So on they went, muttering and praying for water, watching the little ridge beyond which lay fresh air, real soil, and real water.

They crept along a deep gully that led through to the next valley. The black basalt cliffs rose straight up on either side. The sky above was scarcely visible, and what they still could see through the silent leaves was yellow, not blue. Finally they came to the stream. The sick camels lay down beside it and the sick men stripped and plunged in. The water foamed over their brown bodies and black heads, and then silkily onward in its narrow black channel. Layeville brought a jar of water to Mme. de la Scaze in her tent. Her face was flushed, small drops glistened on her forehead. She looked incredibly and wildly beautiful to Layeville at that moment. An ache of longing possessed him for an instant: not a physical, but a sad, intellectual longing. And again he felt that little spark of hatred and contemptuousness in her.

Then he turned and lay down on the cool wet rocks and watched three birds circling slowly high overhead. Soon there were four, then six, then a dozen.

Enemies. All around him were the enemies of man—in the air, in every stone, deep under the earth. Even in those naked shapes lying in the shade—there too they lurked, those watchful enemies, those subtle traitors.

He felt very excited, now. Some sly little danger, some profound, faintly monstrous danger was lying in wait for all of them; he felt quite sure of that. And yet he felt very excited, very expectant, almost breathlessly so, as he lay back on the rocks and watched the gathering birds high above the gully.

5

The Birds

THE BIRDS KEPT ON HOVERING HIGH ABOVE THE GULLY all night long. Layeville counted them, again and again. There were just twelve of them. As the stars appeared and the scenery emerged from the blackness of late dusk into the clear shimmer of deep night, Layeville could still see their black unbeating wings moving ever so slowly from constellation to constellation. They gave to the night an aspect peculiarly menacing and unreal. They too had paused on their way south, perhaps. On their way to those glimmering Tibetan ranges which caught the star-light ever so far away, so far away that they resembled a slender ribbon of foam on a distant sea, incomparably calm.

Akhejon sat down beside him and told him ghost stories, one after another. Some of them were very old tales, full of an inherited magic; others he had invented himself. "Once at twilight I was approaching a monastery on my way to Urga."

"All alone?"

"Oh yes, all alone. I am not afraid to be alone, sir."

"Valiant Akhejon!"

"High up in the cliffs lay the monastery, so high that it seemed to be hanging in the air. I sat down under a tree to rest, and began to pray, for I had begun to be afraid. Not afraid, precisely, you understand; but disturbed. Uneasy. Very well. I was almost falling asleep, out of sheer weariness, when I heard the tinkling of bells. I sat up and gazed skyward. There was the monastery, still bright with the setting sun, looking almost as if it were wrapped in flame. . . ." His voice grew deep and ardent as his imagination sought release in words. "And I could see the High Lama slowly riding up to it on his horse; only a child he was, surely no more than fourteen years. Unbelievably fine his face was, so pure and unearthly, his eyes blue as Indian turquoise, his skin soft as satin! He was dressed in yellow and red silk that almost covered his golden slippers. And he wore a golden hat which hid his hair. He rode on a black horse, though the black shone like gold and silver as if it were on fire. The men on each side were carrying burning censers; I could see the smoke arising from them and hiding their holy faces. For one more moment I could see them, all shining, and the birch trees beside them, and the waterfall, and the high silver hills beyond. Then, at the same instant, the sun faded away and they disappeared among the walls. Everything grew blue and motionless."

Akhejon paused. He was blushing, his eyes were shining, and in them Layeville could see reflected the glimmer of the moon and the flash of the moonlit stream. He could hear the stream, too, rustling and whispering away, delicately, rather mockingly. He brushed his hand across his brow and lay back.

"A pretty little story, Akhejon."

"Oh no! That isn't the whole story! Now I shall tell you the real part of the story. I rose and climbed up to the monastery. But the path, would you believe it, was thick and almost impassable with stones and weeds and creepers. There were no footprints at all. And when I reached the monastery I saw that it was totally in ruins. The corridors were black and charred, cobwebs covered the doorways, birds fluttered in and out of the windows."

"And no one was there?"

"Wait. At first, no one. But then, at the top of a stairway from which the steps had been torn away, I saw the High Lama. Still in his silken robes, his golden hat. But his long white hair and white beard fluttered in the breeze. I couldn't understand it in the least. But it was the same man, the same eyes beyond a doubt, still quite as blue as turquoise."

"What did you say?"

"Nothing, sir."

"What did he say? Anything?"

He paused a moment, thoughtfully. "Yes. He looked at me in a very gentle manner, and then said in a high boy's voice, 'Time is nothing, young stranger; change does not exist. Nothing outside of us really changes. Only one thing matters, and that is the piety and tenderness of your own spirit!' Then he smiled and walked away. And I climbed down the brambled path again and proceeded to Urga, remembering his profound and soothing words."

"Is your spirit full of piety and tenderness, Akhejon?"

"Yes, yes!" He blushed. His voice was full of a sweet and tremorous earnestness, he seemed to be sincerely moved.

★

When they awoke the next morning they found that three of the camels had died during the night. The sky was full of enormous birds. Two more were dying, and only four seemed well enough to proceed. No one understood. "Desert poison?" suggested the old Moslem, Ibrahim, but the rest merely looked sulky and suspicious.

While they were still wondering and planning, three horsemen appeared on the crest of the next hill, a mile away. Akhejon cupped his hands and called. They called back and then approached slowly. They halted a short distance away, and presently negotiations began. Mme. de la Scaze remained in her litter.

"This has happened before," Dr. Liu whispered in Layeville's ear. "This is a difficult place to pass. Camels fall sick for peculiar reasons, and the bandits then do their work."

"Bandits?"

"Not actual bandits, of course. But outcasts, marauders, who are afraid of real danger. So they take our money and in return help us until the next caravan passes."

And that was precisely what happened. Twenty more

horsemen appeared, and they were all led to a ruin hidden
by the slope of the hill. Here they waited for three days.

☆

The strangers looked like hyenas, incredibly ill-kempt,
stupid, truculent. Most of them had no teeth, almost all
of them were diseased and crippled in some way. Syphilis
had found its way even into this empty spot. They all wore
shaggy coats and blue kerchiefs on their heads.

They were proud to be called bandits, though they were
hardly that. They lived on cattle and hunting. They still
managed to sell furs to the traders now and then, but not
often. All they had was a collection of old Mauser carbines
and rusty Berdane rifles; and most of these didn't work.
But they had to serve.

They longed, so they explained, sentimentally, over the
evening fire, for the old days of Ja Lama and the great
robber fortresses. Now they had to be contented with these
ruins which they were too lazy and degraded to repair. The
place was outrageously filthy, perversely so. They appeared
to go out of their way to do their unpleasantness where it
would be most conspicuous. They were wild and filthy
animals, quite simply. And there was an antagonizing
canine look of guilt about their eyes. Also, a certain look
of exhaustion hung over their features and gestures—a sad
and unclean sort of exhaustion, like that of a wicked boy.

But even so, they longed to be friendly, and to be accepted as friends. Some of them even wanted to go along
with the caravan when the time came. "No?" they said

gloomily, and looked resentful and injured, as if they understood why they weren't wanted. In a way, this disguised brigandage was merely a habit with them. They cared little about money or material wealth as long as they had enough to keep alive. But this was an old habit which they were too stupid to resist; it was a form of exhibitionism for them, a relief from loneliness, and nourished the ancient animal instinct of reciprocity. They longed to see and hear and feel the strangers beside them, lost souls that they were. It was their only pleasure, almost. It gave them a tiny, momentary feeling of power.

As they moved south and eastward, Layeville noticed, the men grew smaller, frailer, humbler. They were more shabbily dressed, filthier in their ways, wilder of aspect. More stupid, hopeless, humorless, conscienceless, inhuman. Sleeping in their midst was like sleeping on the ground with a sullen pack of dogs.

☆

On the third day, by some curious accident, two caravans passed at almost the same time; one from the west, passing from Sinkiang on toward Lan-chow-fu, and one from the north, on its way through the Tsaidam to Shigatse in Tibet. Dr. Liu had several hasty consultations with the leaders, and then resolved to join the eastbound caravan, along with his four surviving camels and his porters, and, of course, Mme. de la Scaze.

"You will come too, of course?" he said to Layeville. He said this, for some reason, in a hesitant, silky tone.

[49]

"No. I shall go on to Shigatse." Layeville was half-surprised when he found himself saying these words. But he knew. He understood. He wanted to reach those snowy peaks at all costs.

"You will never get to Shigatse, my friend!" Liu's eyes flickered, his eyelids trembled—with a certain malicious pleasure, Layeville thought. Either he was a very, very wicked man, or he had ceased to have any feeling at all toward life except one of ironical amusement. Layeville wondered what might be in store for that lovely Spanish woman who was now staring at him in such an ambiguous, concentrated manner.

"I shall try, at any rate," he murmured, almost apologetically.

"Ah! You are most unwise. . . ." That was all. He did not try to urge him.

So they said good-by, young Asis, old Ibrahim, Akhejon, Izahk, and the rest. It was all very casual, as if they were saying good-night. But of course they would never see each other again, and the light-heartedness of these permanent farewells was a saddening thing to see. And yet he felt his heart leaping with energy and even a certain delight.

Once or twice, later on, he wondered why he had insisted on going on toward Shigatse. An act of folly, no more, no less. But at the bottom of his heart he understood why. The glow of those distant, icy summits, the brilliant, eager gaze in the eyes of the strangers who were passing on into Tibet. . . . But above all, something in himself, a wild uncontrollable longing, something intense that scarcely ever revealed itself in him, but which really underlay everything he felt and did, everything. From the moment they met the caravan from the north, he knew that he would have to go to Shigatse. He would have to,

that was all; there was nothing else he could do. He did
not even wonder why.

☆

So he found himself among strangers once more, approaching the frightening region of the Tsaidam. These
were Mongols and not Turkis, for the most part, and only
two of them could speak Hindustani.

One of these was a young Torgot named Tansang.
Strong, shaggy-haired, emerald-eyed, quick-limbed: a real
tiger of a man. And, like all cats, oddly elusive, both
valiant and cowardly, both true and false.

He was the son of a wealthy merchant and was a friend
of the leader of the caravan. Why he was going on toward
Shigatse Layeville could never discover. Probably mere
adventurousness. But a strange fellow. Inordinately vain,
too. He wore silks and brocades, his hat and his jacket
embroidered with gold. In his belt he wore golden buckles,
and his shirt was heavy with semi-precious stones.

He instantly attached himself to Layeville. "You are a
student, isn't that so?" he asked. "Yes, I am too." And he
related eagerly how he had studied Buddhist metaphysics
for four years, and the secret Tantric teachings.

Then he told, in a great onrush of confidence, about the
things which he loved and admired. First of all, his an-
cestor, the great Do-rje, one of the greatest of the Torgots.
He had slashed the breasts of his enemies, and with his
own hands had torn out their hearts! He had branded
them, castrated them, blinded them, flogged them to death.
"He hated everything that was beautiful—in people or

[51]

cities or objects made by men. Everything except animals. He loved beautiful horses." Barren women had been brought to him, even in his old age, as he passed from village to village: he made them fertile, just with the touch of his finger. Maidens longed to be possessed for his pleasure, so the story went, and wild animals meekly obeyed him if he glanced at them and touched them. Plagues subsided at his entry, rains descended on the drought-ridden areas, the rats fled, the locusts perished by the millions, covering whole cities as they fell. But toward youth and beauty he felt this terrible old man's hatred. Something unspeakable had happened to him while he was a boy, and the effect of it was still visible in his eyes.

"What had happened to him?"

But the young man didn't answer. Perhaps he didn't know.

Later he told about his own youth. He was now twenty-seven. At seventeen he had killed a male cousin one hot night, by the monastery well at Amur-baishalantu. At nineteen he had handled serpents and walked among the wolves in the forests beyond the great Kirghiz Lake. At twenty-one he escaped from a burning vessel on the Irtish river, at twenty-three he came near to drowning in the Brahmaputra north of Sikkim, at twenty-five he had been sick with cholera in Uliassutai and had cured himself by bathing in ice-cold water. So he said. Then his voice began to grow rather pompous.

"There will be a vast flood in two years, and pestilence will follow, in all of China. I am sure of it. I know. In five years will come a terrible war, and strangers from far-away islands will be seen on these plains. The lakes will wander, the rivers will change their courses, cities will vanish. In six years I shall be dead. All that I know."

He went on endlessly in this conceited and mystifying manner. Yet there was something very ingratiating about him, treacherous and cruel though he plainly was. He would turn and glance at Layeville now and then, with his sly, lustrous eyes. There was a sadistic and possessive touch in that look. As if the loose and ancient East had captured the emphatic West and were toying with it, gently, knowingly.

☆

And so, slowly, they approached that august glittering range beyond which stretched the Great Swamp, the Tsaidam, and Tibet.

Once they heard a strange whirring noise. The rest were puzzled for a moment, but Layeville knew what it was right away. He felt thrilled, stabbed for one wild moment by both delight and regret.

He looked up. Very lovely it looked to him, that huge, unwinging bird, with the sunlight flickering like a silvery snake along its metal tail. So clean, so clear, so cold it was! So powerful, so indifferent! And yet so dear in a way, a recognizable fragment of humanity in that august infinitude.

Tears appeared in his eyes. It seemed to flutter now, like a real bird. They all watched it grow tiny and then vanish over the horizon. Then, without a word, they turned and looked southward again.

Southward, where, little by little, the snows were drawing nearer.

6

The Mad Lama

AND, LITTLE BY LITTLE, AS THEY APPROACHED THE gradual snows they met the warning signals of winter. The torrents were freezing among the rocks at night, and in the sunlight the flood would pour forth again through the armor of ice—nervous serpentine tongues of water flickering out from the iridescent teeth.

The new caravan had brought yaks to carry all the loads. Some of the men rode on these, others on mules. There were only two camels left by this time, and these perished soon after they had left the Tsaidam. They were left twitching at the side of the road, the vultures already down

[54]

on them and plucking at their rolling eyes and nervous entrails.

They passed many dead animals; most of them converted into skeletons in less than a day, others swollen and disfigured, shunned even by birds. Now and then they saw the bones of a man.

Near the top of the Koko-shili pass they began to bleed, both men and animals. The drops froze on their faces, and when they looked at one another they were amazed by the ghostly mottled masks that stared back at them. Nothing but glaciers and snow lay ahead, and of course the eternal cliffs and the everlasting wind.

It was still October, and snow had already covered the landscape. The more distant mountains were a coronet of white foam rising from a huge white sea, nothing more, but of course they were the thing that absorbed all their thoughts, that filled their hearts with both longing and fear.

At dawn they began to climb down again. The porters cried *"Long! Long!"* and they all drank their morning tea in the early darkness. This was the coldest day they had met. They crossed slippery icy streams, one after another. The yaks plowed bravely ahead, but the mules fell time and time again. When they reached the roaring wind that flashed past the edge of the pass they were utterly exhausted. And then came the sun toward them from China, welcome and gentle at first, but soon as sharp as a dagger, needling into their eyes with its agonizing glow.

☆

They crossed these hills for three days. Each day glittered like a vast diamond, quite as hard and as variable. A thousand colors flashed up from the snow: so that white and silver became, as one watched, an absolute wilderness of marvels, crystals of blue, of green, of gold—recognizable colors, but such shades as had certainly never been seen before.

And in the intervening night the snow subsided into real sapphire. But even then the glittering stars were captured in the arms of the snow a million times near by and far away. Again the land resembled a sea at the same time tempestuous and totally still.

As they approached Kagchinar they met horsemen again, silver bells jingling on the delicate gray ponies. Young men, elaborately dressed in fine high Tibetan boots and in cloaks of velvet edged with fur. They wore their hair in tresses on each side, cheeks artificially reddened, and ornaments in their ears and on their fingers. They would pass the caravan slowly, carefully looking at each face, and then turn around in their saddles after they had passed and stare. Some of them stopped and chatted, and two of them sat down and had tea early one morning beside the camp fire. They were garrulous lads, and seemed to talk in an ambiguous and highly ceremonious manner, with a good deal of gesturing. Possibly they were merely curious, possibly it was more than that. There was no telling, of course. Layeville was struck by the soft, furtive tone of their voice and quality of their gaze. Also, they were terrific boasters. Tansang explained afterward.

"All of us know," they had said smilingly, "who approaches and enters our country."

[56]

"How do you manage to know, if you are a three days' journey away?"

"We know," they replied quietly. "Even the blind and the deaf know. That is the way it is with us. We know."

★

On the third day three soldiers rode up to them and asked them to halt. Near by they saw the camp of a lama's caravan which had halted because the lama was very sick. They were quite sure, they explained, that he was dying. He had come from Jyekundo on his way toward the Blue Lake, where he wished to gaze into the water. Why? In order to see reflected there, in the clear blue mirror, the village where the successor to the great Dalai Lama was living. That was the way they would discover the new Dalai Lama, and he wished to reach the lake before his death, so the men said. They were all very quiet, curious, gentle. They seemed to feel no sorrow or anxiety. Quite incapable of regret these people were, as far as one could see. They had been waiting here a week, but he still hadn't died, though he was far too feeble to move.

Layeville was led into the presence of the old lama. He lay among the cushions, wrapped in red and yellow silks —a sly, fragile, lizard-like wisp of a face. Two young men were at his side, tending the braziers. He was utterly feeble and could scarcely whisper. It was a highly mystifying atmosphere that surrounded him; something that Layeville felt sliding past him and eluding him, a dark shape, so to speak, which still fed life to the old man and moved nervously about in the tent, transforming everything it touched into something subtly alive.

☆

They waited two days at this place for permission to proceed. Late in the afternoon of the second day Layeville was amazed when one of the old lama's servants approached him and said that the lama wished to see him again.

The old man lay in the same position as before. It seemed as if only a second had elapsed instead of thirty hours. The brazier was still glowing, and as twilight approached the light in the tent melted into a soft orange glow.

The lama addressed him in a slow and careful Hindustani. "You understand?" His voice was hot and infinitesimal, like a lizard's tongue flickering in the sun.

Layeville nodded.

"Where are you going?"

Layeville hesitated. "You needn't tell me," the lama said softly, as if to keep the two servants from overhearing. "I know. I know." Then he closed his eyes for an instant and an expression of pain, which was at the same time an expression of contentment, crept over his old face. Old, old, he was, obscenely old.

"I know. To a place by a cliff two days beyond Kiytun-shirik. I can see it now. The yaks deep in the snow, the men buried in their cloaks, the wolves, the birds. Yes. I know.

"I know," he went on. Layeville could understand him

only by listening very intently, for he spoke with a strange accent and with a peculiar choice of words. "You are a sick man. You are trying to escape from your sickness as if it were a pursuing animal. That is so. . . ." He turned his head very slightly, so as to see Layeville more plainly. He looked appalling, inhuman. His face was a network of wrinkles and delicate veins that had crept to the surface, like weeds in a frozen pond. The skin resembled Chinese silk, wrinkled and yet serpentine; oddly repellent, for it was purple in hue and resembled a far-fetched sort of mask far more than the face of a man. A few long white hairs hung from the top of his head. There was a certain horrible, ancient majesty about him, a saurian quality, an old subterranean wisdom and endurance.

"Let me tell you about the old religion of Tibet," he said, softly, and his voice was like a strand of silk being slowly and rhythmically unraveled from the silken mask which hid him. "The Black Faith, now profoundly feared by the Buddhist lamas of this land. I have studied it for many years, and I fear it no longer. It is the oldest thing in the world that is created by man. It existed before anything else. It began with terror. That was the beginning of it. The terror of darkness. A great awe.

"It still exists in remote places, in forests and in the out-of-the-way corners of Nepal. Its monasteries still hide here and there, and you will find stone altars to its gods on the summits of numerous hills. There are the White Gods and the Black Gods, you see, and ruled by these are the little demons, who bring storms if they are angered or lead the caravans astray. They still exist, and, just as it was many thousand years ago, it is blood only which will exorcise them. So at least it would appear. . . ." His voice, which had grown quick and breathless, now subsided

[59]

again. "There is a sort of Buddhism, a Tantric variety, devised by the great Padmasam Ghava, which resembles this one in its infinite complexity and penetration. But it isn't the same, for it depends for its life on ritual; the old system depends, as I said, on human terror, on a bottomless awe."

There appeared to be some tormenting *arrière-pensée* behind these confidences. The old man raised his hand one or two inches and then let it fall again. He seemed to wish to convey something—a secret, a feeling, a flash of intuition—which was wholly apart from the province of words. He was quite insane, Layeville now realized; he had abdicated the human limitations of a self-imposed order, of consoling simplifications, even of words. His intuition had gotten beyond control. His ancient, reptilian self was emerging.

The old man lay quietly for a few moments while the two young men watched Layeville motionlessly. Then suddenly he exclaimed, "The happy and pure after their death are lifeless, their bodies soothed by precious oils, quiet and cold as statues!" Though his voice was so quiet that Layeville could scarcely hear the words, yet it seemed to resound and echo within the tent in a surprising manner. "It is the wretched and degraded who still toss, eyes open, lips parted, and forever uneasy. They are wrapped in flame!" These were not orthodox Buddhist tenets, thought Layeville; but they were uttered with complete conviction. "They live in the air, and it is they who are our guardians, our spirits, and sooner or later they will possess us all. They see through us as if we were pools of wax, and with their little flames they stir us into heat and illumination and at last extinguish us.

"It is their mission to pursue and punish," he said, tremulously raising his purple claw of a hand again. "To

[60]

punish the crimes committed in utter darkness. To punish," and his voice rose infinitesimally, "those who have brought suffering without knowing it, those who have never purified with the terror that results from wicked deeds the wickedness that hides in every heart. They have taken human history by the throat and made it bleed, century after century: but no one sees, no one understands, for it all transpires in total darkness. With their terrible whispers, to an accompaniment of music, beautiful and intricate phrases, enchanting gestures, features and limbs enthrallingly lovely, and a crescendo of magnificent battle cries, they have damned us all, these pure ones, not for a lifetime but for eternity. . . ."

Now he appeared to be exhausted; the tiny, desolate music of his voice faded away, and he closed his ancient eyelids once more. One of the porters rose to stir the coals in the brazier, then sat down again in the corner. Both of them looked bored, contemptuous, suspicious. There was a very queer smell in the tent, Layeville now noticed—a malicious, secretive little smell.

Presently Layeville bowed to the mad dying creature and departed. In the morning, when the caravan was allowed to proceed again toward the south, Tansang told him that the old lama had died during the night and that his caravan was returning to Jyekundo.

7

Tansang

AND SO, ON THE FOLLOWING DAY, THEY WERE PER-
mitted to proceed southward once more. The
porters were really worried now. It was too late,
too late, they kept muttering. The snow, the snow! But
there was nothing to be done about it, of course.

On and on. Further and further away from the past,
deeper and deeper into the future. It was a flight of the
spirit, really, as well as a flight of the body. As the suffering
of the body grew more bitter with cold, altitude, and
privation, the disturbances of the mind appeared to lose
intensity. Fear, curiously enough, became a shadowy affair, the revulsions and longings of the past grew unreal,
made sterile and lifeless somehow by the surrounding

peaks of ice. Sickness of the limbs sponged in its parasitic
way the sickness out of the brain. The images of civilization, that intricate and intoxicating vegetable of the tem-
perate zones, could, after all, perhaps be cleansed away by
heat, cold, and their physical accompaniments. Existence
grew rhythmical, painful yet wholly serene. And it seemed
possible at last that the life-long nerve-racking disease of
the cities might be purged away, and that a life free of
disgust, of reveries and recollections, be engaged in. A pure
life, so to speak.

☆

They crossed one range after another. These were the
Altin Tagh, the boundary between the two wildernesses,
that of rock and that of snow, that of heat and that of cold.
Up amongst the crags and gorges of the second range could
be seen the great snow-fields of Chakhalda. Then they
crossed the Shara river on their camels, through the weird
muddy currents that were so bitterly cold that the camels
screamed with anger.

Then, after they had crossed the highest pass, came a
huge plain of gravel. "Now we are in Tibet," cried Tansang. But oddly enough there was no one to stop them,
and two soldiers who met them presently merely nodded
at them and rode on quietly. They could see the blue hills
fluctuating on the eastern horizon. And then a great lake
far away. They saw herds of wild asses as they crossed the
plain, stretches of grass so sharp that they cut into the
camels' legs like knives, dried streams, dried springs, and

soon the salty levels of the Tsaidam itself. Far away they could still see the huge and unapproachable lake surrounded by miles and miles of salt marshes. Everywhere they saw white veins of salt running through the dark skin of the plain.

Then came the sand-dunes: milder regions spotted with grass and low dark rivers: places made traditional by generations of banditry and guerrilla warfare. They cautiously posted sentries here during the night. Nothing happened, but all night long Layeville experienced a feeling of secret life, listeners and watchers hiding betwixt the mounds on all sides.

The next day they found the people of the Tsaidam, dwelling beside the salt lakes and the quicksands reputed to be bottomless. Curious and antipathetic little people; they were far more cunning than the big uncouth Turkis and Mongols who passed through year after year, and whom they had been cheating for generations. Tansang had heard of them far in the north. They were notorious. They had become rich, and dressed with the greatest elegance and lavishness. Their blue shirts, not infrequently of brocade, were trimmed with fur on the cuffs and the collar. They wore great leather boots, white felt hats wound about with bands of violet silk, and all over their bodies they wore elaborate silver ornaments studded with coral and turquoise. Many of them had faces ravaged by exposure to cold, and a number of them were lame. Many of the women had goiters. The women were all dressed in green robes likewise enrichened with fur and silk. Those that were married wore braids, those that were maids wore little black locks. An odd puppet-like tribe; graceful little hunters of wolves and antelopes; lovers of war and bloodshed; almost imbecilic, utterly heartless; they lived in a secret Middle Age of their own, told curious tales, believed and feared everything they were told about the world outside, and understood nothing at all.

☆

Now they could feel winter approaching. The camels moved more quickly into the winds that now began to crawl down from the ranges. The days grew bleak and pale and the colors faded into gray. But the nights, while they became colder and colder, remained lovely beyond words: clear and pure, the stars more flaming than ever and the sky more oceanic. Sometimes the white hills rose distinct, and then it was they who seemed immeasurably remote and the stars a mere three days' journey away. Fiery clouds passed over the steepest summits and they too seemed hard with snow and ice, great waves frozen into a succession of gigantic pearls.

Layeville woke up alone, before dawn, and stepped into the cold gray air. Sleep was a veil, not pierced by awakening nor dissolved, but very gently and gradually parted by an act of the will. He saw the silhouettes of the camels grazing in the distance and the remains of the fire still glowing dimly.

Presently they reached the mountains at the end of the swampland and climbed up slowly toward the higher ranges of the Kuenlun hills. They saw the bears drinking far below them at twilight, and in another valley a great herd of yaks. They were entering the higher plateaus. The

lakes of rain water left from the August rains were beginning to freeze during the cold nights. In the valleys the
strips of quicksand and salty swamp were growing hard
and brittle. Again the country became one of wild crags,
precipices, boulders. Far off at last they could see the
pinnacles of the great Thang-La, cloaked in their meta-
physical snows, the august and traditional monarchs of
Tibet.

The sun was still hot in the daytime, but the winds grew
stronger and the nights grew steadily colder. More and
more snow. So that the eyes began to ache, and even when
they wore smoked glasses they suffered maddening headaches and could scarcely see. Layeville was in distress with
a constant feeling of nausea at this point; and after the
slightest exertion—leaning down to fasten his shoes, climbing over a rock in the middle of the night, turning around
to watch the valleys they were leaving—he felt dizzy and
breathless.

They met strange things from time to time. This was no
new country they were entering, but an old, old one, full
of not yet forgotten spirits, as the men were constantly and
rather glumly impressing upon him. They found the body
of a child in the limbs of a dead tree, torn fleshless by
vultures. And two men beside each other, all but their
flannel boots and tall yellow hats and a few bones devoured
by the wolves. Once they met three tall young men, with
otter collars and pointed hats and big skirts of brocade.
They passed without smiling and in fact without even
seeming to notice them, and disappeared.

"Who were they?" asked Layeville. "Wealthy merchants?"

"No," said Tansang softly, turning his mocking silky

gaze upon Layeville, "they are the *tchen-lam*; spies sent out
from Lhasa, and the cruelest men in the land!"

✫

At night Tansang would ask him questions about the
great cities of India and China. He would listen coldly and
disdainfully, staring at Layeville with his flashing, insolent
eyes. He remained peculiarly aloof during these days, almost hostile at times.

He particularly wanted to hear about the ocean. It
seemed incredible to him that the great oceans really
existed. He wanted to hear how deep they were, and about
the size of the waves during a tempest, and the tempests
themselves, typhoons and such, the coral islands, the various fish, the ships, and so on. He had only heard vague
though stimulating rumors about these matters. His eyes
looked puzzled as Layeville explained to him; full of both
longing and a queer sort of hatred, both desire and horror.

And then in return he told Layeville about the great
cities of his own land. Long dead they were: but, he vowed,
they had been even more splendid and gigantic than those
more recent ones which hugged the edge of the sea.

"Desert covers the land now. But this was the greatest
city of all! Many, many miles in every direction. Canals,
large ones and small ones, flowed past the mulberry trees,
and in them were reflected the silver bridges, the golden
turrets, the high jeweled walls of the palace and the lovely
gardens. That is why the canals were built; so that everything would be seen double, and the magnificence of the
city be twice as grand. The beautiful virgins from Siam

[67]

and India, even from the island of Japan and those other islands where black people live, all were brought here for the Khan's pleasure. The most excellent of silks and of ornaments, and pearls out of the sea of Korea, and carpets, all were brought. And the most excellent of the poets and painters to be found in China. All for the brave and almighty Khan. . . . I am a descendant of that Khan!" He looked at Layeville through his green cat's eyes with a gaze of real hatred. "I should long to be like that Khan, and wash my hands in the blood of the invaders. . . . But everything has changed!"

As he talked on, Layeville felt an odd sort of relief running through him, as if the hostility and secret violence of the young man were in a way disinfecting him, like a hot iron cauterizing the bite of a snake.

"Near the city there was a tower, very high and thin. The floor sloped downward like a sieve, so that the prisoners could neither stand nor lie, but had to suffer one on top of the other until they died of disgust. Here were dropped the traitors, those who desired change and counseled freedom for the vanquished and mercy for the oppressed. I have dreamed about this tower, from time to time! I think that the lamentations of the prisoners surrounded the tower like a veil of mist, now heavy and now subsiding. Both night and day, more shrill in the sunlight than in darkness."

Layeville could not take his eyes off Tansang. There was something disturbing, just a little bit insane, in that wild, lustrous face, that hard and potent body. Very cruel he looked, very cruel indeed, as he turned his glistening head away, in a sly and conceited movement. Each gesture of his slender, finely-shaped body was as lithe as a panther's, as subtle and sexual.

Suddenly Tansang turned around and caught his gaze. A little smile, quite intimate, frightening and yet full of understanding, appeared on his lips. His eyes shone. A very wicked look, there was no denying it.

Then he turned away again, and refused to speak to Layeville the rest of the day. Layeville felt himself beginning to fear Tansang, and to hate him too.

☆

The last herons were passing overhead on their way to Burma; so high that one could scarcely see them. Now and then they saw a group of gazelles, moving as crisply and lightly as autumn leaves blown up by a quick gust of wind. They were climbing the slopes that led toward the great Thang-La, and as the hills which they saw on all sides grew more numberless and lovely the air grew more bitter, the brilliance of the sunlight more dazzling and intolerable.

Around them and below them the hills were still snowless. Across them ran the innumerable vales and ravines, purple veins glowing through the mottled and permanent flesh. Now they were cloaked in a mist that flowed softly over their shoulders like a shawl. Watchers; the rocks; below them the enormous plateau, and above them the stars. Nothing if not strong, and what they refused to condone in this place, so assiduously observant, was weakness; that is, impurity and frailty of spirit.

This was the region, Layeville suddenly remembered, which the dying lama had mentioned in his prophecy. He began to feel very excited. Something was awaiting him

[69]

on that great mountain, he knew. Something intimate and majestic. Something awful, something real. He should feel anxious and afraid, he realized; but he felt, instead, full of alertness, full of desire for those incomparable summits. The white walls up there seemed very personal and meaningful all of a sudden. They seemed to be gazing down at him, waiting for him. They were more beautiful than anything he had ever seen.

8

Snow

LAYEVILLE'S CARAVAN WAS HELD UP AGAIN AT A TRAD-
ing-post at the foot of the great Thang-La. Three
great routes met here, so they explained to Layeville, all going to Lhasa: one from Mongolia, one from
Jyekundo in the east, one from Sining. There were heaps
of refuse lying about, dead mules and yaks by the dozen,
even the bodies of dead men, all half frozen and half
devoured, still odorous. The sky was dotted with vultures.

The officials sat in a black tent beside a glowing brazier,
polite but cool, ambiguous and serene. The leader of the
caravan brought presents to the *nang-so*, a cynical and
acute old man, gaudily cloaked like the rest in heavy purple silk. Silver ornaments—charm boxes, pistols, knives,
bracelets—stood all around him on the table, suggestively.

[71]

Finally, after six days of negotiation, they were allowed to continue. The men were desperate now; it was November, and they were confronted with the discomfiting likelihood of spending the whole winter in the hills. The yaks were growing perceptibly weaker. They would need enormous luck to carry them through to the Brahmaputra. They could not afford to lose a single day.

A truculent dirty soldier accompanied them for another two days, ostensibly to guide them. Once he appeared to lose the way for them deliberately, once he seemed genuinely bewildered when the trail lost itself in impassable rocks. The porters grew desperate at this, torn between rage and anxiety. He lied his way out, indignantly blamed the porters, and spoke insinuatingly regarding Layeville's presence, and the thoroughly bad impression it would make on the intolerant Hill Spirits. The porters conspired to whip the rascal and send him back, but they didn't quite dare. They were all afraid of the Tibetans.

The land was full of frozen lakes, nestling in the arms of the ranges. Their icy mirrors were not yet covered with snow; during the day they were black as ebony, during the night pure silver. The torrents were permanently frozen now, massive tongues locked between the rocks, great white fangs silently guarding the descending hollows. The land grew more and more rocky, more and more full of caves, most of them almost covered with snow.

They obtained fresh yaks at Kiytun-shirik, but now they needed them more and more frequently, and were lucky to get them at all. The local headsmen grew surlier with each station that they passed. The natives here were small and sullen creatures, with inhuman toothless faces framed in long matted hair: more degraded than men but far less amenable than apes. Some of them had to be bribed and then threatened before they would surrender fresh animals.

Once one of the mules grew frightened, leapt and stumbled over a rock and rolled with its rider down a precipice. The rider jumped and clung to a ledge, but suddenly he curled up with pain, appeared to lose consciousness and collapsed, and fell far down, leaping from rock to rock across the steep gravel like a bundle of wheat until he finally disappeared.

Not only Layeville, but some of the others as well, suffered from spells of mountain sickness. They would almost faint, and an insistent perilous drowsiness would trouble them again and again in the course of the afternoon. Layeville's heart would beat so violently that a dose of digitalis had to be given several times a day. The snow grew deeper, the cold grew more constant, the winds grew more penetrating, the yaks grew weaker and more difficult to replace, the scattered inhabitants grew alarmingly hostile, and slowly but quite inevitably the exhausted men began to lose hope of reaching Gyaro.

But the worst thing was yet to happen.

★

Early in the afternoon of the following day it began to snow. The scenery suddenly lost all its depth, the desperate glare of the sun was transformed into a solid gray shadow, and the distant peaks vanished. A delicate white armor soon covered the animals, and the men rode on, heads bent forward, through the descending thicket of snow. They could scarcely see where they were going. Now and then one of them would disappear among the falling flakes and then emerge again, a shape meaningless and silent. The tinkle of the bells sounded as if they were far away or underground.

☆

That evening, at the moment when the cold and the gradual darkness forbade further progress, they halted almost on the edge of a deep abyss. It had been snowing all afternoon; it had almost stopped now, but still, there was enough so that here a great drift had been gathered by the wind in which the yaks were now almost up to their shoulders. They had to turn about again and find a suitable place for the night.

Then they discovered that the Tibetan soldier had left them. Far down the valley they could see the scoundrel moving along on his horse, back in the direction from which they had come. It was odd indeed that no one had seen him depart. But there he was. And suddenly they realized that they had lost their way, that the route lay probably miles away on the other side of the cliff, that they would have to retrace their steps for a whole day's journey; and almost worst of all, that they had been misled, intentionally beyond a doubt, and most probably by the order of Lhasa, that surreptitious and distrustful power which seemed to know everything, which was incapable of mercy.

But there was one thing that was yet more disturbing: it was snowing, the animals were exhausted, the courage of the men had vanished; in short, they might have to stay here until fresh animals could be brought and the trail to the main route cleared again.

They sent out two men the next morning. It was the only thing to do. The rest sat down and waited.

☆

They waited.

There were four yurts—circular tents of black felt, with a hole in the top to allow the smoke to escape. A fire was kept burning in each almost constantly until they found that the yak dung which they used for fuel wouldn't suffice. Then they kept a fire going in only two of the four, and they sat crowded in the fœtid darkness all day long, waiting, until they grew heavy-eyed and feverish with the bilious smells, the bad food, and the utter monotony.

There were eleven men left now. Two of them—Tansang and Ahun—were Layeville's special friends, and the only ones with whom he could converse. They all ate together in the same tent, so that the wretched crusts and muddy tea might be distributed more cautiously. Insects had infested the food, and the tea and coffee and sugar were full of sand. Several cans of condensed milk were left, three cans of meat, and a fairly large can of marmalade. The meat had spoiled, and for some reason the milk had turned gray and rank. They devoured the marmalade in two days, as well as a package of raisins that Layeville found in one of the boxes. They were covered with mold and infested with worms, but still, they were a relief.

Furthermore, the smell of burning dung and ailing humanity had entered into everything: some of them fell sick

[75]

from it and could not eat for a day. But finally everyone
had to eat what little there was; there was no way out.
They grew weak and irritable beyond words. Again and
again one of them would fly into a temper, and then calm
down suddenly, breathless and exhausted.

Their manners grew to be absolutely fantastic. They ate
like wild animals, not like men. They sat hunched over
their little bowls and crusts, pawing, growling, their eyes
flashing from side to side, torn between ravenousness and
loathing. And in other ways, too, they grew wild and
unsavory. They were teeming with lice, of course, and
scratching came to be a sort of excess, an orgiastic frenzy,
with two or three of them. Their hair was long and matted;
their faces were covered with boils and green sores. Even
the faintest pretense of cleanliness or thoughtfulness had
vanished. The men made water wherever they pleased, and
the tents began to stink with urine and worse. Layeville
was the only one who tried to keep the place habitable;
but it was no use.

They slept on sheepskins, and covered themselves with
flannel and fur. Most of them now wore their fur caps and
fur boots day and night. Some never budged out of their
sleeping-bags, except for their bodily needs. Near the end
one or two of them gave up doing even that.

For a while Layeville had shaved regularly, but now he
was wearing a long beard and his hair fell almost to his
shoulders: so that when he stared at himself in his small
pocket mirror one day he thought for a moment that he
was looking at a stranger's face: the eyes still blue, but
blue like ice, the pale long hair, the silky beard, the dark
and deeply lined skin, the hollow and lifeless expression.
He was frightened, and tossed the mirror out into the
snow.

headaches, nausea, insomnia, hæmorrhoids, diarrhœa, and certain visual disturbances. But Tansang had always been the strongest of them all, too haughty to admit sickness and too spirited to experience a defeat of heart. Now he had to lie down beside the other sick men in the largest of the tents. The smell here was indescribable, for some of the men refused to budge all day long. Some of them had developed a chronic diarrhœa, one began to vomit incessantly, amid nerve-racking little noises. Now that Tansang was ill, Layeville tried desperately to make the place more bearable. Each morning he cleaned the filth away, panting with weariness and revulsion, and lit some incense which Ahun gave him. But the air remained loathsome, and yet more impure than the air were the bodies and spirits of the sick men.

Once Tansang leaned over and whispered something in his ear, while he was setting his evening meal beside him.

"You are as lonely as I, my friend." The sparkle, the insolent luster, had faded from his eyes. "We are part of a dying world, both you and I. There is no room for us in the living world. . . ."

He paused. Then he put his hand on Layeville's wrist. "You are a very strange man!"

Layeville tried to hide his feeling. "Why?"

"So full of love," whispered the other one, "so full of kindness and wisdom, and even courage, and none of it used!"

★

There was only one thing really, after this, that kept him

[79]

full of energy during these destroying hours, and that was his obsessive feeling that he must save Tansang's life. At all costs. For Tansang had become a symbol of reality to him, indeed, of life itself, of everything worth saving in life. He began to feel that if he saved Tansang's life, then he would save himself.

The territory all around him now seemed to him more beautiful than ever. Even its total desolation was forgotten under the spell of its terrible splendor. He could no longer resist looking at the snow under the morning sun. He observed the soft slopes very gradually penetrated by the light and transformed from blue into silver. And as it grew more vivid and exact he could detect in the snow the most dazzling ornaments and devices, a million intricate shapes, a pure and crystal world unbelievably ornate and perfect. He could see that the snow was leading a life of its own, precisely like the earth or the sea: but sterile, secret, silvery, its love so to speak turned forever upon fragments of its own self and destined to fruitlessness and silence. A million crystals of infinite complexity, living for nothing else but the gradual destruction of their own perfect selves, growing slowly into each other, moving silkily downward during each moment of sunlight, motionless again at night, and then in the warm sun again becoming amorous and weak, like vast degenerate tribes drifting together, flowing away; demonstrating how close to one another were purity and decay, perfection and death.

And then after a few minutes of pleasure and surprise he would have to rush into the dark tent again and ease the pain in his eyes by staring into the pale twilight that covered the floor and the suffering bodies. Toward sunset he would go out again, breathless and aching. Now and then he could see the snow-partridges whistling and flickering over the slopes, or more rarely, the great winter hares, or the marmots. He would wait for sunset as if it were a moment of ceremony, of revelation.

The landscape at this hour was really indescribably desolate, monstrous beyond all words. The peaks were enormous hooded creatures squatting on the horizon, freshly risen out of another quite unimaginable world, it appeared to Layeville, composed neither of stone nor of metal, white not with snow, alien not with a chemical but with a spiritual whiteness, hazy not with distance but with centuries of inaccessibility, a state of being totally beyond conjecture. Light shone on the western slopes, they seemed to melt, glittering rusty floods appeared to trickle down their sides, the white shadows grew darker and darker in the east. It was then, when he watched these vast distances, the snow, the ice, the icy emptiness of the sky, the snowy clouds, that he suddenly began to long once more, in a subtle, subdued way, for a warm curtained room, the glow of a fire on the red carpet, the approaching footsteps, and at last the intimate touch of a certain beloved hand, awaited for hours with beating heart. The past, the dear, secluded past.

He could not understand it. The ways of his heart were far too intricate to follow. For he had been fleeing, he now realized; fleeing, fleeing away from his past, from the desultory cities, the disintegrating continent to the west, the implacable continent to the east, away from the impurities of a world which, so it had seemed to him, was growing falser, madder, year by year. But now, at the very moment when his flight seemed complete and perfect, that same world seemed inexpressibly alluring, inexpressibly consoling and safe.

He could not understand it, and perhaps there was no

answer. No answer, that is, except this one: that he now knew that these territories he had entered were something he had never conceived of. They were devastatingly lovely; but inhuman, inhuman; and therefore forbidden; and therefore profoundly dangerous.

And then at the moment of sunset the hills grew frail, insubstantial. Now they were only waves, foam-capped, in a vast and reddening sea; graceful as waves, equally ephemeral. Then abruptly the final glow would alight on them, one peak would grow resplendent, then swiftly the whole tremendous range of the Thang-la would flash into fire. Everything became flame for one instant, the clouds, the sky, everything. Then it subsided, a thread of gold fluctuated along the edge of a cloud like the sound of a flute. Then the hills became violet, solid, eternal again. And then descended the relief of dusk, followed, for Layeville, by the mounting calamity of the night.

9

Ice

O N THE NINETEENTH DAY THE FOOD BECAME
alarmingly scarce. The cold was growing more
and more intense, and during the night more
snow had fallen, covering the scattered remnants of the
dead animals.

Three of the men had developed pneumonia. Others
were suffering from frostbite: their faces had become
black, their skin was falling loose and dead, sores spread
across their arms and legs, and the discolorations and odors
of gangrene appeared. Yet they all seemed oddly serene
now. All night and day they would moan very softly; now
and then one would cry suddenly with pain; but none of
them spoke, and in any case all nervousness and anger had
left them.

On the twenty-first day two men died. No one knew it until late in the evening, when one of them returning indoors said quietly that two of the Mongol porters were squatting stiffly in the snow beyond the furthest yurt.

Now the other Mongols began to grow afraid of ghosts. They whispered at night in sudden spells of terror about their snow-covered companions sitting with open eyes on the mountain-side, and wondered what the next few days might bring to the survivors: not of bodily suffering, nor was it death and what might follow death that they feared. It was that they feared ghosts, as they had been taught to do from childhood, and the revenge of those who had perished earliest, in such solitude and neglect.

Layeville was almost the only one who wasn't actually sick. He tried to comfort them, talked to them gently, told them stories. But they didn't appear to listen, and presently he discovered that he was doing this quite simply in order to preserve his own sanity. Tansang was the only one with whose fate he was deeply concerned. He would sit beside him hour after hour, bringing him fresh tea now and again, or telling him stories about Europe and the sea; but more frequently in silence, motionless.

"Are you feeling better, Tansang?" he'd whisper to him, perhaps.

"Yes, my friend," and Tansang would glance up at him and nod. His gaze was no longer shining and insolent, it had grown subdued, almost abject.

"You are very kind," he would add.

"No, no," murmured Layeville.

"Yes. You are stronger than I. . . ."

Layeville felt terribly pleased with these words. "No," he murmured, "I have had luck, nothing more."

"Sh," said Tansang softly, "there is no such thing as luck! I know, I know!"

Then he would close his eyes and seem to fall asleep. But he wasn't really asleep, Layeville realized. His eyelids would tremble, his lips would move.

What these quiet days most resembled was the breathless silence that exists in a room while a storm is raging outside: an added illusion even more commanding in its implications than the reality.

☆

Yet he found here, during these final few days, a profound and indeed comparatively soothing consummation of his spirit; for in these slopes, these glittering snows, these Asiatic skies, he found his own spiritual emptiness and chill reflected, made actual, and thus given a tremendous release. He felt calmer, more satisfied, than he had for many months. This scenery, so still, so cool, so restrained and yet intense, was indeed nothing else than a white, abstract stylization of that green insular landscape which he now beheld whenever he closed his eyes, which he carried with him incessantly locked in his heart.

☆

On the twenty-fourth day Layeville thought that Tansang would die. He lay quite motionless; he had become utterly indifferent. Layeville sat beside him and watched

[85]

him. His face was still full of power, the power of a young man, an old man, a woman, a child, all fascinatingly combined. He seemed to possess the instincts of both great age and earliest childhood. And yet a certain rather ugly imperfection resided in those eyes. Layeville could not recognize what this might be, but it seemed to consist of some profound lack of balance, a prolonged spiritual dissipation, some fruitless vice indulged in by the imagination.

The matter of food was a desperate one now. The marmalade was gone, and so were the cans of meat, down to the very last scrap. They had to use the canned milk, rank and odious though it was, and even the remnants of barley which the yaks no longer needed.

On the twenty-fifth day another of the Mongols had died of pneumonia, but Tansang appeared to have improved. Layeville sat beside him all day and listened to him. He told how years ago he had crossed from Siningfu, and had arrived at the Brahmaputra. There was to him something magical about the Brahmaputra. "We had climbed a high range," he observed, "and then we saw the distant Himalayas.

"We crossed the juniper-covered slopes and the sand-dunes, and saw the tents and sheep. Then we knew we were near the river. And then we reached the swamps and saw the river.

"For two days we followed it, with four mules and four horses. Then we crossed it on a ferry. The water was swift and red. Are all big rivers like that? Dark? Powerful?"

Layeville nodded.

"Then we followed the southern shore of the river until we reached a great mountain valley which was glittering in the clear air. In the evening we passed a steep promontory with a lamasery on the summit, black against the

[86]

starlight. In the morning we saw the great mountains again, and beyond these we knew stretched the hot plains of India.

"The precipices were full of ruins—fortresses, watchtowers, castle walls. We passed a village of unsacred filth. The people were dying in the streets and the dogs were devouring the excrement of the diseased ones, pilgrims to the Holy Lake.

"Then at last we crossed the unspeakable range. It was June. I saw the glaciers, the snow of the peaks; far greater and more adored than these beneath which we are now waiting. I cannot forget that.

"Then later on the rhododendron forests of Sikkim, the deodars, the fragrance of flowers, the singing brooks. The slopes were covered with evergreens in white and pink blossom, lovely after the gales, the torrents, the icy inclines, and the treacherous deserts. Everything became gentle, and again we saw beautiful people!"

☆

On the next day, the twenty-sixth, two more men died, and on the twenty-seventh day Tansang died too.

☆

Layeville began to feel very weak. The throbbing in his head grew less violent, but he saw objects less clearly, and sounds reached him as if across miles of water. There were five men left. Three of these were very sick; the other two helped carry out the bodies of the dead. They were placed in a row in the snow beyond the furthest yurt. The first three were covered with felt, but the felt gave out and the rest were left uncovered. After they had stiffened they continued to look as if they were alive: until, on the following day, Layeville saw Tansang's haughty face covered with ice, glittering in the sun, breathtakingly beautiful. It looked reverent and appropriate. In the distance circled the dark hideous birds, the incomprehensible birds, hovering on the very edge of this pool of silence.

On the next morning he saw that snow had covered them all, and he felt for the first time a throb of real and devastating loneliness. Something had left him. He was alone, alone. He looked at the sky and watched the clouds moving. Some were over the remote horizon, other and vaster ones over his head, passing slowly, shifting, dissolving, expanding, each edge dazzlingly white as it passed over and hid the sun for an instant. The sky itself looked more pure and endless than even the white boundless snow. A bird was floating under a cloud, now still, now poised on the brink of motion, now slowly turning, now a quick arc of delight catching the sun on its wings far, far away, and now disappearing. Up there life appeared to be exquisite, untouched; cold, clear, clean. Below them even the pure snow seemed stained by the thought of humanity and its various modes of loving and dying.

10

England, a Shadow

LAYEVILLE WOKE UP VERY EARLY ON THE MORNING OF the thirtieth day. Through the hole in the tent's ceiling he could see three stars in a sky still almost as dark as the black felt of the roof.

He closed his burning eyes and tried to go to sleep again. But he was feverish. Forgotten scenes, little lovable fragments of the past, kept flowing before his eyes. Then he discovered a strange thing. As soon as he closed his eyes he could see the world slowly turning pale and distinct, as though dawn were actually spreading with an abnormal swiftness.

The present faded, the past grew real. More meaningful, more moving, the past became, as the present subsided into snow and ice. It became, in a sense, a talisman, a key to quietude, a harmonizing power, an isle of safety in this limitless sea of mortal existence.

Indeed, what he saw now, he suddenly realized, was a landscape far more detailed and intimate than any he had seen for months. Flooded, it was, with the secret and familiar loveliness of his childhood. And then, with a stab of intense happiness, he recognized it.

☆

A small stream ran through the garden. For several yards it ran close beside the hedge, shyly and in shadow; then in a burst of open-heartedness, as if it had suddenly discovered that there was surely nothing more to be afraid of, it flashed forth across the lawn, rippled gaily over the pebbles, curled around the flower-bed, passed gently again into shadow: the shadow of the beech tree, whose lowest branches were forever trailing in the flowing water, creating tremulous arrows that disappeared one moment and again slipped into being in the next. Then it leapt with sudden energy and whispering excitement over a rock and passed through the hedge again out into the fields of Somerset.

He knew every inch of this stream, every pebble, every whim; each sprig of moss, each arc of fern, each tiny green cavern and lichened promontory. Here transpired the secret existence of his early childhood. Strange obsessions, and cruel ones: to explain to his father how much he despised him, to torture his mother with a pretended indifference, to climb over the hedge and escape forever into another world. Secrets: how much he really knew, how unpleasant to his gravity and dignity the subterfuges of love did seem, how cloying the phrases and approaches of the old, how gauche and yet how mysteriously arousing. He knew what love was! In loneliness and secrecy he had discovered the power of Love, its prolonged mystery, its unspoken eloquence, making the whole world—trees, cries of birds, half-comprehended phrases, hours of the day—into its symbols and conspirators. And he knew what sin was, too. In solitude he had discovered it, and spoken warnings had been no more than a travesty of that childish awareness. He knew that he possessed the extraordinary powers of the beautiful and the haughty, and already he could suspect what evils would spring from these. He knew already the dangers that surrounded him and the vices of which he was guilty: heartlessness, pride, calculation, self-love. And it was this childish self-regard that turned each vice into actual terror; namely, sin.

And yet, under the protection of how delicate a balance the sweetness of childhood transpired! It was this magical perception of terror indeed that gave to the images of childhood their peculiar loveliness. For, after the real darkness and misery of night, and the nightly fear of death, how exquisite and responsive the hours of the day appeared! How desirable they seemed in the golden afternoon, how melancholy and unreal they became in the silver evening! At times as he sat beside the water in the shadow of the tree he felt an intense and solitary joy, by no means the joy of light-heartedness but rather the calm joy of actual illumination, a perception of the quality of life, so indefinably austere yet caressing. Moments to be lost forever, never even to be resurrected in memory: for they were of so fine a texture that they resembled micro-

scopic fish flowing backward and forward through the
meshes of a net. They would never be caught, for the remembering mind could never quite discern them, could
never know that they had once existed in a life so far more
delicate, pure, and profound than any that later years
could conceivably provide.

Now and then the lawn changed its character, became a
place unfamiliarly formal and aloof; such as during his
mother's garden parties; he could see the big plumed hats,
the sky-blue taffeta flashing in the dappled sunlight, the
feathery lace, the white gloves, the striped umbrellas. And
he could hear again the gentle voices, the undulating
laughter, the whimsical and suave phrases that snipped
their way through the air like scissors, and the tinkling of
the spoons and the saucers. His aunt Gwendolen lifted him
onto her lap and held him there. He could smell the perfume, see the white teeth, the skin coarse with powder and
age, the golden brooch, and the trembling earrings; he
could feel the soft flesh hideously against him and the
warm beating of the wicked heart, and then it was that he
discovered how subtly disguised and yet how casually the
sicknesses of the heart parade themselves: grief and love,
spun by the years into fantastic shapes, baroque postures,
refinements as delicate as lace and cold as ivory, but none
the less intense, none the less agonizing.

The golden days of youth, the days for which life had
created him! The sounds of the seashore at Le Touquet,
the sun on the incessant foam, the bitterness of the salt
water, the intriguing identity of each single grain of sand,
and far away the voice of Mademoiselle, her ribbons fluttering in the breeze and the buttons of her high black
shoes shining bizarrely in the morning sun. The drive in
the victoria between the olive trees, up along the shore of

Maggiore; the villa with its decaying urns, the veined plaster, the wistaria-hung balconies; a ball of pink wool and two knitting-needles left lying among the cypresses by the *gouvernante*; and far below the sailboats like petals in a dark blue saucer. And the quivering constant sounds rising from the city below toward the garden at Mustapha Supérieur, the venous green swords which rose from the soil in the tiny garden, two blue morocco slippers upon the white shining tiles; the curiously estranging odor of the old Algerian cook and of the filthy little Arab boy who stared at him with eyes of such surprise and self-forgetfulness. And the walks in Savernake Forest after sunset, listening to the leaves growing alert before a storm, to his father's quiet and remote voice, no longer alien now, but rich, exciting.

And the days at Eton, when the war was a fantastic rumor miles and miles away, leaving only a strange oppression in the air; the death of his father, for him so unsubstantial an affair that it appeared really to exist only in the nightmare gaze of his mother, her impassioned grief-stricken kiss, her terrible shuddering embrace. The green field with the fives courts at the end, the three red arches of the bridge, the statue of Henry VI in School Yard so inexplicably menacing and hostile, the scent of the freshly-cut lawns, the white flannels, the young faces shining with sweat, the voices calling, the sudden keenness, the jealousies, the adorations, the bitterness and delight. The warm blue snow of Austria that squeaked under his boots at Christmas, the frozen pond at night lit by lanterns, the quiet whisper of the skates and the cries of the skaters, the red cheeks and the flying scarves, the moments of display and of anguished rivalry, the hot chocolate in the log hut, the wet woolen clothes upon the floor, the four boys—

Augustus, Michael, Tom, and Tony—lying in front of the
fire, the hoarse joke, the sudden shyness, the gesture of
friendship so long hoped for and tremblingly received, the
happy journey home, the unforgetful dream.

And Cambridge. Those ingratiating days of hesitation
and unreality! Those platonic hours upon the grass lit by
the rays of sunlight slanting through the leaves, or among
the scattered dusty books lit by the rays that slanted
through the high windows. Their very unreality indeed
gave them a magical and melancholy innocence, not that
of childhood, but that of pure seclusion. The elaborate
pleas for a new order; the eloquent disputations on social
justice; ardors and ambitions which made every moment
seem important and profound. The sound of the oars as
they passed so gravely beneath the bridge; the willows
overhanging the Cam, and the cool academic arches of
Clare bridge reflected in the water; the green lawns at
Fenner's freshly cut and smelling of May, the sound of the
ball on the racket, the feel of a long backhand shot arrow-
ing down the line, the white flannels and the white balls
stained with green and the white lines crossing the green
grass and the green sparkling gut in the racket, all fringed
with delight, blossoming in the sunlight; the odor of rain
in the squash-courts in Portugal Place; the rain, the rain,
and then the green sunlight again, and now both together
caressing the dark passages, the old discolored spires, the
lawns, the whispering trees. The lamplight falling on the
wet ivy, the sound of footsteps hastening guiltily through
the glimmering quadrangle, the suggestive shadow of the
fountain on the moonlit grass and pebbles of the yard; the
silhouette of a tower, of a weather vane against the moving
clouds, the market place by torchlight on Guy Fawkes
night and the roofs under the starlight; the drunken voices,

the whispering gowned shadows passing, the nocturnal smells rising with such sweet punctuality from the wet ground as midnight approached, and the green scent of restless young men not yet hurled into the stagnant floods of existence.

In the gray late afternoons he would bicycle back in blazer and shorts, his face flushed and his moist locks curling over his ears, holding his squash-racket in his hand, looking down Trinity Street for a familiar shape stepping out of the haberdasher's or the bookseller's; and then, still wet and panting, yet curiously elated, he would enter the warm firelit room just as darkness was crossing the court, and there would sit the wiser and softer ones, his friends— tall squinting Clere and fragile Colin and dumpy Oliver— over tea and some cakes from Matthews', comparing Webster and Tourneur, or Menander and Terence; but quicker than any were these very ones (and this was their reward and punishment as well!) to recognize a Grecian loveliness in a certain negligent posture or a momentary glance, and to suffer with an unquenchable longing. In this room, out of the fragrances distilled by Racine or Theocritus or the amorous Sonnets scattered carelessly upon the floor, were spun intrigues so subtle and involved that hours could and would be spent in following their threads. Yet no more than the surface would be scratched, ever. A separate little world, and a dangerous one. The atmosphere was so subtly charged that everything carried meaning—the color of a scarf, the title of a slender volume of poems lying on the table, the position of the tennis clothes tossed on the bed after the return from the field, a hesitant preference expressed in the Court at ten o'clock.

Or gliding up the green mirror of the Cam under the charming bridges—Queen's, Clare, Gareth Hostel, King's,

John's—seeing the flowers of June, and the metallic beeches, and the unanimous ducklings; or, quietly after dusk, down past the last few boys at the bathing-pool, toward Grantchester and Byron's Pool and back again, passing a silent boat and two happy faces revealed for a moment by the light of a match, and suddenly overwhelmed with grief at leaving this place, at surrendering this rarefied and paralytic existence where the turn of a phrase or the turn of a head or a white ball passing to and fro across the net were, truly, all that seemed to matter.

One evening, on a visit after the summer holidays had begun, walking through King's Court, seeing in the distance the misty rococo willows and the peaceful, unassuming cows in King's Paddock, suddenly through the darkness he heard the organ in the Chapel playing Handel's familiar Largo; as he approached he began to tremble, the music so sonorous yet so delicate seemed to rise out of the ribs of the Chapel itself; the enormous dark Chapel itself seemed to be the instrument which poured forth from its old stones this music, up toward the vivid summery constellations; the melody was not a thing apart, it was a tapestry woven out of those buttresses, those willows, those lawns, those silent shapes, and instantly this music acquired the significance of a symbol, intense and unalterable; that is, the utter thrill, the trembling of love, the breath-taking agitation which shortly became a real anguish, while he was listening, represented to him, both then and yet more poignantly later on, the climax of his life, which had been consummated too early, too romantically, too exhaustingly, and above all in an atmosphere of total seclusion and unreality.

Never again! He would never again wander across that green lawn with a quick-beating heart, crossing the shad-

ows cast by the declining branches, toward some meeting-
place in a room or beside the river where he imagined
happiness to lie. But still he heard from time to time
(more clearly of late, it would appear) the echo of those
very same juvenile heartbeats. Nothing was ever totally
lost, of course, and if perhaps the agony of seeing so clearly
what could never again be grasped grew intense and still
more intense—well, he could not help being consoled by
the thought of such a sweet fidelity of the past; which, like
the touch of a woman's fingers, would console him, the
more he needed it, then all the more tenderly.

He learned what England had to teach; England, that
declining and dingy land of adorable scenes and adorable
faces; declining, yet still in a stray phrase, an account of a
distant deed recited years later, one might detect the impulses of a forgotten sort of spirit, a heart still careless, still
private, still contemptuous and fruitlessly adoring. He
learned, like the others in his class, not to care too much;
not to fidget, to fret, to resent, to loathe. Forever open to
new stabs of pain, at a reminiscent phrase, a teasing smile,
a racket and blazer flung on the grass, a voice calling softly
from a window, two figures disappearing among the trees:
little by little he learned, like a true Englishman, not to
care too deeply.

There was the Abbey at Moreton Tracey for instance.
One evening toward sunset he stood in front of those ruins;
and suddenly a flock of gray birds flew out of the tower, as
if they were little memories sent forth across the island to
soothe those scattered English spirits who had once been
here. The silky thistledown, the scent of blackberries, the
sound of yellowing leaves, were now a part of this tower,
and it seemed impossible that there shouldn't be some sort
of human life still clinging to those ancient storm-beaten

[97]

stones, like a shy bit of moss; so that a deserted bird's nest, the flutter of a feather, the sound of a cow, the bucolic voice of Madge the farmer, or the surprised face of Mr. Jelfs the school-teacher, all became a part of this tower; their life was a thing harmonious and inseparable.

Or another occasion, more tender but less self-forgetful, when the Welsh moonlight lay clinging to the creepers on the castle walls, on the casement, on the floor, and glowing across those two bodies, one blond and one dark, desperately locked into their rising tiger-like desires upon the enormous bed. Or, later, that familiar longing to reach through the curtains into another gentler and simpler life, seeing the room grow dark, the curtains parted, the necessary touch of warm limbs, the essential words whispered, the birdlike caress of hair against his cheek, and then the hand departing, the words fading away among the soliloquies of the ivy, the dry and delicate approach of self-knowledge, until at last it seemed inconceivable that love should ever signify anything but bitter sorrow.

And then, more and more faintly, the months in Berlin and Brussels; the shadowy young people who had spent their whole lives in trying so desolately yet fastidiously to devise some reply to suffering, unalleviated and degraded youthful suffering, the most perilous of all. And then, the desperate longing for purity, the detestation of cities, the fear of humanity, the recognition of escape. The new ambitions, the Greek islands, the long daily swims to a lonely rock, his body growing darker and harder so that even the natives turned to watch as he sauntered by. And then, passing more and more swiftly and passionlessly, the years which he spent on expeditions—in Africa, in Arabia, in the Turkestan—with the colorless days in Somerset and London scattered through them like autumn leaves, yellow and brittle in the pursuing breeze. More and more quickly he would fly from place to place, exploring new corners of the world, searching for cities, hills, plateaus which no one had ever visited before, approaching each one with a new thrill of expectancy, hoping for ever to escape from the chill in his heart, the lovelessness, and the loneliness. And it was these years and these voyages that whispered the final bit of eloquence into his ears: Whatever you do, there is another side. For whatever you do that is noble, you must suffer, for whatever joy you pluck out of darkness you must pay. If evil is in you, then nothing will save you, nothing. There is no chance of victory, however adroitly and passionately the sweet self-deception is sustained. You will be punished, whatever you do, whether you join the virtuous or the wicked; whether you subside into the pure and obvious terrors of the evil ones whose faces betray their despair, or join the subtler, more distinguished and more devastating number of those who have succeeded, been wealthy, been good and respected and utterly merciless.

So that, little by little, he became familiar with the chilling pangs endured by those who have lost, somewhere amongst the ardors of childhood and youth, all power to love.

☆

When he opened his eyes again the sun was shining down through the roof of the tent. A circle of light lay quivering on the floor beside him, making everything seem alive again, dispelling all mystery and danger. He felt as if

[99]

he were softly arising out of a deep warm pool—so deep
that he could imagine no bottom, so warm that his limbs
felt thoroughly languorous and longed to slip back again.

The men were still sleeping quietly in their sheepskins;
none of them had moved. He reached out his hand and
began to nibble at a black crust which he had been saving
for several days. It was the very last bit of food in the tent.
But it tasted horribly, he could not bring himself to swal-
low it, and finally he spat it out again.

Then he rose and walked through the door out into the
dazzling whiteness. He moved very slowly, it seemed as if
he must walk with an exaggerated caution, and every step
were a matter of immense significance.

He walked through the snow toward the edge of the
cliff. Far below he could see what appeared to be a path,
and moving along it a row of black shadows; yaks they
seemed to be, slowly crawling across the ice. High overhead the black birds were appearing. But nothing seemed
of consequence, nothing carried meaning.

He sat down in the snow and watched the incredible
valley. The ache had vanished from his eyes, his limbs felt
soft and serene again. He was surprised to see how light-
hearted he was, and comparatively happy.

Then he closed his eyes, and slid back upon the past
once more, that consoling little island, the past.

☆

Yes, all four of the seasons were lovely.

Winter, with its streams still watchful under the ice, the
snow-capped stones; the snow on the fallen logs, on the

dead leaves, on the blackberry hedges, on the walls, the turrets, the icicles dripping from the steaming stables.

Spring, with its eager blossoms, the white chickens venturing further into the fields, the clothes billowing on the line, the glitter of yellow and white on the softening meadows; the willows delicate over the delighted streams, now hanging scarcely perceptible draperies of green over their pointing arms; the air full of excited sounds and scents, the birds growing noisy and impudent, the hedges budding, the cocoons bursting, the salmon leaping, even the fox intoxicated with the air now and again moving brazenly out into the dangerous sunlight.

Summer; the grace of the land grown rich; the hedges shining in the sunlight, still and full, the warm odors curling lazily amongst the berry bushes, the butterflies lying stagnant on a decaying trunk with their velvet-eyed wings wide open and only their gilded fringes moving ever so slowly; and the streams too lie still and mirror-like, and the angler watches the fish darting beneath the fleecy clouds which only now and then are set atremble by the quick flash of a fin beneath; so still, the streams are, that a spider can weave his web from an overhanging twig down to a floating leaf, across the contented silence.

And autumn, yet more entrancing, with the sunlight moving across the red foliage; the grass still fresh and deep, hiding the tiny sleeping furry creatures, the dew heavy on the hedges until late in the morning, the scent of night still clinging to the blades; then noon, full and contemplative, the trees laden down with fruit, the red apples falling with only a quick whisper into the deep grass and presently the first leaves likewise beginning to fall; the roe deer and the fallow moving slowly through the hazy purple wood; the delicious scent of hot tea-cakes flowing out into the approaching twilight; spring the time of longing but happy, autumn also a time of longing but sad; everything departing, nothing to be done, and for a few exquisitely changeful moments the enchantment is still held captive on the twigs, about to spring away and vanish.

Oh, England, England! your faces so gentle and singular, your touching landscapes; dreaming, misty island, land so afraid of being young and of seeing too clearly; dusk now descending, hour most subtle and bewildering of all; so casually drawing across the countryside its enchanting vapors, a gesture of tenderness before the sullen winds and cold fogs arrive. The willow almost touches the pool, indeed its lowest yellow leaves are already floating in the black water. The last green moths hide in the crevices of the bark, frayed and weary, ready to die quietly. A final gleam of sunlight still hovers hesitantly over the barnyard, the dovecote, the winding path, the sleepy soft-eyed cattle, the oaks, the castles, the spires. The birds are leaving. Southward from Westmoreland and Lancastershire, down across Devon they go, through Exmoor and Dartmoor Forest toward the scattered misty isles, and then far south toward Portugal. In Somerset the soft wind still carries a few last fragments of cobweb and pollen across the fields. Then the air grows quite still and ever so loving, caressing the russet leaves like the touch of a mother's hand on the golden hair of her departing boy.

☆

Once more he opened his eyes. But only for a moment. A feathery softness fled through his body. His arms seemed light as snow, pale and cool as snow, beneath the furry cloak. He felt that he could fly, if he chose. Fly on and on, amid those ethereal peaks, high above the world, one with the light and everlasting sky. The snow looked very dear to him. Desirable. Intimate. As if his own body were made of snow too, and longed to enter the snow all about him in a final ecstatic and all-consuming embrace.

Then he lay back, closed his eyes, and felt the snow rise up and caress his cheeks, his lips, his eyelids.

BOOK TWO

Serafimov

11

The Men at the Inn

DAY AFTER DAY THEY WOULD SIT, THE RUSSIAN AND
the Belgian, beside the fire in the *caravanserai*
and watch the strangers passing in and out.
Weeks passed, the autumn faded, the days grew cool. Some
of the men grew presently to be strangers no longer. But
every day, until the big winter set in, there would be newcomers whom they had not seen before. The refugees from
Russia were daring less and less to speak of their one great
hatred; communist officials of one kind and another would
troop in from time to time, smiling to themselves, or looking very superior; but occasionally some one—like old
cross-eyed Varanin from Odessa, or blond young Smaratkinov from Tashkent, would flare up drunkenly and cry

[107]

out all that he had suffered so unjustly. During the winter that followed both Varanin and Smaratkinov disappeared.

Serafimov knew enough to keep his mouth shut. It was no use complaining. Hostages—that was what Dr. Liu had called them; but actually no one seemed to care what they did. The whole incident of their arrival in Aqsu had apparently been forgotten. They had to pay a few pence to the keeper of the *serai* now and then, that was all. They could do what they pleased, they could go where they pleased. No one ever spoke to them. They were prisoners, but it was the winter that was their gaoler, and the snow. As soon as the warm weather arrived, he said to himself, he would hurry off toward Shanghai with the first caravan.

One evening as he lay on the floor, half-asleep, he saw a face peering through the window. He was startled, the face looked so familiar—rather like the face of the Frenchman de la Scaze; but this man wore no *pince-nez*, his face was paler, his eyes were more piercing. However, it set Serafimov to wondering what had happened to de la Scaze, and to his beautiful wife who had gone off on a mad trip with a slender Englishman and a weary-eyed Chinese; and to the other two, the young and handsome ones, Germans apparently, who had been imprisoned in Aqsu? There was no way, really, of finding out.

The crude Turkis and Mongols would lie like dogs on the floor all night. Gloomily Serafimov would watch the light from the single candle, which flickered with each gust that entered through the open door and created nervous little shadows everywhere—on the crumpled newspapers, on the empty red bottles, on the spotted floor, the huge bow-legged table, the broken chairs, the men's faces and their coarse clothes. Flea-infested, these clothes were, worn far too long, so that they had lost the quality of cloth and had become like leather, a sort of second skin. Their boots, worn into grotesque shapes and smelling like a stable, were wrapped about and patched with bits of cloth and string. They were animals; no more, no less. The locks of long shining hair, hopelessly matted and louse-ridden, fell over each pimply pock-marked face like the mane of a wild beast. Their noses were shapeless, constantly running, sometimes blackened with blood, and the snoring breath would set their nostrils vibrating, the curling hairs within them swaying to and fro like saplings in a storm. Their mouths would open wide, two black enormous teeth would jut out from those alcohol-scented caverns, and if he had looked closely he could have discerned, beyond a doubt, the enamored lice and the fleas meandering gaily to and fro in each soup-stained thicket of beard. Their hands were hardly hands at all; swollen and brutal paws they were, the nails torn, the knuckles bleeding, and there was no end to the startling variety of sores that disfigured their skin. Hideous utterly, most of them, until one of them would open his sleepy eyes, colored a rare azure, perhaps, like certain Russians, or tinted with that lustrous knifelike gray of the Kirghiz tribes, or the cool sharp black of the Buriats, or even the deep and languorous black of the people south of the Himalayas; and perhaps in the naïve animal gaze Serafimov would see something that warmed him; he would feel closer to them, and by and by feel comforted by their cruel, tender, jocular imbecilic ways.

*

There was Sorje, for example. Sorje, the lovable, the

[109]

filthy, the swollen-faced, the weak-willed. He would come tramping in morosely, wearing his Tibetan boots and dirty homespuns, his ornaments and necklace, and in a few minutes his face would gleam with delight, and forthwith he would bubble over with drunken reminiscences, homely chatter about families and ancestral prophecies, meaningless tidbits plucked with affection out of the muddle of his past.

He would explain to Serafimov how to lead a good life. Serafimov listened earnestly, feeling pleased, somewhat like a teacher whose pupil has learned his lesson well.

"Sleep, but not too much," Sorje would say. "Work, but not too much. Drink, but not too much; be regular in your drinking ways, and once a week you can go further than usual. Lie with your wife," he would say gently, "twice a week. Be kind, but not," and his voice grew firm, "too kind. Work, but do not think of gold. Desire peace with your neighbors, but not with your enemies. A man cannot live without hatred, that is his destiny. Beget five children," he hinted cautiously, picking his nose with a dirty forefinger, "or perhaps six or seven; never more than twelve; and pray that most of them will be boys! Learn from what others tell you, but do not be swayed by them. Strive to please only those whom you both love and respect. Travel to the neighboring villages from time to time; but do not go too far, do not stay away too long. . . ." And so on.

Then there was Kostya, with his blue-black locks hanging over his perspiring forehead, and his pig eyes peering eagerly now at one man and then another. He took a fancy to both Serafimov and Goupillière, and tried to impress them with his vulgar little tales. He spoke in an elaborate citified accent which Serafimov found amusing. "I was in

Moscow, you know, five years ago," he would say from time to time. His great misfortune, clearly, was that he was born ugly; there was nothing, deep inside him, that he longed for except just that one thing—beauty; romance; love, in short. But he had to do without it, and he became picturesquely sensitive, lascivious, depressed, useless, and all in all rather contemptible. He lacked any trace of strength, so it appeared.

He loved to tell about his experiences in love: lies, one and all, but it didn't matter. How he found, when he was six years old, a little girl lying in the bushes one evening at sunset, and in a surprising access of desire held her in his inexperienced arms; how, a few years later, a shepherd boy, seeing him daydreaming beside the well, suddenly seized him by the arm, kissed him passionately, and poured out his overflowing heart to him; how he glimpsed his sister one afternoon lying in the arms of a dark young stranger, in the birch copse at the bottom of the hill; how the stammering girl whom nobody loved one morning ran up to him and covered him with hot caresses. These imaginary tales constituted a whole miserable little love life of their own, touching but not quite tragic; and, in a way, they were real enough; after all, they comforted him somewhat; but only, of course, when he was reciting them to others—that was the sad, degraded thing about it.

"When are women loveliest?" he would ask romantically. Or, roguishly, "When are they wisest?" Or, in a philosophical tone, "When are they most dangerous?" Or, "When they are most incomprehensible?" Or, "When are they most unkind?" The answer to all of these was, inevitably, "When they are making love!"

"Some day, when I am old," he announced with an assumed bitterness, "I shall climb to the top of the highest cliff in the world, and cry out, so that every continent and island can hear me, about the perfidy of woman!"

The Russians in general, Serafimov was able to observe, were apt to be sentimental, bigoted, colossally provincial, totally irrational. They spoke of wars in foreign countries, of riots, of strikes, and so on. Now and then one would speak of Marx, or Lenin; from their words it might as well have been Nebuchadnezzar or Xantippe they were apotheosizing. They appeared to understand nothing at all, nothing that involved even the faintest trace of logic or pertinence.

Soviet officers appeared, rather surprisingly, from time to time. Ill-mannered, conceited, stupid men, yet at the bottom full of a certain magnanimity, an authentic animal generosity. They weren't really selfish or self-absorbed, that was the important thing. They wore the hammer and sickle on their peaked felt caps, and small pictures of Lenin on the buttons of their gray uniforms. They wore their hair very short, which gave them a look quite dazzlingly stubborn and fanatical.

One or two of them were different, naturally. There was one from Tashkent, an enormous bear of a man, with one ear missing. He wore black leather boots fastidiously polished, loose riding-breeches, a filthy gray blouse, and when it grew colder a pointed cap with chin flaps. A determined and not ignoble face, which dissolved sometimes, very rarely, into a boy's shy smile. A creature of instinct entirely; his eyes were the eyes of a madman, and he could see for miles, he could see a bird flying three miles away or a horseman crossing a distant range of hills.

He too was interested in theories. "Where is this world going," he would inquire in a husky voice, "where are we all going?"

"Eternal joy, of course," simpered the old Dane, Asplund.

"Ah, truly? You really think that?"

"Oh," muttered the shaggy old Dane, "yes indeed. Oh yes. There's no doubt of it. The world is growing better every year—wiser, kinder, safer. Mm-m."

And then he would suddenly lose his temper. "Civilization," he howled, "civilization! It's not a matter of progress. You've been quite wrong. It's simply a matter of wanting something new. Humanity grows bored so easily, you see, that's the whole trouble. Yes. Our dear kind brotherly human race. So we invent toy after toy to please us. The toys are becoming rather desperate, rather distorted and horrible, you know. We pretend they're useful, edifying, exalted, and so on. Nonsense!" His fine Scandinavian eyes flashed with fury, his lips trembled, a streak of saliva ran down his beard.

"Toys, no more than toys, to keep us busy! Women are better off than men; they always have something to keep them busy. But we men must invent toys to give us a feeling of importance. And we call them civilization, just why I don't know, except that it is a good resonant hypocritical word, not inappropriate to our rotting hypocritical little bodies. . . ."

There would be terrific drinking bouts now and then. No one seemed to know where the liquor came from— vodka, most of it; it just appeared, a new supply of it every so often. And the men in the *caravanserai* would go boasting, flattering, insulting, accosting, threatening, raging, attacking; maudlin and vicious with drink.

After the cold set in they quarreled more and more. Every little thing—the way one of them snored, or another wore his cap, or another belched, or another scratched, or another stank, or another whimpered—it all grew more and more difficult for them to bear. The atmosphere became one of a constant furtive hostility.

☆

Once Serafimov told Goupillière the story of his escape from Russia. How he had left his beloved native village of Dolya and had gone to Odessa, how he had met a group of students, editors and "intellectuals," how some years later one day two young officers came to his house and arrested him, and he was tried less than a week later with four others for espionage and treason, condemned, and sent to Siberia two months later. He described the interminable journey through the *taigan*, the great belt of primeval forest beyond which rose the white peaks of the Saigan range; the village of log houses, the muddy streets, the diseases, the famine, the cold, the wolves; the summers too, the meadows and the haystacks and beyond these the forests of larch and spruce; the nights in the cottage by the river, the men and the boys drunk, singing bawdy songs, quarreling, celebrating, hating, growing old and rotting away; his escape two years later in a troika, past rocky gorges, frozen streamlets, innumerable sheep heads and great horns scattered in the snow, past caravans and carts motionless at night, past villages built out of pine logs, deep valleys, endless plains, past Biisk and then snowswept Altaiskoë in a tinkling sleigh, and then the frightening border, the prowling wolves, the frozen forests, the military post, the blond-bearded officers in their pointed caps and their long coats trimmed with red velvet, and at last Mongolia, which he had thought would mean freedom, the

mere sound of whose name had always suggested liberty,
equality, release from the bonds of thought and tradition.
Goupillière would listen carefully and watch him with
glittering eyes.

☆

And he in turn would watch Goupillière. He looked like
a very wicked man to Serafimov. His sharply featured face,
his big black eyes, his curly blue-black hair that flickered
as if it were alive, his delicate olive skin, his fine restless
fingers. But above all, that plum-colored scar which slid up
from his mouth toward his left ear. Alive, that scar seemed
to be; it looked as if it were leading a malicious, snake-like
life of its very own. A symbol of discord, of naughtiness.
Serafimov kept wondering what Goupillière could have
done to acquire this scar. It changed his whole face profoundly. The face of a thief, Serafimov kept thinking. The
face of a whisperer, an eavesdropper, a conspirator.
He longed, intensely, to confide in him. For he was the
only man in the *serai* who had any share whatever in his
past. But he didn't quite dare. He distrusted him, of
course. But that wasn't the true reason. He began to admire him, all against his will. He looked so very intelligent, full of self-control, competent, shrewd. And at the
same time so very fragile. Serafimov could have twisted
him in two with a flick of the wrist. But this knowledge,
far from giving him a feeling of superiority, made him feel
a little bit helpless. For Goupillière possessed a curious and
impressive sort of nervous strength, like that of a rodent,
dangerous in its way. His glittering eyes, cold and yet fiery,
began to disquiet and to alienate Serafimov.

12

Solitude

EARLY ONE EVENING, SOMEWHAT WARMER THAN THE rest, Serafimov stepped out of the *caravanserai* and went to bathe in the little brown stream that trickled around the outskirts of the city.

For the first time in weeks he felt, as he stepped out of the shallow cool water, free once more, and clean, and really natural. He stood on a flat stone and looked down at his reflection trembling in the water below him. He could see his toes, reflected against the very edge of the rock. And below those the reflection of his ankles, his thick strong legs spread far apart, happy to be unclad and alive again; and between these that traditional shape, that magical and terrifying bit of flesh and blood whose behavior was so full of caprice, so far past all conjectures; which gave him strange and unexpected orders from time to time, creating a sudden breathlessness, or a quickening of the pulse, a spell of gloom or a wild spasm of pleasure, a bout of weariness or an uncontrollable fit of trembling, moments of stormy anger or, again, periods of warm and jovial tolerance.

And far below, beneath that tawny belly and that enormous shaggy chest, deep in the water so it seemed, he could see his face, in shadow: a coarse, shapeless sort of face: but it meant nothing to him: it was his face, that was all, something he wore, like a piece of clothing, neither handsome nor repulsive.

But, from this moment on, he felt profoundly and bewilderingly aware of his body. He felt the water drying on his skin, and as he stepped back into his clothes, he felt for the first time that they were a shell, shameful and unreal. And on his way back to the inn he was aware of his muscles moving beneath that shabby cloth, and his real existence, the warmth and movement of his limbs, progressing there so secretly yet powerfully.

☆

He began to feel restless after this. His body troubled him.

He proceeded to withdraw more into himself, since life had become more complicated, a matter of uncertainties and conflicts. Nevertheless, he was drawn constantly to the company of others; partly because they comforted him, but chiefly out of instinct quite simply, just as a bear or an ox

[117]

or a lion will feel drawn to the company of his own kind.
To be with the others at the *caravanserai*, to see their faces,
to smell them, to hear their laughter and buffoonery, all
became a need.

Still, little by little he began to realize that there existed
in this place, this climate, this isolation, something which
alarmed him.

☆

On some nights he felt, as he awoke from a troubled
sleep, completely overwhelmed with desire. To lie alone
became suddenly intolerable to him. So he would bundle
up a few clothes—a coat, or a blanket—and arrange them
primitively into the shape of a woman's body. He would
then press this effigy to himself, cover it with kisses, caresses, whisper to it, clutch at it in a supreme spasm of
adoration, and finally, somewhat calmer now, fall asleep
once more.

All this grew worse and worse. Presently he took to exercising like a madman all day long, walking, running even,
performing in the morning and the evening that quaint
repertoire of knee-bends, push-ups, and so on, taught to
him years ago by his spruce and military uncle Ivan in
Odessa (who had been somewhat of a dandy, actually, and
could not tolerate the sight of his figure year by inelegant
year subsiding beyond control).

But, in the long run, all this sort of thing didn't really
make much difference. If anything, it ended only by making matters worse, and his body, groomed into alertness,
became more imperious than ever. He began to think al-

most constantly, even while the others were arguing noisily, even while he was panting back along the street after a run out past the city walls, of the shape of an imagined woman, perhaps not even conspicuously attractive, but still a woman and therefore inexpressibly desirable and enchanting. He never ceased wanting her, and once or twice he even fell on his knees, at night, and prayed while sweat ran down his brow that these torments be relieved.

✻

In the meantime, life was not becoming any more pleasant at the *caravanserai*. November arrived, and with it the general cold and snow and ice and tempest, all of a sudden. That meant that the men grew more reluctant to leave the inn, unless there was an especially good reason. They grew lazy and slovenly. The *serai* began to resemble a prison. The inn yard grew filthier and filthier, and it reached such a point that a snowfall was really a profoundly welcome thing, since it covered all the disgusting refuse in the streets with an aseptic white shawl.

That, of course, was by no means the only unpleasantness. A fire had to be kept going constantly, the air grew stagnant and fœtid, and the vermin gathered together in the central room where now everyone took to sleeping, since the rest of the building was too cold and damp. Cockroaches were forever dashing officiously in and out of every crevice in wall or floor, looking very servile and sleek in their shining black uniforms. There was no one, naturally, who wasn't troubled with fleas and lice. Eventually they grew not to mind these so much, but those unpredictable

[119]

visitors, the cockroaches and the rats, became all the more execrable.

Now and then some one fell sick. One man turned green, and the fragrance distilled by his sores became quite unbearable; he was moved to another room. Some had trouble with their digestions, though it wasn't so bad as a casual observer might have expected, to tell the truth, considering what the food was. Serafimov had contracted a sort of eczema (it first appeared two days after his bath in the stream) but this disappeared again after a few weeks. He made every effort to keep himself clean, and to wash his clothes now and then, but this grew more and more beset with difficulties, and furthermore the rest began to make fun of him, and even more so of Goupillière (who, fortunately, could not understand some of the insinuations which were uttered apropos of his continuous and really heroic regard for appearance and cleanliness).

There were now about a dozen men sleeping at the *caravanserai*. Each one of them had his little vices, little habits that made living together progressively exhausting. One took opium, and that was all; in every other way he was thoroughly ingenuous and mild of disposition. There was one, of course, who drank too much. He was regularly carried into one of the rooms upstairs and there locked in whenever he went too far, which was about once a week. This one had money; he was able to bribe the townsmen into bringing him vodka on the sly. There was one who was a glutton: he made of eating an elaborate and resonant ceremony, his eyes grew glassy, his tongue lost control, his lips grew wet and noisy: all this might have seemed relatively trivial, but in the long run it grew quite peculiarly trying, and if there was one whom the rest especially detested, it was certainly this thin reptilian Turki.

There was one (old Varanin) who constantly bragged; there was one (Kostya) forever talking about women; there was one (young Smaratkinov) who uninterruptedly imagined himself sick, afflicted with outlandish ills—stones in his brain, worms in his finger tips—a puny little hypochondriac; one was malicious, and ended up by inventing fantastic lies calculated to set them all against one another, till at last no one took him seriously any more, and then he gave up all pretense at credibility and his lies became merely preposterous; one stole; one whined; one imagined himself a spy, took to eavesdropping and, with elaborately furtive air, scribbling on bits of paper: no one paid any attention to him at all. And one began to make a habit of bringing his women into the general room late at night and there, in front of the rest of them, performing his blatant and distasteful amours. This last created a general restlessness, and those among them who led unfulfilled lives were driven into frantic desires of one kind and another: women were brought in—some of them palatable and lively, some of them shabby and inert—and there were nights of drunkenness and violent promiscuity, when the lamps were upset and the darkened room was filled with the murmurations of a highly variegated but utterly loveless lovemaking.

And yet, week by week, in this place where the utter despicability of man caught in a state of helplessness and stagnation was so constantly demonstrated, Serafimov felt growing in him a certain understanding; a certain feeling of brotherhood, almost of love. The more he saw, the more fully he began to comprehend, and there soon was almost nothing that he could not have brought himself to forgive. Man is the instrument of his surroundings, he reflected: no crime or shabbiness is to be condemned absolutely,

[121]

everything is relative, one can never know everything—if one could, then no doubt one could bring oneself to love even the most hideous, the most contemptible, and the most corrupt.

In this way, and in this shabbiest of companies, Serafimov felt how his tormented heart was growing, little by little.

✫

But, significantly, while the spirit was so anxiously learning to grope about, the flesh grew impertinent and capricious.

He was growing lazy, for one thing. He would lie there in the morning, listening for half an hour, an hour, two hours, to the others indolently shuffling about. Then finally he would turn over, open his eyes, sit up and watch. But it wasn't until an hour or two after this, when the rest were awaiting the bowl of green broth which was about to appear on the big table, that he finally rose, arranged his clothes, fastened his shirt at the neck, tied the strings around his boots, and slopped three handfuls of cold dirty water over his face.

And, along with this, grew various little private habits: he avoided stepping on the cracks in the floor; he would run his fingers along the rough surface of the wall whenever he walked; he picked his nose, scratched at his scalp, plucked the hairs out of his ears and chewed them, all with great intentness. It grew so that he could scarcely move, or even sit quietly, without indulging in a little ritual of his own, dingy yet tyrannical.

He was growing fatter now, and he would run his finger

under his clothes along the deepening crease in his belly as he sat there, with mingled apprehension and resignation, even with a certain satisfaction. He would suffer now and then from the agonies of conscience. But not often. He took to daydreaming more and more: Explorations, airplane flights over oceans and continents, exploits of astonishing courage, plans for human welfare on a grand scale; and, especially, spells of endurance, bodily pain, and spiritual suffering, too.

"I am a weakling," he would murmur to himself. "I am destined to suffer. I must suffer before I grow strong again."

☆

There was one thing, however, which tugged at him in another direction. Fear. He could never have explained this to himself. The fact was that he continued to feel more and more mystified by Goupillière.

Goupillière seemed remote, elusive. Serafimov couldn't help rather admiring him. He was gifted, incredibly efficient in his way, brilliant in his power to preserve himself intact under the most adverse circumstances. He never submitted, even for an instant, to his surroundings. Everyone began to fear him, many obviously began to envy him and hate him.

Everything he did was graceful, purposeful, alive. His black eyes never lost their watchful sparkle, his slender body never lost its animal nervousness. And strangest of all, his face never changed. He was the only one who ever shaved, for one thing. His vanity was unbounded; he resorted to any effort and stratagem to preserve his appearance; and he succeeded—his smooth cheeks, his fine skin, his silky hair, his energy, all remained miraculously with him.

In this place, where men's faces were so apt to become horrible and hateful masks, this was most conspicuous. The rest of them, though their bodies may not have remained lonely, nevertheless displayed an utter isolation in their faces; not merely ugly, these countenances were rather of that very kind that repels affection most—gluttonous, stagnant, half imbecilic.

But Goupillière's face was different. It glowed with energy, with intention. He seemed to be forever planning, forever thinking sharp, surreptitious thoughts which he kept to himself.

It was disconcerting to look at him. Seen from the right, his profile looked haughty, serene, as beautiful as a woman's face, really amazingly beautiful in contrast with the bear-faced creatures all about him. That side of his face made Serafimov feel very strange. It made him feel humble, protective, almost desirous. But the other side, the left profile, filled him with distrust. Predatory it looked, watchful, and haggard. Really hideous. And then, seen from the front, the two halves merged into an expression of terrible irony, a discordant mixture of calm and agitation, of coolness and of delicate ferocity. Very magnetic, that face was.

What, Serafimov kept wondering, was the strange power that Goupillière possessed? That animal grace filled him with surprise, that extraordinary cooperation which seemed to exist between his body and his spirit, such as one usually finds only in children. Magic, no more, no less: that was how it struck Serafimov. That tranquillity of manner, that shrewd and intimate gaze, that slow mag-

netic voice, the challenging and uncapturable fire that
seemed to animate him, making him both close and remote. Everything about him was delicate, precise—his gestures, his hands, even his finger nails. He was, Serafimov
reflected, full of a very rare sort of electrical energy; everything he touched flashed into life and yet he controlled it
always; it was as if he were guiding events, and the other
people were no more than marionettes whose gestures and
words he could have manipulated to suit his own whimsical vanity.

He wondered what Goupillière thought of him. He was
so gentle, so restrained, so even-tempered. "Does he like
me?" thought Serafimov. "Does he trust me?" Then it occurred to him that he himself, of course, did not in the
least trust Goupillière.

In this hothouse atmosphere, where they all began to be
absorbed so much in the varied manifestations of man's
baser instincts, Goupillière alone seemed alert to the tormenting processes of the spirit. He would talk to Serafimov
about their companions. He knew, or suspected, almost
everything, seeing far more than he would say, seeing, as
clearly as if they were pebbles under a rippling stream, the
desires and devastations that fluttered beneath each murky
mask of flesh. And more than that. It seemed to Serafimov
as if, through this knowledge and his flexible magnetic
power, he could, if he chose, control all these lives. Not
benevolently, perhaps; indeed, Serafimov began to feel
that whoever came under the régime of that keen spirit
was, in a sense, doomed.

One evening he asked Goupillière, rather casually:
"What is your greatest ambition? What would make you
happiest?"

Goupillière smiled. "Ah, Alexei, my friend," he replied

playfully; "to kill my enemies, to strangle them, to torture those who have caused me unpleasantness!"

Serafimov was deeply impressed by the poise of a man who could joke about those impulses which, at the bottom, really seemed to inspire and govern his whole existence.

☆

Our lives transpire, perhaps in loneliness, Serafimov would murmur to himself, but most unquestionably and everlastingly, in solitude. One must grow accustomed to it, it is no use bluffing and pretending, in the long run.

Surrounding all of us rises a barrier of air, he would reflect, as he sat in the half-darkness by the hour, and then a barrier of skin. It is best that it should be so, no doubt. Dismiss the barrier of air, press body against body, and loneliness may vanish. But the barrier of skin will still remain, solitude will remain. Only now and then, very rarely, the imagination will cut through this and achieve supernaturally a glimpse of the spirit that lurks within another body. It is a horrible experience. It is like seeing a man's bowels beneath glass; it is like smelling another man's blood.

It did not comfort Serafimov to feel himself drawing closer to this subtle Frenchman. Far from creating a kinship of heart, it created, very gradually, the beginnings of a secret and consuming hatred.

13

Madame Tastin

THERE WAS A RUSSIAN WOMAN FROM HARBIN LIVING in Aqsu about whom the men at the *caravanserai* used to chatter on certain occasions. She was thirty-five or so, they would say—some claimed that she was older, forty, forty-five, even fifty!—nor was she particularly pretty; but there was something about her, so Serafimov gathered, which intrigued them immensely. Not a mere prostitute, by any manner of means, but a woman of considerable wit, elegance, and ingenuity. So they said.

However, Serafimov never thought much about all this until one evening, as he walked about the streets glumly he happened to pause in front of the old gray prison. This was where they had locked up those two young students.

A very depressing place. He began to feel very sorry for them. Then he passed on. Not far from the prison stood a house in which only a single window of the second floor was illumined. In front of this hung a curtain. But outlined on the curtain, as distinctly as if the figures had been cut out of black paper with a fine pair of shears, he saw the figure of a woman languorously and very deliberately undressing, first unbuttoning her dress at the waist, then slowly sliding the whole thing over her head. He could see the points of her breasts and the flawless curve of her back. And then he watched, with extreme physical excitement, her amorous posturings and the approach of a soldier, a regular brute of a man—he could see the shaggy beard, the unbuttoned uniform, his cap still sitting incongruously on his head, the clumsy pawings all silhouetted with the utmost precision. The two figures fluttered upon the curtain as they twisted and turned in their preliminary skirmishings. Then they disappeared to one side of the window and, though he waited breathlessly for a long time, he saw them no more.

When he returned to the inn the drunkards were noisily arguing about a recent murder in the city.

"Should he have killed her for being faithless?" shouted Smaratkinov.

"Certainly," argued Kostya, the bleary-eyed. "She deserved to be killed, if not for being faithless, then at least for giving him her disease!"

"Nonsense," muttered old Varanin, "he was sick already, as all of us are. You are indulging in sheer sentimentality, no more, no less."

"Oh, women!" cried Kostya, in mock despair, his ugly little eyes beaming from his flaccid face. "Oh, beautiful, dangerous race! Oh, the naughty ways of love!"

They yelled, they screamed, while outside the cool wind from the mountains was singing gently, rustling the dead leaves that hung from the single tree in the courtyard.

Presently Serafimov mentioned, in a casual manner, the scene which he had just witnessed and which so preoccupied his mind. They laughed. The house which he had just passed, they explained with many digressions, innuendoes, parenthetical elaborations and categorical cross-references, was assuredly the house of Madame Tastin.

Serafimov resolved, as he lay in his corner that night, unable to fall asleep, to visit Madame Tastin's house the next evening.

☆

He entered the room and was amazed. A very comfortable room, all in all—heavy red curtains, a magenta rug, somewhat worn, an old picture of two languid ladies in Grecian costumes on one wall and on the other a large painting in very crude colors of the Bay of Naples by moonlight, Vesuvius smoking in the distance. Obviously some attempt had been made to give it an appearance of respectability and European sophistication. On a table underneath the picture of Naples stood a big round bowl with two Japanese fantails swimming back and forth through a little Japanese castle and some water ferns that swayed gently with each movement of the fish. Beside this stood some china cups, also Japanese, and a plateful of wafers and raisins. In a corner, upon a pedestal, stood a small bronze bust beneath which Serafimov read the word *Voltaire*. He was impressed, for he had frequently heard

[129]

people refer to Voltaire in admiring tones, during those "intellectual" days in Odessa.

Madame Tastin was charming, he thought. She sat on the sofa in her black taffeta dress. Bewitching, thought he, and he could scarcely control the trembling of his hands and the hoarseness of his voice. Soon his eyes began to water, so that the whole room, Madame Tastin included, looked rather blurred, as if it were a huge goldfish bowl.

But Madame Tastin behaved very coldly when he rose and took her hand. He was at a loss. Madame Tastin smiled. She removed her hand and looked at him teasingly.

Then she began to simper. "No, no," she exclaimed, in a sing-song voice. "You are too big and strong! You are a regular lion!"

She lowered her eyelids. They looked like the wrinkled petals of a tearose which has lain for years between the pages of an old volume.

"I am afraid," she whimpered, with a leer, "so afraid, of your strong teeth and your big heavy paws. And I am still more afraid of your wild eyes and yellow mane and hot blood! Yes, I am afraid of you, my man!" Her eyes looked big and empty, and a bit uncontrolled; now and then she would shiver a little. She seemed very absent-minded.

Serafimov decided that she was drunk. He felt very discouraged and unhappy suddenly. "She doesn't like me," he thought. Suddenly, in a new onrush of passion, he was seized with a desire to humiliate her, to hurt her, to crush her to the ground.

But he didn't dare, of course. Instead he simply rose and said "Good Night." She didn't seem surprised or disconcerted in the least, and smirkingly bade him farewell.

"Come again," she murmured softly, and then quickly

she smiled at him, a new and unexpected smile, full of a sweet tenderness, he thought.

Serafimov turned away and stepped out into the street with aching heart. Suddenly and inexplicably he was almost in tears. As if it were a precious jewel to be buried deep in his heart he hurried off with this smile still imprinted on his senses. The big room in the inn was empty. He threw himself on his blanket in the corner, trembling. Infinitely happy and infinitely torn, feeling as he had never felt before, he murmured, without knowing what he said, over and over again, "I love you."

Not much later Goupillière entered. Without appearing to notice Serafimov he sat down at one of the tables and called for some food. The old hag brought him a few crusts and a tumbler of wine, then disappeared again.

Serafimov watched him eat. He ate very slowly and cautiously, and with great precision, like a cat. Everything was chewed carefully, even though he manifestly did not relish it. The wine was sipped drop by drop, with an air of calculation and disdain. Serafimov lay back, pretending to be asleep, and peered at him as if he were an actor on a stage at the moment which the author has chosen to reveal his real self. Serafimov could recognize him in the act of guarding himself, preserving himself, so to speak; everything was being handled with caution and distrust—even the black bread, even the wine.

After he had finished he leaned back in his chair and began to pick at his teeth. Then he picked his nose and slowly ran his fingers through his hair. Then he coughed, two or three times—a curious, choking ineffectual little cough. All of these things annoyed Serafimov unspeakably.

Then he remembered that Goupillière had allowed himself some ironical comment regarding Madame Tastin on the night before. And then it occurred to him, dimly and sickeningly, that perhaps Goupillière had been successful where he himself had failed. He was overcome with a terrible jealousy and disgust. He began to feel dizzy, the sight of Goupillière's body became completely intolerable, and he turned over on his side and closed his aching eyes.

☆

During the days and nights that followed, desire became more and more powerful in him. If he lay down, desire would overwhelm him, the earth would appear to rise, breathe on him, fondle him, and he would become utterly limp and breathless. Even as he walked along the street an accidental movement of the thigh or forearm, the momentary brush of cloth on a particularly sensitive part of his body, or the touch of skin against skin, would arouse abruptly the most irresistible longings, his heart would beat, he would feel weak, he would lean against a wall or sit down and close his eyes, and the recurring impulses of his boyhood and early youth would once again invade his mind and his limbs, much more powerfully than ever. He would run his fingers along the wall or caress the tablecloth as if it were a body—his own, or a woman's. He would feel feverishly breathless until once more the spasm would approach and transpire, quickly, violently, a moment brief and sharp and yet exquisite, possessing a quality beyond all other senses, though profoundly flavored by each in turn—by the delicacy of a color, say, or an aroma, a note of music or the soft sound of a voice, the accompanying warmth, the rhythm, the unutterable pain. And even then the quietude would be no more than momentary. He became increasingly aware of his body, each part of his body, as if it were an alien thing; it fascinated and absorbed him, just as it had done when he was a boy entering the visible stages of adolescence. And since the ambiguous shape of Madame Tastin in its graceful ballet postures was never far away from his thoughts, he finally murmured to himself one evening, in real despair, "I have fallen in love."

Elaborate scenes of one kind and another were thereupon enacted periodically in his mind. Scenes of enslavement, first he the utter slave and then she; scenes of tyranny, of torture, of suspense, of extreme tenderness, but always ending in the same way. He would walk past her house several times a day, sometimes glimpsing her through the window but more frequently not, and he would long now to perform an act of sacrifice and veneration in her behalf, now to subject her to the utmost cruelty and suffering. He felt that he had to be near her. This became, by and by, not so much a matter of physical desire as a psychical necessity: he had to know that she was not far away, to know that in his moments of anguish he might creep past her dimly lit house and know her to be there and feel her nearness bringing an end to his agonies, feeling a joy both illusory and real in knowing that only a bit of clay and mortar, after all, rose between her and him as he leaned against the wall. He grew obsessed, likewise, with a constant tormenting fear that she might go away, that somehow that house might become empty of her person. All this lasted for several weeks. But always and fervently he continued to call it "love." Night after night he lay there, his whole body stiff and feverish, whispering over and over again to the filthy odorous blanket, "I love you. I love you, I love you!"

14

A Russian Idyll

SERAFIMOV SAT BY THE WINDOW OF THE "SERAI" ONE evening and looked toward the Russian church. The sunlight was slanting upon the round spire, liquid and golden. It almost blinded him. His eyes grew blurred for a moment. Then he thought that he saw the flickering sunlight through his eyelashes, lingering not upon the cold hard ice, but on a summer cloud, a field of wheat, a brown arm. He was deeply touched by the unexpected sweetness of a sudden remembrance, descending upon him in such a gentle caressing way. His heart grew full of a homesick longing.

He turned away from the window and leaned his chin on the palm of his hand. Little by little, with a great bewildered effort he tugged at his memory as if it were a huge rock unmoved for years; and there, beneath it, he glimpsed a twisted network of grasses and roots, flattened, pale, but still alive. . . .

☆

The farm near Dolya! The pool, and the ducks floating upon it, all snowy white except for the one with the iridescent purple head and the clean gray wings, the bright and knowing eyes, his own pet. The scents of summer, and the little tumbledown summer-house smelling of decayed wood, the boards falling apart and allowing a golden blade of light to glide into the odorous darkness, tipping here a spider solitary in his web and there an old hornet's nest tucked among the rafters. And the fragrance of wet wood, of leaves after rain, of the heavy dripping trees, the hot sun on the wet earth, the water dripping from the berries and from the young bodies kneeling beside the pond, the birds quarreling outside, the musical trickle of water over the dam, the rustling twigs, the breathless whispers, the excitements, the delights. Far away the spire of the village church rose from the flat land, and on either side of it, on the very edge of the village, the copses. Behind one of these lay sick old Semenenko's estate.

Once, when he was a boy of ten playing beside the haystack, one of the harvesters, a leering young man of twenty or so, passed by and beckoned to him.

"Come along, I'll show you a thing or two," he whispered.

Stealthily they approached the woodshed and peered

through a knot hole in the door, first the one and then the other. The chap kept tittering and winking his gray eyes, but Alexei could not understand why, until at last he discerned two shapes in the darkness, lying upon the sawdust, kissing and clutching at each other's bodies—his cousin Zofja and the handsome young officer Piotrowski from Kharkov who had been loitering about the village so much lately.

He caught his breath. He did not understand. But one thing he grasped—the hint of a debased yet sweet excitement, so it appeared to him. From that moment on he could not rest for curiosity and a wistful sort of envy. Everything took on a new significance—the women with their silky hair and their rich soft flesh, the older men, all brown muscle and hair, with their bellowing voices.

"I'll be as strong as that one day," he thought. "A soldier, maybe, like Piotrowski, with a mustache and a uniform. . . ."

And there were moments, a year or two later, like the one when he sat with the men out under the trees beyond the field and the girls brought out the food in yellow baskets, and Anna sat down beside him, hot and breathless, leaning back and closing her eyes, her blue skirt rumpled, her forehead pearled with sweat, and he could see her smooth young legs as she raised her knee, and her thighs, mysterious and dark.

And another time too, not long after, when he sat beside Anna in the hay-cart as it rumbled along the road toward Yelenovka at dusk, the air full of the farewells of autumn, the chirping of crickets, the humming of insects. They sat dangling their legs over the dusty road, the sun had set, he could see a single star, just one, no more. He felt the itching of his arm as it rested in the warm hay, and then, as

Anna turned to one side, the brief caress of her hair upon his cheek. Then suddenly he put his eager brown arms around Anna's slender waist and placed his face upon her neck, closing his eyes, feeling her warm skin upon his lips, hearing her laughter, her teasing voice slowly growing more tender.

And later, again and again, he would imagine Anna in his arms, his heart full of this warm autumn confusion, his body quivering with sweet and puzzling desires, the air full of insects, full of desires too, and the quiet darkening sky, the stars beginning to appear, and Anna's silky soft hair, her warm soft arms, and her teasing laughter growing soft and warm.

☆

One August morning, six or seven years later, he was walking through the copse behind the Semenenko estate when suddenly he stood stockstill. There, on the leafy path before him, stood the most beautiful creature that he had ever seen.

She wore a big pink hat with flowers on it, and a silky white dress, and she was carrying a parasol. Her sleeves reached down to the elbows, and her forearms were paler and softer than those of the village girls. Her hair was blond, her eyes were blue, her cheeks were rosy. She looked very delicate to Alexei, like a flower or a butterfly.

At first she didn't appear to see him. He stood beside a tree, hand pressed against the bark, and waited breathlessly for her to pass. She walked in soft timid steps with her eyes lowered toward the ground. Her slippers were tiny and

[137]

shimmering gray, unlike any he had ever seen, so delicate and foreign-looking.

Then she raised her eyes suddenly and looked at him. A gaze as gentle and calm as that of a deer, but inexpressibly lovely to him, full of a certain fire too. His heart beat wildly. It seemed that a momentary smile crossed her lips as she passed, a friendly yet dignified smile—or was it more than that? He couldn't be sure, he could be sure of nothing at all now, for the world had suddenly grown new, tremulous, and full of magic.

☆

He saw her a second time, and a third, walking through the copse, and by discreet inquiries he discovered that she was a distant Austrian cousin to Madame Semenenko. Her name was Maria, he found, but her family name he never knew. He now felt that he had come closer to her: no longer a silken evanescent creature out of a fairy tale, but human, sweetly tangible.

One day, seeing her hurrying with a bouquet of bluebells through the garden toward the big white house as it was beginning to rain he suddenly cried out to her, softly, joyfully, "Maria, Maria, Maria!"

And in the deceptive whisper of the rain, for a moment, he thought he could detect her hushed reply: "Alexei! Alexei! Alexei!"

A few days later he found her sitting upon a tree trunk at the side of the village road, her yellow hat on the grass beside her. She looked hot and tired—but, with the beads of moisture on her brow and the wet curls on her temples, lovelier than ever. He stopped near her with an aching heart. What, oh, what might he say? What might he whisper in her ear, to tell her how deeply he admired her, how he longed to kneel at her feet, to write a poem to her, to send her a present of roses, to protect her from the cruelty of the world? He approached, eyes lowered, glanced for one moment at her with an intense shy longing, and then passed on down the road. His heart was overflowing, yet he had said not a word.

But he had seen enough. He had seen, for one celestial and unforgettable moment, her blue eyes meeting his own, the sweet glance of friendly recognition beneath the row of blond little curls that fell upon her forehead.

As he approached the farm he began to leap with joy, he wanted to sing, but then remembered that his voice was hoarse and displeasing. However, he stopped beside an old poplar tree, leaned his head against it for a moment, and then planted upon it a quick happy kiss.

☆

Several days later he was sent to the big white house with a basketful of cherries for Madame Semenenko.

But instead of waiting in the courtyard he was led by the footman along the mirrored and marbled hall into a large brocaded room.

"Wait here," said the ugly old footman in his conceited Polish accent.

Through a half-open door he could see into the next room—a large yellow room with dark-green hangings. In the middle of it sat two army officers playing chess, one old

[139]

and the other young. He couldn't see clearly, but the young one very much resembled that man Piotrowski from Kharkov.

There he stood, with his sunburnt arms hanging bashfully out of the torn blue blouse, alternately blushing and blanching in expectation of he knew not what austere or enchanting arrival. He waited five minutes, ten minutes. Then, the basketful of ruby-red cherries dangling from his elbow, he looked about the room more curiously. Everywhere were little Chinese figurines, bits of ivory, exotic vases and toys and such. Upon the mantel in front of a large mirror lay a marble boy, with the long curls and ripe breasts of a girl—on the pedestal underneath he read, letter by letter, the mystifying legend, *Sleeping Hermaphrodite*. A great fire screen stood in front of the hearth and on it were painted in the most charming colors a shaggy man with legs like a goat's and a woman lying under a willow tree, naked and smiling, eyes lustfully fastened upon the other's body. Alexei found this picture deeply exciting. His heart beat more quickly, and the room seemed suddenly full of strange shadows, visitors out of a curious and fabulous unknown. A great cabinet inlaid with ivory roses and cherubs stood in the corner. Pink ladies rested on golden clouds that were painted on the ceiling, and upon every wall hung paintings framed in magnificent golden frames. He looked at one—another naked lady—and under it he read the name "Guido Reni." An Italian, he thought, or a Spaniard perhaps, and his heart leapt with the thought of a sunny Southern land where men had goat's hooves and women were forever willing and boys were shaped like girls; and where such lovely unclad figures went leaping across a landscape of ruined towers,

streams lined with gnarled trees, grazing sheep, and countless flowers.

Presently the door opened and Maria appeared on the
threshold. He was overcome by her beauty, so ethereal, so
far beyond his reach. She looked at him gently and without a word. She appeared much younger than he had
thought. She wasn't, after all, so very much older than he,
perhaps. Her skin was smooth as silk, her eyes were clear
as a blue April morning. He caught his breath, stricken,
and a sweet melancholy instantly filled his soul.

He nodded, gave her the basket, and mumbled an awkward explanation. How kind she was, how gentle and full
of understanding! Her smile was free entirely of that
robust irony which twinkled forever in the eyes of the
prettiest village girls.

"Thank you," she said, in a soft accent, somewhat outlandish yet charming and amiable. "And come again soon,
do!" Then she blushed.

☆

Oh, those enchanted and light-hearted days! The delight of arising early in the August morning, stepping into
the out-of-doors where the sun was already beguiling each
leaf and flower; the rambles in the field where the silky
bullocks, their hoofs wet and shining with dew, stared at
him with their big stupid eyes; climbing the fence, leaping
over the brook, skipping past the haystacks and through
the orchard, full of the morning's joy and the summer's
profusion, and other subtler joys still anticipated. Youth,
with the spring in the ankle and the fresh young juice in

the knee-joints, the limbs still clear and pliable, the chest firm and smooth, the ribs like soft waves in the warm resilient flesh, the hips slim and white as marble, the hair glowing, the gait careless and graceful, the eyes quick, clear, responsive, innocent, the lips firm and pure, the voice soft and expectant, the spirit so self-forgetful, so ardent! The eyes, the ears, the skin, all were overjoyed to be alive, quivering with delighted surprise at everything they perceived, the green dewy grass, the rolling fields of rye, the infinite blue sky, the travelling clouds which assumed strange shapes—a sleeping giantess, a wild boar, a crumpled glove, a wig, an enormous lyre, glowing against the blue so brilliantly that for a moment he longed to be there too, in that soft white world where no mortal harm could ever reach one and where, beyond all doubt, a continuous heavenly music echoed in one's ears!

He would reach the edge of the wood: the dark level wood of Russia, the ageless, tangled wood where trunks of a thousand years ago were still rotting away and a thousand pale mushrooms guarded their black remains. She would be waiting for him at the edge of the path beside the gate, hidden from the fields and the houses. Then she would take his hand and walk with him through the orchard, her hair fluttering in the breeze and her straw hat hanging on her shoulders by a satin band around her neck. He would watch her, scarcely able to believe her beauty— her flower-like cheeks, her satin neck, her exquisite lips across which she would quickly run her tongue now and again. Even on rainy days she would solemnly wait for him under an umbrella, and they would creep into the old summer-house and sit there, telling old tales, whispering reminiscences. Once she fell asleep there, and his eyes wandered across her face, pausing now at her eyelids, now at her temples, now at her lips still smiling ever so faintly, like a traveler in a fairy-tale landscape who cannot believe that those trees are truly out of gold, those leaves of emerald, those diamonds naught but daisies.

Suddenly, with a glow of surprise, he whispered to himself "I am in love! I am in love!" Then he leaned over and placed on her cheek his first kiss, as timidly as if it were a flower out of the meadow that he was placing in her hand.

And then, those late September evenings! Those prolonged kisses, those impatient fingers sent on their familiar journeys, caressing the fragrant muslin, each new treasure so sweetly attained with wildly beating heart! In the perfect black mirror of the pond he could see reflected the hanging leaves, the darkening sullen clouds, even the devout spire in the distance, all with a filigree precision. She would point these out to him, as well as the leaves falling slowly into the water and the fragrance of the fallen leaves. He would be full of surprise at things which he had never noticed before—all the details of this dusky landscape that flowed gradually into such a novel existence before his eyes. The mere color of the leaves seemed miraculous and touching. That, yes, that was love, so unbelievable, filling the world with intimacy, making it all his own, as if the Lord had tried to please him above all other creatures in creating this intoxicating variety.

And she beside him seemed now no longer an individual, but a perfect song created out of all the rest of the world; no longer Maria, but one with the trees, the water, the subdued rhythm of the oncoming night. Oh, lovely, lovely, she was! The loveliness of woman seemed mysterious and marvelous indeed, as variable as the glitter of water, as fresh as the scent of ferns, as consoling as the sound of a violin in the village inn on a cold night. The

porcelain hands, the silken hair, the glowing cheeks, all
assumed the indefinable hues of mother-of-pearl—like that
shell from the Caspian Sea which lay on his mother's dress-
ing-table—as she leaned back on the grass and smiled.
There only, in those opened arms, did all peace and sweetness of the world seem to be united, while the vast clouds
moved above their heads and the trees grew darker and
darker.

☆

But September passed, and October too, little by little.
The leaves in the copse turned red and the harvesters returned at evening from the barley fields. Little by little he
felt his light-heartedness vanishing, his delight endangered.
He no longer understood the things that went on within
him—the wild ambitions, the longing for glory, the gnaw-
ing uncertainty, the quick moments of panic and hopelessness and longing to hurt which later on he learned to call
"jealousy."

Once they quarreled—about nothing at all, about the
hour they were to meet on the next day, perhaps. Full of
despair, he crept around to the big white house that night
and stood outside her window. It began to rain softly. He
could see the lamplight falling on the curtain which was
drawn across the window, and now and then a momentary
shadow cast upon it. Then he climbed the chestnut tree
and crept along the wet branch almost up to the window;
by reaching out his arm he could almost touch the casement, but not quite, for the branch began to creak omi-
nously and he didn't dare climb further. Through a small

opening in the curtain he could catch a glimpse of the room. She was sitting by a table, her back to the window, turning over the pages of a large photograph album bound in green velvet; at one page a dead flower fell out and fluttered to the floor, and for some obscure reason he felt a sickening twinge of grief in his heart—perhaps to see this fragment of a different love out of a different past so very casually fluttering into oblivion, perhaps because his own heart suddenly recognized how little one can ever possess, how frail and brief the ownership must be. He admired the glow of her hair under the lamplight and the lovely curve of her neck as she leaned over. He longed to touch it with his lips and yet, for the first time, there seemed to be something cruel and perverse in that beauty which he had never yet tasted quite to the full, which still was veiled in mystery.

He broke off a twig and tossed it at the window, and then another. She rose and turned around, with a curious expression on her face. He lost sight of her for a minute. His heart beat madly, for it occurred to him that she might leave the room. However, a moment later the curtain was drawn aside and she stood at the window, only three feet away from him. Yes, there was an unmistakable look of mischievousness in her eyes as she gazed at him and her lips melted into a smile.

He called to her gently, "Maria," and slowly she opened the window, reached out and touched his hand. Then he crept forward and clutched at the window sill and leapt into the room.

"Look, your clothes are quite wet, Alexei," she said softly, "you will catch a cold. . . ." She looked incredibly lovely, never before had her beauty seemed so irresistible, so flamelike, so tormenting.

[145]

"Here, slip off your wet things," she whispered, and held out a blue dressing robe; "put this over you."

He took off the wet blouse but did not dare put the silky thing over his wet shoulders, so he sat there, half-naked, unable to think of anything to say.

But, seeing that she had forgotten their quarrel, and seemed indeed more gentle than ever, though he understood nothing at all, himself least of all, he knew that he felt terribly happy, relieved almost to the point of tears to see her being so kind to him. He longed desperately to put his arms around her and press her wildly to his heart. All he dared do, though, was suddenly to run his fingers over her hair in a burst of childish delight.

She smiled, and sat down on the edge of the bed. "You heard the singing in the village tonight?" she asked in a soft low voice.

He nodded ecstatically.

"Wasn't it agreeable?"

"Oh yes!" he whispered with enthusiasm. Actually it had only increased his sadness two hours ago, to hear the sound of the accordion and the singing voices coming from the inn; but now in retrospect it seemed to him wholly delightful.

But as she waited for him to say more, glancing now at the floor and now at him, a little smile was forever lurking behind her lips like the clown in a play who peers through the curtain between two acts. And during these moments which he never forgot, it did not occur to him that a subtle imperfection existed in this joy. All he knew was that there was something he longed desperately to say, but since words were always very difficult things to him and since no words in the world would have been more difficult to utter than the simple ones, "I love you," he remained silent.

And presently, carrying his wet blouse in his hand, he was again walking through the orchard on his way home. Now and then he felt an apple being crushed under his heel.

The rain had stopped, the leafy darkness was full of the smell of rotting apples and wet autumn foliage. Once he heard an apple falling softly into the grass. The frogs were singing down by the pool, in the deep rushes. High overhead he saw the clouds moving, some stars suddenly appearing, even a little sliver of a moon. Never before in his life had he felt both so unbelievably happy and so inexplicably sad.

☆

Two mornings later Maria departed from Dolya. She was wearing a dark hat and a dark coat, and long dark gloves. She looked quite old suddenly. Her two trunks were placed in the carriage beside her, and off they drove. She turned and cast a hurried smile at the servants who were standing in a row beside the stairs, and hardly seemed to notice Alexei at all. Piotrowski was sitting beside her. She was going back to Austria, they explained, where she was to marry the son of an alderman.

He turned and ran to the old summer-house, full of its sweet and fragrant afternoon remembrances. He buried his head in the darkness, but even the power to burst into tears had quite forsaken him. He felt very ignorant, very helpless indeed.

And he never saw her again. All he had left of her was a little miniature portrait which she had given him a week before, in a leaf-shaped mosaic frame designed with infinitesimal roses and forget-me-nots, and tucked behind the picture, a lock of her hair and a bit of fern that she had once pressed to her lips. And even this small object he could scarcely bear to gaze upon, it hurt him so. He took to wearing it on a red string around his neck until one day a friend of his teased him about it as they were undressing to go swimming in the Kalmius river. "A moon-struck calf," he called him, and "a sentimentalist." After this he simply carried it in his pocket, reaching in to feel it there, ten, twenty times a day. But he rarely looked at it, even long after, for he couldn't do so without feeling an overwhelming longing that ran through his body and an ache of sadness clutching at his heart.

15

The Voluptuary

FINALLY, ONE NIGHT SERAFIMOV COULD BEAR IT NO longer: he leapt up from his blanket in a fit of violent desire, buttoned his clothes, threw his coat over his shoulders, and dashed out into the cold night.

The stars were out, high over Aqsu. The night, it occurred to him, was unutterably beautiful. "Such a beautiful night," he kept muttering as he strode along rapidly; "so beautiful, so beautiful." The snow glistened in the starlight. Far off—were those the snowy mountains he saw, those waves, those shapes so imponderably far away? Perhaps. He felt, for some reason, very much moved by this thought.

The snow creaked and whispered beneath his feet. He

could feel the cold wind rushing through the openings in his coat, but he didn't think about it. He felt so hot that sweat ran down from his forehead along his temples and his cheeks.

He felt weak after he had walked a short distance, like a runner after a race. There was an ache in his side, his breath came stiflingly, his heart beat wildly; a novel sort of weakness crept through his limbs. He had never felt like this before. It was, he thought, as if he were turning into some sort of wild animal, fugitive, panic-stricken.

At one point he suddenly stopped breathlessly. It seemed to him, as he turned his head by accident, that he had seen a figure crossing the street behind him. It was an ugly moment. He was sure that it was Goupillière. His fingers twitched with a peculiar desire. Then he grew calm again.

"I must have been mistaken," he muttered to himself.

He passed the old tumbledown prison, where the two young Germans had been sent. He had forgotten their names—rather odd names, they were. He wondered whether they were still there. He shuddered a bit. A hideous place—no one could survive there long, he felt sure of that. It looked far shabbier at this moment than it had ever looked before.

As he hurried along he noticed again a certain feeling that he had experienced lately, from time to time. A sense of helplessness, of powerlessness to control some instinct deep inside him. What this instinct was he was far too muddled to comprehend, but he felt it to be something evil, a terrific hidden energy of some kind that would drive him into a state—a thought, an act, a fear, perhaps—which would be full of dangers, real dangers. But this feeling was so troubled and so vague that it never occurred to him to control it, and to turn back.

At any rate, he was soon standing in front of Madame Tastin's house. It was quite dark, like all the other buildings, not a window was lit. It must have been about three o'clock. The façade looked less dingy than usual in the icy starlight. For a moment he stood quietly in front of the house, head bowed. To a passer-by it might have seemed that he was praying.

Then he turned and walked along the side of the house. A double wall stood between him and the little courtyard behind the house. He leapt over the first wall, which was no more than five feet high. Then he climbed to the top of the second wall. This one was higher than his head.

He sat down on top of the wall. He had bruised the palm of his right hand against the rough clay, and it was bleeding. He raised it to his lips and licked the wound. He was amazed to notice how cold his hand was—like ice.

"I should have worn gloves," he thought; then he reflected, "But they might have been in my way later on." He didn't feel the wound in the least. The taste of blood on his tongue was interesting and soothing.

He looked into the courtyard—its leafless little shrubs, its empty little pool, thrilled to see it for the first time. Then suddenly he grew wild with suspense, for a second he almost fainted at the thought of what he was about to do.

He stood up on the top of the wall, which was about a foot and a half thick, and stared at the four black windows. He wasn't quite sure which one was the window to her bedroom, but he thought it might be the one furthest away. So he walked carefully along the top of the wall all the way around the garden to the other side.

Here he paused for a moment. A heavy curtain was hanging over the inside of the window. His excitement grew, irresistibly, reminiscently, at the prospect of forcing an entry into that mysterious recess where the sweet and intimate consolations of love were awaiting him. He measured the distance up to the bottom edge of the window with his eyes. He might leap up from where he was standing on the edge of the wall, and with a bit of luck he might reach the ledge which projected below the window. He felt very calm now. He bent his knees three or four times to prepare himself for the jump. Then he decided to take off his sheepskin coat and lay it on the top of the wall.

Then he jumped. It was just as he had thought, he was able to grasp the ledge, but for a split second he relaxed his grip and one of his hands slipped. He came within an inch of falling upon the paving of the courtyard. But with an inspired catlike effort he drew himself up until he was resting on his elbows, his belly against the ledge, his face against the window.

He pushed against the blind with his shoulder. It gave, unexpectedly, and with it the window too. What had happened was that the wooden blind was loose on its hinges, and being quite old and rotten gave way and promptly broke as it was pushed inward. For a moment it hovered bizarrely on the edge of the window sill; then it fell down past Serafimov and crashed upon the ground below with an ugly, splitting noise.

Serafimov held his breath. The mere echo was enough, he thought, to have awakened the whole city. He didn't move, but still clung to the window sill, poised on his elbows, feet dangling, head leaning into the room which now was accessible to him. He could smell its warm stuffy smell of old rugs and stale perfume and vodka, welling forth in a wave into the icy night.

He strained his ears. He thought, at once, that he could hear something moving in the room. He peered into the darkness, and finally detected one or two shapes—a table, a gilded clock on a shelf. It was her "parlour," he realized, not her bedchamber. He listened again: he heard nothing, and decided that he had been mistaken the first time. He noticed with some surprise, at this moment, how very deliberately and rationally his mind seemed to be operating.

Then he noticed another thing—that he had torn his right hand again and that it was bleeding profusely. He could see by the starlight how the blood had created a large triangular stain on the gray sill. He wondered whether it was the loss of blood that made him feel so weak and dizzy.

He pushed the window open a bit further and noiselessly slid over the sill and into the room. His footsteps made no noise whatever, for his boots were of felt, and soundless as the paws of a tiger.

He stood still for a moment and tried to think things over. But he realized abruptly, with a twinge of fear, that while his mind had moved simply and lucidly while he was acting, now that he was at rest, safe for the moment, it became thoroughly jumbled, he could think of nothing at all, his mind and heart were plunged into a vast hot nocturnal confusion.

It was chiefly in order to rid himself of this feverish confusion that he tiptoed across the room toward the doorway that led into the bedchamber. He thought of Madame Tastin again. He was surprised to realize that he had, during the last fifteen minutes, quite forgotten about her. Now that he thought about her again, he was staggered at the reason for his presence here. He leaned against the wall beside the doorway. His breath came convulsively, and his beating heart ached as if a powerful hand were gripping it.

And then, at the vision of Madame Tastin's luxuriant yielding body which was automatically conjured up before his mind, he grew cool and active again. The word "voluptuary" occurred to him, quite irrelevantly. "I am a voluptuary," he muttered to himself pointlessly, naïvely. The word filled him with loathing and yet—with a profound excitement as well. He took a deep breath, and drew aside the curtain which hung over the doorway.

For some reason he was not really surprised at what he saw. Everything that night, however grotesque, had a calm and logical air about it. So it was with this.

What he saw was Madame Tastin standing with her back to the wall, facing him, with an expression of the most desolate, insomniac horror on her face. Her hair hung about her face and over her neck in disorderly shreds. He saw her only dimly, by the snowy starlight which filtered past the curtain into the room. But he saw her quite clearly enough. She was wearing a red nightcap. Her nightgown—torn, perhaps by some impetuous lover earlier in the night—hung like a silly rag about her, revealing ludicrously a naked shoulder and a naked calf. Her cheeks and chin were sagging—she looked very old, very rumpled. He hardly recognized her, she had become so lovely, little by little, in the course of his meditations. A heavy scent of vodka filled the room.

She didn't cry out; the only sound that came from her was a low clucking sound, a rhythmical rattling little noise, a sound of drunken terror.

He turned around, hurried through the other room toward the window, leapt down upon the wall as lightly as a panther, and in less than a minute he was out in the cold blue starry street again.

He hurried back to the inn. The idea of pursuit was now uppermost in his mind. He was convinced that he was being pursued—perhaps by Russian officers, perhaps by inarticulate Turkis, perhaps by noiseless Chinese. The air was full of danger, even the stars looked ominous, signals for an impending calamity; the wintry landscape looked hostile and feline.

It was growing lighter, little by little, and everything was breathlessly still. He felt very cold; his jaws were immovable; the hairs of his beard seemed stiff as needles. His hands and feet were quite numb, but his wrists and his ankles were still full of a fiery ache.

A lamp was at that moment being lit in one of the houses, and the flickering light filtered through the frosted pane and fell softly upon the snow in the street, shabby and timorous as an orphan. He saw a huddled shape moving about slowly in the dark blue room. Ahead of him he saw a dog furtively crossing the street and disappearing in a narrow passageway. Far down the street he could recognize the sleepy old walls of the *caravanserai*, streaked with weather and urine and a spontaneous corruption of its very own, and at this very moment ever so gently kissed by the first golden haze of the morning.

☆

And then, quite suddenly, as he hurried along there, he had a vision.

What he saw now, in this silent street, from which the

night was withdrawing her shadows and upon which the
golden day had not yet intruded, had only begun to peer,
to breathe, was this. Life had been sharpened, in this
instant between night and day, to a point, an exquisite
surgical point. Yes, he could see them all; the shapes
emerging from their sleepy little houses, hundreds of them
arising out of the calm and pastoral morning shadows, each
one staring at the others with grave, beautiful eyes which
seemed at first, in the blue snowy haze and under the
masklike shadow of their cloaks, merely dreamy, but in
which he presently discerned a positively maniacal hunger
and intensity. They were moving about, whispering very
softly, performing meaningless little follies and obscure
gestures, but wholly without delight or enthusiasm, never
really succeeding in revealing their hearts to any other,
however bizarre and increasingly bizarre their stratagems
—the last, the most corrupt and triumphant of these, of
course, being death.

They were constantly bleeding, he then observed; from
the eyes, the ears, the mouth. But even more disturbing
than this was the fact that he could not tell, in gazing at
their misty moss-like faces, whether that widening of the
lips and wrinkling of the eyes indicated laughter or anguish. The two seemed fused in a profoundly desolate way.
At any rate, in none of this—their gestures, their passions,
their endurances and extinction—could he detect the
tiniest shred of meaning. There was a dreadful voluptuous-
ness about it all, and the only thing about them that kept
them from resembling waxen dolls was this: the obvious
and corrupt persistence of their desires.

It was at this point that he realized that they were really
human sacrifices, offered ten or a thousand or ten thousand
years ago. It was the gigantic Past which he now beheld,

as he had never seen it before. Sacrifices. But sacrifices to what? To the ancient imperfection of man? The cruelty of God? The ruthlessness of nature? The everlasting distortions of love?

He trembled and closed his eyes. Now he understood Madame Tastin, Goupillière, and the rest, it seemed to him. All those others—Piotrowski, and his cousin Sofja, and the beautiful Maria, and the Frenchman de la Scaze and his Spanish wife, and the tall Englishman whose name he had forgotten; and himself too: he understood them all, now. That was what they all sought—love. Oh, love! What could it be, this power from which all magical joys and glow of warmth had always sprung, from which all terror sprang likewise, if it went the least bit astray?

The desire for death, he reflected, in a moment which he knew to be more lucid than any he had ever experienced, is one of the many disguises of our forever wandering sorrow, our forever wandering love; because, in all that we do, we are so enchained by place and time, so local, so ephemeral, that what we desire more than anything is to burst through into the infinite and eternal, to flee into another land, another age, to acquire a traditional grandeur and immortality, and thus to discover our true selves. It is an inevitable longing. And the final indulgence is to wish to send others and then to send ourselves into those remote, enchanting realms where the spirits of ages past and future now reside.

It is no doubt this glorious yet tragic longing which gives such a profundity of terror to our existence nowadays, it occurred to him: the secret realization that we are, forever and forever, surrounded by the endless, nomadic, conspiring hordes of those who have already died and vanished, and in whose arms we may eventually discover the immensity of our fate.

He opened his eyes again. The morning was gently arising. In the distance, beyond the shadow of the *serai*, and the ermined roofs of the town, he could see the clouds reflecting the sun.

"I'll recover," he murmured to himself, "I'll survive."

★

Lying in his blankets again at the *serai*, utterly exhausted, sweating and sleepless, he tried to think. It required a long and painful effort to bring his mind under control.

He felt, he had always felt, really, that there were two people in him. One, deep below, a sly watchful being, but quite helpless in a crisis; all that this one could do was to warn, no more, for he was never very active or energetic. The other one saw far more clearly, and was able to make plans; he was the wild one. They never worked together, never, and no matter what he said or did, he always had an inkling that deep down in him, he really knew better, he really was capable of dealing with matters more shrewdly.

He turned and looked at Goupillière. An ever so faint glow was left in the hearth, and by this he could detect the outlines of Goupillière's face. Very dimly at first, but then the face grew clear and bright, almost as if it were illumined by a light within.

Serafimov was deeply moved by this. For it seemed to him that this face was a representation of that wiser and

[158]

more rational being deep inside himself, who had never protected him or guided him. The face acquired magnitude and meaning, the features took on a doomed and diabolical look, and the red light which shone on the two discordant halves of the face gave to it the symbolical and utterly revolting appearance of evil, true evil.

The real cunning, he saw there; the real animal slyness; the hidden power, the courage, the endurance and self-preservation of the rat. His loathing at this moment became almost unendurable. He turned over and lay on his other side, staring at the black wall in wild despair.

16

Wolves

THE MEN LIVED LIKE WOLVES. THEIR THOUGHTS AND actions were no longer human. Snow was thick in the courtyard, on the window sills, on the very threshold. The cold out in the streets was murderous— even the briefest opening of a door allowed the entry, sinuous and metallic to the touch as a knife, of the desperate winter's wind.

Most of them never left the *serai* now. They sat, huddled and silent, full of smells, despairs, and compensating visions, on the floor or on their beds—figures out of such a dream as all of us no doubt have once or twice, thought Serafimov, which we never quite arrange to forget, which the simplicity of our minds never quite survives, which affords us a glimpse of that cistern of profound loathing which dwells so secretly and prophetically within every last one of us.

Indifference: that was the thing which, by the delicate chisel of each cold expiring hour, was engraved more and more deeply on every face. Whether they ate or slept, whether they sat alone or in perfunctory couples or trios, whether it was a new lust or a new loathing that abruptly summoned them out of isolation and silence, it didn't really matter, it didn't matter at all. Assuming curious postures, picking with bloody paws at their itching temples, their hair, their noses, their ears, their discolored eyes, their afflicted and tormented parts, devouring what was set before them brown and stinking like savage dogs, shouting wildly or whispering with excessive softness, infected with all the varied tyrannies of half-starvation, gradual disease, utter filth, protracted loneliness, constriction of the heart —nothing that happened to them really mattered in the least. For they were hibernating; their spirits, and bodies likewise, had fled into a musty lair, invisible and undiscoverable; they would, of course, survive, and in the spring again start on their trying journeys to Tashkent, Yarkand, Urga, Khotan, Srinagar, Shigatse, Kashgar, Uliassutai, Kobdo, Lhasa, even Pekin or Novosibirsk. They would be the same as they had been the year before, amused, stoical, merciless, shrewd. And the period of half-living during the months of ice would not be remembered, because, to tell the truth, it had never actually existed for them. Fortunate creatures, in a way, since for them the desperate afflictions of a moral degradation and collapse could never really assume a concrete meaning and a concrete power.

✫

Once there was a fight. Two men suddenly leapt out of
the muttering quiet of the night and like two beasts in
the black jungle tore at each other, snarled with a catlike
frenzy, rolled on the floor, sobbed unrepeatable words,
moaned with rage—it was all, extreme though the passion
may have been, performed in a sort of emotional twilight
—the sounds were muffled, the motive was unfathomable,
the movements were meaningless. In the morning Serafimov learned that these two (young Turkis from Maralbashi) had actually been life-long friends; and, indeed,
now they were sitting quietly side by side again, placid as
ever, only a trifle more exhausted-looking than before.

Once an old man rose out of the stagnation of the late
afternoon and gave an impassioned speech. The world, he
explained with glowing eyes, would presently be enveloped
in total and eternal darkness; and "we must prepare ourselves for this time by pious and sedate thoughts of our
ancestors, of our own nothingness, of the mighty pacific
vastness of the One and Everlasting. . . ." Then he
smiled and sat down again, relieved and apparently quite
happy.

Other incidents too. A fit of weeping, a spasm of tenderness, an odd confidence, a prolonged prayer, a significant
lie, a refusal to speak, a dramatic inability to eat or sleep
or make water. One evening the youngest of them, a dark
boy with only one eye, Nulja by name, disappeared and
was not seen again. One morning a man was found in the
courtyard, his throat cut wide open, frozen into a fantastic
posture. But both affairs were forgotten on the following
day, for each night was very much like a cloak, covering
completely the body of the previous day, so that the passing
days appeared in retrospect, however various and amazing

they might have seemed at the time, as no more than a
forlorn succession of shapes, uniform, dark, and empty.

☆

Serafimov thought more and more about Goupillière.
His distrust, his revulsion, grew more reasoned and elaborate.

For several days he was obsessed with the idea that
Goupillière was a spy against the Soviet; commissioned,
possibly, by one of the Fascist powers in Europe, or even
by Japan. There were moments when he was quite certain
of it: every detail in Goupillière's behavior—his reserve,
his power to survive, his vanity, his care for his health—
strengthened this suspicion. Also, he noticed that Goupillière appeared to have a certain amount of money—he was
able to buy food in the nearby shop—little black biscuits,
sweets made of almond paste, tins of broth and of meat,
freshly baked bread; the others would watch him with
jealous loathing, but he never gave any of it away.

When Serafimov finally forgot about these suspicions, it
was not that reason compelled him to do so. Rather it was
this: that all this became an irrelevant consideration, beside certain new impressions—irrelevant because living
here in the *serai* was no longer a social matter, a matter
that involved the world outside, the world of other men,
of Asia, of Europe; the world for Serafimov was the world
increasingly minute and intense, like the gaze of a micro-
scope, of this town, this room, this bleak and bitter cold,
this feline awareness that flickered between two men, this
electrical loathing.

Now and then, at night, he would suddenly wake up and see things more lucidly. He would decide that he must leave as soon as humanly possible. For Shanghai, preferably. There he would be able to collect himself, to make plans. . . . But then, when the day arrived, he would forget all about distant Shanghai, and it would seem to him that he had lived here in the *serai* all his life.

Sometimes, as Serafimov sat watching him, Goupillière's appearance would seem to change. In the shadow of approaching evening, or by the flicker of a candle-light, his finely shaped features would become sharp and repulsive. His nose would seem to be hooked, beaklike, his teeth pointed and irregular, his eyes would glitter like those of a rodent. His scar would look like a mad, exaggerated grin. He always looked alert, whatever he was doing—even while he lay asleep.

Everything he said or did had a curious air about it—as if his words and deeds sprang never from within, from what he thought, but simply from a desire for manipulation, so to speak, as if he were sending forth his words and gestures like little waxen marionettes into the theater of another man's heart, masqueraders, unreal and yet gifted with the power to disturb and to harm. He would sit and watch the others quietly, draw little designs on the table, tap the floor rhythmically with his little feet. It was all a game, perhaps, but a narcotic and dangerous game. And why he did all this Serafimov could never guess. First he thought it to be the performance of a spy. Then, merely a sort of restlessness. Then, more subtly, a form of vanity. There did seem, indeed, to be something almost sensual about it all.

Asplund, the shaggy Dane, once spoke to him about Goupillière. "A dangerous type, my man," he said. "He may be your closest friend, perhaps, but he'll never do anyone any good. . . . He's servile, he fawns, he coquettes and flirts; but there's something else beneath it. I've seen them before like that, in cities. It's the life of the cities that has ruined them. Power, that's what they want, power. And when he gets it, do you know what he'll do? I'll tell you, quite confidentially. First of all, revenge. Revenge for all that he suffered, years ago. He'll be corrupt, like all the other rascals, buffoons, gorillas, and lunatics who govern the world. . . . Well, perhaps he'll ruin himself first. There's always a possibility of that. He's not really strong, you see. He may meet his master yet. . . ."

☆

One night Serafimov hurled himself upon his bed in a spasm of despair. He lay there sobbing, his face buried in the moist unsavory blankets. Far in the distance he heard the wolves crying in their hills. He felt like a little boy, badly in need of comfort. He felt afraid of something, as he had years ago, when he was a child staring through the misty window pane at the black clouds and the lightning drawing nearer over the fields.

He heard Goupillière come up and stand beside him. "Alexei. . . . Can I do something for you, my friend?"

Serafimov's heart leapt. The voice in which his name was pronounced was so gentle, so friendly, that for a moment a wave of homesickness swept over him; he felt as if comfort and companionship were almost within his grasp. His heart was filled with humility and forgiveness.

Then he turned his head and looked at Goupillière. He

was leaning over, staring at him, his lips moist, a little smile playing about his mouth.

Serafimov closed his eyes. He felt as if he had glimpsed a forbidden vision. He began to tremble, and, without quite knowing what he was saying, he muttered to himself, "He must be killed, he must be killed. . . ."

These few minutes of intense feeling had so exhausted him that he thereupon fell asleep almost instantly.

17

The Murderer

IN THE MIDDLE OF THE NIGHT HE WOKE UP. IT WAS AS
if a gong had been struck: he felt as soon as he opened
his eyes that there was something he must do, a mission demanding to be performed.

For a few moments he lay quietly and deliberated. During this pause his mind felt very clear, very impersonal.

"Is this a crime?" he asked himself. "One is what one
is, that's certain; what one does springs from what one
is. . . ." He felt as if his thoughts were climbing a stairway, each litle conclusion leading to the next, in an orderly
yet fascinating manner. "Well then. A good man feels a
natural detestation for evil. Just as a healthy plant hates a
rot, a poison, a parasite. That is only right. He should do

so. But then: if he hates evil, he must place himself on the side of nature, he must struggle against evil, try to conquer it, kill it. Yes, kill it! Otherwise he is a traitor to his own natural spirit. And so, what he then does with his hands is good or evil only as his spirit is good or evil. Murder itself, separated from the spirit of the murderer, is meaningless. Isn't that so? Of course it is. . . ." That was the first time that the word "murder" had really occurred to him; but now that it had, it did not repel him in the least; indeed, it rather soothed him.

"And besides, in my heart, in my dreams, I have already murdered him. Murdered, that is to say, my image of him. . . . But then, after all, that is all I know of the world—my image of it, what I see with my own eyes. That is all that exists for me. And how else can I act except by obeying what I see in that image? I alone am real to myself, that's the truth of it; my heart and my thoughts are the things that matter to me. I must obey them and do whatever they tell me, or else go mad, dwindle away into nothingness!"

Through the little window beside the big doorway he could see the starry night. The night was his own now, the stars were his own. "Ah, Alexei," they seemed to say, in a voice indescribably tender and with a calm and loving smile like that of his mother, "Alexei, we understand you. You are one with us, at last! We are gazing into your heart, and we understand you, ah yes, we do. . . . And we love you. Be calm, be true to yourself, Alexei our child, and we shall watch over you forever. . . ."

He rose. With a certain nervous surprise he observed that Goupillière was not sleeping in his accustomed place on the other side of the hearth. He glanced hurriedly around the room. He saw dimly the usual shapes in their usual places, but Goupillière was nowhere to be seen.

But he understood. He knew where Goupillière was. He felt very calm now.

He slipped his heavy cloak quietly over his shoulders, laced his boots more tightly, crept quietly across the room, opened the heavy door inch by inch, and at last stepped out into the icy night. Quickly he crossed the courtyard. It had snowed early on the previous morning, and the snow still lay scattered lightly all over the gravel and the stone. It glittered, incredibly white in the midnight stillness, upon the window sills and the top of the wall.

His footsteps made no noise at all. Never had he felt so calm, so certain. It was because at this moment, for the first time in many, many years, for the first time since his early childhood when full of delight he used to go leaping toward Dolya over the grass still wet with the morning's dew, he felt himself to be one with the natural world about him—the unsubtle earth, the patient sky, the florid clouds, the affectionate stars. This feeling was so exquisite, so harmonious, that he seemed to be gliding rather than walking. A whimsical old song about the "girls of Cherdakla and the flowers of Yalta" kept running through his head.

At last he arrived in front of Madame Tastin's house. He stood beside the gate, eyes fastened on one of the dark windows, and waited, confident, full of a warm and vigilant understanding, aglow with a new sort of pleasure. He felt sure that Goupillière was there. He thought of Goupillière's shape, somewhere behind those walls, that quick lithe nervous body so alert yet so fragile, and of his face, as subtle as a woman's, as ambiguous as a thief's. A wave of tenderness and pity swept through him; he felt that no one in the world could possibly exist who did not deserve infinite love and infinite understanding.

Suddenly he found that his nose was bleeding. The warm trickle crept through the hairs on his upper lip; he could smell it. He raised his arm to his face, and now the elusive odor of snow and cold flannel reminded him of something—something distant yet almost suffocatingly sweet. He felt as if he were in love; he felt young again; once again the fragrances of his youth sprang up around his aching heart.

His hands felt curiously restless. "I cannot understand this world," he muttered to himself, profoundly moved. "But we must do as we are destined." He noticed that he was trembling. His enormous hands were itching with nervousness.

And then, at that instant, he glimpsed through an alleyway that led through the purple walls before him a small dark figure moving quickly out toward the white slope that rose above the edge of the city. His heart leapt.

He raised his eyes for a moment up to the Asiatic sky. The clouds were vast, the stars were almost hidden. He was stricken with awe. All over Turkestan, that sky extended! From every mountain, desert, valley, plateau, men who opened their eyes from sleep and stepped into the night would gaze at those very same stars!

Then he stared again at the house across the street. "It is all destiny," he repeated, "it is all destiny," and little by little he began to feel calm once more.

Quietly he walked toward the alleyway, then up past the shabby little prison toward the treeless hill in the distance. A wind was coming up, the stars had vanished, snow was beginning to fall lightly.

BOOK THREE

Goupillière

18

The Sleepers

IME PASSES. NOTHING APPEARS TO HAPPEN, RE-flected Goupillière, nothing at all. Though it is cold winter, the world seems swaddled in sultriness, it is like the hot sun lapping against a fruit which hangs from a twig, gently urging it to ripen, to fall, to burst. Things seem so very quiet, one can almost hear the insects humming in the hot shade, eternity would appear to have been captured in one instant, like a continent on the tip of a needle, and the world appears stagnant indeed.

But time does pass, very surreptitiously, behind a sort of veil. Things do change. The incessant pantomime is performed, though we hear and see nothing, and the climax is again approaching. The drumstick is slowly being raised, is about to descend and shatter the globe of stillness.

*

Yes, though it was winter, it all felt more like a breathless tropical summer's day. Goupillière sat and listened to the buzzing of voices, the conspiracies of the rats beneath, the ceaseless soliloquy of the fire, the creaking of the rafters. Nothing new ever entered the room; now and then a blast of wind or a scattering of snow, but nothing to change the spirit of the place. He watched the men growing filthier and filthier, their beards growing longer and shaggier. They had become less talkative, and their movements were almost mechanical now. They were hibernating, just like bears. And he himself was hibernating too, he realized. Waiting for the winter to pass, so that he might return at last to Shanghai.

He would glance, then, at Serafimov, and begin to wonder. He would smile. He had heard several rumors recently through Asplund, the big Dane, whose ears were always wide open. One, that the two "young Germans" had escaped from the prison in Aqsu but had lost their way in the desert as they fled. And then, that his wealthy friend de la Scaze was slowly starving to death in his little room in the middle of the city. And finally, that Dr. Liu's caravan had been captured by brigands and no one knew what had happened to them all—perhaps they had been imprisoned, perhaps killed.

And then he would smile. He himself, at any rate, would

[174]

survive. He would see to that. If only—and he glanced
uneasily at Serafimov's powerful, clumsy body: but no, that
man would perish too, he was too stupid, too impetuous.
He, he himself, would be the only one to survive. . . .

✫

The food would be served in a huge red earthenware
bowl—a pool of grease in which stray bits of meat were
floating, curious and unrecognizable fragments hysterically
torn, so it seemed, from some extinct variety of beast. It
might have been camel meat, actually. A horrible smell
rose from this mess, but still the men jumped madly for it
and dipped their fingers into the hot gravy and fished
avidly for the tatters of meat.

Then they would go to sleep again, most of them. The
majority were camel-drivers or minor tradesmen who had
nothing whatever to do during the cold months; and these
were types who, having spent most of their time moving
quietly and patiently across enormous stretches of land,
had lost the desire, or at least the power, to talk. One or
two, it was true, made up for the rest and talked incessantly. But most of them, especially as the winter wore on,
said hardly a word all day long.

So they would sleep, since there was little else to do—
like those other dark and shaggy animals who lived in their
wintry caves up in the hills all winter in deep slumber.
But even in sleep they found no peace, most of them. One
snored desperately, asthmatically; one whined, one
had frightening visions; one sat up and moved his

[175]

hands to and fro with his eyes still closed; one would rise suddenly and cry out in a fit of persecution mania; one would get up groaning in the middle of the night in the torments of dysentery.

They developed strange little habits. One became colossally devout—he had suffered a good deal, and had lost his family only three months ago. One began to steal—nothing of value, simply odds and ends, bits of paper, rags, buttons, a stray old sock, a broken knife, a piece of string, never anything of consequence. One would reminisce all night long. And so on.

Wretched as this sort of existence was, nevertheless Goupillière little by little recognized, with his sharp eyes, how at last in this ceaseless monastic twilight of sleep, half-sleep, and whispers, paradoxically a curious but genuine and gentle happiness crept over them, slowly, and over him too. A sort of religious calm, a resignation, a relief. It showed in the softening of their gaze, the softening of the lines around their mouths. They had nothing to lose, here and now; sleep held no terrors for them any more, nor did the thought of pain or extinction. Nothing mattered. The stage of wrath and violence had been passed, apparently.

☆

And so it hardly seemed to mean anything when one of them fell sick and was taken away, and they were told three days later that he had died; or when one of them burned his fingers one evening at the fire, and the smell of burning flesh filled the room; or when one of them broke his arm and the swelling grew larger and larger until it became evident that gangrene had set in and that the man would have to be taken away; or when one of them went a little bit mad, and talked of nothing but the rats below them, and how they would some day rush out in a horrid battalion and devour them, one and all, every last untidy bit of them.

Nor did it seem to matter that the older ones lost all interest in the world, or that the young ones in their lonely beds would dream all night long of their women, their sweet recollections, and that their manhood was going to waste, drop by drop; or even that now, in this isolation, as each one turned to his own spiritual hiding-place, the presence of others grew almost unbearable, their shapes, their hair, their eyes, their gestures, their voices, all grew loathsome, and pale ineffectual hatreds sprang up all over like white mushrooms.

These Turkis and Mongols and Russians lying about on the floor, drunk, some of them, the black juice of dyspepsia flowing out of the corner of the mouth of one: they looked to Goupillière like the shapes on a deserted battlefield. All dead, or dying. Neither happy nor sad about it, feeling nothing profoundly any longer, as tenuously suspended from the grandeur and anguish of living as dry autumn leaves hanging from a tree. For one instant he thought that he had been afforded a glimpse, just one quick glimpse, of the real nature of human life. He closed his eyes. He heard the sound of frozen twigs caressing the roof, ever so softly: like the sigh of lovers, lovely beyond words, this trivial sound was; like the early morning babbling of children far away, the sound of feet on the market

place, church bells ringing, dogs barking, pigeons fluttering; a trepidation, a mischievous yet loving little sound,
infinitely far away.

☆

One evening they all began to talk of a certain Madame
Tastin. Serafimov seemed particularly interested.

So, in a moment of curiosity, Goupillière went and
visited her. She was what he had expected, more or less. A
silly, pompous, ridiculous female, with the most vulgar of
European mannerisms. She gave him tea from a copper
samovar that stood on the table. Then she took him into
her bedroom. She seemed very anxious to impress him. All
over the room, in every corner of it, lurked certain feminine smells—oils, facial creams, cheap perfume.

She sat down beside him and began, rather nervously, to
tease him.

"My sweet young boy," she simpered. "Well, you are no
more than a boy, really! Such lovely skin, such soft hair,
such pretty eyes. The type that I really like best, when all's
said and done. Almost like a girl! But there, that annoys
you, doesn't it? Yet it's true, you know. Yes, I could kiss
you, I could kiss your pretty body, every bit of it. I'm sure
it is clean and smooth and white all over, isn't it? But I
shan't! Not yet. . . ."

And so she went, on and on, giggling affectedly, trying
to impress him and yet allure him, a difficult combination
sometimes. He could smell her breath: she had been
drinking.

Then she undressed him and combed his hair. She began, at this point, to assume a maternal air. Doubtless her instinct told her that this would be the most persuasive tack; that her strength lay in that direction. He began to smile to himself, with a certain feline pleasure. He felt the power ebbing out of him, all against his will he felt himself purring like a kitten as she caressed him.

But presently she grew restless and plaintive. Something seemed to bother her. An intense expression appeared in her eyes, and her gaze was shifting nervously to and fro.

"What is troubling you, my sweet," she whimpered, "are you afraid of me? Do you think I'll bite you? Do you think I'll eat you up? Oh dear," she laughed, in a flat metallic way, "you are still very young, all in all. . . . And yet I'm a bit frightened of you, you know! Why am I? I can't help laughing at you, and yet I am frightened of you! Frightened to death! Dear, dear," she murmured in a low hollow tone, "I think I really love you. . . ."

Then suddenly she turned away and burst into tears. "No wonder. You think I am ugly, don't you? Of course you do. Old and ugly. And you're right. Oh, my life is slipping away, slipping away from me like a little white ghost. Believe me, I was lovely once. So innocent, so tender! Golden hair, eyes that looked as if they were gazing straight into heaven. A real angel, I was. . . . Look at me now. Hardly an angel, do you think? I've been around, let me tell you! Venice, Warsaw, Paris, Shanghai, Harbin. . . . Yes, I've seen life as it is lived by the rich and elegant aristocrats. I've drunk champagne with the best of them! Yes indeed. . . . Oh dear, everything is gone, nothing is left, no one loves me, and still I am so full of love! It's the one thing left of me, the one thing. . . ."

Goupillière felt repelled yet flattered. He wondered

[179]

whether Serafimov had slept with this woman, and then began to feel rather triumphant.

✳

The next morning he watched Serafimov bending over a bowl of water, washing himself. He scrubbed his neck, his eyes were tightly shut and gave to his face the expression of a child about to burst into tears; he looked like a great animal, with his ugly pock-marked face, his huge stooping body patterned with hair, little curling flecks of it on his breast, his belly, his shoulders, his swelling forearms.

Then he dried his face and stretched himself. He opened his eyes. Amazingly beautiful these were, as blue as the sky, and as candid. His hair stood out grotesquely all over his head. A thick beard covered the lower half of his face.

His body twisted to and fro as he did his silly exercises—recently resumed, for some reason; supple as a tiger's, the fine grace of a body totally confident of itself and its powers, fearing nothing in this world, nothing tangible at least. "How innocent," thought Goupillière, "and yet how helpless, how weak, after all, how ill-equipped in spite of all his simple strength, in this crafty world. He seems brutal, crude, resilient. But how deceptive that is! Underneath that coarse body, which I envy yet despise, beats a soft heart, a tender, stupid, impulsive, pitiless, sentimental spirit. The world is full of creatures like that. They always defeat themselves in the end. They never come to much. They need to be guided. . . ."

Goupillière felt hot with resentment. Resentment for

the other's free, strong and simple mind, resentment suddenly against his own peculiar type of weakness now so plainly revealed, against his own youthful years of stratagem and chicanery and worse. "He is a man who can have only one thought in his mind," he reflected, "and that will govern him utterly. I am moved by more hidden, more conflicting considerations. He is warmed by a single flame, I, by a thousand embers."

He wondered how old Serafimov was. Forty, he thought. Possibly two or three years short of forty. His hair was very rich and black, like that of a young man.

He noticed that Serafimov, as he was dressing, made a habit of glancing for a moment at a miniature portrait of a woman in a tiny mosaic frame, the shape and size of a birch leaf, and then slipping it back into his pocket. He wondered who it was, and felt curiously fascinated by it. He wanted very much to look at it more carefully. He made a mental note to this effect.

Then he saw Serafimov glancing up at him. For a moment their eyes met. Goupillière felt disturbed. What was that huge stupid man thinking? What did he feel toward himself? A flash of shrewdness, and of something more than shrewdness, had entered his animal gaze. Suspicion? Jealousy? What was it? The man seemed to be uneasy about something.

✳

That night he noticed that Serafimov was shifting to and fro beneath his blanket. He heard him moaning now and again, almost sobbing—with lust, he would have said. He had noticed signs before this of the poor wretch trying to work off his passion. He must have been very heavily gifted by nature, for he seemed to be almost constantly on the alert, sexually; every touch and glance appeared to disturb him; sweat would appear on his brow at the slightest erotic reference. He himself had taken to reciting obscene anecdotes, full of picturesque detail, simply to observe their effect on this stallion of a man. It amused him to see the signs of excitement invariably and punctually appearing there.

But on this particular night something rather odd happened. As he was watching, by the light of a glowing log, he saw Serafimov's slumbering face suddenly grow tense, his lips pressed together, his eyes twitching. Little bubbles appeared at the corner of his mouth. This continued for two or three minutes. Then he uttered a little cry, his teeth showed, and his body twisted: his expression became wolflike for an instant, and terrifying. Then he sighed and relapsed again into a sound sleep, and his face was once more that of an ugly child.

All this puzzled Goupillière. He found that he no longer quite understood what went on in this simple sentimental creature.

And simultaneously he began to be somewhat afraid of Serafimov. There was something rather dangerous there, and he didn't quite understand it; something moving about uneasily, waiting to break loose and to emerge.

19

The Fox

YES, SOMETHING WAS ABOUT TO HAPPEN, AT LAST.
He knew it. The atmosphere was that of a jungle,
a deep and torrid jungle, where absolute stillness
reigns but where anything might occur without warning—
the arc of a lithe golden shape leaping through the air,
the tearing of flesh, a brief cry, or the flash of reptilian
hatred suddenly disturbing the centuried stillness of a
pond. Every detail carried a heavy significance, so Goupillière observed, every gesture, flicker of an eyelid, simple
phrase, casual departure or arrival, was observed, and took
its place in the intricate web of relationships in the inn.

He watched Serafimov more cautiously now. "That man
is a fanatic," he thought, "simple but really dangerous in

his reactions. Those eyes indicate a natural tendency toward obsessions."

He would watch him washing himself each morning, with a certain envy. He looked like a great ape, his legs spread, his arms reaching out, his shaggy torso curved over the bowl. The domination of the body over the mind, he reflected. All that is born in those dark loins, that traditional middle region of the body! Cities burned to the ground, provinces changing hands, thrones desecrated, the most beautiful of our things created and others destroyed in rage; the flames ravaging the countryside, the violence of young soldiers, the death of horses, the migration of tribes, the decline of a kingdom—all because of that tormenting area, that restless tugging and itching of the seed!

And, in a certain spirit of spitefulness, he would tell Serafimov little stories in the evenings before falling asleep. He knew quite well how dangerous this might prove to be, but he could not resist the desire to torment that restless body.

"Oh, she's a passionate one," he'd say. "Be cruel to her, be disdainful, that's the way to treat her. And she'll come begging for it. The worse you treat her, the more she'll do for you. Call her names, accuse her of all sorts of things. She loves it! You should see her." He would watch the poor fellow's eyes water and his lips tremble.

"She'll burst into tears, as likely as not," he'd go on, leeringly. "That's always a good sign. But don't let it bother you. Laugh at her. Torture her. Pull her hair, rip off her silky things, call her a revolting old hyena, and then finally when she is on the very edge of hysteria, creep up to her, bury your head in her lap, ask her forgiveness, kiss her ever so gently, implore her to be tender. Oh, she'll be tender then, tender is no word! . . ."

And presently Serafimov would wipe the sweat from his brow and dash out into the street to seek some sort, any sort, of relief.

But he envied, deeply, that big Russian. The glow of love in his eyes, in everything he did, the constant leaping of warm masculine energy through his limbs.

And, of course, he also realized that little by little the man was losing control of himself.

★

He could scent in Serafimov, as the winter wore on, something entirely new and disquieting. As if he were a great cat, divining things through his senses alone, things generally incalculable by men; so that the air, the actual air, between the two of them seemed charged with an electrical vitality, and their attitude toward each other was no longer a matter of words or deductions but a matter of incomparably delicate apprehensions, compared to which the most subtle of phrases would have seemed crude, irrelevant. Life was becoming real, in a very profound sense. No longer a tissue of words and devices and compromises conceived by generations of men; but an animal thing, covert, and wholly inexpressible.

He could observe constantly, as he had often observed before, how extreme suffering and unrelieved conflicts carried the stupid far above the boundaries of their minds, and gave to them a peculiar vision, intense, gleaming, and in its way penetrating; just as, in a forest so dark and thick that light only rarely reaches the ground, the scene be-

[185]

comes brilliant only in the sudden extreme illumination of a huge fire which thereupon destroys everything.

Late one evening Serafimov suddenly rose, thumped his fist on the table, and cried out, in the midst of a general silence, "This land isn't Asia! This is the land of the damned!"

☆

A night or two later Goupillière was telling the company some succulent anecdote about the "harlot from Harbin," when suddenly Serafimov interrupted, and shouted to him, eyes flashing, "Don't be the devil! Don't be the devil!"

Hours after they had all gone to bed he woke up and heard the big Russian arise and creep out into the street. He waited in suspense. He could guess where the man was going. He could see him dashing along the empty streets toward Madame Tastin's house. And what would happen there, he wondered? What sort of relief would he find?

About two hours later he heard him returning. The fire was almost out now, dawn was drawing near, and he could see, through half-closed eyes, the big lumbering shape approaching through the darkness, tearing off the enormous cloak, stumbling heavily into his blankets. Then, listening intently, he heard the poor wretch groaning to himself, whispering softly, "I'll survive, yes, I'll survive," and then suddenly exclaiming, in the curiously trite and ugly accents of a passionate distress, "Oh God, have mercy on me, have mercy on me!"

It was, actually, this incident which warned Goupillière of the really dangerous state of the Russian's mind, and

[186]

which presently led him to suspect something of his intentions.

✯

The next morning Serafimov appeared to be calm enough. He seemed, in fact, preoccupied and rather mild. His eyes were bloodshot and sleepy but quite gentle, as if he were thinking of something far away or long past.

But this didn't really deceive Goupillière. Not by any means. He realized that Serafimov was more resourceful, and in fact more intelligent, than he had supposed. Swiftly and quietly he began to make plans of his own, and to prepare himself, as a fox does, for the approaching crisis.

20

The Thief

GOUPILLIÈRE SAT BESIDE THE WINDOW AND stared out into the courtyard of the *serai*. In the distance he could still see the gilt spire of the White Russian church rising above the squat gray hovels of Aqsu into the dusky sky. Flakes of snow fell across the window—the near ones swiftly and capriciously, the more remote ones deliberately, stealthily, in utter quiet. The men in the room were deep in slumber, not one of them stirred. It was almost dark outside, the night was descending with those flakes, soft, still, cold, drawing its subtle sleep-bringing veils one by one across the city. Inside it was quite dark. Only one candle was burning on the table, and the shapes on the floor were now scarcely visible—only a boot here, and a lock of hair there, or a half-opened hand clutching at a ray of candlelight. The inn was built in the Russian style; a winding stair with railings of carved wood led to the cavernous darkness upstairs. The snow blew in through the crevices in the window, but in spite of this the room was hot. He could smell the sleeping men, he could smell their warm dirty bodies clumsily dreaming of voluptuous and festive worlds.

Now it was dark outside. The golden spire had vanished. Even the flakes of snow could no longer be seen, except for a stray one now and then flashing as it captured the candlelight for an instant. He saw himself reflected in the black window pane, his face illumined by the trembling flame. He stared at himself, immensely fascinated. His eyes were aglow with memories. The hideous scar on his right cheek vanished, as he stared at himself. His face grew young again, the face of a boy. And as he watched, it actually seemed that through the alien monotonous darkness behind him the shapes and landscapes of his youth were moving, one and then another and then another. . . .

☆

The past! That echoing history of hatred, subterfuge and chicanery! Where did it start? How did it start? He remembered his "grandmother," wearing her stiff black cloak and long black gloves, leading him down the hill toward the old church in Ronce. She wasn't, to be sure, really his grandmother at all. She and her husband were childless; they had taken him in and had given him their name, that was all, and he despised them for it. He had always known this, he had always known, though he didn't remember how, that he was an orphan, that his mother had been an Italian servant-girl, and that his birth was a thing best left uncontemplated. There had been something horrible; his mother had been found murdered—no one had told him that, but he knew, he knew. He had always, as far back as he could remember, known more than anyone could tell him.

He remembered how, on one particular afternoon, on his way back through the holly-lined street, the tall strong boys picked up bits of dirty snow and hurled them at him. "Bastard! Bastard!" they cried. He went running home, eyes fiery, cheeks striped with burning tears.

"What!" cried Madame Goupillière. "Crying on Christmas Eve! Naughty child. . . ." And then she ran her long fingers through his hair and sat down to read to him—from the *Oraisons Funèbres*, the sheer resonance of whose clauses filled her with pious emotions, or perhaps the *Maximes* of La Rochefoucauld, which, though "immoral," were thought to "stimulate a reflective and cautious nature."

And then the next morning he dashed down the cold gray stairs in his nightgown, expectant, his heart beating with calculation and avarice. Yes. There they were. The stockings hanging above the hearth; and in his own, a bright red apple, polished till it shone like glass, a wax doll, a pair of slippers lined with rabbit fur, a box of red cinnamon *pastilles*, some postage stamps from Algiers, Guadaloupe, Madagascar. Full of restraint, full of dignity he gazed at them, proud but disappointed; no better, after all, than last year. No tin Senegalese soldiers in their gay uniforms, no train with automatic signals, tunnels, and the rest. He began to pretend that it wasn't Christmas at

all, and stared with intolerance at his "grandmother," who
was somehow infected by the lovely occasion: alert, excited,
full of memories of former Christmases too, and then,
unhappy soul that she was—though there was nothing in
her heart of hearts that she desired more than to press his
pretty head against her shrunken bosom and cover it with
passionate kisses—instantly trying to kill off all tender
recollections as if they were flies buzzing about, disturbing
her rigid skeletal calm.

Yes, he saw passing through the darkness behind that
staring face all the whimsical images of early nights and
early days; the noises of the storm, the gray shape stooping
above the bed, the long hungry corridor; the church, bleak
and fragrant with stale incense and wet boots, visited early
on blue snowy mornings; the bare courtyard behind the
house with its one dry quince tree; and school—the eva-
sions, the "botanical" and "geological" excursions, the sly
symbolical games, the revelations in the copse, the games
in the forest, the whispers in the schoolyard, the knife
discovered in the lavatory, the illicit pears plucked beside
the ruined chateau, the tin soldiers stolen from the sweet-
shop. And scattered, unforgettable visions—a dead cat
lying out in the rain; a design, repugnant yet fascinating,
scribbled upon the fence; a coffee spoon lying in a dirty
saucer; a wild cry in the street suddenly springing out of a
tower of imprisoned desires; the rhythmical sound of
wooden boots on the cobbles; a portrait of the Sacred
Heart, flaming and passionate, upon the wall; a lamp beside the window—and in these signs, already, with a child's
native visionary sense of guilt, he was beginning to discern
the shape of the appalling and everlasting struggle between
Good and Evil.

He recognized a certain morning—the girls all dressed

in stiff white tulle and artificial flowers for their First Communion, so very innocent and pure with their freshly scrubbed cheeks and their yellow hair in taffeta ribbons and braids. And he recognized a certain evening—the dark shapes along the undulating road which led from the town out to the cemetery; the stiff ugly houses of the wealthy and the stingy hiding behind their foliage and their walls; the alley of huge chestnut trees; and beyond this, the row of leering shops already quiet and black—the butcher's, the baker's, the stationer's, the draper's, the grocer's; nothing could be discerned, life lay hidden there, and over everything hung a gentle but estranging veil.

He knew that he was the bastard son of a murdered girl from Genoa; but he also knew that he was more clever than any of the boys in Ronce, that he could sing more sweetly, leap further, run faster, steal more deftly, learn more quickly, lie more glibly, than any of them. And so, one day after he had been whipped in school for writing a scurrilous poem about M. Barillot the Latin master, (who at that point was particularly intent on his own dignity, since he had unsuccessfully been trying to find a publisher for his newly completed translation of Horace's *Epistles*) he ran away to Paris.

☆

The great city. He would never forget the endless, aimless posturings of its wicked and frustrated ballet—the sleek young waiter returning from the sumptuous silver platters of the Ritz to the dingy complaints and suddenly undesired caresses of his wife; the ugly invalid stifling in

his iodine-scented room with the acute longings for greatness—the power, say, to sway dark multitudes and conquer
torrid peninsulas—which might compensate for his intolerable isolations; the hack-driver sleepily listening to his
wife's tale of a murder trial, a rape, a conflagration, an outrageous swindle in Rumania or a flood in China; the young
bookseller's apprentice with literary ambitions setting
out for a walk in the Bois one night from which he is not
destined ever to return alive; the unsatisfied young wife
of the banker, lying in her lavender silks beside the tele-
phone, expectant and peevish and drenched with perfumes; the handsome and intelligent Jewish student, collecting statistics for a time to come when all will be equal,
none will suffer, injustice will be punished by unutterable
agonies, and he himself will be asked to coffee in the best
salons; the paralytic among his twilit first editions, planning devastations, inventing martyrdoms, imagining hatreds, shaken by a hopeless passion for the ripe young body
that lives on the floor above him.

Sitting in front of his blistering mirror one morning, he
realized that he had suddenly become very good-looking.
This discovery changed him a little, but not very much.
He grew more vain, that was all. He would sit in front of
the mirror and stare at his beautiful face, day after day.
He fell more and more deeply in love with himself. He
would gaze with pleasure at his dark, sparkling eyes, at his
long lashes, his silky curly hair, his fine olive-colored skin,
his graceful, cat-like body.

One evening as he walked along the Quai Voltaire a
woman picked him up. It was really as simple as that. Not
particularly pretty, she was. But, he realized, rather
wealthy. She took him home. She pretended to take an

interest in his "career," his religion, his reading, his clothes, his political views, his curious Flemish accent.

On his next visit she wore a thin gown of scarlet brocade; behind her hung a mirror, at her side stood a bowl of jonquils. He kissed her, dutifully. Thereupon she caressed him, ran her fingers along his neck, and spoke to him about his character.

"I don't understand you," she murmured, "You are so pretty yet so sullen, you are always changing. . . . I think you must be a thoroughly deceitful boy! Either that," and she smiled lasciviously, "or very ambitious. . . ."

On the day of his third visit, it was raining heavily. She put a shawl over his wet shoulders, put his feet in a hot mustard bath, gave him some spiced wine to drink. He felt creeping over him a feeling of luxury, of desire for himself, of a sudden and devastating hatred for her. An hour later he lay beside her on the bed. He lay there for hours, confiding to her, pouring out for the first time a whispered history of his soul. He felt her pressing against him, running her fingers over his face and his neck. He kissed her once or twice—on her eyelids, on her shoulder, on her nipples. But that was all; there was nothing more.

That was the last he ever saw of her. He kept a little souvenir to remember her by, however—an emerald ring and a diamond bracelet which he had slipped out of the table beside her bed when she wasn't looking.

He continued to steal; he felt no sense of guilt whatever, no twinge of shame, no fear. If he felt anything at all, it was pleasure. It was simply a game, a sort of flirtation with those who had wealth, position and power. He stole from shops—cheap bits of jewelry, underwear, perfumes, socks, gloves, even silks and furs. Once he was caught and clapped into jail for three nights. But everyone instinctively liked

him; they all smiled, they seemed almost to take pleasure
in his youthful corruption. They would call him a "pretty
boy" and smile at him, lecherously and contemptuously,
and all he could do in return was to loathe; loathe with a
constant and calculating ferocity.

He stole love, too. Chiefly to gratify his vanity, but also
out of a delight in cruelty, a curious sensitive desire, conceivably, to avenge all that had been endured, through the
machinations of love, by his mother—the only creature,
though he did not even remember her dark suffering face,
for whom he had ever felt what might be called, not
love, perhaps, but a certain loyalty of heart.

Then there came an unsavory period of two years. He
contracted gonorrhœa, and was tended by an old cocotte.
And worse. He lived on the vices and follies of others,
light-heartedly, quite gratuitously. And now the worst
desire of all grew on him—the desire, not for physical love,
but for spiritual love. For power over the souls of people.
For the power, in short, to corrupt the human heart.

And all the while he fell more and more deeply in love
with himself. All the while he felt, secretly, that something
thrilling, something thrilling beyond words, lay in store
for him.

☆

He grew afraid, it is true, just a bit alarmed, now and
again. He would seek out the company of certain women
(he was happy only with women, they were the only ones
with whom he felt at ease and in whom he ever confided)
and would allow himself to be flattered and soothed. He

had affairs with some of them, of course, but these were the ones he left soonest. But still, he at last began to wonder what sort of creature he was, and why he was what he was. Lonely, tempestuously ambitious, wildly unscrupulous, immensely proud, incurably calculating. Sensual but without tenderness, sociable but without loyalty, tormented but never by a feeling of repentance. He could ask himself quite plainly, was there anything in him that was good?

At any rate, he did see clearly once in a while. "Everything false and treacherous, everything evil that you do," murmured a curious little hidden voice within him, "changes you. You may think 'If I do this one thing, it will be trivial, it will be forgotten presently.' But ah, you would be deceiving yourself! It is momentous, it will last forever and forever! You have changed yourself, you will never be the same again, and, whatever you may think, you are not the same person that you were two hours ago. It will show, at first faintly and perhaps not unpleasantly. . . . But later on, more revoltingly, in your eyes, your lips, your hands, your voice, your manner of making love, and worst of all, your endless tormenting restlessness. No subterfuge will avail. You will eventually become afraid of yourself! Eventually you will lose out in the endless struggle for survival. You will think, perhaps, that you are winning. But a nasty surprise will be lying in wait for you. . . ."

★

Then, one July evening, something happened. Everything changed for him, everything. Nothing was left of the old life; a new life began.

Towards sunset he visited one of his little friends, a *grisette*, Didi Boucicault by name. A pretty thing, she was. Red-haired, impudent, full of life, with a body as quick and nervous as a squirrel's. But a terrible temper as well. He would tease her each time that he saw her, and watch with delight how her eyes grew fiery, her body trembled, her voice grew shrill. But, at the bottom of his heart, he really hated her.

This was what happened. He began teasing her. "You're still pretty, my love, but not so pretty as you once were! A bit of the freshness is gone, a bit of the sparkle. . . . Oh well, we all grow old. . . ."

"Indeed!" she cried. "Don't I please you? Is that it?"

"I didn't say that, my love," he murmured softly. "No, no!"

She spat with rage. "Oh, I know! I know where your tastes lie, my pretty boy. You haven't deceived me!" Her eyes were aflame, a little vein in her throat began to vibrate queerly. She tore off her dressing-gown and stood naked before him. "Look!" Her whole body was glistening and trembling with rage and violent desire.

"It doesn't suit you?" she snarled. "A bit of the freshness is gone? A bit of the sparkle. . . . Well," and she flung herself at him and began tugging at his shirt. He smelled the hot perfume of her body. He couldn't take his eyes off the little throbbing artery in her white throat. "I don't please you, is that it? Well, I know why, my little columbine! I know why! I know, I know. . . ." Her voice had risen into a scream, a vibrating, lust-ridden, nauseating scream.

Suddenly he sprang up from the bed and threw Didi

into a chair. He thrust his body against hers, and in a spasm of desire began to press his fingers against her throat. Against that quivering pink artery in her snowy throat.

Didi coughed hoarsely. Then she began to yelp like a poodle. He relaxed his grip and laughed loudly. He rose and began to tear his clothes off. He felt violently passionate now. Then he turned toward her again, and reached his fingers toward her neck.

She began screaming with fury. A pair of finger-nail scissors was lying on the boudoir table beside the chair. With a gesture incredibly swift, a feminine, electrical gesture, she snatched at them and plunged them into his face. He saw the flash of the tiny blade, and for the briefest moment felt the odd, chilling frenzy of the metal tearing across his cheek.

Then he saw, heard, felt nothing. He thrust himself forward in a blind, ecstatic rage, and plunged his fingers into her throat. That was all. He felt, heard and saw nothing at all.

But several minutes later, when he saw Didi lying all askew on the chair, a ridiculous broken doll, her tongue clamped like a little red rag between her teeth, her eyes bulging like those of an idiot, he knew what had happened.

He wiped the sweat from his body. All desire had flowed out of him in that terrible, obscene moment. He dressed, carefully and thoughtfully, walked out, locked the door behind him, and sauntered homeward. He felt very calm, profoundly relieved. The trees in the park looked hazy and aglow with tenderness.

When he sat down in his room and glanced at his face in the mirror, he shivered, felt faint, his hands began to tremble. It was a strange face, besmeared with blood, half of it disfigured into a staring hyena-like ugliness. He knew, then, that life had changed for him. Changed totally and forever. He was one of the unlovely now, the unlucky, the unloved. One of the afraid.

Quietly he rose, washed out the wound, painted it with iodine, and applied a bandage. Then he sat down again. For the first time in years, he began to sob.

That evening he took the train for Marseilles.

✫

He stayed in Marseilles for four days. That most astonishing of European cities; a shimmering, shadowy background for the most desolate and plantlike of vices; the edge of another way of thinking and living; the edge of Asia; city of anonymous arrivals and frightening departures, of mystifying instructions and absorbing apprenticeships. Under those tangled roofs, along those surrealist streets, where odd little parcels freshly arrived from Port Said lay hidden among the meats in a butcher shop, waiting to be purchased by red-slippered, dark-skinned girls with hoarse voices and flower-like bodies. Those streets which seemed to lead, through incessant archways and enormous shadows, into an eternity of their very own, that jungle of alleys, those whispering chambers lit only by stars or the occasional flicker of a match or the glow of a long, slender pipe. It charmed him, at first. He thought that he might stay here.

But something was wrong, he presently discovered. Something was profoundly and sickeningly wrong. There was something new tormenting him. Fear. Every face he saw was that of an enemy. Around every street-corner, beside him in every latrine, opposite him in every little café, he saw the face of an enemy. Watching and waiting. Hour by hour he grew more afraid. Finally, in a moment of panic, he decided quite simply to run away. Far, far away.

So, after four days in Marseilles, he sailed on a freighter bound for Saïgon. It was in Saïgon, weeks later, that he met a wealthy Frenchman, de la Scaze by name, and agreed to fly with him and his wife in a private plane to Kashgar.

"The end of the world!" he thought to himself, when he saw the staggering colors of the Chinese Turkestan unfurling far below, mile by mile by mile. He felt excited, full of a tremendous calm and a tremendous expectancy as well. "The end of the world!" he whispered to himself. . . .

☆

The sleeping men were still lying motionlessly on the floor of the *serai*. The candle was flickering, but the red glow of the fire still fell on their cheeks, their straight lips, their long flat eyelids, creating there an appearance of warmth and preoccupation, as if a fire were glowing inside them too.

Now the door opened and another one entered. He sat down beside Goupillière and smiled drunkenly. Then he began to sing softly. He seemed to be intensely moved by his own song. To Goupillière it seemed a hideous song, profoundly empty and desolate, like a sigh rising out of a depopulated ravine; yet the words appeared to be concerned with love, passionate trysts, tender caresses, home, children, and uxorious contentments! Presently the old fellow fell asleep.

And soon Goupillière began to fall asleep too. He closed his eyes and began to smile. He felt a happy little flutter in his heart. He was thinking of all those truculent and helpless human spirits scattered about, in such a disorderly fashion, upon the world of which half was forever in shadow. He couldn't help feeling amused and intrigued. He frequently had feelings like this before going to sleep. Even as a child he used to have them. His heart fluttered like a little bright-eyed bird, and his body felt nervous and alert with pleasure.

Then, as he turned over, he caught sight of Serafimov lying near by, face to the wall. For a moment he felt thoroughly shocked. There was something very eloquent about that huge sleeping figure, something powerful, something monitory. Goupillière felt an impulse to get up and run away.

Perhaps, it occurred to him, he should leave the *serai* right away. After all, he had a bit of money left—enough to find a little room for himself. He might find de la Scaze, for example. . . . But no, he then decided. It wouldn't do. The thought of de la Scaze depressed him. He would think it over tomorrow morning, he said to himself.

Then he fell asleep.

21

The Pursuit

HE WOKE UP QUITE SUDDENLY IN THE MIDDLE OF the night: it was with that feeling of suspense and intuition which exists in the outskirts of a dream that he opened his eyes. The darkness around him was veined, tactile, like the flesh of a man. Straining his ears, he thought he could detect the beating of another man's heart not far away.

But he could see nothing strange. Nothing was moving at all. He could discern, dimly, the pale shapes lying along the four walls, some prostrate and others hunched up bizarrely. Serafimov was lying with his face to the wall. He was by far the biggest man in the room. He looked, lying there so quietly and enormously, like a statue that has fallen from its pedestal, crumbling and corrupt.

Then he raised his eyes, still groping his way through that region where past and present merge ever so tenderly, both whispering softly and pointing out curious likenesses never before observed. He could see a small semicircle of sky through the little window beside the door. At first it appeared to be a fragment of blue only slightly less dark than the color of the ceiling. But then suddenly it began to glitter, he could hardly believe his eyes, and an incredible fiery brilliance leapt across that small semicircle. There, through that opening which seemed from where he lay no larger than a finger nail, the complete and gigantic night suddenly shone down upon him. It was, more than anything, perhaps, the effect produced by those glittering wintry stars, which he now noticed for the first time. Indeed, for the first time in his life he perceived how miraculous their golden power was, piercing those black solitudes, entering a tiny window somewhere between the Altai and the Celestial Mountains, shining down into his eyes with such unmistakable energy and passion. He instantly remembered his childhood again—how he had walked across the cobblestones of Ronce with dark and revengeful heart, and had noticed the stars in the sky; or, glimpsed through the window, the sinuous sheen of midnight gliding like a serpent across the roofs of the Belgian town, and entwining itself among the branches of the quince tree in the courtyard, and then slipping past the curtains upon the rose-patterned carpet in his room.

And now, as if the anxiety of those moments had flown like a bird across two continents and twenty-two years, he felt, as he had then felt, a real fear. That lurking, sickening fear of the unknown. He listened to the beating of his heart, and the stars seemed with their flickering to accompany perfectly this fragile rhythm.

Then quickly all these vague associations scurried into the darkness, like mice when the cat is approaching. His fear grew definite, for at this very moment he had the feeling, though nothing in the room had moved, that another person had entered, a figure quaint and silent, watching quietly.

He looked around in alarm. But of course, the rest were all lying asleep. No one had entered.

"How late is it?" he wondered. "After midnight? No doubt. Too late to go to Madame Tastin's. But then, what does it matter? All the better. She'll be all the more pleased; I needn't even worry about an excuse, just restlessness, I'll say. . . . And then I can think things over in the morning. . . ."

He knew now what he was afraid of, of course. It was that silent powerful shape that lay there, statue-like, staring at the wall. He was almost sure now that Serafimov was not asleep. Terrifying, that vast prostrate statue looked to him. He felt a wild impulse to leap up and run.

But then his mind grew alert. He began to make plans. He knew, in short, that Serafimov was lying there, thinking of murder.

With infinitesimal precaution he rose, inch by stealthy inch, gathered his heavy clothes, and crept noiselessly across the floor to the door. He crouched there a moment and glanced about the room for a last time. This was where his ambitions had been imprisoned for so long! This fœtid desolate cave! Never again would he enter this place, never again! He knew it, somehow. He was sure of it.

Then, without a sound, he opened the door and slipped

out. And, once he had reached the street, he ran quickly toward Madame Tastin's.

*

After Madame Tastin had fallen asleep again and had begun to snore softly, he walked across the bedroom, drew aside the curtain, and looked out into the street. A wind had come up, and clouds were beginning to cover up the stars. But the night was still clear as a crystal. He saw, far, far away, summits of hills that he had never seen before, even in bright daylight. There was a very faint wind, and it sighed as it hastened along the street. He began to feel excited, for the night seemed so very brilliant, so nervous, so alive.

Then he saw a shadow on the opposite side of the street. He almost fainted at this momentary vision. He closed his eyes.

Then he looked again. Now he saw clearly the dark cloak, the fur cap, the thick boots. He recognized the huge shoulders and the queer, stooping gorilla posture. The name "Serafimov" did not cross his mind, but he knew, even before he had actually seen him, at the mere glimpse of a shadow upon the wall opposite, that his senses had recognized him. Just as, standing in a meadow, one can foretell by a tingling of the skin or a brightening of the eyes the coming of a storm long before the first black cloud is visible; and then, a moment later, by the curious shadows, the strange reflections in the leaves.

He was fascinated; he could not move. His heart beat

[205]

wildly, half in terror, half in a curious, senseless sort of enthusiasm.

But then, at a tiny movement in the figure below—a mere flicker, no more—he suddenly grew electrical. He did not even stop to think. He crept across the floor, hurled his cape over his shoulders, and without a moment's pause flung aside the window that opened from the back of the house, and leapt upon the wall that surrounded the little courtyard. Then he hastened down the road, out across the snow, past the old gray prison, past the group of deserted buildings in the western outskirts of the town.

22

The Tower

H E MARVELED AT THE SOFT SOUND OF HIS FEET
in the snow. The air was like fire, so sharp and
pure. In all these weeks at the *serai*, this was the
very first time, it occurred to him, that he had stepped out
into the actual country beyond the town, the first time
that his feet were stepping on unfamiliar territory.

He was panting. Even in this complete darkness he could
see his steaming breath. The sky had grown quite black
now, and the landscape was visible only by that snowy illumination which even in the darkest winter night allows
shapes to emerge from the velvet background.

He paused on the slope of a small mound. He could see
the whole city, extending from north to south. Unspeak-

ably desolate it looked, and now that he was standing outside it for the first time, it seemed really unbelievable that he could have survived in that desolation there, that lifeless vacuum. Curiously enough, he had forgotten about Serafimov for the moment, and though he was still trembling with excitement he had now grown reflective, as a man instinctively does when he sees a familiar scene from a totally new angle, no matter how crucial and violent the occasion.

A ruined tower was standing on the very top of the mound. Only a broken circular wall no more than twelve feet high was left of it. Goupillière crept up to the pockmarked base of the tower, leaned against it for a moment, and then crouched down in the snow, breathing heavily.

☆

Squatting there, sweating and panting with exertion, he felt totally aloof from everything all about him. From the snow-clad city, the barren snow-white slopes, the distant mountains deep in their snow. All his agitation was gone. A perfect calm settled on him. He began to think about himself in a painstakingly deliberate way.

"I am being pursued," he said to himself quietly. "Some one is at this very moment wanting to kill me. But I'm not afraid. I'm not afraid!"

There was something deep within himself which he presently began to understand, which surprised him, which elated and, a moment later, frightened him. He was unconquerable, so to speak: that was it. No one would ever be really victorious over him. He was, in his little way,

unattainable, impregnable. Neither through hate nor
through love, not even through death, would anyone ever
conquer him. And there was one simple reason for this. He
loved himself too much. Not only with vanity or pride;
but deeply, excitedly, untiringly, absorbingly, calculat-
ingly, indeed passionately, almost as a boy loves his first
mistress, or as a woman adores her clandestine lover; so
that all ardors were locked securely in a world of his own—
surprisingly varied they were too, full of iridescent intrigues and subtle surprises. He was able to contemplate
the rest of the world with a smiling indifference. Other
people didn't really matter to him at all. They could never
really hurt him, those others. They might try to punish
him, starve him, torture him, kill him. But he would
remain secret and powerful.

"There is only one force," he thought, not without a
certain pleasure, "capable of ruining me. And that is
myself!"

He was filled with a glow, a welling of energy. But he
did not feel happy. Everything seemed more involuntary,
more uncontrollable, more meaningful, more loaded with
destiny, than even an hour ago.

He leaned his head back against the ruined wall. "I
have never in my life been really happy," he murmured.

Then he noticed that there were snowflakes falling—so
few that for a moment it seemed that five or six little white
moths had suddenly flown out of the tower and were fluttering softly to the ground. A moment later he heard a
rumble of thunder in the distance, and then by a quick
sharp flash of lightning saw the whole landscape leaping
into a new existence, an excited, pale, quite hysterical
kind of existence.

There was something in that jagged vein of fire which

thrilled him, made him shudder with a dagger-like yet
deeply harmonious delight. This white assassination which
tore across the night—unlike anything else in the world, its
roots and consequences shelled in darkness—was a symbol
of a pure, climactic inner hatred, that was it. He could
feel its electrical power pervading him, instilling in his
limbs its own alertness.

But the immediate reason for this queer thrill of recognition was not that glaring light which suddenly flooded
the snow-swept valley and the misty pinnacles; nor the
walls of Aqsu which shone forth, suddenly luminous,
skeletal, intense. It was this: from this empty whiteness
the black shape of a man emerged, his fur-capped head
bowed down as if scrutinizing the ground, moving very
gradually through the slow veil of snowflakes, up the
mound in his direction. He could at this moment not have
been more than two hundred yards away from where
Goupillière was sitting.

With perfect intuition Goupillière seized that brief
pause of intenser blackness which followed the blinding
flash of lightning, and ran swiftly around to the opposite
side of the tower, so that the ruined walls now rose between him and Serafimov. He felt full of an entirely novel
energy—a bodily delight, almost, an animal's control over
the body and an animal's ability to calculate through the
senses alone, instantaneously and unerringly.

He glanced at the wall, touched it lightly with his hand;
then quickly, with flawless judgment, leapt up toward a
crevice about ten feet high, simultaneously setting the tip
of his right foot on a slight projection, and then unbending
his knee, again raised himself so that he could grasp an
opening where the top of the wall was somewhat lower
than elsewhere. And thus, after a single flowing movement,

like that of a squirrel sliding up a tree-trunk, he suddenly found himself on top of the wall.

He gazed for an instant into the circular interior of the tower. Snow lay flickering there, cold and alert as a great reptile, some eighteen or twenty feet below. A fragrance of desertion and antiquity rose from the cavern. He lowered himself by his hands, hung once again for a moment from the top of the wall, then dropped elastically and noiselessly down to the floor within the wall.

He walked across the space—it was the size of a large room, the size of the common room in the *caravanserai*, perhaps—and there, in a corner somewhat darker than the rest, beneath the highest section of the wall, he crouched and waited, while his steaming breath took shape before his eyes like a little ghost.

☆

A long time passed, so it seemed to him. Half an hour, perhaps. But he felt very calm. The only excitement he felt was the rather pleasant tingling of perfect watchfulness, as if a curtain were about to be raised, and the footlights about to flash on the final scene of an exciting play.

The thunder began to rumble again. The snowflakes had ceased falling, and it seemed to Goupillière that the night was growing lighter, ever so faintly so, and that dawn, still far away and gentle as a dove, was now approaching slowly. He could hear the wind rushing around the tower like an arriving flood and filtering through innumerable little crevices in the wall.

The rumbling of the thunder was a mighty thing. From

a small dark cavern in the sky, a sleeping secrecy, forth rolled these gongs, these terrible globes of music, each one cobwebbed, like the bottom of a wave, with a sort of speaking quality, a delicate frightful utterance. What they were saying no one knew. But there they were, these fragile whispers trembling upon the monstrous drum of thunder.

Then there was a sudden flash of lightning. By this flash Goupillière's mind and body were welded into a perfect and glowing unit. For what he saw by that flash was the silhouette of a man standing, motionless as a pillar, on top of the wall, at the exact spot where he himself had stood not so very long ago. He could see the stooped shoulders, the horrible doglike intensity in the posture of his body. He could see the bearded profile, and one hand held forward, in a gesture of suspense that looked almost like a gesture of benediction.

A spasm of guilt shook him and frightened him. There was something disgusting, really disgusting, about this gradual approach, this abject and inevitable *rendez-vous*. He could see the cloak billowed in the wind and the flannel of the boots. He could even see the sweat on the forehead and, he thought, the quiet gleam in those beautiful, ignorant eyes. Behind him, by the icy glare of this brief flash of lightning, he saw the whole blue bowl of the sky suddenly transfixed, arrowed through by this vein of fire. He could imagine perfectly, though he could not see, that mercurial gleam flowing over the windy landscape, flooding the valley and the hills, and washing every alley in the town white as chalk. Quite clearly he could picture these— valley, hills and town—for they were in a profound manner linked with this degraded statue which towered above

him. The illumined town, the hills, the valley, all sprang
into being through the passion of this black shape. Sparks
seemed to flash from his eyes, his hands. He was no longer
a man, he was more than that.

But his motionlessness was only momentary. And during
that subsiding period, infinitely brief, when the light faded
again and darkness leapt swiftly back from every side, he
saw Serafimov hovering, hesitating, leaning forward, poised
in the air with his arms extended; then instantly losing
tenseness and shape, suddenly ugly again, collapsing as a
loose stone crumbled away beneath his feet, and rushing
down into the pool of darkness. The scene was entirely
black again before Goupillière saw him reach the ground.
But he had seen by this glimmering echo of light the wild
clutch of the arms, the helpless angle of the head as he lost
his balance and fell. The sound of his body on the stones
below was subdued and ambiguous. But a moment later
Goupillière experienced a totally new feeling, one of
relaxation and almost of despair. And by this little feeling,
rather than by the evidence of his senses, he suspected that
Serafimov was dead.

He rose and walked across to Serafimov. He knelt beside him, gazed upon his closed eyelids, touched his warm
wet pock-marked forehead. There was a deep gash in his
forehead. He felt the warm blood clinging to his finger
tips. A terrible longing filled his heart. And instantly he
understood that this unbelievable moment was of course
the closest he had ever come to self-forgetfulness; to real
pity, real fear, and real devotion. In fact, what he felt for
one inexplicable instant was almost a kind of adoration.

Then suddenly he remembered something. Quickly he
knelt down beside the Russian's body, reached under his

cloak and deep into his right-hand pocket, and drew out a small object in the shape of a birch-leaf, and some coins.

☆

But just at the moment that he withdrew his hand from Serafimov's pocket, a thrill of terror, a very complicated and complete sort of thrill, intoxicated his mind and every limb of his body. It was as if he had been drugged. He sat motionless, appalled, utterly resigned; more than resigned.

For he had seen the tiniest tremor in those eyelids. Not the flicker of a wounded or a dying man, but that of a powerful, watchful, crafty animal, a real murderer. The man was not dead, after all. He was alive, terribly alive. In that one tiny movement of the eyelid and glitter of the eye he glimpsed the weeks and months of hatred, of suppressed violence, and the immeasurable energy in the man's heart.

He felt utterly helpless. He knelt motionless as an idol. All feeling had left his body, he could not move a single muscle. His eyes began to ache, for even his eyelids refused to close down upon them.

There were little flashes of lightning every few moments. Not huge and penetrating glares, but fluttering, bluish undulations. The fur of Serafimov's cape, the great creases of concentration in his face, his open eyes, the black snow-flecked cloth of his enormous cloak, all flickered in this throbbing, sea-blue light. And as Goupillière stared with aching eyes, their outlines grew blurred. It was like a scene under water.

How long he sat there he did not know. Ten seconds,

ten minutes? It didn't matter, of course. Time and space meant absolutely nothing now. Years, miles, all flowed into one. It crossed his mind, as he knelt there, his hands poised rigidly over the prostrate figure, that he might be praying. Praying in some secret, prehistoric manner, with a wisdom and passion so intense that it could not be recognized in human terms.

Then he saw Serafimov moving. Quietly and deliberately the huge man drew back his arms, raised his back, pulled up his knees and arose. Without effort, in a single movement it seemed, like smoke arising from the ground. Then the shape grew solid and still again, like a black pillar towering above him.

He closed his eyes. It was almost sweet, this calm, this veneration, this martyrdom. His life was complete, now. He understood. A little smile fluttered upon his lips.

He smelled the dangerous odor of the Russian's body approaching and engulfing him. He did not resist, he subsided gently, when he felt the touch of those vast hands upon his throat.

BOOK FOUR

Wildenbruch

BOOK FOUR

23

Prison

THEY WAITED AND WAITED. THE DAYS PASSED. BUT
nothing happened. As they sat by the prison window each day, they saw how the spire of the Russian church began to cast longer shadows; and how dawn
approached more hesitantly, and dusk arrived more swiftly.

Then Wildenbruch felt sure that they had been tricked.
But he didn't know by whom. By Dr. Liu? By the government of Sinkiang? By Soviet agents? There was no way of
discovering. The ugly bison-jowled gaoler couldn't even
understand what he was trying to say.

Each morning he woke up and began to hope for something novel—for a bit of news, a notice of release, and
finally, anything at all, a new face, a new kind of food, any-

thing. When he was stricken with toothache one day, it was almost a relief.

He would wake up very early and sit by the tiny window. The sun would rise on his left, slowly it would encroach upon the twilight of the distant sands, the dunes would begin to cast dark blue shadows, a thin film of silver would glide across the hillocks and the gravel over which, many days ago, he and von Wald had watched Dr. Liu's caravan slowly fading into the distance, eastward bound.

Then the little stream that ran down from the cemetery hill would begin to glimmer, it would grow alive, its red water would run flickering down the valley. A sheen would settle nervously on the late autumn foliage in the mulberry grove; each leaf would be a fragment of copper dangling from a twig. The stones in the cemetery emerged, each one gazing luminously toward the east and darkly toward the west. And then the shapes of the townsmen slowly began to appear, some clad in loose and brilliantly colored garments, others in dark jackets and shaggy boots. They would wander along the river or through the grove or up toward the cemetery, each one performing his customary morning errand—a prayer, a jugful of water, a morning lamentation, a visit to a relative.

And then the roofs of Aqsu and the walls of the old city would catch the light, and the golden spire of the Russian church would flash blindingly as the clouds parted and the whole blazing globe of the sun rose over the limitless waste. The little Chinese temple on the hillside, half-buried in foliage, would display its slender eaves and its delicate golden dragons through the lucid airs.

And then, as he turned his head slowly toward the west, he would see the miraculous slopes of the Mountains of Heaven, still cloaked in the mists of dawn, a little cloud perhaps poised on the loftiest peak like a coronet. The snow, the everlasting snow! How pure it looked, how powerful, how dictatorial and austere! Hugo's lips would harden, his gaze would grow intense and bitter.

Then he lowered his eyes again. There, down the blue street, hardly a quarter of a mile away, lay the *caravanserai*. He would begin to remember once more, and to wonder. What had happened to them—to the stupid Russian, the contemptible little Belgian, the effete Frenchman?

He would wonder. And then he would stop wondering. He didn't much care. He despised them.

☆

During the first week in the prison he had merely waited. It never occurred to him that they might have to stay more than a few days. He would sit and talk with his friend Joachim most of the time—about everything, about anything, about Europe, about God, about geology, about music, about people. About the people they had recently been separated from, for example. He himself had disliked them all; all except, perhaps, the Englishman Layeville. And even about Layeville there was something, a certain intangible something, which had risen between them like a wall.

But Joachim was more lenient. They would argue. "You are too severe, Hugo," Joachim would say, with a sly smile. "You must not expect too much from people, we all have our failings."

But Hugo disapproved of that kind of outlook. "Certainly," he would reply with energy; "certainly we have

our failings. But in the first place, have we the energy to
discipline ourselves? And in the second, have we the
strength and purposefulness beneath which will make us
real men?"

"Strength?" Joachim would murmur; "purposefulness?"
He would turn his golden head and look vaguely out of
the window. Hugo decided that Joachim did not understand people; that is to say, he merely accepted them; he
passed no sort of judgment, he had no discernible scale of
value; he was too young, too inexperienced.

"That man de la Scaze, for example," Hugo would say.
"I watched him carefully. Full of sensibilities. As sensitive
as a flower. No, no. I dislike that."

"He looked like an unhappy man," Joachim observed
gently.

"Certainly. Weakness never brings contentment. He
will always be unhappy." And then he remembered how
ill de la Scaze had looked. Possibly, it occurred to him, he
was still sick; possibly he was really badly off, possibly he
was dying.

"His wife," observed Joachim, "was very beautiful,
wasn't she?" His curly blond hair glittered in the sunlight,
his blue eyes looked thoughtful, a certain tenderness lay in
the curve of his full lips. Hugo would feel a brief little
ache of envy, and of deep friendliness too, when he glanced
at him. Just a puzzling, momentary touch of longing. But
then he would grow hard again. "He needs order," he
would say to himself. "Order. Discipline. Ambition."

And then his mind turned for a moment to de la Scaze's
wife. Yes, she was beautiful. Very beautiful. He would feel
a certain tingling in his breast when he thought of her, he
would grow restless, he would almost feel a blush coming
into his cheeks.

"But not the right type," he muttered. "That rich, southern kind of beauty." He grunted with disdain and disapproval. "No, no. Too heavy, too lifeless."

They would talk of the others too. Neither of them liked the little Belgian very much. Joachim didn't quite know why. But Hugo gave a snort of disgust. "A real degenerate," he said. "Not an idiot, like that Russian, I'll grant you, but a worthless character. I tell you," and his voice faded into a whisper, "I distrusted him. From the very beginning I distrusted him. . . ."

But they disagreed about Serafimov. "A fool," said Hugo.

"But a kindly sort of soul," said Joachim. "His eyes were like those of a little boy."

"Little boys are useless unless they grow up. Unless they are guided, controlled. Now that Englishman, for example . . ." There was something in Layeville that impressed him deeply. The aristocratic mien, the hauteur, the Spartanism.

Joachim wrinkled his brow. "He seemed so very lifeless. So cold, and a bit hostile too. Frightened of something, defiant, bitter. He looked back at us in a very curious way, I remember, when we separated in Aqsu. . . ."

But Hugo didn't answer. He was thinking about himself, now. His hands trembled with impatience and nervousness.

Impatience with time, above all. But with everything else too.

Above all, the prison was unutterably squalid. Not grim, not nocturnal or terrible. Merely shabby, ridiculously, farcically shabby. Everything was askew—the floor, the windows, the ceiling, everything. The plaster would rustle all night long and a constant gray powder descended like a

[223]

whisper from the ceiling. Infested with mice, for one thing, and slowly succumbing to the years and the climate, for another. It looked a thousand years old, even older, as old as a cave in the hills.

And then, the food. Meager, stale, insipid beyond all dreams. And the stupidity of the guards. Neither of the two guards could understand the fragmentary Hindustani that he and Joachim spoke. Furthermore, they were gratuitously surly. One of them was particularly odious. He would watch them through the door and grin, and perform puerile, indecent gestures. Once he accosted Joachim. Then Hugo lost his temper, shrieked with rage, and the scoundrel ran for the door. An obscene fellow. He stank like a wolf.

☆

The days passed somehow. Evening would finally arrive, each day a few moments earlier than the one before.

Once more the low shabby buildings of the city, and the *caravanserai*, would slip into their cloak of dusky blue. The glow would fade from the golden spire of the Russian church, little by little. The mountains, the beautiful Tian Shan, would again cast a veil of mist over their shoulders, and clouds would flow across their peaks once more. The little Chinese temple would hide behind its darkening foliage, the golden dragons would close their wicked eyes and go to sleep. Slowly the townsmen wandered homeward again, the mulberry grove withdrew into its shade, the cemetery became bleak and deserted except for a few disconsolate mourners. Stealthy shapes now emerged into the streets of the city, new and furtive activities blossomed forth like night-blooming flowers. In the east the dunes lay covered with twilight, and the air grew cold, so cold that Hugo would start to shiver and would begin passionately to curse the frailty of human flesh, the emptiness of the human mind, the utter shabbiness of the human soul.

24

Escape

AFTER A MONTH IN THIS WRETCHED PLACE, HUGO became obsessed with the concept of passing time. Minutes, hours, days, weeks: they crept past like little gray shapes, like mice. But beyond them hovered the months, the years—bigger and more ominous, fat squatting animals, hippopotamus-like. Things moved slowly in central Asia, and ambiguously, and very carelessly. The passing hours grew dangerous. They had tiny nibbling teeth, there was poison in their flickering tongues. There was no telling what might happen. He had heard stories before. Prisoners whom the government no longer wished to think about—as much out of boredom or embarrassment as out of malice. Every day he would rack his brains for possible modes of escape.

But for a long time, for over a month, he could think of nothing.

*

But in the meantime he devised a strict régime, to quiet his nerves.

He still had his fine Swiss watch with him, and he learned each morning to wake up at exactly the same time —six o'clock. For the first few nights he did it only approximately—within fifteen minutes, that is, or half an hour. After that he grew to be almost exact. Within five minutes of six, every morning, he would open his eyes, glance toward the window, and then peer at the watch which lay on the floor beside him.

Then he would hang the watch on a little hook, and the rest of the day would pass like clockwork. A certain exact hour for breakfast, a certain hour for his bodily duties, and for his morning exercises, and for relaxation, and finally the second meal of the day, quite as inedible and colorless as the first. And then two hours of what he called "meditation"—that is to say, the making of plans, occasional talk with Joachim, daydreaming. Each of these was performed within a minute or two of a rigid schedule. If the food came in early, then it had to wait. If it came in late, he pretended not to notice. By that time the sun had set, the skies had finally grown dark, the stars had appeared, and at promptly nine o'clock he lay down on his black mattress and closed his eyes.

*

The whole thing became rather feverish after a time.

He would try to vary the monotony by writing in a little diary. It was a tiny leather book two inches high, intended for expense accounts and addresses. He would sharpen his pencil painstakingly and fill one-half of a page with a handwriting miraculously minute and regular. But there were only nine pages left in the book, and before long they were full and he had to give it up. But when he reread the entries he found that, after all, they had been quite hopelessly dull and pointless.

He thereupon resorted to other tricks of one kind and another. He would count the number of people that passed in the street below the prison, for example, and to keep an exact record on the wall: mornings, afternoons, evenings; men, women, children; and so on. He imagined a certain scientific importance to lie in these figures. In the morning, he found there were more women, in the evening more men. Women grew fewer as the days grew cooler, and children still more so. But finally, with a gasp of horror, he realized one day that the whole proceeding was frighteningly empty and absurd.

Then he took to exercising like mad. Every morning and every evening he would go through the routine: forty push-ups from the floor, forty knee-bends, and all the rest. At first he enjoyed them. The feeling of stiffness and weariness calmed his nerves. But one day he discovered that they had become too exhausting; the food had been too bad, and he had no energy left. And so, with a feeling of real bitterness, he decided to give them up.

After that, he simply sat quietly most of the time. He began to feel quite unwell. His digestion was growing worse and worse, he found that he was permanently constipated, little pimples appeared all over his face and his back, and he was troubled with piles. A feeling of violent hatred, and of sorrow too, accompanied the gradual realization that he was growing weaker. He began to be afraid that what was left of his youth—he was twenty-eight now—might suddenly vanish.

☆

Once or twice something happened to relieve the monotony.

One evening Joachim called him to the window. "Look," he murmured.

Hugo looked. Some one was passing hurriedly in the street. He recognized that huge physique, that stooping gait: it was Serafimov, beyond a doubt. "Where is he going, I wonder?" he whispered, full of excitement.

They watched him. Finally he disappeared in a house further down the street. They looked at each other and smiled. For they knew what the house was. That stinking knave of a guard had explained it to them, in a kind of obscene sign-language. A brothel. But then, a moment later, Hugo turned away from the window with disgust. And that was the only time they saw Serafimov.

But once, as he peered through the grille at the street below, he saw another shape that he recognized. De la Scaze. There was no doubt about it. The loose and uncertain gait, the pallid face, the thinning head of hair. Even though he wore a green robe and was without his *pince-nez*, Hugo was sure of it. Sadly and hesitantly the figure wandered out past the twilit cemetery, and disappeared from sight. Hugo felt uneasy—the Frenchman's face had looked so haggard and fever-ridden, his tread was so uncertain. He looked almost like an old man. Willfully Hugo brushed him out of his mind, as if he were a troublesome fly, and did not think of him again.

☆

And then, one day, he had an idea.

It was so obvious, he was ashamed that he had never thought of it before.

He had noticed that the tall, heavy door into their chamber was locked on the outside by a simple iron latch which operated by being raised up and down. That was all. It was sufficiently effective, for on the inside there was no handle whatever, and when the door was closed it was like a part of the wall, except for a small hole in the middle which served as a window, with a covering which slid to and fro and was generally kept barred from the outside. It looked fairly impregnable.

But then, one morning Hugo noticed that there was a crevice almost an inch wide over the top of the door. And he had an idea.

All day he worked feverishly. He unraveled a long black thread from his shirt, then he took a large pin that he wore in his collar and bent it into the shape of a fish hook. Then he tied the pin to the thread. Every now and then he glanced up meaningly at Joachim, who was watching with childish curiosity. Then he would whisper cautiously, as he nodded toward the door, "Be careful! Don't let them see you. . . ."

Finally, he scrutinized the latch very carefully while the

guard brought in their usual crusts and broth in the evening, and immediately after the door had closed on them again, he crept up and scratched a mark on the door at precisely the place where the latch was on the other side. He felt full of energy, he almost felt well again. For the first time since he had arrived in Aqsu he felt excited with life.

Every hour or two the shaggy Turki guard would saunter past the door, unbar the little window, and peer in sulkily. Finally it grew dark, and they knew that he would not return. Joachim's eyes were shining, Hugo felt his heart beating wildly.

He tiptoed toward the door. For two or three minutes he listened carefully. He could hear his watch ticking away in his pocket.

Then he asked Joachim to kneel down on the floor, and stepped on his shoulder. Now he could reach the top of the door. Cautiously, breathlessly, he measured the distance from his little mark up to the top of the door. Then he made a knot in the thread, at the proper distance. Thereupon he slid his impromptu hook through the crevice. This was difficult, for the door fit snugly; but finally he managed it. He heard the hook dangling against the outside of the door, as he held the other end of the thread. He lowered it until he felt the little knot between his thumb and forefinger, at the top of the door. Then he knew that his hook was resting against the latch.

He paused for a moment. His hand was trembling. He felt his feet shaking precariously on Joachim's shoulders.

Through the little window he could see the night sky. By the cold white light on the metal grille and on the gray stone of the window sill he knew that the moon was out. Vast, that bit of sky appeared, and inaccessible.

He breathed deeply several times, to steady his nerves.

[231]

Then he began to manipulate the hook. For two or three minutes nothing happened. Then it caught. Gently he tugged at the thread, and heard the latch beginning to creak.

At that moment he heard footsteps. He didn't dare move. He was torn with anguish, he almost burst into tears with nervousness and premonition. But the footsteps lumbered away in the distance, and all was quiet once more.

He found now that the hook had lost its grip. "Wait," he whispered to Joachim. "Don't move." Cautiously he began to turn and twist the thread again, to raise it and lower it. For several minutes nothing happened. Then it caught again. Infinitesimally he began pulling the thread once more; the latch creaked gently, then it clicked delicately as it began to slide out of its home.

But at that instant the tension on the thread suddenly relaxed: the thread had broken. Hugo almost collapsed with irritation and suspense. He stepped down from Joachim's back and leaned against the wall. He noticed that his clothes were wet with sweat. His head was aching violently.

For several minutes he said nothing. He wanted simply to close his eyes, to go to sleep, to forget all about it.

But then he saw that Joachim was busily drawing a heavy white thread out of his own breeches, and that he had already fastened one end of it to a round piece of wire.

"Where did you get it?" he whispered, happy and alert again suddenly.

Joachim smiled and pointed to his pocket. Hugo could not help admiring at this moment, Joachim's ease, his calm, his unruffled control.

So they did the whole thing a second time. This time it worked very easily. The wire caught the latch promptly, and a moment later Hugo heard the little staccato squeak, like the chirp of a cricket, as the bolt was released.

The door was unlocked now. Of its own accord it began to open slowly and noiselessly. For a moment Hugo stood motionless, still poised on Joachim's shoulders. Then he stepped down and peered into the corridor.

Far down at the end a green oil lamp was burning. He heard two voices, rather furtive they sounded; one of them was the voice of their guard, the other was a woman's voice, a bit giddy and alcoholic, more than a bit flirtatious.

Quickly they tiptoed down the hall in the other direction, where they saw the stars shining through the open doorway. They reached the door, climbed down a black flight of stairs, and found themselves in a small courtyard, underneath the open sky.

For a moment Hugo felt frightened. But then he realized quite suddenly that they were at last free. It seemed too easy, too simple to be true. The courtyard was empty, and a sagging half-open gate led into the soundless street.

It was cold, and over everything—the earth, the walls, even the moon itself—glimmered an icy sheen. Winter had arrived! The place looked suddenly different; this was not the city he had watched day after day from the little window overhead; the simplicity and serenity were gone —it was a vast and inexplicable place, full of surprises. He had entered the world again.

He leaned over as they stood for one moment in the shadow, and shyly put his arm around Joachim's shoulders. The beating of his heart sounded like beautiful, distant music. Joachim's face looked as beautiful, as gentle and pure and protective as that of an angel. "My friend, my friend," he murmured softly, with deep feeling.

Then they crept through the gate and hastened toward the empty, gravelled, starlit slopes in the distance.

[233]

25

Flight

THEY FLED ALL NIGHT ACROSS THE HILLOCKS. THE stars overhead looked down on them as if they were long-lost children, and the gravel under their feet uttered a perpetual caressing whisper. Joachim beside him walked slowly and regularly, as if in a dream. And as for himself, he found after two hours that he was sick with exhaustion. He had grown weak, his muscles ached with the unfamiliar motion, and the pebbles began to drum forth little blisters upon the soles of his feet. Finally he lay down under a small tamarisk and fell asleep.

But even in his dreams Hugo was haunted by the notion of pursuit. First a single dark figure would seem to cross the stretches behind them inexorably—the shaggy, perverted prison guard, it was at first, and then the huge Russian Serafimov, and then de la Scaze with his tentative, frightened footsteps. And when he looked again, the shape had multiplied, the townsmen of Aqsu were pursuing him, until at last the barren land was black with the shapes of these inarticulate, pursuing hordes. What did they want? Why were they following them? What had he and Joachim done that they should be captured and imprisoned and forgotten? He didn't understand at all, he had never quite understood. And yet, a little tremor of guilt trickled through his body.

✳

It was very cold when he woke up. The landscape about them was as gray as old age, and as forgotten. He trembled with cold and hunger. Joachim was still asleep beside him, his face buried in the crook of his arm—only his curly blond hair was visible, like a dandelion in the middle of the desert.

When he raised his eyes again he saw a black thread being drawn across the mounds in the south. He sighed with bitterness and relief. It was a caravan passing northeastward.

Quickly he woke up Joachim, and they hastened across the gravel. An hour later they reached the caravan.

"Kuchengtze," murmured the leader of the caravan, when Hugo shouted a few fragments of broken Hindustani at him. Then he nodded his head. Finally he smiled.

[235]

And so they joined them, and began to move slowly
northeastward.

☆

After the black barrenness of Aqsu itself the regions to
the northeast, the plains toward Dzungaria seemed full of
suggestiveness, scents of the past, hints of a passionate
tradition. They passed some little villages nestling in the
reddish desert, then a valley with a torrent, several smaller
oases sprinkled with poplars and willows, then more desert
again. At nightfall they entered a village; dim blue shapes
could still be seen shifting aimlessly to and fro in the
bazaar. The *serai* was hot and filthy, so they slept in the
courtyard. The horses were tethered here, and all night
Hugo heard their gentle movements, the sound of their
breath.

The village looked very different the next morning. He
discovered that everyone, everyone in the village, was sick
with syphilis. Many were terribly wasted, some were suffering with malaria, some had terribly infected eyes, covered with little green flies which they had finally grown
too lazy to brush away. Their faces were spotted with
fresh sores and deeply pitted with the scars of former
ones, their features were simply a collection of knobs and
indentations capriciously composed, made into a unit by
nothing more than their pure ugliness and their constant
expression of malice. Yet it was odd that here too, though
rarely, a shape of the most dazzling perfection would saunter past; all the more lovely, indeed, as if in compensation
for the general squalor all the beauty had been concen-

[236]

trated into the body of a single woman: the bronze limbs, the musical grace, the limpid voice, the unfathomable gaze.

☆

Several days later they entered Kuchengtze, the great caravan center. Here all the caravans from China, via Urga, collected. The town was full of rumors. A great new Chinese army marching northward; a new ultimatum sent by the Japanese; more trouble with bandits, involving the capture of an old American missionary; a revolt in Inner Mongolia; guerilla raids on the Manchurian border. Everyone seemed pleased with all this. No one seemed worried. No one ever mentioned the Soviet.

After three days in Kuchengtze Hugo and Joachim joined another caravan. They had to pay two hundred and fifty *liang*, an outrageous price; but Hugo still had a good deal of money with him—most of it in Mexican dollars; and there was no alternative. This would be the last eastward-bound caravan before winter, the men said.

Besides, Hugo did not want to wait any longer in Kuchengtze. Best to leave Sinkiang as soon as possible. The thought of Aqsu haunted him.

And so, presently they entered the real Mongolian lands, the most brutal and unlovely they had yet seen.

☆

Progress was very slow. Again and again they had to

[237]

stop, crossing dunes or a wilderness of rocks or shrubs. Each time they heard the boys cry "Yabonah! Yabonah!" and then, after long hesitations and complaints, the irritable Bactrian camels would be underway again.

Once, while they were still fat and nervous, the camels rebelled. A crate fell off one of them, the panic spread, the boxes and baskets went spilling and crashing in every direction, and it was hours before they were collected and put in order again. Later they grew more submissive, after they had entered the more difficult territories. Then they would pass long chains of camel skeletons, and exhausted opium caravans driven by indifferent doll-eyed Chinamen.

They presently began to wear long heavy goatskin gloves, felt boots, and great goatskin helmets over their necks and around their faces. A quick spiral dust storm rushed down on them once, a miniature cyclone, hissing, warm, maroon-colored. It hurled them about for a while, shattered a crate or two, covered everything with a sticky sheen. The sun looked like a dim little apricot glowing through the fog. Their eyes ached and their skin smarted with the little stones that came hailing down on their helmets as they lay face down on the ground. Then it passed on, a mad preoccupied thing, whisking away across the desert.

They passed beautiful gorges, and little conical hills topped by *obos*. In the distance they saw tremendous mountain ranges, conjured forth by the mirage—huge purple serpents gliding through the water, these might have been. "The bears are sleeping there, in profound peace," murmured one of the men.

"What is this place called?" asked Hugo.

"The Reeds on the Yellow Ridge," explained a cross-eyed old Russian who had joined them at Kuchengtze.

And later they passed "The Boundary of the Wild Camel" and "The Place of the Evil Mountain Spirits"—merely a broken tower, perhaps, or the site of a battle long ago.

There were few animals. The fleet-footed, slender-horned antelopes, now and then; or black foxes; or a gazelle in a mountain-ash forest; or a stray wildcat. Once they passed a group of hunters. And once a poor pilgrim on his way to Urga, to the cloister of God, his holy scrip rolled up on his back, his hair tangled with lice.

Once they passed through a village, sweet and peaceful on its dreamy, willowy banks, its faces calm with patience and stupidity. Some horse-adoring, bow-legged Buriats lived here, wearing their long gay mantles. They traded in brick, tea and wool from Uliassutai, and musk, and furs, and *dunsa*, the pyramid-shaped pellets of tobacco which they carried about under their wide sashes. There were some lamas here too, on a hill near by, dressed in red and yellow, with high fur caps: cynical fellows, mild, timid, inefficient. Some of them were very, very old, and dying. Vicious dogs guarded the decaying monastery.

From this place the caravan road ran on and on like a yellow ribbon fluttering upon the waves of a desolate brown sea. They could see for miles and miles through the still glittering air.

Then came the foothills of the Altai, several days later. And then canyons, wind-swept plains, and tiny villages of *yurts*, each with a little red flag flying from the roof. Now, at last, they were on the road to sacred Urga.

*

It was growing cold.

Far off they saw the Altai. This was the land of the great migrations, the wanderings of a thousand and two thousand years ago, the place where hooves had been tramping back and forth, where hordes had been sweeping to and fro like the ripples in a great gusty lake; toward the Caspian and the Euxine, and further yet, and back again. This plain, north of the Celestial Mountains, south of the disquieting Altai, was really the heart of Asia; the heart of those ungovernable upheavals, springing out of the remotest and most isolated spots.

It was still unsafe, so Mordovinov, the lively cross-eyed old Russian who had attached himself to Hugo (and who spoke surprisingly good German) explained to him. Kirghiz brigands, for instance, who thought less than nothing of killing, worst at the border of course, between the Chinese and Russian frontier outposts, but troublesome everywhere.

Whether it was for this reason or for another, they began to travel mostly at night. Hugo would watch the grotesque silhouettes of the camels, monotonous and eventually meaningless, trailing their abject fluctuating shadows across the slopes, so pale and barren in the starlight that snow seemed suddenly to have surrounded them. And he would hear the bells in front and behind, bells of all tones, some deep and some delicate. The camel-men would walk along mechanically, not human beings now but the inevitable accompaniments to the sound of the bells, the shapes of the camels, the light of the stars; no more. Others would lie asleep on mules, and now and then they would stop and build a fire and kneel down. They would then begin to chatter, the fire would shine upon their ruddy faces, they were men again suddenly, suddenly the land became a setting for human excitements and rumors.

Once Hugo saw a white camel running across the hillocks in the distance, quickly and softly like a ghost. He had never believed that a camel could run so rapidly and so lightly, and he asked Mordovinov about it.

"It is bewitched," said Mordovinov with a smile. "Demons.

"You see," he continued, in his low, eager voice, "this occurs occasionally with camels, as it does with everyone else."

"What will happen to it?"

"It will run another hundred miles, or another two hundred. Space has become meaningless to it, its spirit is demanding release, the body has almost ceased existing. Finally it will lie down where no one will ever see it again, and suddenly it will be nothing but a heap of dust which the wind will disperse forthwith. Demons, you see."

✶

"Demons," he muttered later: the word had clung to his mind like a bur. "Oh, demons still exist! I know, I know! I have seen them in men's eyes. When I was a child my mother told me about them; how at night they spring forth from people's sleeping eyes, escaping through the lashes, flying together from all over the world in the sky above, weaving great prophetic tapestries of coming events which presently descend like clouds and engulf the land. Ah, if you young ones only knew!

"No, no, my boys. The big struggle won't be as simple

as you think: it won't arise out of a desire for money, or
food, or equality, or dignity: it's death that they're really
hankering for. No one will quite understand. But a terrible demoniac madness will possess them all, such as this
world has never seen before. The great, final migrations
will have begun!"

A real character, Mordovinov. His long hair and his
long beard were gray, almost white, and his skin was as
dark and wrinkled as a walnut. He must have been almost
eighty. But a surprising fire shone in his gray, uneven eyes,
and his low voice trembled with power and intimacy, like
that of a man in his prime.

✱

They now slept in sleeping-bags of sheepskin. They
would find a thin sheet of ice over the pools in the
morning.

Now and then, very briefly, they would see a gazelle far
away among the shrubs. Or perhaps, still further away, at
twilight, some wolves gathering around a dead mule. They
passed caravans several times, most of them on their way
from Urga or Uliassutai to Kuchengtze. Once they ran
into a blizzard. Everyone bowed his head, the wind pierced
the skin like needles, and for the first time the thrilling
thought of actual winter occurred to Hugo.

They met no towns at all. A cluster of *yurts* at the very
most, and these only rarely. They would find, here and
there, a handful of Kirghiz tribesmen with their cattle,
dark men, brave, alert, powerful, with wild-looking eyes
accustomed to scanning great distances. They crossed sandy

stretches, regions of sharp stones, small forests now and then, and bit by bit they drew closer to the Altai range. They would see the wild pigs digging for roots or basking in the sun. Or squirrels, in their fine gray coats, or white arctic hares among the willow scrub. Once or twice a lynx, or a silver fox.

26

The Hut in the Woods

ONE EVENING THREE MEN APPROACHED FROM THE north on horseback and joined the caravan. Buriats these were, big insolent brutes, with their heads shaved, pompous bullies. Hugo noticed how Mordovinov kept peering at them suspiciously. Something seemed to be wrong, but he didn't know what. He began to feel nervous, and spoke to Joachim about it. But Joachim smiled light-heartedly and remained silent, as usual; nothing ever troubled him; even after the sojourn at Aqsu he seemed unable to think ill of anyone, or suspect ungenerous motives.

That night Mordovinov whispered to Joachim and Hugo: "Better watch out, my boys. There's a bit of trouble ahead. But I'll keep an eye out for you. . . . I've taken a liking to you two, and I understand these things, you know. . . . Trust me."

Hugo could scarcely close his eyes all night. He would hear the noise of pursuing hoofbeats, or of whispering conspirators. It annoyed him to see Joachim sleeping so soundly, so trustingly.

☆

But apparently he was quite wrong. Nothing at all happened that night. The next morning was the coldest they had met. Winter was really arriving, and the first snow-flakes came blowing down at them from Siberia. Frost had stiffened everything, the grasses crackled like glass under the camel's hooves. Enormous black clouds were approaching from the north, and suddenly the land seemed to have been deserted—no trace of any animal, no hares, no birds, no insects even, except, of course, the vermin that devoutly infested the clothes of each and every one of them.

Toward noon the clouds vanished, it grew sunny and warm again. They crossed a gully in which it still seemed to be summer—the greenery was still fresh, the air was warm, the water was sweet to taste. They killed a gazelle here.

But then, the road grew worse and worse, and late that afternoon they suddenly discovered that they had taken the wrong way. They would have to go back to their camp of the night before, or strike out for the south on the chance of meeting the road to Urga. Mordovinov explained all this to the two Germans.

So they finally pitched camp without more ado. Mordovinov appeared to be a bit puzzled, and he didn't know whether they would retrace their steps the next morning or turn southward. He seemed sulky and reticent.

*

And the next morning they understood why.

They had been deserted. The caravan had departed at dawn, and Joachim and Hugo had been left behind.

"Two reasons," explained Mordovinov gently. "Orders from the north. The Soviet. You must remember, you are enemies of the Soviet. You are lucky that it wasn't worse . . .

"And then, the Buriats distrusted you. They thought you brought bad luck; that was why they lost their way, they thought. You must not blame them. They are not treacherous by nature, all of them. But the soldiers had their orders, you see. . . ."

"And you?" asked Joachim.

Mordovinov looked at them slyly with his crossed gray eyes and smiled. "I will protect you, my lads. Trust me."

*

Two weeks later, after the most exacting and painful hardships that either of them had so far endured, he brought them, late one afternoon, to a cabin on the shore of a river. The land had changed. The valley was still and beautiful. Both shores of the river were covered with trees.

Winter had come at last. Snow covered the ground, the river was frozen over.

"My home," observed Mordovinov. "You will be safe here."

He said it in a very casual manner, but Hugo could hear his voice quivering and see his eyes shining with excitement.

He explained to them that the hut was theirs to live in, but that they must be very careful.

"One can never be too careful," he said, running his fingers through his gray beard. "Even here there are watchers and listeners. Enemies. Spies." He chuckled a bit. It seemed to amuse him.

His own hut, he explained, was a mile or so further on. Then he said good-by.

"Be comfortable, my lads," he called back, as he wandered into the woods. "I'll take care of you!"

*

They stood quietly, the two of them, and watched old Mordovinov disappearing among the trees. Then Hugo raised his eyes to the hills on the other side of the frozen river. The black forest rose out of the snow, still hooded in snow, extending its ten thousand black branches edged with snow, almost motionless but not quite, shedding with an invisible tremor a fragment of snow now from this twig and now from that, so that even from where he stood he could see these ghostly white moths fluttering softly from

[247]

the topmost branches, resting for a moment on some intervening twig, hovering, breaking, scattering into a veil and then subsiding, suddenly invisible, into the soft motionless snow that covered the earth.

Together they walked into the hut. A fire was blazing in the hearth, and on the table in front of the fire stood a bottle of wine, a loaf of black bread, a bowl of cheese, and a big red sausage—all of it planned and arranged for them by kind old Mordovinov. The hut was a tiny place. Moisture had blackened the rafters, the walls were streaked with fungi. The damp sour smell of months still lingered in the room, not yet dispelled by the fire.

They sat down together and began to eat, at first without a word. Outside, through the veined and frosted pane, Hugo could see the great valley winding northward among the hills. The endless northern hills, the immense northern forest. "The very darkest, the most silent, the most fragrant and beautiful valley in Mongolia," Mordovinov had said; "and I have seen them all."

A thrill of happiness ran through Hugo. He breathed deeply, and stretched his arms. His body felt alert and elastic again, his heart beat eagerly, like the heart of a boy, with a pleasure not yet identified, not yet named.

He glanced at Joachim. He too was happy. Ah, thought Hugo with a glow of affection, no wonder he is happy; he does not know what torment or conflict is, he loves everything just as it is, he wishes nothing to be even the least bit better; there is no selfishness in him, nothing can hurt him—his lucky heart flows out to the trees, the earth, the sunlight and the animals, and he becomes a part of them.

An odd fellow, he reflected. Gay by nature, yet so gentle, so childlike and reflective, that a certain surprising melancholy seems to hang over him always, like a soft shadow.

And now and then, in spite of all his cheerfulness, his calm and happy acceptance of every situation, a sudden little note of despair seems to enter his voice—as if he knew that, entrancing though the world is, there is no use, no use whatever, in hoping for more; that beauty is as brief as the flash of a falling drop in the sunlight, and love must do its improvident best, must struggle along from moment to moment, never sure where to turn next. . . . Or did he know better than that? Was there some secret that he had discovered?

The golden head of hair, the crystal-blue eyes, the healthy glowing skin—yes, reflected Hugo, he was almost angelically handsome. He felt a twinge, ever so faint, of envy, even a tiny inexplicable pinprick of hostility.

But only for a moment. There was in Joachim's eyes so sweet, so patient, selfless and gentle a gaze, that no one could feel resentment for long in his presence.

"And yet," thought Hugo, "if he were only more disciplined, more intent, more ambitious. He needs to be guided. . . ."

✫

Late that night, after the fire had died and the room was in total darkness, he woke up and heard the wolves howling softly. High above the river, in the wild ravine.

He opened his eyes and gazed out of the window. Nothing more beautiful existed than this night, this sky, this snow. The snow was a gigantic thing now, a sea. A vast sea surrounding the hut, lapping up at each twig, each tree, each hill, each range, scattering its spray into the wind, encrusting each twig with its foam. And yes, a vast sea surrounding every action, every hour, every sound, thought, hope, apprehension; all of these lay floating upon the vast white sea like tiny fragments of seaweed, or flecks of foam, or momentary ripples.

He crept out of bed and walked to the window. A bit of snow had crept through a crack in one of the panes and lay in a delicate ridge upon the sill. He ran his finger through it, then raised it to his lips and tasted it. The pure cool snow. Outside, a soft and gentle blanket. It looked very beautiful to him—so cold, so clean, so severe, so calm and victorious. Mordovinov's footprints were still visible, leading away from the doorstep into the copse.

27

A German Boyhood

AND SLOWLY HUGO FELT HIS HEART MOVED, AS HE stood there, staring through the window at the still Mongolian night, by feelings which he couldn't in the least understand. Caressed into being, they were, so to speak, by the gentle surgical fingers of an earlier day, a sweet and cruel past. He was so bewildered suddenly and so shaken that a flood of similar little excitements again ran through his blood, conjured up out of boyhood by the sympathetic tremors of a desire which he had felt then and which he felt now, very poignantly indeed: a primeval, vehement, northern desire for some sort of "heroic ideal."

And, one by one, all the ardors of his boyhood reappeared. . . .

☆

There was, of course, the nestling village on the Chiemsee, the decaying watermill, the old rowboat under the willow tree along whose slippery branches he had climbed so often. They would arrive here from the Ludwigstrasse every summer. And sometimes even in the winter, and then there would be snow on the bushes, warm lights in the windows, skating at night by the light of a lantern hung on a willow twig, and the tinkling of sleighs, steaming breaths, red cheeks, laughing faces, happy voices and then afterwards hot chocolate poured out into the big red cups in the kitchen. There would be Klaus, the gifted, the beautiful and strong, the expert skater, the swimmer, the diver. It was Klaus, the gay one, whom he admired and envied. But it was blond Waldemar whom he really worshiped. Waldemar, who led him through the woods, taught him to swim, to climb hills, to endure without exhaustion, to suffer without wincing, to worship the austere and natural powers of the wood; to be strong, in a word.

Those summers on the Chiemsee! Those walks through the wood, in search of adder, rabbit, chipmunk, squirrel, shimmering butterfly or terrifying beetle; climbing the trees, feeling very much like a Red Indian, cunning and muscular. The calls across the dusky lake, the nights on the shore. The telling of manly tales, the bodies still hot from exertion, the gentle rain falling, drawing its shimmering film across the birches, the arabesque ferns, the iron balcony, the boy's eager body and smiling upturned face.

He wanted to achieve great feats, just to please Waldemar. He would climb the highest trees, capture a new and malicious sort of beetle, swim further than ever before, cling from perilous ledges on the hill, dive from the highest of the three diving-boards. All, of course, in order to make himself worthy in Waldemar's eyes. To be sure, he wanted very much to be a good boy, a clever boy, a loyal and praiseworthy and important boy; more than anything, though, he wanted to be a strong, proud boy; and, some day, a strong man, a stern and truly strong man, with muscles and heart and will of iron.

One warm August night he went rowing on the lake with Waldemar. The air was so mild, they stripped off their clothes and laid them in the bottom of the boat. The reeds glistened along the shore. Far in the distance he could see the walls of the castle of Herren-Chiemsee, steeped in moonlight. And in the water, as he strained his naked little body, he could see the brilliant circles which each plunge of the oars left floating there, one after another, until they melted into a spangled path which led away into the darkness of the lake. The boat halted among some willows. Waldemar rose without a word and dove into the water. He stayed hidden so long, Hugo's heart grew tense with worry and adoration, the thought of such a glorious death intoxicated him. And then Waldemar reappeared. He climbed into the boat and stood there, Grecian and superb, the drops glistening on his bronze body. No longer a man, but a god! Hugo's heart beat wildly. A sob rose in his throat; it was the most exalted moment of his boyhood. O valor, he thought, moved almost to tears; O heroism of man, worthy of any sacrifice, any at all! He felt overwhelmed with a desire for greatness and glory. He resolved to swim daily, never to smoke or drink, to remain a virgin, to train his muscles into iron, to dedicate himself to some noble cause.

When he left Waldemar at the end of the summer, to go back to the Ludwigstrasse, he was torn with sorrow: he wanted to cry, he longed to have Waldemar lean over, put his arms around him and comfort him: but that would have been a shameful act of weakness, and he smiled and shouted from the phaeton, his heart flooded with a mysterious and ennobling passion, "Good-by, Waldemar, good-by! I will write you a long letter, some day!"

But he never saw Waldemar again.

☆

There were three further incidents in his boyhood that he recalled forever after more clearly than all the others—trivial, perhaps, but in their way, no doubt, allegorical.

The first of these was the visit to his great-aunt, the Margravine, who lived near Bayreuth. That he could never forget, for even his mother lowered her voice in awe as they walked down the great corridor, past the *orangerie*, the strange mirrors crusted with sea shells, the brilliantly hued Empire chairs, the heavy old yellow curtains. Through the huge windows he could see the beautiful trees in the park outside, and the spotted statues, the dry fountains, the decaying grotto. Overhead hung the monstrous candelabras from a ceiling painted silver and blue. And everywhere, in every corner and every whispered word, lurked the angels of the past, the baroque, the darling, the venerable, untouchable, frightening past.

Grosstante Amalie gave him a little wafer shaped like a Bavarian lion out of a gilded jar, and then leaned over and placed her hand upon his head. As he glanced up he could see her little black mustache, the hairs on her chin, the warts on her neck. A displeasing odor of dead flowers emerged from her body. But he had been told that she was a woman of grandeur and power, and accordingly he adored her, and felt profoundly honored.

His sister Annaliese rose and minced across the mirror-like floor to play some Chopin. His face went aglow with pride to see her pigtails victoriously flying, with their big pink hair ribbons (worn only on very festive occasions) as she tore, with such energy and emphasis, through the A major Polonaise! And then, when she rose, hot and blushing, they all praised her, and she strutted triumphantly back to her plush chair.

His uncle, the Herr Doktor, sat beside the Baron, discussing etymologies in a deep and learned voice, the customs of the Polynesians, the dialects of Java and Borneo. The Baron wore a black velvet jacket and smoked an enormous pipe; he heard it whispered later that the Baron was a poet—*ein berühmter Dichter!*—but that was all he ever knew about it.

And quietly by the window, the rays of the setting sun caressing her beautiful sorrowful head, sat his mother. She looked fragile indeed, and he felt, even then, a boy's intolerance of such submissiveness. "What will they all think of you," he wanted to whisper to her, "Grosstante Amalie and Onkel Adelbert and the Baron and the rest, if you burst into tears again!" He felt rather grown up, already, beside her. And when she held him in her arms,

on the drive back through the whispering red autumn
trees, and kissed him with such intense and lonely kisses,
he felt almost like a father whose child has not yet learned
control, the first, the simplest and most important lesson
of all.

But there was one thing in the great house near Bayreuth that he never forgot. That was a statue of a golden
warrior sent from China—a present from his father to the
Margravine. How disdainful, how ornate, how remote and
worshipful he looked, this golden warrior out of China!
His father had died in China five or six years ago, during
the war. He had guessed in a child's way that his father
had been a glamorous figure, brilliantly gifted, handsome
and so on; and, by some sort of inference, that his mother
had married beneath her station; but in his heart of hearts
he had always carried about with him a picture of his
father, his own invention, of course, but one which stirred
his heart and filled him with heroic ambitions. And when
he saw this golden warrior he was seized with a fierce ad-
venturous desire to sail to the remote ports of China.
That was why he felt impatient with his mother's kisses
that evening: his heart was filled with other things.

*

Then, in the second place, there was the voyage to
Baden-Baden for the Grande Semaine.

What a lovely, haughty place! He would look through
the fluttering lace curtains of the Stephanie, and watch
the moping willows above the pool, and the sleek foliage
of the chestnut trees reaching down toward the sparkling

regimental wavelets in the stream below. His mother would take him along to the red tennis-courts, dressed for the tennis, in her white blouse with its high collar, wearing her white tennis hat in which was stuck a hatpin with a golden rose at the tip, and carrying her pear-shaped racket. On the sunny terrace of the little tennis pavilion stood big red umbrellas, and underneath these the white tables where coffee and coffee-cakes were served. He would sit here with his sister Annaliese and old faithful Mathilde in her yellow straw hat and bright blue dress, eating apricot ice out of little canoe-shaped biscuits, sipping chocolate with whipped cream from the cups which he admired so much, since they had a pattern of wild strawberries running around the rim; these last reminded him of the Chiemsee and of Waldemar, and he felt, with a little twinge of shame, a wave of happiness suddenly sweeping over him. In the distance the baroque fountains were playing beneath the huge English elms, and beyond these the white marble bust of the Grossherzogin peered quizzically through the shrubbery. Beyond the hedge he could hear the laughter of little girls drifting, like rays of sunlight, amongst the innocent leaves. And out on the tennis-courts his mother was playing with a stranger, a young Austrian count, very smartly dressed in white flannels and a white silk scarf.

Later he saw her in a coach driving along the Lichtentaler Allee with this same stranger, who was now dressed in black, with a pink carnation in his lapel. She looked incredibly lovely, he thought, with the feathers of her hat flowing down over her shoulders. And somehow he contrived, young as he was, to see something new and strange in that beautiful, fragile, contemptuous face; he saw that there was a life remote from his own glowing there like an Indian pearl, still passionate, agitated, mystifying.

That evening he and Annaliese went with old leather-faced Mathilde to the Kursaal to listen to the music. They sat down under the trees at a table with a green checkered cloth and listened to the Casino band playing with infinite feeling into the August night—*Ein Frühlingstag in Garmisch* and bits from *Die Puppenfee*. And then, when they returned, he crept happily into his mother's silken room to kiss her good-night, and found her cheeks hot and wet with tears.

He could not understand all this. But he learned presently how, while for most men in the world is many-sided, so that they can change their interests from one to another without too deadening a despair, for most women the world is really a single simple thing; they are guided by one passion, and forever contrive to remain loyal to it, and hug it to themselves as if it were a child, and even when it is fatally ill or proven false, or limp and dead, with a terrifying devotion they still clutch it to their hearts, obey its slightest whims, perhaps all the more desperately if it is deserted with a shrug by all others, a poor and shabby thing as far as anyone can see.

✶

And then, school in Munich. Through the big window in the classroom he could gaze upon the red geraniums outside the window sill, and the military fountain below, and the pigeons on the cobbled street, and the lady in the baroque residence across the way incessantly playing her

Scarlatti sonatas behind the green lace curtains; and further away the pond where the children sailed their little
boats, and the bright, budding foliage of the Englischer
Garten, and the Chinesischer Turm. There was the sadistic
master, of course, with the clipped gray hair and the bright
gray eyes; there were the military excursions, the narcissus
lies, the provocative wagers, the fascinating jokes; von
Thaden, with his yellow curls and his Swabian accent, but
full of nervous energy, forever restless—he wanted to be
a soldier, nothing else mattered very much, and that, of
course, was what charmed them all; and the affectionate
teaser, Krusius, and blue-eyed Kaulbach, the little cheat,
the tell-tale, the cruel instructor, the treacherous one, the
flirt. In the summer they went on a bicycle trip, and they
would lie in a glade at night, or on the slope of a hill,
among pines, or even higher up, where the air was cold,
and the Bavarian Alps wove their brisk fragrances around
the tent; they would watch the stars while von Boeckmann
played *Freut euch des Lebens!* or *Ich hatt einen Kam-
eraden* on the lute, and they would sing, rather softly—
softly because, after all, they were a little bit afraid. Afraid
not of the mountains, nor the night, nor the cold, nor even
of one another; but of a certain something else; a singular
boyish fright, now and again, at what this business of
growing older might bring to them all. Kaulbach would
tell them about Berlin; about the cabarets, the illicit
resorts, the gestures in the Tiergarten, the murders
unexplained, the body of a woman found wrapped in
newspapers beneath a street lamp at dawn; about the un-
adorned vices, the swaggering negroes, the fat profiteers,
and all the rest of those horrifying orphans who dwelt in
the shadows of the war; his eyes would glitter; his excitements, his leering curiosities and hatreds infected them

all. His eyes were curious, gray, magnetic, wicked; they asked for blood, for terror, for treachery; he was the powerful one, the one whom they all wished to please and to obey, Hugo as well as the rest.

Yes, he too wanted to obey, and blindly. What he longed for was the simplicity of ignorance, the animal, the child. Boy though he was, he suspected already that to devise his own system was an exhausting affair, fraught with perils. What he glimpsed ahead, while a terrible uncertainty coiled itself around the future of a sickened nation like a cloud, was dark and dangerous indeed.

The next summer he went with his Onkel Adelbert to Rügen. His mother had died that spring, of tuberculosis.

There they lay, the two of them, naked in the sun on the willow-crested dunes or among the bird-flecked rocks. His uncle would sit at an improvised table, twenty feet or so from the salty sea; and there, wearing nothing but a *cache-sexe* and a pair of blackened glasses, his brown body shining with walnut oil, he sat and worked at his Oscan and Umbrian etymologies. And then, the morning's study done, they would throw the ball, or run, or swim, and finally, thoroughly happy and exhausted, lie down on the delightful sand. And there his uncle would speak to him in a low hard voice, tell him about the golden ages of the past and the everlasting strength of great men; of Goethe, of Hebbel, of Andreas Hofer, of Nietsche; of Greece, of the warriors, the athletes, the poets, the philosophers. "A world of the spirit."

"A world of the spirit?" Hugo echoed.

"The spirit of the Noble and Victorious Hero!" Hugo shuddered with joy when he heard these words.

A vague but sweet excitement filled his heart. He too longed to be strong, superb, obedient, keen, with eyes of steel. A life of dedication, of utter and heroic loyalty. That was the only way to be truly a man, explained Onkel Adelbert. To struggle, to grow muscular and potent and merciless in the struggle, to become instinctively heroic, to be one of many comrades in a life purged of all doubt, distrust and introspection, a life intense, pure, and austere.

He felt inspired, lying among those dunes, watching the vast white clouds float down from the Baltic, hearing the angry murmur of the surf. No longer, for him, the simple life of the child. For him, pain, privation, death! How he longed for them, to prove his true nobility and ardor! The masculine power of the Spirit—that was everything, and nothing else mattered beside that.

Onkel Adelbert read him a poem by Rilke as they sat together in the warm sand after sunset. He could not understand it at all, but through the wild and wingèd sound of the lines he could detect the flash of a sword or the trumpet-cry of a warrior, and as he lay in his bed that night, listening to the waves, he longed also to be one of those who ride with their fellow warriors through the forest night, blowing their trumpets, their leonine hair flying in the wind, the torchlight reflected on their shields and helmets; summoning, with the sound of their trumpets and the beat of the hooves and the flash of the sword and the fire in their hearts, a mighty echo out of the deep forestal past, which would with its power shatter the cities, and set the villages crumbling away, so that finally none but the heroes would survive.

He had been groping blindly in the darkness for something to adore, on which to expend all his love and all his power. Now he had found the path, so it appeared, and he was overwhelmed with energy and delight. He would spring up from his hard narrow bed in the morning, run down to the sea, leap back and forth along the gray misty beach, plunge naked into the frothy bay, longing for the cold painful bite of the sea, and would finally emerge again, breathless but shouting with joy, skipping back among the dunes to the tent where the smell of bacon and coffee beckoned to him. And he would see his Onkel Adelbert peering at him out of the corner of his sinister gray eye, appraising him; but he approved, that was the thing that mattered; and beneath that cold, lupine face he knew that love, pride, and ambition existed, alert, waiting for the moment to act, gathering strength for the superb and victorious effort, longing for the hour when he might inflict and endure pain, watching the world with the cold bright eyes of a madman.

28

The Handkerchief

NOW AND THEN, DURING THE WEEKS THAT FOL-
lowed, Hugo and Joachim would walk along the
frozen river, not where the path led to Mordovinov's cabin, but the longer way, where no one else
ever walked.

There they would see the tracks of the roe deer in the
snow along the shore, and here and there, perhaps, a delicate yellow comet imprinted on the snow where one of
them had paused to make water. And then they walked
deeper through the woods, over the great trunks of the
fallen and decaying larches, and through the sparkling
thicket, which as they passed through it dropped petals of
ice upon their caps and cloaks, or embroidered upon their

sleeves its feathers of snow. Then they would reach the ice of the river itself, now white, now green, now wholly black, and now, where the sun fell like a bursting bubble upon an iridescent crevice, sparkling with all the colors of the rainbow. They might see, on certain days, small cascades forced up through these crevices, water that actually seemed to be boiling, exhaling its steaming breath into the icy air as if it were alive. A million icicles hanging from the bushes on every side caught the sunlight, and their eyes would begin to ache with this blinding glitter until presently they walked underneath the larches once more, and even here a network of silver was perpetually being woven among the branches by the filtering rays of the sun.

Or, if they walked all afternoon, on a day less chilly than the rest, they could climb over the field where the old grave-mounds were, and past the torrent, until in the distance they could see the smoke rising from the little wooden village on the other side of the range.

They didn't dare go further. Mordovinov had warned them. "There are enemies everywhere, spies everywhere," he had said; "even among the just, the ignorant and the gentle ones." So they would pause, enchanted, hidden among the trees, and hear perhaps the sleigh-bells tinkling faintly in the valley below, or even discern through the heavy branches a moving sleigh, or the roofs of the village, or the black shape of some old Mongol carrying a bundle of sticks down the path toward his home.

✫

Once they even waited foolishly until the sun had set, and then suddenly the landscape grew blue and hazy, two, three, four little lights appeared in the scattered huts, and the lantern of a sleigh moved like a glowworm through the lilac-colored dusk. Then they walked back through the darkness, stumbling wearily over the fallen limbs and sudden hollows until late in the night they finally glimpsed the light in Mordovinov's hut.

He welcomed them noisily, ecstatically. "Oh, how happy I am to see you! What a pleasure! Sit down! Warm yourself, Herr Wildenbruch. Your face is red as a beet, Herr von Wald! And your fingers are like icicles! No, no; that won't do for a young man. A young man should be always warm and glowing, ready to drink and make love. . . ."

He poured out some vodka for them, his hand trembling with excitement. His old wife was sitting in a corner, knitting, and by the fire a young stranger was standing, leaning carelessly against the mantel, playing with his gloves.

"Youth, youth!" cried Mordovinov, rubbing his hands together, casting his eyes to the ceiling reminiscently, "there is nothing else in the world that is worth anything. Only youth. And it is gone so soon, so soon!"

He walked up to Hugo, placed his two hands on his shoulders, and gazed into his eyes with great seriousness.

"Do you know what I regret now?" There was a certain agitation in his voice, and his eyes betrayed some disturbing *double-entendre*.

"Do you want to know? Let me tell you. You'll be surprised. It's this. That I kept myself so pure when I was young. Even as a boy. I didn't do what all the other little boys did, the lively pretty robust ones. 'It's impure,' I whispered to myself, full of torment and hurt feelings. I knew I was ugly. Oh yes. 'It's wicked,' I whispered. And then later, when they ran after the girls and went out on picnics with them and crept into the bushes, I still kept

[265]

my eyes lowered. 'It's improper,' I murmured, almost in tears. Well, perhaps it was! And perhaps it wasn't. But they followed the natural commands of their blood, with their young boys' bodies, as well as they knew how. Oh, yes indeed! They had subtle sly ways, young as they were. But I'd blush, and run away. Well, I'm sorry for it. I was a silly goose, and I'm sorry for it . . ."

His voice trailed away and grew quiet. Then Hugo heard, emerging rather gradually from the dark corner at his side, the voice of the old woman, delicate, wavering, as different as could be from the voice of her husband; and yet at the same time profoundly similar.

"—and then he took me to Baku, on the Caspian. . . . I was no more than a child. . . . The beautiful seaside, the shore full of little children, orphans I think, for their parents were nowhere to be seen. . . . And the mother-of-pearl glistening in the water, magical, magical! The pebbles were smooth as glass, and the water came creeping up on the white sand, I declare," and she tittered softly, "quite as if it were making love, running its little fingers between the pebbles, entering each nook and cranny, kissing the sand with a long soft kissing sound. . . ."

"Do you know why we were so wicked, all of us?" bellowed Mordovinov, and Hugo could smell the alcoholic fumes of his breath as he leaned forward, his eyes glowing. The blond curly-headed stranger beside the fire looked very contemptuous. He was staring at Hugo in a curious hostile way. Perhaps he is drunk, thought Hugo.

"Do you want to know," continued Mordovinov, leering, "why we slit up our best friends behind their backs, and love to see the young and lucky ones meet with disaster? Well, it's because of those hours we spent ourselves being so unhappy and hurt, feeling the injustice of the world. . . . It's a shocking thing, for a child to discover injustice. And it's something he'll never forget. . . ."

". . . and all day long, lying in the sun," whimpered the old woman in a voice as empty and pathetic as the sound of a breaking icicle, "we'd watch the foam curling up on the rocks, and then fading away again, fading away, all day long, forever. . . . Oh, we're older now, we're dead or ready to die, the ones whose lips were firm and fresh as roses then, whose eyes glistened like stars, who trembled at the mention of a name or the touch of an arm. . . . Yes, yes, you're young now, you lovely lads, but you're like the foam curling up on the rocks, in an instant you'll fade away again. . . ."

The young stranger was smiling now, but his pale features looked sick and unhappy. He looked frightened and nervous. Something was wrong with him. "Perhaps he's a fugitive from the Soviet," thought Hugo. Then he noticed suddenly the resemblance between him and Mordovinov. One was handsome and young, the other old and ugly, but beneath it, there was a curious resemblance. And it was the young one who looked exhausted, stale, lifeless, the other who looked fiery, alive, quivering. Cousins, perhaps? Or, perhaps, father and son?

Soon Hugo and Joachim said good night and left.

"I'll come and see you tomorrow," cried Mordovinov after them, as they walked down the glistening path. "Good night, my lads, good night! Sleep well! Be happy! Fear nothing! Good night, good night. . . ."

★

It was only a mile from Mordovinov's cabin back to their own little hut, but it had suddenly grown bitter cold again. The melted snow had frozen into the hard ground, a wind came chattering through the twigs.

Then he found that his feet were cold as ice, and he shivered as the cold wind penetrated his moist shirt and caressed his throat and chest with its cold, steely fingers.

He lay down when he reached the hut. He felt a curious weakness sprouting in his chest and spreading, budding forth, encroaching. His face was aflame, his feet were numb.

Then he began to cough. A soft, wet cough that rose deep inside him and slid upward quite gently. He pulled out his handkerchief mechanically and held it to his mouth for a moment. Then he slipped it into his pocket again.

But as he slipped the handkerchief back into his pocket something caught his eye. He drew it out again, and unfolded it. There, in the very middle of it, he saw a little red stain.

He felt stiff all over now. He knew what it was, of course. His mother had died of it. He closed his eyes and lay motionless. Everything grew dim and gray. The room seemed to rise and fall, as if he were being carried along on wave after wave toward an unknown destination.

☆

After that, life became for him a matter of new terrors, new desires.

BOOK FIVE

Von Wald

29

Ye Mountains of Gilboa

DURING THE DAYS THAT HUGO LAY RECOVERING
beside the fire Joachim would walk alone
through the forest each afternoon. It was February already, the cold was still frightful, but on certain
mornings and evenings the sun would shine forth with an
unexpected brilliance, and the scene of snow and ice
would be transformed into one of a rich and almost tropical profusion. Among the black ecclesiastical columns of
the forest, trunk after trunk casting across the snow its
parallel shadows, blue as a field of irises, would ripple and
leap the jets of light, as nervously as they might across an
Alpine lake, or a flower-decked Austrian hillside. The
colors would be there, conjured out of pure blinding sun-

light, nothing more, and they would expand and emerge upon a scene limitlessly varied, incessantly changing. Above the trunk a more exciting web of pure colors was forever being tremulously knitted across the pergola of ice-crusted twigs, the sunlight was in fact woven into a dazzling lattice-work, harboring blossoms of every imaginable color, flashing forth from the black diamond-braceleted branches, until at last Joachim's eyes became dizzy and would turn again toward the long and restful blue shadows which flowed away from the trunks. He would turn from the trees down toward the slope above the river. And there he would suddenly see the sleepy and illusory outlines of a lake, with its shore—the feather-crested waves, the white rippling pebbles, the concave radiance of mother-of-pearl captured in a shell of ice blown down from the limb of a larch tree. There was no reality in all this; the color was only a manipulation in the atmosphere, the variable richness nothing but a conspiracy between the ice and the sunlight. Yet the very fact that all these splendors sprang from such a restraint of shape and hue, from a mere wintry longing, so to speak, made them seem all the more compelling. It was the very fact that the Alpine lake, the flowered slope, the pebbled shore, didn't really exist at all that made them seem so paradoxically touching, as if the image of the cliff or the garden or the beach were distilled out of the pure soul, the spirit of these things, rather than from simple earth, sand and stone. And somehow the rarefied and unattainable quality in these scenes also wrapped them in the most moving glow of all, that of memory. So that when Joachim went walking across the snow he felt the same innocent happiness as the playing of a violin or the singing of a familiar

[272]

song might have evoked; an image was conjured forth in all its purity, and the joy he felt was correspondingly pure.

☆

Hugo mystified him, more and more.

He had never felt at ease with Hugo really, or very intimate. Hugo was too cold, too intolerant, it almost seemed to be bitterness and deep disgust at times. Yet, as weeks passed, he grew more and more puzzled, and fascinated too, both impressed and repelled. For Hugo began to change. It was odd that this should happen, in such a lonely, simple place. But it was true, disquietingly true.

Hugo regained his strength very swiftly now. He would cough less, his face would look less flushed and unnatural, and less tubercular. His skin grew clean again, and dark and ruddy. His hands lost their whiteness, they too became brown and strong once more. His tread grew elastic, and his tight-rope body became hard and narrow as iron once more. With his clipped hair, his dark, shining skin, his gray immutable eyes, he looked like a sort of idol, startlingly Oriental.

His body was very broad at the top—shoulders so wide and a chest so deep that it looked almost like a coat of mail, and then leaping inward at the belly, like that of a wolfhound. And then, above that thick hard neck, loomed forth a heavy, protuberant chin and a shallow, narrow skull. He had a receding, rather primitive-looking forehead, that sloped down toward the immense eyebrows, under which the gray eyes lay motionless and watchful. A fighter. And yet, another man too; a watcher, a cautious,

[273]

stealthy figure, with a menacing curve to his lips, with
restrained and catlike motions. Secret plans, unscrupulous,
merciless, patient plans lay hidden there. Waiting, watching. Yet over it all hung a certain dignity, a masculine
dignity and power.

"We must always do things," he said once. "Do things,
do things. Plan. Look ahead. That's the way to acquire
power, to survive!"

And once he said, "What does it matter what we learn
through science? What matters is what we feel; the ideal
that sets afire our spirit; our immersion in a greater whole,
a burning cause!"

At those moments his face would glow feverishly, his
body would seem to grow, he would look taller and more
imposing than he really was. Joachim would feel like a
child beside him. And yet, he himself was a good three
inches taller. Wildenbruch was really a small man, trim
and agile; not more than five feet seven or eight.

☆

He rarely said more than a few words at a time, but
once or twice, at night, beside the lamplight, in the wintry
silence, he would begin to speak. When he spoke each
word seemed to be an effort; his temples would begin to
vibrate, and the muscles in his jaw worked nervously.

"Yes," he himself had said, "life is trying here, Hugo,
but at any rate it's simple, isn't it, and clear? . . ."

Hugo's face had something haggard, frightened in it.
"Nothing is clear," he said, staring down at the floor, quite

motionless. "Nothing is clear, nothing is simple." He paused rather timidly. He was usually very shy of words.

"We long to place things," he continued, not moving his gaze, "to arrange and label them, to achieve unity. To snatch a meaning out of the air here and there, out of our remembered past, our immediate sufferings, our hopes and fears for what's to come.

"But there's a power that ignores our systems," he continued in a very quiet tone, almost a whisper, "and at the most intense moments we see the perfect circle of our thought being crushed, shriveling away. . . . And nothing, no device in the whole wide world except blindness, and the extinction of everything that is most real and precious in us, will make life simple or smooth again. . . ." He seemed to have forgotten Joachim; he was talking to himself; muttering a bitter, crucial little monologue. His face had grown dark, pale creases appeared in his forehead, his lips were almost white.

"What can we do, in this overwhelmingly tragic and sinister age? We see too much, too much! Where can we look? What can we think? What can we do?" His voice rose, Joachim could see the veins in his temples throbbing. "Life has changed during these paranoiac years for all of us, of that I'm sure! Europe, Europe! Something quite incalculable lies in wait for us all! Perhaps we shall bear it, perhaps we shall be purified by it, perhaps the world will discover a new kind of simplicity and cleanliness. Perhaps. And perhaps the decency of our whole life depends on hoping and believing. But I don't know, you don't know, no one can know. . . ."

He coughed. His eyes closed for a moment. He pulled out his handkerchief, and Joachim noticed the quick little movement, the little red stain on the handkerchief.

He himself, at these times, would feel very hazy, very empty, passive, heavy, and quite lost.

But bit by bit, in the course of that anguished lamplit recital, something emerged which excited him. A faint suggestion, say, of the plight of a man, in conflict with society and yet in subtle and touching harmony with the flood of history; a man under extreme conditions, and not without terror, learning to recognize himself as the designer of his own destiny; gradually made more profound, more exact and meaningful, by the battle between body and mind; learning, in short, to discover his fate in action.

At that moment there was for Joachim something very thrilling and heroic about Wildenbruch. He watched those narrow features, those hard, aquiline eyes, with a feeling almost of adoration.

☆

The only book he had brought happened to be a very tiny, slender edition of the Bible which a middle-aged aunt had sent him from Vienna, just before they had started off on their expedition. Hugo asked him to read aloud from time to time. Joachim read his favorite passages for him—"Ye mountains of Gilboa, let there be no dew, neither let there be rain, upon you. . . . I am distressed for thee, my brother Jonathan"; or presently, "And the King was much moved, and went up to the chamber over the gate, and wept. . . ." He himself preferred certain passages from the Book of Psalms and from Ecclesiastes, but these Hugo appeared to dislike, so that Joachim presently lost interest in them too, and considered them less touching than those others of which Hugo was so fond.

30

The Storm

THERE WERE TRYING MOMENTS, OF COURSE, FOR NO
two men can get along calmly for very long, and
at times Joachim would find Hugo irritable and
dreadfully nervous. It occurred to him, as he looked at
Hugo's restless eyes and parted lips, that it might be physical desire that was troubling him; and this, since they were
both real and mature men, was a thought which both
touched and estranged Joachim, and he would at these
times prefer to leave Hugo alone. So he would go off and
visit Mordovinov, or if the day were less cold than usual,
walk across the snow toward the hill that overlooked the
village. He never grew tired of this. Each time he found
something new to admire or reflect upon in the landscape.

He might be entranced, for example, to find on the way home how the stars had suddenly appeared and under the dark sky the snow still continued to shine, how indeed it seemed to have gathered to itself at this moment whatever radiance was left in the land and with this concentrated glitter to have become liquid, mercurial, alive, so that the tree trunks appeared to rise out of an icy sea. The sounds at this hour would become more subdued yet more audible, each footstep would almost seem to utter the word "Hush!" and a distant twig brushing against another in the slight breeze would make a sound like glass, but soft, secret and intimate, as if some fond parent on Christmas eve were hanging from each branch a tinkling ornament, so cautiously that the children in the next room might surely not overhear. And now and then, late at night, on his way to his cabin, he might find a fresh track in the snow, the delicate circling print of a prowling animal, which with a thrill he would stoop to examine. The wolf! And suddenly the intricate web of shadows on the gleaming snow would appear more alert, more watchful, a tiny fragment of snow fluttering slowly toward the snow-covered ground would assume the nature of a subtle warning, and on looking up the stars would appear like a million watchful and adoring spirits. He would feel full of delight, then, convinced once more that Nature felt a special tenderness for him, and the rest of the journey home would be full of new discoveries and charming mysteries.

And then on passing the river, the ice might have been blown clean of snow, so that it looked bottomlessly black, and on stepping on it he would remember certain brilliant nights long ago, and take pleasure in sliding about and losing his balance and gliding down upon his side, his gloves and boots flat on the ice, his eyes gazing into this ebony mirror which reflected the blinding moon and every single star, and under the shallow ice he might discern little bubbles and crystals or even the frozen stalks of reeds, each vein, each hair flawlessly retained in its prison of glass.

Once or twice he passed strangers, but they seemed friendly and preoccupied—woodcutters, in their gray fur caps, calling to each other again and again with wild and melancholy voices, or hunters on their way back to the village ten miles away, silently carrying the limp furry bodies on a blood-stained stick between them.

Once a storm came up as he returned from one of his longer walks; for half an hour or so the wind was terrific, it tore like a mad band of kobolds through the woods, the larches trembled, the frail hysterical birches broke against each other, twigs were torn, snow was whirled about in great circles, and the sounds of the tempestuous North appeared to have been unchained—the gnashing of teeth, the moaning, the sobbing, the shrill wailing, and the tireless diabolical whispers of the mischief-loving trolls during the occasional moments of pause. Snowflakes were driven against his face with such power that his skin seemed aflame, and he turned his back to the wind only to find a moment later that it had wheeled about and was attacking him from another side. He sat down under a large tree and buried his face in his furry gloves.

Presently the storm subsided, and when he finally approached the cabin only a few flakes were still falling. The lamp was shining through the frosted window pane upon a snowdrift outside. He saw the flakes falling slowly through the glowing circle of lamplight, glittering for a moment like silver; and the flakes near by appearing almost captured, almost motionless, moving to and fro through the atmosphere with the gradual and lilting motions of a dance, still faintly reflecting the saffron glow that was falling through the window upon the snow.

He could hear faintly through the fur that covered his ears how a ripple of wind was running through the trees, setting the limbs atremble, flicking with its army of delicate and invisible fingers the fresh feathery snow from the slenderest twigs, so that silently these petals of snow fell, one after another, through the winter night upon the gleaming drifts of snow.

☆

One night Mordovinov arrived at their hut, a little bit drunk. He tapped at the window.

"Let me in!" he cried, his ugly grinning face peering through the snow and frost.

Joachim unbarred the door and in he swept, capless, his long gray hair and beard wrapped in a veil of snowflakes.

And then, once indoors, he began talking. For a while he raved on blasphemously about the state of the world. There had just been a battle, a week before, on the Manchurian frontier; both sides had crossed over and opened fire. Only about fifteen or so had been killed. But it had been a conspicuously needless unpleasantness.

"There's no end to trouble!" he howled. "First there's this Japanese cancer breeding away poisonously in Manchuria. It's already crept into Inner Mongolia, it's working away in its twisting busy fashion. Then there are the Mongolian rebels fighting against their dear Soviet-governed Republic of Outer Mongolia." He laughed gloomily.

"And of course the Manchurian rebels against *their* dear Japanese-governed fatherland. Believe me, there's evil brewing in these places, and just where you'd least expect it, too. They're all making plans, getting ready bit by bit. You'd shudder if I told you about the spies. . . . And to the west, there's Sinkiang. Well. They're busy enough with *their* local rebels too, at the moment. But then it will be the Tibetans, or the Chinese, or the British. They've learned to get along with the Russians at least, bless their idiotic little souls! And you'd be better off not looking to the east into China, my boys. That is a bizarre tangle if there ever was one, and the very saddest of all. . . . Ah, no country has suffered more than ancient celestial China! Yes, if China were a great country again, the world would be a finer place, I assure you!"

He leaned back, spread his legs far apart, and closed his eyes. "The countries are hysterical, one and all. Ruled by paranoiacs, they are, so it's little wonder. They behave like a pack of disreputable schoolboys. All ready to fight, as ridiculous as roosters, flaming with envy and conceit and bombast. Nothing will do any good. Strike them down and bit by bit they'll recover, and even before they've regained their balance they'll be off again. Revolting. Don't you agree, my two young Apollos? And the worst of it is it's contagious. Yes, Evil is always contagious, which is one thing that can rarely be said of Good.

"Ah, I used to chatter away to my dear friends; 'Listen,' I'd exclaim, 'do you want to hear the real, the basic solution for it all? Understanding. M-m-m. Just that. Oh yes, if one could only look straight into other people's hearts, hatred and grief would disappear. Eternal joy and love would rule the world. For there would be peace. For it is misunderstanding which brings discord, from which all minor evils rise. . . .' That's what I used to say, would you believe it?

"I feel a bit differently now, I regret to add. If we could see straight into each other's hearts, well, it would hardly be peace which would cover the world, but rather a murderous insane pandemonium. I'm sure of it."

He opened his crossed gray eyes again. Like two little tempest-ridden skies, they were. A constant storm seemed to be raging in that heart. "And there's another thing I used to believe, in my student days in Kiev. The grandeur of logic. I believed that in all of life the only thing worth preserving at all costs was the pure, the adorable, the subtle, the everlasting flame of reason.

"Well, it's easy enough to laugh now, of course. Now I have lived, in my little way; I have, my pretty children, been torn by wolves, blinded by snow, tortured by hunger, thirst, enemies, and worst of all by my own unfulfilled sinfulness. And do you know what I sometimes think? Just this. That seeing truthfully doesn't matter a jot. Being well fed, happy, free, and so on, doesn't matter a jot. The only thing that matters is what you see in my hideous old face, a bit of it still left—the fieriness that should set our lives aflame, even if it plunge us into doom. We should be lifted above our lives, high above the things we see and touch; our spirits should grow intense and passionate. To feel, to endure, to be purified by fire! Yes, grief, violence, pestilence, slavery, all of these are preferable to the infinite but hidden terrors of stagnation, the life of the clod, the true inertia."

His face, thought Joachim, torn as it was, deeply lined, irregular, broken and bitten and stained, seemed nevertheless profoundly pure, almost gentle, at this moment. For the power of his spirit had mastered the flesh, for just a moment or two. And that hideous mask was suffused with the harmonious perfection of the visionary, the beautiful, penetrating gleam of madness.

"Life has become unreal, in this modern world, this gigantic octopus city; for everything has become public, tangible, materialistic. Even the most remote pastures of the Congo or the Caucasus—even they are only corners, little lamplit parks and squares in this vast city. Because, after all, it is not what we see and know and love that unites us all nowadays, but what we fear. And the instincts of fear are supernatural, they leap over oceans in the twinkling of an eye, they flash into hidden cellars, nothing can any longer be hid from them. They are the power that will guide our lives, you know, henceforth!

"Yes, even our noblest emotions, our loves and loyalties, are now false, the glib result of music, pictures, and words, words, words. Words! Have you ever considered how ghastly they are, these little mushrooms that cling to our life, sponging it up little by little till nothing is left to see or feel? Love, the divinest of our powers, lovely love is no longer a passion of the blood, but rather an expert jumble of words and images, dictated by the horrible traditions of our various orators, our merchants in words. You know them as well as I. Tolstoi, Turgeniev, Baudelaire, and that incredible Englishman of whom we know so little. And a thousand others. Do you see what I mean? What I mean is a very awful thing, which I can never quite understand. I prefer not to think about it too much, I'll confess.

"There has only been one cure, ever. And it's to be found only in solitude, our real solitary selves. Study, learning, discipline, privation, quiet—they all help. Cease

watching others, cease regarding your own body, entrancing though it may seem. Be natural. . . .

"And yet, the great nations say, Join together, be one,
be equal, be unified in spirit. Ah! the most utter terror,
the most vile deception, lurks in those simple words. But
so secretly that they do not see it, and most awful of all,
they will not know it even when it has arrived, but will
subside into its delicate annihilations with a sigh of relief.
Death."

He turned and gazed at Joachim. Joachim felt more
torn at this moment than he had ever felt in his life, and
Mordovinov's face now seemed to him aglow with a supernatural fire.

"Do you know what they have told me, those impudent
morons? 'You are an escapist,' they say. 'You have admitted
defeat, and are trying to escape from reality,' and all the
rest. An escapist! A defeatist! P-f-fh. How imbecilic and
loathsome they are, how blind! I have a word or two to
say to them. Yes. It is *they* who strive so incessantly and
verbosely to escape, who are too paltry and vain and sentimental to see what is true, the emptiness of their spirit,
the spiritual emptiness of the world. Yes, yes. Men will do
anything, anything, nowadays, to escape from the terror of
their own minds. Secretly they know, these mad material-
ists, that they will never succeed completely. No materi-
alist can ever succeed completely, it is impossible, that is
their punishment. And, of course, they are afraid. Afraid
of the primeval terror of thought, of contemplating the
vast inhuman laws of the universe.

"Their whole life, all of 'civilized' life"—and he uttered the word with a violent spasm of disgust—"is a
subtle and degraded escape. Music, paper, print, oratory,
fast movement, alcohol, crowds, racial and economic the-

ories, and all the rest. The Middle Ages look very dignified and profound and orderly to me by contrast. Marx-
ism, fascism, yes, all of them—some on a fine, idealistic
basis to be sure, others on a terrifying legendary basis—
but it's all the same, deep down. Oh yes! they can't bear
modern living, they try desperately to make it into something endurable. But they can't quite! You wait and see.
They seek to escape from what stares them in the face:
namely, death at the hands of an everlasting power which
will tolerate these silly and conceited insults not much
longer.

"Defeatist! I laugh!" He shrieked with rage. "We will
see. *They* are the ones doomed to defeat, I rather suspect.
They will be the losers, the sufferers, the relics of the past.
And there will be nothing heroic in *their* annihilation. It
will be a sound like tin and broken glass, just as hollow
and desolate. Nothing will be left. I at least will be able
to smile. I've made plans. I've learned to suffer, far, far
more than they. There's an invisible creature hiding in
me, call him a soul if you wish, and he'll survive.

"The world, the world! They talk of war and money
and starvation and injustice and all the rest. But the reality
is much bigger, more profound, more terrible than these
by far. Do you want to know what it is? It's this. The love
for death. Yes, haven't you noticed? It's becoming quite
an infatuation these days. Life has become too nerve-
racking. Men don't really care about most things—women,
art, music, books, and so on. Yes, they use them, of course;
they're opiates. But only one thing really matters with
these western people like you and your friends. The desire
for annihilation. It's secret, it's subtle, it masquerades in
a thousand whimsical costumes, it hides underground like
a serpent, it gazes from clouds like an eagle, it mutters

from the depths of the sea or the depths of a prison. But whether they dress up like airmen or sailors or spies or martyrs, it's all the same thing, really. It's there. It's the world. I *know*."

He closed his eyes again. His face now looked utterly different; almost the face of a child. The lines of endurance, the fire, the hatred and conceit, had melted away. The storm had subsided. He'd fallen asleep, and presently Joachim blew out the lamp.

31

The End of Winter

A S THE DAYS PASSED, AND THE WINTER FADED, HUGO began to grow haggard again. His sickness was once more rising up in him. The veins in his temples beat like little red drumsticks, and long blue petals blossomed forth under his eyes.

He began to cough more frequently and his handkerchief grew spotted with crimson stains. A certain defiant, fierce look slipped into his eyes. He would sit silently for hours, and the lines of his chin would harden, his lips would grow thin and pale. Now and then Joachim was filled with uneasiness, when at a casual word, or a trivial gesture, Hugo would suddenly look at him with eyes that seemed inflamed with a wild, piercing, animal hatred;

until, a moment later, he would realize that it was not toward him that this glance was directed, but inward, toward the world that lay bleeding in Hugo's own heart.

Occasionally he would seem to be better. He would go tramping through the snow, hunting, setting traps, collecting wood, cutting through the ice, all with energy. A fresh glow would enter his cheeks, and Joachim would feel relieved.

He would say strange things, though. Once Joachim tried to comfort him. "We'll get out soon. We must stay hopeful!"

"Hope!" murmured Hugo. There was a certain intensity in every word he uttered, as in every gesture he performed, so that it acquired a new meaning, a meaning associated not with the mind but with the blood. "There is no such thing as hope, except in the minds of children. One lives, one does what one is created to do, one wonders, one loves, one struggles, one endures, one decays and dies. Hope is like a fish leaping out of the water. A certain longing drives every man to it, but he's better off below."

He hated almost everything, almost everyone. He believed in no sort of God. He seemed, at times, to be infected with some of Mordovinov's nihilism. And most people he seemed to think wildly contemptible. "There are things in everyone's life so loathsome, I've gradually discovered, that they become a cancer, eventually they kill the little infinitesimal spark of the godlike in everybody. I have never known it to fail!"

At times his body seemed to grow small, his face shrank into a savage, scared nakedness, his lips looked as narrow and sharp as two knives.

"Growing old," he would murmur. "Horrible. . . . That's what I can't stand thinking of. . . . I hope," he said slowly, metallically, "that I die before I am forty. I should rather kill myself than watch myself growing weak, submissive, afraid, resigned, contemptible. . . ."

Once he said, "I must get back. Back to Germany. I am already growing afraid. Time is passing, I must get back. . . ." A terrible bird-like nervousness shone in his quiet eyes.

"Afraid of what, Hugo?"

Hugo glanced up. But he did not seem to see Joachim. His gaze grew more and more remote. "Of the devil," he said. "He's lying in wait. . . ." He pointed to his chest. "In here." He began to laugh, then; he seemed embarrassed, perhaps terrified.

In everything he said, during these final days of winter and frozen ground, hovered a flash of malaise, of sickness. He would shiver, his voice would grow vibrant. It was a kind of nightmare that he lived in, a nightmare by sunlight, and yet icy.

☆

Once when he returned with some firewood he found Hugo kneeling beside the window, weeping silently. He turned away as soon as he saw Joachim.

But Joachim was torn with grief, for he understood the terrible qualms Hugo must have gone through before he allowed these tears, and the hopelessness in them, and the intense despair with which this fatal weakness would forever after be regarded.

He longed to help him, to whisper a word of comfort

and encouragement to him. But of course, he did not dare;
and besides, it would have been worse than nothing.

✫

It was in the following week that they resolved to leave
for Urga and Pekin, even at the risk of still meeting a
period of intense cold on the way. The end of winter was
in sight, and the days had already begun to smile.

So they visited Mordovinov for a last time.

Mordovinov was lying on his couch, drunk. A copper
samovar was steaming and bubbling by the fire. The
steam curled up past a weather-stained icon on one side
and a dirty faded picture of Lenin on the other. The old
woman was sitting in the corner silently, doing nothing.

"She's dying," whispered Mordovinov with a leer. "She's
sick. She knows she's about to go. Ah! How she loved me!
She is the only woman left in the world now who loves
me; or man either, for all that. I'll be alone!"

Joachim looked at the old woman. Her eyes were closed.
She was dying, there was no doubt about it. She had the
unmistakable look of those who are approaching death—
peaked, intense, so personal yet so remote. One could see
in that mad and suffering face what human nature, really
drawn to its limits, can endure; as the extremities are approached the features lose humanity, and in that very
transformation comes a new and unexpected source of
strength, the magical power of those who are about to die.
She had grown terribly ugly, her skin was infinitely wrinkled and of a curious hue. An utter shabbiness hung about
her like a filthy rag; a vile smell came from her body. Yet

[290]

over all this, unexplainably enough, appeared a really terrifying beauty, the beauty of complete abdication, but more than that, the beauty of the incessant dream of mortality, of man at the end of all fear, hope, desire, or even the beauty of love, perhaps, in its final stages; it was hard to say.

They told Mordovinov that they were departing, and thanked him. They felt curiously shy, all of a sudden. It was because they both realized what was happening to Mordovinov, and the loneliness in his old heart which hankered so wildly for love and understanding.

He was silent for a while. Then he explained to them in great detail how to reach the caravan road to Urga. It would take them perhaps three days to reach the road, not much more. They might reach Urga in two weeks if they were lucky. But it was a risk, of course. Not only the cold, but other things too.

"Things are unsettled, and getting worse. The Japanese know they can't wait much longer, you know. Or it will be too late. They've got to strike while the great bear is still rubbing his sleepy lazy eyes. Yes. . . ."

And then he went off again, rather despondently. "The behavior of people is an absolute tangle, I tell you. A complete tangle. Reasons are invented, but no one understands the dreams and memories hiding years beneath the surface, which really control the postures of this tragic ridiculous dance of death. You can laugh, but it's not so simple. You can't judge it from the outside. It's a labyrinth incredibly subtle. Love, that's what I used to think would help, no matter what happened. That would give meaning to it all. But the hate buried in the hearts of men is infinitely more violent, I can see now, than I had ever guessed!

[291]

"Well, there is a great force, I say, a sort of fire, in every man. Turn it one way and it's good. Turn it the other way and it's evil. You could call that fire 'love,' I suppose. Do you see? It's really the same fire, whichever way it goes. And that is what is so absolutely terrifying. It's this frightful perversion which has crept across Europe, and Asia too, like a gas."

He rose up and stood in front of them. There were tears flowing out of his rheumy eyes. "Listen," he whispered, "listen. I know one thing. Only one thing. And that is this. The people in the world that I have seen with my own eyes are merely shadows. Breaths of nightly wind, vapors: blow at them, and no matter how strong or beautiful they seemed, they vanish away, my boys. They move across the land, some with considerable energy and others with weariness, but what they do, say, think, and endure, these millions of beating hearts, is as far as my silly eyes can see quite without real meaning. Oh, forgive them, I say, for they know not what they do! They will undergo, I dare say, the most awful of martyrdoms. They will speak in the most diabolical tones or utter the most excruciating litanies, they will perform the most exquisite sacrifices. But all in order to relieve the anguish of living a life without the old things which they cannot unlearn so soon, hope, I mean, and faith, and charity, and the rest of those outdated sentimentalities. Oh, it will be a thrilling period in our history, the world will melt together into a single intense nothingness, at last!" His face had flashed into life, the muddle and sentimentality had vanished. Apparently he really believed what he was saying. His eyes glittered, his tangled gray hair flashed, it seemed alive, and he himself seemed young again.

"Yes," he said at last, "now I shall be alone again. I have loved you, my lads, as I love everything young and alive. Well, good-by to you now, good-by. Perhaps you will meet me again, after all, in some distant city! I am still young, you know!"

32

Landscapes

THREE MORNINGS LATER HUGO AND JOACHIM FOUND
themselves climbing the low range of hills that
wound between valley and valley, among the various tributaries of the Selenga.

The sun appeared over the tree-tops. And then the
caress of morning fell upon the clouds which directly
assumed the contours of living creatures, huge oblique
birds, flamingoes, sauntering at that instant through the
bright air on their way from some southern pool, still gray
in body, their gray claws trailing in the current of departing twilight, and their breasts displaying a pink as soft
as feathers, then a sharp edge of ivory emerging as the
light grew clearer and each silhouette more precise. But

of course, thought Joachim with delight, they are not birds at all, they are the careless emblems of the world's journey toward the east, gliding her hidden charms one by one into the embrace of the morning. The enchantment of that moment was the same—and it was this that so especially touched him, no doubt—as that which, on a morning long ago when he awoke beside his two sisters on a meadow beside the Salzach, had filled him with such a childish bliss, and the sudden wish had occurred to him that he might engrave this adored scene upon his heart and that he might thus carry it with him forever, to be plucked forth and contemplated in moments of loneliness, and in this manner insure his future happiness forever. For after all, it had occurred to him even then, how long could this happy care-free life continue? He held happiness in the palm of his hand, it shone there as vividly as a butterfly's wing. But what lay ahead? How build an armor for it without drowning it in darkness, or allowing the passing days to wear its shimmer away? And it had occurred to him, just as a child thinks that by pressing some furry animal to its heart at night the terror of darkness will be made tolerable, so the presence of this Austrian landscape would prevent any unhappiness from ever invading his heart.

But then he looked at the sun. Everything else faded into triviality. There it was—the ferocious golden eye of eternity. He could see the arrows of fire fluttering outward from it, its gaze transformed into something alive, more than alive, the very creator of all life. All energy in the whole wide world lay flickering on those bursting, blinding rays of gold which now created little tremors of love in every tree, each blade of grass, each creature warm or cold.

[295]

It was growing warmer, and though the night had been cold, the icicles were already melting, drop by glittering drop. Each one, as the sun gathered strength, grew tenuous, and broke, until the patches of snow were covered with the glitter of these icy fragments, shaped variously like sea shells, some long and pointed, others hollow and semicircular. Everywhere Joachim could hear the trickle of melting snow, the nervousness and eagerness of the million streamlets flowing together under the subsiding blanket of snow, and promptly entering the earth. The air was like a crystal. And toward noon they found that in the open glades the earth had already grown soft, and when they stepped upon the snow it yielded entirely. Their boots were wet from entering these little puddles which lay hiding under the snow. Rivulets were veining the slopes, and the sound of an incessant secret whispering and kissing rose from the ground, as if in every nook and crevice the resilient water were making love exuberantly to the yielding earth.

That evening they came to the edge of a slope of pastureland, the southern slope of a range of lower hills which ran directly from east to west, and here they saw, in the ruddy haze of sunset that hovered like the glow of golden curls over the feminine undulations of the land, a shepherd and his flock slowly wandering home. This was the first man they had met, and they rested contentedly in the edge of the wood and ate their last bits of crust and cheese. Hugo was more contented now, the labor and sweat of the day's march had set his troubled heart at ease, and as for Joachim, he felt happier than he had for many weeks. He saw some birds traveling northwestward, and in his pleasure he thought of their pleasure too, their flight through the empty skies, over the restless seas, the seventy ranges of China and the thousand valleys.

That night while they slept in their sheepskin bags the twigs of the birches and the alders were full of little whispers, hundreds, thousands of them. Whispers of expectancy, of anticipated delights, no doubt, and in the distance Joachim could hear another happy sound, that of a stream released from the bondage of the winter's ice and little by little nuzzling its way among the stones once more, finding numberless channels, new ones with every new minute, winding its way through a thousand freshly discovered crevices.

On the following morning, indeed, the hills were full of infinitesimal songs, innumerable little chants of liberation. Joachim woke up just as a streak of golden light was bursting through the clouds. He rose and walked down the hill. On every side he could hear this clamor echoing and reëchoing in the dappled morning air, the various hosannas of arriving spring, some distinct, many so subdued that they could scarcely be detected, but all quite unmistakably proclaiming one theme above all others, the simple one of delight.

Torrents came roaring and foaming down the steep hillside opposite, carrying along with them small rocks, clusters of leaves, small twigs, debris of the long rigid months, all sorts of things, mortal creatures too, furry ones, eyes opened wide in terror, captured alas when their days had scarcely begun, before they could share these very powers and joys that were springing up on all sides and were in fact now carrying them onward and downward in their happy merciless flood.

Fog, a silver veil, still hung over the woods on the north-western slope, and as the sun grew stronger he could still see these lacy fragments clinging to each hollow, each shady copse, shimmering there until the warming, brightening air dispelled them too, and the day established itself in every single nook and cranny all over the countryside.

He watched the sun grow brilliant and dictatorial. For a while clouds still hovered over the horizon, and their shadows, fragments of snow and ice, still lay in dark protected places among the trees. The land seemed infinite and ungovernable at this moment. But then a glow of light, mother-of-pearl, slid across these areas of snow, the shadows wavered, they rippled like little waves on a shallow beach, and then the ruddy finger of the sun sent them scurrying away, the growing alertness of the wood now grew serene and dominant, nothing was left of night or of secrecy or of lonely imprisonment, the day had come, the warming, the lovable and loving day.

☆

They felt very hungry, and resolved to follow the path along the river and stop at the first tent and beg for breakfast. They could already see a flock of sheep moving across a hill in the distance.

They felt the dead leaves of centuries under their feet as they walked along. The earth was elastic, odorous, and out of the darkness of the decayed leaves and branches tiny green things were already appearing, curling tender ferns, still sticky, a little cawl of babyhood still clinging to them for another hour or two. The change was one that the eye could not quite discern, but the subtler senses could, and Joachim felt intoxicated with this atmosphere of renovation and eager, blissful energy.

As the river turned and flowed from east to west for two or three miles, they entered a stretch of spruce forest. It was much cooler here, the ground was still hard and silent, and entering these shadows was as brisk and sudden as entering cold water. But here too the sunlight was dappling the ground, the open glades glimmered through the tree trunks like golden carpets as they approached, and in these the new grass was appearing, and occasional flowers too—early ones, small and bell-shaped.

Then the river broadened out into a lake, and from the right a small brook came rippling down the slope. On the shore a mile away or so they saw a *yurt*, and a plume of smoke rising from it. They lay down beside the shore in the warm sunlight and rested.

The lake was clear as crystal, and a flock of wild geese passed overhead, each one reflected perfectly in the mirror of water. Joachim knelt beside the brook and cupped his hand to drink; the water was cold as ice, so nervous and fresh that even in his hand it shivered and seemed alive, trembling with eagerness to be on its way again.

Delight was now, and had always been, like a brook running through the landscape of his mind. Sunlight and shadow trembled over the water, were reflected on the green moss and the porcelain-white pebbles beneath: one as inevitable as the other: and true joy had its roots in solitude and thoughtfulness as much as in a golden indolence. Spring came leaping down the hill on these coruscating wavelets, it hesitated at a thousand different places on the way—a pebble on the shore, the shell of a snail, the wing of a moth or a dragon-fly, a single drop resting on a leaf or a stone.

Landscapes ~~~~~~

Yes, he thought, a landscape is a spiritual thing, there's no denying it. A landscape is a state of the spirit, it is a constant longing for what is about to come, it is a reflection incomparably detailed and ingenious of what is everlasting in us, and everlastingly changing. Each scene is dear to us, more than dear, the dark as well as the sunny, the cold as well as the glowing. If his heart were opened to view, he knew, then all these landscapes would come rippling out, one after another, full of sunlight, full of the sound of laughter, of brooks, full of the scent of grass, the accidental caresses of the wind, of foliage beneath which he himself sat hidden, breathless, alone, or confiding to another, perhaps, one of those eager secrets of childhood. . . .

33

Austria

JOACHIM'S HEART LEAPT WITH DELIGHT. YES, THE vision had been captured. Suddenly he was filled with a loving vitality, an overwhelming love for everything alive, that glittered, that fluttered, that moved and was warm.

There they were again: the buttercups in the meadow, each petal a water-smooth golden bowl, and the clover with its furry blossoms; in the hedge the berries were beginning to appear, the days had flown past, summer was already smiling through the glades with her fists full of flowers and her apron full of fruits. The sheep, the geese, the dandelions were covering the fields, and in the stream the ducks were gliding to and fro, whilst a solitary frog sat basking on a lily pad near the footbridge.

Gently he opened the gate and stepped into the garden through the ivied arch—gently lest indeed the gate be revealed once more as that miraculous portal leading into a land where hours are like flowers, profusely intermingled, each to be plucked at will and light-heartedly savored, and where there is nothing at all to fear, nothing at all. There they were—the forget-me-nots, the larkspur, the daisies and the roses; and beyond, in the shade, the violets and lilies-of-the-valley, all the more poignantly eloquent since they were so small, hidden away in grass and shade. Through the leaves he could see Rosa in her strawberry-pattern apron, bringing the coffee-cups and the big yellow cakes into the arbor. He raised his head. Two huge red feather pillows were hanging on the balcony railing, and Annamarie stood leaning against them, combing her golden hair. His heart tightened, for she was smiling at him.

And then he heard a voice singing; but, as he listened, he saw that it was not a voice but the sound of the oxen weaving their sleepy path along the lane, under its canopy of leafy sunlight, and the tinkling bells of the cows in the field, and the singing brook. Now he could glimpse through the chestnut leaves the earnest little tower of the St. Gilgen church, and the mirroring lake with its boat; he could see the cherries red in the trees, the flowers like stars in their cloudy fields, the clouds like vast unfurling flowers in the sky. And wandering along the road he could now see the deer among the beeches, and the girls dressed in blue, the frank and childlike color of the morning sky and of forget-me-nots, plucking the warm strawberries; and the little white sail on the lake, pointing toward still lovelier islands, the magical joys that lay hidden in the tremendous shadowy groves of the future; and clad in a more mysterious blue, the blue of hills, of seas, of irises, of despairing love-letters, the harvesters among the golden hay, where the sweet warm odors of Austria were forever kissing their cheeks, thus surely preventing them from ever feeling the slightest sorrow; and now entering the village, he could see the fruits, the vegetables, the limp feathery fowls and shimmering fish all laid out in the market-place beneath their red umbrellas; and the bronze fountain playing, the lad with his violin, and idling through the sunlight the curly-headed boys in their leather breeches and the golden-haired girls, the handsome children sprung out of the sorrow of war; and now at nightfall the tables were carried indoors, the checkered tablecloths were folded, the lamps were lit in *Zum Weissen Hirsch*, and the lovers went sauntering down the road, two by two, singing songs to the sweet sob of the lute, the boys caressed by the scent of the elderberries and the touch of wind-blown locks, the girls full of teasing laughter and sweet expectations.

Now it was night, and he stepped indoors. Yes, there was the old oblong piano, and the cuckoo clock on the shelf, and the scent of Rosa's freshly-baked black bread. Beside the clock stood an immense gaily-colored platter, on which he could read the words, *Bewahr im Herzen Sonnenschein, und trag ihn überall hinein,* and now indeed it seemed to him that this sunlight alone in the whole wide world was real, warming our hearts, illuminating our days, carving across the darkness of our still and thoughtful hours. Good and evil meant nothing in themselves, he then supposed: it was the presence of this golden vitality alone that determined a man's power, a man's joy, a man's goodness.

Ah, those days were gone forever! But it hardly seemed

to matter; he remembered them with pure delight, without any touch of regret. And of course they could never really vanish away, wherever he might be, whatever he might do, since they had always existed only where they were now still to be found—in his spirit; our daily life, never quite clear to our gaze, is forever most deceptively interwoven with the colored strands of our past; so that what we do, say, feel, is a marvelous tapestry construed in part out of the moment and in part out of our infinite recollections; and after all, what could ever seem beautiful to us, or move us unawares in any way, if it did not whisper into our ears that single word whose manifold echoes it thereupon sets ringing in our mind?

And yet, how treacherously! We are moved more and more deeply in accordance with our power to remember; but these things could never have existed so potently in our childhood and youth as we now imagine; it is the years, the saddening, exhausting years, that have designed this tender resonance, and in fact memory is not a recollection of what has happened, but rather the portrait of these early scenes and desires sketched by our capricious heart, surrounded and made forever more fabulous by layer after layer of new longings, like the ripples flowing outward from a pebble tossed into a pond. And, of course, the treachery is made more cruel still by this: that what we recall is not a field, or a copse, or a room, or a smile, or a magical phrase, but rather something that has indeed escaped us forever: namely, that veritable moment when we lay breathless in the field, or sauntered through the copse, paused on the threshold, imprinted our first kiss, or listened to an acceptance of our love. That, *that* is the fragile and Euclidian moment, caught in the web of the torrential years, which we shall never again see as it was, so pure, so simple; but only as a talisman, an "Open

Sesame," which discloses for the hundredth time our melodious joys and adorations.

✫

The cock crowing at dawn, the flowered aprons ballooning on the line, the smell of the bread in the oven, the dew caught on the cobwebs below the windows, the geraniums in the sun and the lilies-of-the-valley in the shade, his grandmother reading on the bench under the chestnut tree, the glittering pebbles in the walk, the spaniels in the sun, the onion-shaped spire in the distance. And the songs, the songs! *Bakke, bakke Kuchen,* Rosa would sing, and clap his little hands together: and he would see instantly the baker's kitchen, the enormous cakes, the bowl of eggs, the pitcher of milk, and the baker with his towering white cap kneading the florid dough. Or, *Die Tiroler sind lustig, die Tiroler sind froh,* and there would be the tables covered with the amber-hued glasses of beer, the men in their shining black breeches singing and dancing, the girls wheeling around with their bright skirts flying; or, *Fuchs, du hast die Gans gestolen,* and promptly the green countryside would unroll itself, with the grazing deer in the distance, the wicked red fox lurking among the saplings, the snow-white geese, the playful hares; or, *O Tannenbaum,* and there in a solitary word would hover the spell of Christmas, the green glittering needles, the sled entwined with holly, the blue-eyed angels who climbed from star to star and sang their loving carols.

✫

There would be hot wine at Christmas, and a suckling pig with a lime in his mouth, and smacking kisses beneath the mistletoe, and songs, and red-faced visitors with snow still clinging to their caps and mittens. And a steaming pudding was set aflame, and then the children waited breathless and expectant outside the door until the little bell rang out, whereupon they rushed in and discovered their presents under the tree—the wide-eyed dolls, the surprising animals, the tin soldiers and cannons, and the little toy village, all smelling of pine needles and of dripping wax. Gilded apples and pears and walnuts hung from the tree, all aglow in the candle-light, and little waxen angels, and silver birds, and lions of red sugar, and St. Nicholas with the snowflakes glistening upon his venerable old beard.

Joachim would prance gaily into the kitchen on his wooden horse, where Rosa and Lisl and Annamarie were whisking about with shining eyes among the glistening pots and pans. On the blue oilcloth beside the sink stood a big yellow bowl full of dough, and a smaller bowl full of hazelnuts, and a still smaller one in which four egg yolks pressed tenderly against one another. Sprawled upon the raw, scrubbed wood of the kitchen table lay the shimmering entrails of the goose which was hissing inside the oven, and beside the oven, in her basket, Miezchen the cat lay purring amid her five nuzzling kittens. Fat Lisl in her big red apron cried in mock anger when she saw him, and picked up the flour-bespeckled rolling-pin in her big, red, dripping hand.

Joachim fled to the window and gazed through the misted glass at the blue waves of snow extending as far as the forest, so infinitely still and silent behind the glitter of candles mirrored in the window pane. And then sud-

denly the night flashed into life, three sleds sped down
the hillside, lanterns appeared in the path, the door
opened, and Rosa dashed past him with a cry and a great
bowl in her arms, from which the steam curled upward
like a benevolent little ghost.

And then presently Easter would arrive, fresh as a daffo-
dil. They would go hunting for the colored eggs, a tan-
talizing bit of blue shell glimmering here between the ivy
leaves, or there a glimpse of red in the hollow of a tree
trunk, or something yellow peering through the shadowy
stems of the rose bush. In the evening Rosa would read
them the familiar fairy-tales in her lovely voice, out of
his dead mother's big *Märchenbuch*, still inscribed "Für
Maria, Weihnachten, 1897," raising her soft gray eyes to
them now and again, smiling sadly, the five garnets in her
ring glistening mysteriously and fatally, emblems of something remote, incomprehensible, another land, perhaps.

There was Aschenbrödel first of all, her rags abruptly
transformed into satins and ermines, her chaste foot pointing toward the silver slipper; Schneewittchen, *"Schneewittchen über den sieben Bergen, bei den sieben Zwergen,"*
imperially beautiful as she lay dead, with her coal-black
eyes, her rose-red lips, her snow-white skin; Dornröschen,
her silken locks entangled amongst a thousand roses, roses
strewn upon her crimson gown, her hands enchained with
petals and cobwebs; and Rapunzel, high in her tower, in
the depths of a forest full of nightingales and mystery,
allowing her incredible golden hair to flow over the sill,
yard after yard, into the clandestine night. He would
wonder for hours about these lovely princesses, casting
about in his mind for a clue to the momentous problem
of which of these four might truly be the most beautiful;
now it seemed to be Rapunzel with her braid, now Schnee-

wittchen on her bier, now Aschenbrödel the shy one, now Dornröschen among the briars. He loved them passionately, all four of them, as well as that odd multitude of dwarfs and fairies and witches and wolves which haunted all such enchanted territories—kingdoms in which he could still discern an imagined sea of glass all aglimmer with mermaids, a sky of violets, a meadow of gamboling lambs, a forest of huntsmen green as clover, a town full of fat rolling millers and bouncing cakes, a castle eloquent with the rustle of satins, the tinkle of jewels, and the distant sound of a silver violin. It was out of all this, indeed, that sprang the magical inverted heaven of childhood, the well of infinite love and desire; the land where all creatures are amazing, where all things are possible, where nothing is too glorious or gentle to be within easy reach.

☆

He would wander, years later, along the lake with Annamarie, toward St. Wolfgang, or up over the hills toward the Attersee. They would sit together with beating hearts and glowing cheeks, on the shore of the lake or on the top of the hill, he in his *Lederhosen*, she in her *Dirndlkleid*. They would sing songs together, or tell old stories which both of them knew by heart. There was no need ever to say anything new, since each passing hour was new and gleaming, and an old song became new again each time that it was sung. He would watch her with shining eyes, her braid now wound around her head, her rosy cheeks, her sparkling smile.

In the winter they walked home from school arm in arm

through the leafless wood, and he carried their books bound together in the same strap; they walked along the snowy path past the old mill and the glassy willows and the water-wheel, all of them now still and silent. Once he cut off a lock of her hair, and they quarreled; and once again they quarreled, he never quite knew why, and it was then that he discovered how she loved him. And after this the whole world changed: when they went strolling together past the forest pool the air and water and sunlight were but the delicate agents of desire, and the leaves and flowers but symbols of tenderness and expectation. He would lie beside her, aching and enormous with desire, her garments breath-takingly eloquent, each button in her dress a uniformed guardian to the delights of this world; he would blushingly glance down at his own brown legs, his own hard young body moving and throbbing restlessly beneath his leather shorts, and then when he raised his eyes again and saw her lids lowered, whether in modesty or cunning he could not tell, love seemed almost within his grasp, a sweetly visible and tangible thing about to yield itself once more to his hot touch.

And now he was desperately in love, at nights he could not rest; when she was not beside him he waited only for the moment of meeting; and when he was at her side once more, at the lake, or on the hill beside the waterfall, then too he was forever tormented, her cheeks, her neck, her arms, all seemed miraculously sweet to his lips; and at the thought of what further secrets might await his lips and arms his brain reeled, he caught his breath, and his whole body seemed immersed in a new, celestial element, incomparably caressive, magnetic indeed. He would roll the word over upon his tongue, "love, love, love," the leaves twinkled their eyes at him, the sound of the stream aroused extravagant memories, each house he passed and each handsome couple seemed bejeweled with secret joys, and the heaven shone like a vast bed of flowers intended for love and love alone.

☆

Yes; how forget the stream curling over the dark moss and then suddenly flattening as it reaches the fall, spreading like a silver fan, plunging into the deep black pool; or the scent of the moist earth at morning, the bluebells opening, the new leaves of the ivy shimmering like satin in the fluctuating sunlight; or the thousand leaves of the poplars and beeches, each one infinitesimally perfect, each one holding a feather of sunlight in its green palm; or the quiet moss-covered pebbles forever quivering in the light of the ripples passing above them—the green stones which are vast grottos and precipices to the tiny fish who lie by the tens and hundreds in the cool water and now flash past, almost invisible, and are gone; each little wavelet looking back at him, so it seemed, as it approached the waterfall, whispering a dear good-by; or the bee, hanging motionlessly in the sweet-smelling air, then flashing away in a sudden access of delight; or the butterflies—the red admirals, the peacocks, *vanessa io,* the tortoise shells, the Hesperides quick as humming-birds, the sulphurs and the cabbage whites, and the subtle tiny blues; the over-cautious caterpillars, the amiable ladybirds, the modest ants, the patient spiders, the querulous wasps; or the constant rustling of invisible creatures—field mice, grasshoppers, the metal-green beetles who climb to the edge of a stalk which then bends with their weight, dropping them softly into the vast jungle through which they wander all day long; or the noise of birds, invisible except for a quick excited flutter now and then, or the glint of a bright black eye watching him through the swaying foliage; or the young foal approaching the water, leaning its firm young neck upon his shoulder, asking for caresses, tripping away coyly but forever returning, flattening its silky ears, blinking its black eyes so full of perpetual surprise; or the yellow wheat-field, all flowing and curling this way and that in the breeze, like a lion's mane, and the dark, crisp wood beyond through which the trunks of the birches glimmered like the limbs of slender, timid girls; or the lichen-covered stone bridge on which he had sat by the hour, filled with a delight so pure and golden that his heart would swell, would beat more quickly, his hands would tremble, his spirit grow dizzy with tenderness and longing for something which he could never fully grasp; but overwhelmingly happy to be alive, unutterably in love with every impulsive, shining, nestling thing he heard, saw, touched: how forget these? Ah, how could one ever be unhappy in their presence?

*

His thoughts were like birds, they created a curious sensation of flight, and simultaneously the past grew more and more real. Far, far from being an escape from the world, this meditation grew indeed to be a condensation of all profound experience, intense, intransigent; and presently no longer a flight from the present but an instrument creating in the present an ever greater clarity and meaning. These symbols became real, since life is all in all so intense, he knew, so torrential and moving on the one hand, and on the other so fragmentary and so tormented by unfulfilled dreams, that even at best it can be grasped only through symbols, whatever these may be. Indeed, in what other guise can the desires which govern our lives appear to us, he wondered, than as those shapes which we, in our brief and straying lives, have learned to recognize with our own hearts? Otherwise we should see only emptiness in the powers of good and evil, life would carry no logic, no continuity, no deeper meaning for us at all.

Two longings had, all his life long, lain warm in him: that for a home, and that for a distant land: that for the gentle past, in other words, and that for the exciting future. But how, he wondered, form out of these two a single desire? So that little by little the past might assume lucidity, the present grow meaningful and stirring, the future fall into place, and time lie so controlled by the spirit that neither past, present nor future should ever grow totally possessive, and that instead they might become harmonious, single, substantial, mature.

34

A Spring Journey

THEY WASHED THEIR FACES IN THE LAKE AND THEN were on their way again.

Soon they arrived at the tent which they had glimpsed half an hour earlier. An old woman, preposterously wrinkled, smiled at them with sparkling malicious eyes, and gave them some tea and bread. Two enormous young men were lying on the ground, wrapped in blankets, blinking lazily and sulkily.

The woman sat down and watched them. Suddenly Joachim discovered that her face had grown soft and tender, her gaze had become gentle, modest, rather shy. When they left she unexpectedly began to weep. It seemed mechanical, a ritual almost, a shudder rather than an emotion; she was growing too old, that was it, perhaps, and no one loved her.

Presently they reached the main road and joined a caravan of cattle and donkeys on its way to Urga.

☆

They crossed the great river in the late afternoon. The March floods were descending, the ice had broken up: down they came, these great white ruins of winter, crashing, groaning, spouting. They waited for two hours before they dared make the crossing. Finally they poled their raft of blown-up sheepskins across; tied the sheep and goats together and sent them off—surprisingly agile these were, coöperating with an instinctive efficiency; cautiously led across the donkeys, clumsy and surly by contrast—one of them stumbled, fell, disappeared under the waves and was abandoned. Mud and stones rushed past them in the lap of the foaming exuberant water. Little whirlpools circled about them, surprising isles bobbed up into existence now and again, green and shimmering in the setting sun. Everything was jubilant, full of triumphant noises, everything sparkled, sprays glittered in the red light, the shore was lined with the season's detritus—twigs, roots, whole shrubs and saplings, needles, leaves, rocks, limp furry shapes even, and feathery ones too: until perhaps a whole promontory suddenly crumbled and dissolved as it was whisked away by the emphatic torrents.

The other shore seemed already to have subsided into the new season. Carpets of flowers were strewn across the slopes—primulas, gentians, ranunculus, and the innumerable tiny yellows and whites. The exhausted men and animals lay shivering down to rest in the last rays of sunlight. A rabbit skipped past, two magpies began chattering. A marmot lay basking in his golden fur beside his burrow on a mound near by. Everything shone, the pebbles, the clusters of green, the raw gravel, and even that multitude of sounds and scents, wet and green, which sprang out of water, earth and air, unfurled themselves on the breeze, conjured forth into every vein a love for living.

One of the boys began to sing. It was clearly a song about the recovery of the earth from winter. About the saucy chattering of the birds, so Joachim imagined, about the new springs bursting forth in the heart of a tree, the new blood moving in its new veins; the rabbits born in their caverns, mute and pale-eyed, nuzzling amid the warmth of fur; the new leaves, sticky and shining, and the new flowers, gentle and velvety, covered with a down incomparably delicate, white as the snow near by or blue as the sky which too seemed fragrant and familiar; and then the birds again, the warm birds fluttering, stretching their light, miraculous, careless feathers, whistling, quarreling, dodging and darting about, then suddenly soaring up and away into the endless heaven.

Sunset was weaving like an old woman her fine eastern shadows into the hillside—dourly and inexorably, however feathery these graceful pencilings may have been; and soon it was dark and cold again. Here and there a birch trunk gleamed through the shadows of the opposite, the western, shore. In the glitter of the drops which circled through the air wherever the torrent curved and recoiled, the tints of sunset still trembled briefly.

*

They were approaching holy Urga. This was the grassy country, the land of emerald slopes and feminine hills. Far off they could still see, for a day or two, the snowy peaks and forests where the wolves roamed and the two great rivers were born; but then no longer.

They passed little temples, many little mud huts and felt tents, and met caravans going toward Irkutsk—long-horned oxen and Mongol drivers with faces quite startlingly innocent and obvious, eyes which, from scanning enormous distances day after day, had something of the purity and wildness of childhood, when similarly the eyes are still adjusted to certain infinitudes of space. It was never a "pure life" which created this purity of gaze, so Hugo observed, but rather freedom and fearlessness; which indeed among these happy children were not infre-quently accompanied by practices which in the cities of another land might well have been called vicious and corrupt.

They passed some camel-carriages, whose occupants wore hats which resembled little temples; and two or three motor-trucks too, as they drew near to Urga, and great numbers of donkeys.

☆

They arrived in Urga at twilight—the hour of mutila-tions and of memories. Animals were being slaughtered in the yards, the men were disputing in the square, the lamas in red and yellow, wearing their pointed head-dresses, were turning their prayer-mills in the filthy market-place. Some of the women, wearing their hair in the shape of a cow's horns, appeared to be perfunctorily cleaning the hovels and tents. Scavenger dogs were prowling about in the alleys. This must be the filthiest, ugliest, most desolate city in the world, thought Joachim.

But then came night. He left Hugo and walked alone toward the great palace beyond which rose the forest and the mountain, and toward the Cloister of God. He passed the weary pilgrims with their sacred books, some crawling along, some lying in trances; and the restless young men—the Khalkha Mongols in their purple cloaks and peaked hats, the Chakhar Mongols in their yellow cloaks and round hats, the Torgots in their green coats and sandals, the Soyots in their beautiful silks and furs. They looked contemptuous and hateful, every last one of these spoiled and indolent young ones.

In one tent, visible by lamplight, sat the fat musicians; in another the wicked dancers with their masks and head-dresses; in another two scrawny scholars amid their in-numerable manuscripts; in another the cavalrymen dressed in khaki, smelling of dung; in another a group of adventurers from central Europe, crouching over their maps like ravens; in another certain women, lying quietly, freed forever from the rejoinders of the soul, smelling of southern forests, their finger nails painted gold; in another some lamas, with their bells and silken things and prayer manuals and bowls of incense. Some of the lamas were sounding the conches for evening prayer; others were pray-ing; others were talking—gossiping perhaps about the usual rumors of a new Incarnate Lama.

In the cemetery of Mai-ma-ch'eng, the wooden coffins of the unburied poor stood in rows. Here the dogs were wandering to and fro, snatching and tearing at those cas-

kets where the wood had begun to rot, then disappearing
among the trees whose tiny leaves were now beginning to
burst into a nightly glory. The clouds, black plumes of
warriors edged with fire, moved inexorably across the
minute conflagrations of the sky. This was Tartary, the
prehistoric center of the world, from which the vast migrations, conquests, hot disorders once took their power, and
would, so chanted the prophets, soon take it again. Everything was still, the night was tranquil and meditative, like
a poet considering his lines; and then, a moment later, it
was far more than still, for the moonlight seemed to have
frozen each leaf, each ominous shape, into absolute im-
mobility, and the holy city was immersed in a cataleptic
trance: time now appeared to have been no more than
that breeze which a moment ago still lingered in the budding twigs, and the vastness of space too had vanished into
shadow when the moonlight emerged and the stars shone
like flowers on an adjoining hill.

✱

From Urga they proceeded rapidly northward into
Siberia. The route southward to Kalgan, through the real
Gobi, they heard, was still too dangerous.

They were very lucky to reach Verkhne Udinsk. The
men at the frontier were soothed with a small bribe, the
officials outside the city of Verkhne Udinsk were lazy and,
after hastily glancing at a few ambiguous documents, let
them pass. In Verkhne Udinsk they took the train. It was
expensive, but Hugo still had a number of Mexican dollars

left. They rode into Manchuria, down to Harbin, and from Harbin finally to Tientsin.

In Tientsin they visited the German consul, and two days later, with renewed funds, took a boat to Shanghai. From there, Hugo explained, he would sail to Hongkong and then back home. "Back home," he muttered. His eyes glistened, his haggard face shone. He could hardly sit still, he could hardly keep his hands from trembling.

But Joachim knew that he himself would stay. The thought of Shanghai filled him with excitement.

✶

Now and then he would glance at Hugo, as they approached Shanghai.

There was, even now, an extraordinary power about Hugo's narrow face; or rather, not precisely power, rather a sort of pure, masculine dignity, a resoluteness, a metallic precision.

And a kind of devotion too, a really curious selflessness. He had changed during these months, changed utterly. Joachim felt sure that Hugo would give up his life without any hesitation, without any expectation of reward or any twinge of bitterness; give it up for his ideal, that is, the ideal of loyalty of spirit, of endurance, of discipline. He had, in a curious way, while hammering himself into power, lost his individuality.

Joachim suddenly realized, as the waters of the Yellow Sea moved past him, how close to him Hugo had grown to be. And then he looked at him again. His lips were

[319]

white, and the pupils in his gray eyes had grown extraordinarily small and piercing.

A secret power was waiting behind those eyes, those lips, still struggling against death. And at the same time, drawing him more and more magnetically toward the single desire, the single ideal, that lay behind his every feeling and thought: death.

BOOK SIX

Olivia

35

Dinner with Dr. Liu

SOME THREE WEEKS AFTER THEY HAD LEFT LAYEVILLE, Dr. Liu's caravan arrived at Lan-chow-fu on the Hwang-Ho. Here Madame de la Scaze suggested that she leave him and take a boat down the river, or perhaps a motor-lorry, and so proceed toward Shanghai.

But Dr. Liu wouldn't hear of it.

"Unsafe," he murmured, "impractical and unsafe. Come to Lu-chow with me, and there you can take a boat down the Yang-tze."

And so, three days later, after they had rested, and leaving the caravan behind after making arrangements to have the cases shipped on later, they proceeded southward toward Dr. Liu's destination.

For days they bumped along the road, Dr. Liu in one *tzao*, Olivia in another, swaying lightly to and fro on the coolies' shoulders. They moved in long, regular strides. Squat, smiling men, they were, with wet blue rags on their heads, which they would besprinkle with water whenever they passed a spring or a stream. They were experiencing the last spell of autumn heat. Now and then they stopped and rested for a moment in the shade of a mulberry tree, and wiped the sweat from their bodies. Or they would pause beside a brook, lie on their bellies, and drink the red cool water from Tibet. Their bodies were thick and corrugated with muscles. All brown, quite hairless, and shimmering like satin.

They crossed over rivers and hills, followed the valleys, passed two or three monasteries whose gongs they could hear echoing across the golden valleys. It was still warm. Only a piece of ragged burlap shaded her from the sun.

Presently Olivia began to feel ill. Perhaps it was the bad food, perhaps the monotonous swaying of the *tzao* on the coolies' shoulders, perhaps the heat. She felt feverish. Her head was aching constantly, her body felt very limp and weary. She began to bleed a bit, now and then, at unexpected intervals.

However, they finally arrived at Lu-chow. Lu-chow was Dr. Liu's home. He only went to Shanghai, he explained, for two or three months a year. He had a house there too, but this one, the *kon-kuan* in Lu-chow, was his real home.

Olivia went to bed as soon as they arrived at his *kon-kuan*, buried in greenery on the outskirts of the city, overlooking the Yang-tze in the distance.

After a fortnight she recovered. But it was growing colder now, and Dr. Liu explained to her that she must spend the cool days in Lu-chow. He was very persuasive. It would be dangerous for various reasons to proceed to Shanghai at this time. Above all, she was still very weak, he observed with a smile.

So she stayed. She felt uneasy, and what Dr. Liu said, and the way he said it, made her feel still more uneasy.

But there was only one thing to do. So she stayed.

☆

She would sit in her room and watch the sunlight in the garden. Long ribbons of light went sliding across the shrubs as the hours passed. Fragments of snow appeared there from time to time, and icicles. Then everything would glitter. So lovely it was, at these times, that as she sat by her window this flashing and sparkling of sunlight on the snow and ice would seem to create an actual melody, a high quivering tone, so to speak, and yet serene, elusive, as if a samisen or a flute were being played out there in the little garden pavilion.

Every morning Wu, the servant, came in with the brazier and placed it beside her. A warm orange circle lay coiled and shimmering around it on the matting. He stood for a moment, hands piously folded in front of his belly, smiling expectantly. Then he slipped out again.

☆

Dr. Liu would appear occasionally and chat with her.

They would talk about various things; about politics, the changing ways of the world, of men, of women.

"Always, Madame de la Scaze, one must remember," he would observe demurely, from time to time, with a sad smile of resignation, "that some women are made for child-bearing, others for bodily delight. None for both."

"And so I have a wife," he would add, amiably, "and three concubines. My wife is tender and submissive. My first concubine is gay, full of pretty laughters, and mischievous glances. My second concubine is very adroit in the ceremonies of love. My third concubine is devout and refined, skilled in the most engaging gestures and praises. That is all precisely as it should be, my gentle lady. . . . At other times, when I am in Shanghai, for example, I go into the city," he added airily; "that, of course, is more expensive. The young actors, for example. Very expensive, but it adds variety."

His wife was a plump and drowsy lady who rustled along the corridors now and then in heavy silks, her delicate wrists loaded with whimsical ornaments, tiny dragons and lions suspended by silken threads. Olivia saw her only rarely.

The concubines she never saw at all except once, later on, from a window, while they were gathering early plum blossoms in the walled garden. Thoroughly genteel they were, as far as she could see, sorrowful exquisite little ghosts which drifted aimlessly to and fro across this secluded landscape.

☆

Little by little Olivia recovered. She still felt weak, but the fevers left her, and the headaches.

She was now wearing some Chinese clothes, which Dr. Liu had lent her—pale silken pantaloons, a jacket of blue silk, slippers embroidered with apricot blossoms, a little tortoise-shell comb.

Weeks passed, and then months. The winter trailed away, April arrived, and then May. She began to feel at home almost. It was all very quiet. Now and then she would wonder about getting to Shanghai, but Dr. Liu always gently reassured her.

It was a rather old house, and was slowly disintegrating. A smell of decaying wood and decaying silk and decaying straw filled the rooms. The stairs groaned as she stepped on them. Moths fluttered out of the crevices in the floor and the walls. The eaves and the worm-eaten shingles whined and whispered all night long.

From her window, every night, she could see the incense candles glowing in the little *litang*, the prayer-room, and then in the morning she watched the gardener bringing fresh spring flowers for the vases. He filled the stone basin in the courtyard with clear rain water, and she could see the silver fish and gold fish darting to and fro in the morning sun.

In the distance she could see the orchards and the fields. The mulberry trees, and the peach and apricot trees too, were blossoming. Little girls, dressed in blue (since it was spring again) hopped about under the trees, giggling and whispering. Old men would bring out their flutes and play wispy, mouse-like songs. In the fields the boys would fly their kites, and the plowman with his cows would slowly cross the glimmering rice-fields. And in the distance, the

[327]

shepherd and his slender sheep, so tiny that she could scarcely see them, would climb the sunny hill.

Once or twice she grew really worried. Worried, of course, about her husband, and her friends far away, and her family, and the future in general. And worried about something else too. About Dr. Liu. She didn't quite trust him. He evaded her questions, and told her lies. She had grown to be a little bit afraid of him.

✩

One day, perhaps it was his birthday, a particularly festive dinner was served. Silver flagons filled with heated Chinese wine, rose-scented, appeared on the table. His wife appeared too, dressed very stylishly, in a sheathlike robe of silver lamé. But she didn't say a word all evening.

Fried duck-giblets were served first, and ducks' eggs, green from having been buried so long. The yolks were like a liver *pâté*. Then a soup, with little cubes of melon, slices of water chestnut, bamboo shoots, bits of lobster, mushrooms. Then slices of some sort of large clam, and rice, and a mulled wine. Then squab, chopped fine, and then pork, and then chicken, and then duck, with all sorts of vegetables—cabbage, lettuce, mushrooms. And then an almond broth.

"Come," he said, after dinner was over, and led her into the next room. An elaborate object was standing on a low lacquer table at the end of the room. It was a little pavilion set in a garden, done out of gold and ivory: ivory ducks floating on golden waves, ivory flowers, golden leaves, golden dragons coiled along the ivory eaves.

"Such artifice," he murmured, "such unreality! Ah, I should like to change into something out of beaten gold, or watered silk, or graven jewels, or porcelain, when I die! All things that are truly beautiful, truly serene, are created! Serene and beautiful because nothing can alter them. That is true beauty. The tranquil, the everlasting. 'The tranquillity of the heart is the very crown of creation,' said the great Lao-Tse.

"We all," he continued, his keen eyes peering at her from under their purple crêpe-like lids, "we all live in little pavilions. Even you in the west, Madame de la Scaze, live in little pavilions. We need protection. The sun and rain of our existence are too severe. And each one builds his little pavilion. With some it is devoutness, with others, learning, and with the great few, poetry. And in that way, little by little, we perfect ourselves. That also the great Lao-Tse explained. Give up desire, perfect yourself! True learning, true poetry, those are the things that matter. Events themselves do not matter. They are quickly forgotten, never worth remembering, perhaps. Events alone do not teach us. It is not history that survives, but legend. What does our past matter, except as it has fashioned our spirit? It is legend which is the history of the spirit. What signifies is not a great battle or the death of an emperor or the fall of a city a thousand years ago, but the poetry and wisdom which men have created from these, and which blossom in our minds forever, and move us to serene reflections."

She gazed through the window and saw a coolie hurrying across the courtyard with a lantern. The eaves, the twigs of the nutmeg tree, the stone basin, his cheeks, all caught the glimmer of the lantern. A sinuous golden line flickered along their edge. Beyond the gray of the garden walls stretched the fields and hills of China, and the waters of the Yang-tze.

She glanced at Dr. Liu. He was watching her. Then he smiled. Suddenly she felt, somehow, as if she were waking up. A little bit dizzy.

"I think I shall leave for Shanghai next week," she said. She was surprised to hear her own voice, it was so faint, so empty.

He shook his head slowly. "No," he murmured, "I think that would be unwise. No, no, I think you should stay, Madame de la Scaze!"

Her heart began to beat violently. The look of those ancient eyes, those nervous reptilian eyelids, suddenly filled her with acute loathing.. Her brain went spinning around.

"I am afraid," she thought to herself, "I am afraid."

☆

Late that night she slipped out into the courtyard. All she carried with her was the little bit of money that she had left. Breathlessly she opened the gate from the court-yard into the vegetable garden. It creaked sharply on its rusty hinges. She glanced back. A light was moving in one of the windows.

Limber with fear, she fled through the vegetable garden and across the wet rice-fields. Her slippers kept clinging to the sucking mud. Quickly she slipped them off and ran barefoot, carrying them in her hand. The pebbles dug into her tender soles until she longed to lie down and cry.

Once she sank knee-deep in the slime. Her robe was heavy with moisture and mud.

In the bamboo grove beyond the field she rested for a moment. The *kon-kuan* looked very small and quiet and dark, half hidden by foliage. She could hear the frogs singing in the wet fields.

Then she saw a light appearing in another window. Sobbing with exhaustion, she ran on along the edge of the grove, down toward the road that led to the shore of the river.

Finally she reached a little grove of trees on the edge of the river. She lay down on the dry leaves and fell asleep.

☆

When she awoke it was growing light. Through the tree-trunks she saw the reddish waters of the Yang-tze flowing by.

She felt ill. Her arms were twitching with the cold. When she rose she found that her whole body was stiff and aching.

Her head dizzy and aching, she walked slowly through the trees and then down the road toward the place where the boats landed. An old man was squatting on the shore, smoking a pipe, eyes half closed.

She held out a coin to him and pointed down the river. He nodded and rose, without a word, and walked along the shore toward the town.

She turned and looked at the river. The water was red, streaked with yellow: red and foaming with the rain and gravel of Tibet. The shouting fishermen were gathering their fish-pots. The hills along the shore were covered with red and yellow blossoms.

Half an hour later the old man returned, and rowed her out in his *sampan* to the rather shabby but freshly varnished junk with patched sails which stood anchored some distance away from the shore.

"Shanghai?" she cried to the young pilot as he watched her approaching.

He nodded his head slowly and smiled. She noticed how handsome he was. His white teeth glistened, his eyes shone. He was shirtless, and his chest shone like ivory.

An hour later they started off, and the flower-covered slopes began to move past them slowly. Off they sailed, into the mottled provinces of China.

36

The River

ON AND ON, THROUGH THE TORTUOUS PROVINCES
they sailed.

As they moved eastward Olivia slowly began
to feel calm again. Her panic left her. Now and then she
felt a twinge of fear; it would occur to her that she was
being pursued. But then presently she would feel calm
again, and safe.

They passed pagodas, monasteries, porcelain towers that
crowned the hills along the shore. And pink-walled towns,
villages nestling in the coves, and great cliffs, and numberless groves between the hills.

Once they stopped beside a monastery. The monks,
shabby and gentle-eyed creatures, ran down the stone stair-

way and gathered along the shore. They looked very dirty, many of them were scarred with sickness. They hardly expected presents, for the junk was a small and modest one; but they were hoping against hope. The *laopan*, the captain, gave them some old newspapers and a tattered book.

"*Hsieh, hsieh!*" they cried, shrill with gratitude. "*I lu ping an!*" And so they wished them a peaceful journey.

☆

Olivia would watch the shore all day long. She would lie in the shade motionlessly, a pillow under her head, a coverlet across her body. She was really sick now. A racking chill would seize her periodically, and then a few minutes later she would lie flushed with fever. But as the days passed, she grew better again, and she could eat more.

She would see at twilight the women beating their blue linen on the shore, the soap glittering in their wet wrinkled hands as it caught the dying sunlight. The bamboo groves would glow as if they were on fire. And then, as night approached, they would melt away, hazy and feathery, until once more, as the moon appeared, they grew distinct and their leaves shone like silver knives.

The men would fish at night. The little corks bobbed about, circles of silver spread outward gently, until the cork suddenly disappeared and a moment later the fish would come flashing up into the air, caught on the end of the line, leaving an arc of silver drops behind him, and then, still swishing about madly with his tail, vanish again in the darkness of the boat.

And then morning would come again, with the bluish smoke arising from the fishermen's huts, and the mist fading away in the glens and greenish valleys and under the dark cliffs. Loud and foaming water, cool hills, fleecy snow-white clouds, all would grow clear and bright.

Each day was a little warmer than the one before. The hot sun flowed down upon the boat at noon, and the oarsmen stripped and sprinkled water all over their bodies. When the breeze fell and the current grew less swift, they would pull at their heavy galley oars once more, and the sweat would start dripping from their arms and their thighs.

On the boat, in addition to the coolies, there were the *laopan*, the captain, with his dark wrinkled face and bald brown head; and the handsome young pilot, whose name was Ling; and a very old, very fat, very sleepy moon-faced silk merchant; and a young Chinese woman.

Ling, the young pilot, was the only one she could speak to. He spoke French, rather haltingly. Very handsome indeed, he was. He slipped off his sky-blue jacket when it grew hot, and stood there, in his canvas trousers and white slippers, his huge metallic chest shining in the sunlight. His face was dark brown, but the rest of his body was clear and hard as ivory. He would sing, as he stood there, in a low, gentle voice, eyes twinkling, turning his head now and again to catch Olivia's gaze. Then a smile would spread across his face, a mocking, sparkling smile.

He told her stories, in his odd halting French. One windless night some bats were fluttering about the mast. He came up and squatted beside her.

"Those," he whispered, "are the souls of the unhappy ones. Of those who have never been soothed by love, by marriage, by the gift of children. They are the malicious,

loveless spirits, and must be placated from time to
time. . . . You see," and he sprinkled some incense on the
deck, and lit it, and beside this placed an old silken slipper
and a paper flower and set fire to these: "You see, it is
they who bring disasters, floods, famines, plagues! Never
become one of them!" He turned and smiled at her. His
face was glowing in the flickering light of the momentary
flame.

Then the flame died, but he was still smiling at her, his
white teeth glistening through the darkness.

☆

In the morning Ling would sometimes bring her a bowl
of boiled vegetables and pickled radishes. He would sit
beside her and talk about the others on the boat.

"Those oarsmen," he would murmur, "they know nothing at all, nothing! All they possess is a big straw hat, and
some canvas breeches, and a tattered jacket, and some
shabby slippers, and a little sacred thing, perhaps, a carved
animal of some kind, which they can fondle and love.
That is all. And yet," and he would nod his head gently,
"it is they who will soon be ruling China!" Ling's voice
was low and fluid. It was very pleasant listening to him.

He also told her about the young woman. Now and then
she would appear on deck, dressed in her blue trousers,
and her blouse buttoned on one side, embroidered with
waves and flying birds. Extraordinarily lovely she was,
thought Olivia; even lovelier than Dr. Liu's three concubines. Her hair fell in silky bangs over her forehead, and
in the back she wore a comb of tortoise shell. She never

spoke. There was no expression in her features at all. Yet there was something profoundly touching in that modest, exquisite face. So harmonious, so pure.

"Her name is Tu Tiu-en," he explained. "I have heard all about her. Our *laopan*, Sung Tsi Wu, bought her in Canton when she was eleven years old. I know the whole story. . . . At first his *tai-tai*, his wife, hated little Tu Tiu-en. She beat her, spat on her, made her do all the work in the house. She washed and ironed the linen, and later she learned to read and write. Very intelligent, little Tu Tiu-en was.

"After a few years at Sung Tsi Wu's house, she grew stage-struck. She wanted to go into the theater, or perhaps become a glamorous dancing girl in a Shanghai cabaret. She grew restless. Then, one day, she fell in love with our *laopan*.

"But our *laopan* had bought a slave-boy in the meantime, a very handsome boy, and this one was now his favorite. He cared nothing for Tu Tiu-en. She had to dress in simple linens, and all the while the new slave-boy was dressed in silks and jewels, until he finally grew discontented one day and ran away to Hong Kong.

"And she is still in love with our bald *laopan*. But he does not love her. Wherever he goes, she goes too. But he does not love her any more.

"That is how the world is," he said quietly, grinning at her, his white teeth shining in the sun. "That is how love is. It is never quite right. And even when it starts off in the right way, it never stays right."

"Did she tell you all this?" asked Olivia, after a minute's silence.

"No, she speaks a different dialect," murmured Ling,

[337]

"she speaks Cantonese, and I do not speak Cantonese very well. . . . I have heard it all from our *laopan*."

☆

He also told her about the moon-faced merchant. "He speaks the Szechuan dialect," he explained. "He is very sick. He is going to Shanghai to die."

"To die?"

"Yes. He is going to die very soon."

Olivia glanced at the old man. He was preparing his opium pipe. He drew a drop out of a jar with a needle, heated it at a lamp until it was bubbling, then rolled it into a ball and placed it in the bowl of his pipe. Then he lit it. His pockmarked face grew flushed, his mouth opened, his eyes closed. His head looked like a huge, decaying tangerine.

☆

There were still times when Olivia suddenly grew faint, and the landscape danced eerily before her eyes. Then she would lie down in the shade and try to go to sleep.

But she knew that it was more serious than that. All sorts of thoughts crossed her mind, all sorts of suspicions and anxieties.

The food, for one thing. The food was really very bad. Rice, boiled green cabbage, cottage cheese, a bit of salted fish now and then. It was set before her in a white bowl, and then she was given a pair of chopsticks. The food that the others ate was even simpler. But in any case, it soon grew so that she could scarcely bear to look at it; each mouthful was a tribulation; so that she ate less and less.

And the filth. A heavy stench of varnish and tar and stale fish was forever lurking about. The coolies had been fairly tidy at first, but for some reason or other, the growing heat perhaps, they were growing very slovenly. The garbage lay about on the deck, flies would accumulate, the smell of decaying food joined the other smells of the boat. The coolies would spit anywhere at all, and some of them were none too particular about where they made water; others neglected to wash, and the acrid scent of their bodies grew daily more trying.

And the river. Everything imaginable was to be found in the river. Bits of charred wood, dead animals, old rags, offal, leaves, flowers, old discolored newspapers, discarded old books, tattered hats and slippers, torn paper fans, bits of bamboo, poems printed on colored paper, sheets of propaganda. All of these, and innumerably more, were to be found bobbing about in the capricious red currents of the Yang-tze.

And the heat. Each day was a little hotter than the one before. Spring was really turning into summer before her eyes. Every day toward noon the sun would begin to penetrate everything—the landscape, the boat, even the water. Little electrical highlights glittered on the varnish, on the oars, on the mast. The shore lay bathed in a stagnant golden haze. And in the salmon-colored ripples incessant spirals and zigzags of light went flickering across the waves. Olivia would find her eyes aching intolerably, and even when she closed her eyes the blinding light seemed to furrow its way between the lashes and through the lids.

And then, something else too. The anxiety, the queer frightened suspense which she had felt during those last few days in Dr. Liu's *kon-kuan* had not quite left her. A certain distrust and bewilderment still found its way into everything she thought, everything she felt. Toward the bald, ascetic *laopan* particularly. And even toward Ling. It was not impossible, it occurred to her crazily, that they were all in collusion with Dr. Liu; perhaps Dr. Liu was pursuing her; perhaps he was already in Shanghai, waiting for her; perhaps the *laopan* would hold her captive. There was something odd, something watchful and ironical, in their attitude.

But above all, something was happening inside her. Something was slowly flowing out of her, hour by hour. She was growing limp. The water was carrying her along, further and further eastward. Nothing mattered, after all. The days and nights were smooth as glass, still as sleep. Now and then she would hear the sound of whispering, but that was all.

☆

One morning Ling came up to her in great excitement. "Tu Tiu-en has left us," he said, in a rather sad tone.

Olivia asked what he meant.

"She has left us. She has slipped away into another shape. . . ." He explained that she had leapt overboard in the middle of the night, in a moment of quiet despair. It was too late now to look for her body. It would sink, he reflected, to the bottom of the river. And then, in a day or two, it would rise again. Passers-by from the villages of Szechuan would see it, and would wonder who she was.

37

The Black Cities

ONE BY ONE THEY SAILED PAST THE CITIES OF Szechuan.

The river was growing more populous, Olivia observed. Fishermen and beggars would stand in throngs along the shore, and the coves would be full of little children playing about in the mud and gathering clams. The thatched huts grew more numerous along the shore, there was a temple or a monastery or a ruined fort on almost every hill. Sampans dotted the water, which was darker and filthier here than further up. Steamers passed them— American steamers, French steamers, English steamers. They would hear the shrill music of cheap bands as they slid by, and hear, perhaps, the rattling noise of the *mah jong* players. At night they would see little lights flickering all along the shore, like glowworms, each one duplicated as a tremulous arrow in the black water. Now and then the flash of fireworks would spring in a great arc across the sky, and as it fell would rejoin its ascending reflection in the river and so complete its fiery circle.

☆

Twice they stopped: at Chungking and at Wanhsien.

They approached Chungking at twilight. Three whole hills were covered with its black, insect-like dwellings. They landed, and Olivia was carried up the interminable stairway in a wooden box by two coolies.

This was the real Chinese antiquity. They might have been entering a city of a thousand years ago. Except that at the very moment they entered the city, two airplanes passed overhead. They looked unbelievable. It seemed to Olivia, for a moment, that they must be enormous birds of prey, swooping down on them out of a legendary past.

There was an atmosphere of incessant agitation in Chungking. And yet, at the same time, an atmosphere of timelessness, of utter stagnation. Everything was quivering with a furtive, desperate vitality: and yet, at the same time, the black ages, the lost centuries, the ages of violence, of pestilence, of sieges and superstitions, still lurked in these streets, in every alleyway, in every doorway, in every face. Everything had changed, and yet nothing had changed. Everywhere the men were still building up their hazardous, pathetic refuges against life, and everywhere they were still tearing them down, opening themselves up to novel encroachments. One thing, of course, was constant:

[342]

the unalleviable suffering of the poor, and their incredible power to endure this purposeless, endless, rewardless, beautiless, mindless suffering. Slim boys were fanning the stranger in their palanquins. Tiny, flower-faced children were carrying their buckets of filth along the sewer streets out to the fields. The sun had set. Lanterns were being lit, one by one. New shadows crept across the streets. New faces were caressed into being by the gleam of each freshly lit lamp. Now Olivia could gaze into the shops. By the dim bluish flicker of a kerosene lamp each shopkeeper sat crouched beside his wares: fish, spices, curious sea foods, great polyp-like vegetables, dried and salted objects, innumerable tins and bottles, chinaware, bowls, vases, incense-pots, lacquer boxes, and all the rest, all of them visible in the dim bluish haze of the oil-flame. More and more people filled the streets. Thousands and thousands, it seemed to Olivia. Fat merchants with the sweat rolling down from their eyelids, wicked, oily-faced bonzes, cancerous, hunchbacked old hags, impudent, imbecilic soldiers, one-eyed beggars, raddled with disease, young beauties already fatally tainted, harlots clad in silver lamé, their faces white with powder, their eyes black as pitch.

The next morning they loaded up with the product of the great flourishing poppy-fields that stretched beyond the city—opium, to be smuggled down to Shanghai.

Then they sailed away toward Wanhsien.

*

Wanhsien was similar to Chungking, but more impressive. High up, set upon the rocky slab of a mountain-top

[343]

like a vast castle, looming darkly over the river. Great hornèd towers rose from the thick of the city. Here too the coolies carried their palanquins up and down a steep stairway, up and down, year after year, up and down until they died. Fragile, these coolies looked. But all of them, even the old gray-haired ones, had muscles hard as stones and eyes hard as beads.

Olivia was carried past an enormous cemetery, and past a field from which the stench of human excrement rose like a fury. The streets too were fœtid. The doorways were covered with a black sheen, as if thousands of hands had brushed against them in the course of countless years. Here, in the whispering dusk of the streets, sat a girl as lovely as a flower, and here a creature hideous as a dragon. Time, time: the years, the years: where were they? They no longer existed! Or rather, they were all here, topsy-turvy, inextricably intermingled, overlapping and inter-twined, the past a thing full of threats, the present already a legend, the future fading into the mists of prehistory. There was a scent of incense, a sacred kind of fragrance, and the scent of sickness too, and the scent of violence. Hunger and love walked past her, arm in arm, and all the thousand sins.

There were the old women. Most of these were starving, very quietly, very gradually. Their dreams had come true at last. They were little girls once more! Their limbs had shrunk, their breasts had shriveled. Twisted, imbecilic little girls, their fleshless arms moving in a strange dis-cordant manner, like the arms of marionettes. Some dragged themselves along, spasm by spasm, as if they were mortally wounded. Their voices were bleak, hysterical, quite empty. Courtesans or virgins, it didn't matter now. They were all the same. Except perhaps for the very faintest glimmer of recognition in their eyes. Perhaps, after all, they still hoarded, like misers, certain clandestine pleasures at night, destined for their own eyes only!

And the blind, the numberless blind. A film, a pink haze, had crept across their eyes, and had turned them into sleep-walkers. This was the real depravity, thought Olivia suddenly; this darkness, this everlasting and inevitable resort to a land of private visions; for it is from watching that all truth must spring, just as all falsehood springs from listening; only what is seen, is pure; what is heard from the lips of others is tainted. And it showed, this vice of listening. They were forever treading delicately through blackness, with bizarre gestures, longing forever for certain pleasures, the lucid pleasures of the eye, the delight of seeing what is heard and touched. This longing was reflected in their groping mouths, their imploring hands.

The slim, elusive, light-footed adolescents hurried by like gazelles. Their eyes were eager and wide open, but they stared in wonder, not in self-regard or desire. Their gaze was therefore a lovely thing, still fresh as the gaze of an animal. Their cheeks were still smooth and fresh as apricots, their skin was still warm with the day's sunlight. But they were terribly thin. They were beginning to starve. They were about to learn what life was, their spirits were about to be whipped and hammered and frozen and drugged into submission.

The whores swayed past with heavy eyelids. They all looked the same; graceful and slender, a comb stuck in their black silky hair, their feet encased in tiny embroidered slippers, their bodies sheathed in pale silk. They were trying desperately to disguise themselves, that was it. Cheap ornaments dangled from their ears and wrists. Each of them wore a paper flower. Stupid, unutterably stupid.

They lived in a world of touching, nothing but touching: until their finger tips, their lips, every soft convexity and concavity of their body, all became alive in their own way: those were their eyes, their ears. With them they groped their way past reality. Nothing else was left of them. Nothing left in the heart, nothing in the mind. The only things that mattered, aside from the flesh, were their senseless little toys—bits of silk, bits of leather, semi-precious stones, bracelets, bottles, paper flowers, whips, cigarettes, opium.

They were the ones Olivia watched most closely. They looked so quiet, so far away, even while their bodies went gliding past like panthers. Their eyes glimmered cold and hard as jet. She could not take her eyes off them. She longed to run up and touch them, almost to be one of them. Something, not in their bodies, but in their eyes, attracted her like a magnet.

*

Now came the great gorges of the Yang-tze. The river was only three hundred yards from shore to shore here, and the water had turned into a deep red. Great bronze-colored walls, ageless and majestic, rose from the swift, foaming water. The surface of these towering rocks was dented by quarries—so high, so far away that they were almost invisible, and the sound of the mighty hammers was only the tiniest vibration, the sound of a humming-bird's wing.

The junks which were headed upstream were being towed past the most difficult stretches: oars and sails were

not enough for these swift currents. The towing-paths
followed the river like little threads spun into the immensity of the cliffs. Dozens and dozens of coolies, stripped
down to their loin cloths, were tugging at the ropes. They
wallowed in the ooze, they clutched at the ledges, heads
hanging, muscles bulging, faces distorted and snarling.
They grunted and chanted in unison. *"Hai! hai! ho! ho!"*
they sang, dragging their feet across the rocks and the
gravel.

For days Olivia remembered these haulers—their faces,
their bodies, their endless chant. She would close her eyes
and imagine herself in their midst. She felt the rope
against her body, the gravel under her feet, the cliffs
towering above her, and the sweat upon her throbbing
temples.

Her fever was growing worse, she realized.

38

Ling

LING WOULD SIT DOWN BESIDE HER, AS THEY DRIFTED past the towering cliffs of the Yang-tze, and tell Olivia about the sorrows of China: the convulsions of war, the plagues, the famines, the floods.

"The soldiers swept over the countryside," he exclaimed when he told her about the Taiping rebellion, and the Pekin-Nanking disturbances, "crushing the budding harvests! Their eyes were burning, like the eyes of tigers. They would tie their enemies on the stakes with their entrails hanging and their bones broken. They would hang their heads from the walls. . . .

"Oh, the plagues," he would murmur in a tone of awe; "they descended from heaven, they swept from city to city like an army. Much worse than an army of soldiers! But the disorders from heaven are caused by the disorders of man."

Then he told her of the great Hopei flood. "The foaming yellow water swept across the country, mile after mile. Towns were carried away, big waterfalls swept down the valleys. Herds of horses would swim down the torrents, through the rains and fogs. In the open fields the water lay like a pink sea, a bitter-smelling sea. Here and there a tree or a temple would rise out of the water. Thousands and thousands of corpses floated across the rice-fields. The junks went sailing where towns had stood before. Those who survived sailed about sorrowfully for many days in their sampans, or on old trunks, fragments of shattered walls, broken doors. They flocked to the hills and the cities, and became beggars. There they would live for weeks on rice and bran, hundreds would sleep in the railway stations of the towns, wearing only their cotton trousers and straw hats. Women saw their babies hanging from the limbs of trees, children watched the swollen pink bodies of their mothers floating eastward.

"And thus," he explained, "the great famines were created. Like the great famine of Shansi. The crops were ruined. Only an endless bog stretched where the fields had been. The people fell down in the streets, weak with hunger. The beggars scratched among the offal, children were devoured by their parents, rats were roasted. . . ."

"Terrible!" sighed Olivia.

"Ah yes," he observed softly, "but it must be so. There are too many people in the world. . . . And, if there were no disasters, then we would lose our humility! We would forget the meaning of privation and of death, we would not understand what life really is, we would grow fat and blind, we would turn into fools. . . ."

[349]

Then he told her of his great love for China. His black
eyes would sparkle. Enormous China, bounded on one side
by the Siberian woods, and on another by the endless
desert, and on another by the simmering tangles of Indo-
China, and on another by the curved Pacific. Great rivers
flowed down from the roof of the world and ran through
her fertile fields, and past her mountains and her demon-
haunted groves. In these limitless sceneries lived the helpless multitudes. Their only defense against the natural
elements was a brief and fragmentary ritual: a ritual of
paper prayers, fire-crackers, flowers, bowls of rice, little
white pills, sticks of incense, cups of tea, the sound of
laughter, poems, porcelains, legends of another life, and,
of course, gunpowder. Those were their refuge!

"In this big country, you see," he murmured, "we are
afraid of the great unknown. For we live in an endless
land, among numberless people. What lies hiding in those
endless mountains? What, we ask ourselves, lies lurking
in those groves, beside those rivers? What lies hovering
over the countless years that have passed, the years to
come? What mystery?"

☆

The heat grew heavier daily. She grew really afraid,
now. She wondered how much longer she would be able
to bear it. The scenery danced before her aching eyes at
noonday, all aglimmer and ashimmer.

"How many days to Shanghai?" she asked Ling. But he
shrugged his shoulders. He didn't know.

[350]

Then, in the late afternoon, a certain relief would come. The shore grew still and green once more. Old women would come down to the water's edge with their laundry, the children would go bathing, their smooth, rosy bodies splashing about in the red waves. Petals of mist would appear in the groves and the vales.

Sampans passed by all day long, some large and some small. The naked oarsmen stood upright and moved to and fro, three men to a pole, chanting monotonously into the gathering shade. Temples went gliding past, and forts, and great rocky towers.

Then night flew down on them once more, with its glowing joss-sticks, its prayers, its songs, its whispers, its mosquitoes. Olivia woke up again and again, and opened her eyes on this delicate nocturnal world. She wondered what she would do in Shanghai. What lay in store for her there?

And then morning would arrive, and once more the sun would rise higher and higher, and set her temples throbbing.

☆

Ling asked her question after question. He would lean over her, in a sort of glowing, naïve suspense. His eyes would glisten. There was a gentle solicitude in his gaze, a softness; and yet, at the same time, a certain duplicity, a sly, covetous look.

"Your family. . . . Are they mandarins? . . . Are they all black-haired? . . . Are they all as beautiful as you?"

[351]

He would smile, his lips would part, she could see the arteries beating in his warm brown neck.

Or: "Where is Spain? Is it an island? Like Japan? . . . Oh, islands are wicked places! Nothing is real in an island, no one sees life clearly on any island!"

She would explain that Spain was a peninsula, but she had difficulty making him understand what a peninsula was. "Like Korea," she said. He nodded his head and grew thoughtful. He did not seem to know much about Korea, or to think very highly of it. Peninsulas, he seemed to think, were almost as bad as islands. Perhaps worse!

Presently he grew more intimate. "You are very wise, I think," he said pensively.

"No," she replied slowly. "I think not."

"Wise, and wicked. . . ."

She shook her head.

"Yes. . . ." he said, rather sulkily. And then, "Have you loved many men?" His eyes glittered insolently. "Perhaps! But I think not. . . ." He turned his back toward her and rose. His back sprang upward and outward from his slender waist like a fan. Every movement would set little muscles rippling under the silken skin. "Maybe," he murmured, "you will fall in love again, soon. . . ."

Then he told her about Shanghai. An incredible city, he said. People gathered there from all over the world, from every country. Even in the brothel quarter, he said, there were women from every land—Koreans, Japanese, Scandinavians, Mexicans, South Americans, Slavs, Hindus, Latins, everything. "The European ladies are in great demand. The brothel-keepers pay high prices for them."

"They buy them?" whispered Olivia faintly.

Ling nodded his head. "Yes. . . ." He kept gazing into her eyes. Soft, tender, that gaze was, and yet at this moment the faintest glimmer of uncertainty and conflict appeared there. A certain anxiety, a certain secret torment.

☆

That evening he sat down beside her. He placed a bowl of incense between them, to ward off the mosquitoes. Then he began to play on his bamboo flute. A thin yet fascinating little song. "About love," he explained.

"Love," he whispered presently. "Do you know what love is?" He paused. His voice was low and quiet. There was no breath of wind, no sound. "People are like spiders," he went on. "They weave little silken threads between themselves, to and fro, to and fro. Sometimes the threads assume one pattern, sometimes another. . . . But always, there is something the same in that pattern. Always."

"Yes?" Olivia felt excited, and almost happy.

"And that," he murmured, "is love. It is here," and his hand pointed across the boat, and then up toward the sky, and then across the river, and down toward the black water—"and here, and here, and here! Everywhere!"

He turned and gazed at her. Then he pointed toward his breast. "And here. . . ."

He rose. As he rose, he touched her cheek very lightly with his finger tips. It was electrical. She felt that light burning touch all night long.

☆

She felt very weary the next morning, and yet very nervous too, very excited.

The days seemed to be converging, more and more quickly, toward a point. Life was being accelerated, the scenery passed more and more quickly, more boats covered the river as they moved slowly toward Shanghai, more people lined the shores. There was a constant tingling in her body—no longer one of fear, precisely, nor of pain. Rather, a certain intermingling of expectation and resignation. The future lay eastward, at the mouth of the river, like a great flower. Already she could detect its dangerous, enervating fragrance.

On and on they drifted. They passed through Communist territory, and the thin, bald, wolf-eyed *laopan* looked nervous. But nothing happened. There were machine-guns standing on the hills, but they were never fired. Now and then they heard rumors of atrocities—especially at Ichang, the most troubled of all the cities. The longshoremen's union at Ichang demanded that all the cargo be unloaded and then reloaded. But nothing serious happened. The *laopan* paid a small sum, and that was all.

And yet, the feeling of danger remained. There was something inextinguishable and everlasting in even the most trivial detail—a glance, an arm pointing shoreward, a paper flower floating past them. Perhaps because they were all symbols of her flight. She was fleeing, fleeing: but where from? Where to? And the same thing was true of everything around her—the glance, the pointing arm, the paper flower. A flight. But where from? Where to? There was no answer. The water was glowing under the sun, people were moving their paper fans to and fro. Everything was very still.

She wanted to lean back and close her eyes. That was all. Simply to lean back, to close her eyes, to be carried along endlessly down the river.

39

The Shores of Spain

ENDLESSLY, ENDLESSLY DOWN THE RIVER THEY drifted, toward Shanghai.

Early one morning, as they drew close to the shore, Olivia was awakened by a shrill, flamboyant call: *Ki-keri-ki! Ki-keri-ki!* And, as she lay there, still half asleep, she was transported into a distant land; a sunlit peninsula bound to these passing landscapes by nothing at all, so it seemed, nothing at all but the eager and insolent call of the rooster. . . .

*

One dies a little every day, of course, thought Olivia. Even in childhood, perhaps then most of all. In the morning one is awakened by the chatter of sparrows or the cry of the cockerel, the sun falls through the vines across the bed, imprinting there the restless pattern of the leaves. Out-of-doors the tiles of the courtyard are still wet with dew, the yellow breakfast cups on the table gleam as if they were flowers freshly opened.

Early in the morning she would awaken, when she was a little child, and for several exquisite moments still watch the sunlight and listen to the birds.

A strange feeling would stir within her, both quiet and unquiet. The morning was so bright, so inviting, so profuse, the foliage all aglow, the curtains trembling in the Mediterranean breeze. It was, during these brief minutes, as if she were in a world of her own. She felt a warm fluttering in her heart.

She knew what it was. Happiness. She felt alone, utterly alone, the day had not yet begun, no one had spoken to her yet, no one had laid eyes on her, no one had touched her. Nothing could hurt her during this sacred, glowing interval, nothing at all.

Then softly old Antonia would open the door and call: *Olivia! Olivia!* And that was the signal for the beginning, the real beginning of the day. Antonia would rouse her out of bed, and wash her face, braid her hair.

After breakfast they would wander together into Torremolinos, she and waddling old Antonia, and there they would buy the day's groceries. Antonia would dawdle over the meats and vegetables, drawing out a cucumber here or a carrot there with her crinkled leathery fingers. And she herself would wander among the jars and the bottles. She would stare at the pickled peaches in their sauce, and the combs of honey, and the bluish, wrinkled prunes, and the crisp, yellow baskets full of nuts. Or she would lean over the melon-crates and inhale their sweet green fragrance. Perhaps, if it was a special occasion, Antonia would buy her a sweet, a bit of almond paste, perhaps, or a slice of sugared ginger; or a ribbon for her hair, or a cheap piece of jewelry—an earring or a bracelet, whose gaudy stones she would thereupon imagine to be turquoises, rubies, emeralds, opals. And then they would saunter homeward again, along the white, dusty olive- and almond-lined road. A black sow with hanging dugs might pass them there, or a goat, or a priest in his long black robe and flat black hat, or a peasant with his ox-cart. And the sunlight would go pirouetting across the beach and over the Andalusian fields and over the terraced vines on the treeless hillside.

She would sit on the beach in the afternoon, hour after hour. The waves would wander gently toward her, one and then another and then another, each one bearing on its crest a coronet of pearls. Sandpipers would go hopping across the sand where it was still left wet and shimmering by the retreating waves, and would leave their delicate clawprints on the dark sand until the next wave ascended and licked them away with its glassy tongue.

Now and then a fish would lie stranded on the shore among the seaweed, or a big sea shell, or an iridescent jellyfish, or a starfish. She would see them right away, the moment she appeared on the beach, for all morning she kept hoping that some new surprise might await her there. If it was a fish she would lean over it curiously, gaze into its unseeing eyes, touch lightly its shimmering armor. Or if a shell, then she would wash it clean in the water, and raise it to her ears: that was old Triton's horn that she heard, Antonia explained, being blown in the deep bottom of the sea. But who old Triton was she never discovered, nor did Antonia know; a fisherman, drowned many years ago, she suggested, or perhaps a great warrior, from the time of the Moors.

Then she would wonder what the bottom of the sea looked like. As she listened to Antonia's old tales, she longed to be a mermaid, she loved the water so much. She longed to swim forever among those sunny waves, and to dive again and again deep toward those blue and shadowy realms where the corals trembled in the currents like gigantic flowers.

She would sit in the sand, hour after hour. Antonia would sit near by in her big straw hat, knitting stockings or babbling with her friends. And as she listened to the voices and the steady click of the knitting-needles, and ran the beautiful dry sand through her fingers, a sweet, golden joy filled her heart. But then, as the minutes passed and the waves approached and retreated, again and again, another feeling followed this one; one of melancholy, and of fear. Something welled up from the dark, remembering realms of her little being, a feeling of eternal solitude, perhaps, but more than that; a feeling of approaching disorders, of excitements, of raptures; of change, in short. That she could not bear to face. That this sunny existence should ever change! And she would burst into tears, and when Antonia asked her why, she would not know. She would look around, glance at the palm of her hand, her feet. Perhaps a wasp had bitten her? No, no, it wasn't that. Then she would run off again, down toward the water.

She grew older. Life lost its simplicity, little cloudlets of bewilderment and longing threaded their way across the pure blue sky. She would lie in her bed at night and listen to the shrubs outside her window, eloquent with transitory voices of one kind and another; the little white roses, the two orange trees, the melon-beds, and the hydrangeas where every night the sphinx moths would gather, swift and vibrant as humming-birds.

And then the warm, sun-drenched days. She could remember a lonely spot among the rocks that gazed, so Antonia explained to her, far out toward Africa. From there she could see the sunburnt bodies dotting the beach, and the cedar trees, and the sparkling boats moving across the bay, and the ships, threading the horizon, sails white as pearls against a sky profoundly blue and cloudless. She would sit in the shade of an almond tree and watch the boys among the waves—those cruder and more slender shapes, with their hoarse voices and mocking expressions; and one of them, the rowdy son of a peasant, perhaps, might sit down beside her, whispering inquiries, challenges, pleas; and she would see his black laughing eyes staring into hers, and would feel the sly touch of his fingers upon her hair, experienced for the first time, with trembling and something of terror, a deep and thrilling premonition.

One April, when she was sixteen, her aunt from Barcelona took her to Mallorca. A governess, a thin lady in black, Señora Arquès, went along to teach her French and English, and perhaps a bit of water-color painting. She had learned much in the meantime, she had begun to understand the ways of men and women, and now on her first day in the streets of Palma, she felt herself possessed by a vague yet tremendous feeling of romance, of intrigue. Each well-built young man that passed betokened a potential adventure; each graceful gesture, each turn of the head or casual smile, as she walked along the sun-bespangled Rambla, seemed eloquent; as if to say, "There, perhaps, lies love!"

And so, accordingly, she fell in love. One day she saw a young fisherman repairing his nets down by the shore. Very serious, he was, never smiling. But when he noticed her, he grew very polite, and asked her something which she could not understand—the language he spoke was not Spanish, it sounded more like Señora Arquès's French to her. She fell to blushing and shaking her head. He gazed at her gently, with soft, melting eyes. Then he turned away and bent over the fish-nets again—small and slim as a girl, and, it seemed to her, celestially beautiful.

Every day she walked down to the shore, and presently she discovered where he lived, who his mother and sisters were, what he ate at noon, who were his friends, and she would glance through the window or the open door, seeing perhaps a dark shape in the shadow of the room or hearing laughing voices which filled her with jealous longing. The smell of boats, of fish and seaweed, and the breeze across the bay and the sound of waves—all these seemed a part of her longing, paraphernalia of love, so to speak. And even long afterwards, the sound of water and the scent of a boat would set her heart beating again with that same aimless tenderness.

Once she saw him coming up the narrow street from the shore, and she suddenly turned and began to walk back toward the plaza, so that for a moment she experienced the feeling that he was following her. And then, as she turned a second time and still saw him behind her, his eyes, indeed, fastened inscrutably on hers, so it seemed, she turned abruptly into an alley and stepped through an

[361]

empty doorway, waiting there in the alien darkness, half frightened, half fascinated. It was nightfall, and a lamp suddenly appeared in the window opposite. Some one began to sing. An old woman limped by, almost touching her and yet not seeing her. The scent of southern flowers, jasmine or oleander, suddenly brushed past her, like a beautiful woman on her way to some breathless *rendez-vous*. And she waited, until at last with bitter disappointment yet relief she hastened feverishly to the plaza, glancing from side to side in search of his blue trousers, his dark shirt, his graceful and ambiguous gait, his eyes which knew so much more than they would say; and then at last sank down in the shadow of the fountain and began to sob.

She fell in love once again, three years later, in Palma. A more complicated tale this time—a meeting in a café, a discussion of the plays of Calderon (his father was Spanish, his mother an Englishwoman living in Andraitx) followed by walks, assignations, and petty love-making. He was a small, conceited man; but very lively, very gay and persuasive. Until, one day, among some pines on the hill behind the Castle, she suddenly leaned her head back into the warm, odorous pine needles, closed her eyes and yielded herself.

The following October she heard, in Malaga, that he had married. But then when she returned to Palma seven months later, she saw him alone on the Rambla one evening, and when he asked her politely though casually to visit him the following afternoon at his villa, she consented. His wife, he explained, had gone to Madrid. And then, when he accompanied her back across the empty field at sunset the next day, after absent-minded conversations and a feeling on her part of surprising but sure indifference, he suddenly grasped her hand and held her in his arms. The old pastoral tenderness overcame her without warning, and even while she murmured to herself that she did not love him and had never loved him, she yielded as he drew her down into the tall wheat beside him and submitted again to the old caresses, the familiar and irresistible ritual.

About a month later she met the Frenchman de la Scaze at the Victoria, and, shortly thereafter, when she saw him again in Italy in July, she married him.

Everything seems—it occurred to her later—so natural, so logical, we explain things so neatly. "Oh yes," we say, "he and she couldn't get along for such and such a reason, he failed for this reason, she killed herself for that reason": but when one looks closely, all these reasons disappear, and only a hopelessly mysterious fact remains which defies all efforts at understanding. One might watch as in a dream, seeing the fanciful figures passing by, moved either to a feeling of charity or to one of bitterness by the momentary glimpses—glimpses, say, of a loathsome suffering, or an aged malevolence, or a destroying love. It is a subtle and seductive dance, if one is able to watch casually, full of half-formalized steps and unexpected postures; or, on the other hand, it may appear as a terrible, eternalized procession, if one gazes too closely and is moved too deeply. But if one tries to understand, to achieve lucidity, to discern a pattern and a purpose, one is lost!

She remembered one summer night on Lake Como, two or three days after they had been married. The boat lay motionless, he leaned cautiously over the edge and stared at the water, leaving the oars to creak aimlessly in their locks. The lights in the Villa d'Este were being extinguished one by one, a mist was creeping across the opposite shore. Another boat came up beside them, then passed and disappeared in the shadow of the hills—two naked peasant boys, singing and laughing. She could feel the vitality leaping out of their voices, the humor and delight sparkling in their dark backs and restless arms, the youthful power alert in their black hair and black eyes. Then she glanced again at de la Scaze, bewildered and curious. He had never loved her, she felt sure. He had, for all of that, never loved anyone passionately. And then she began to detest him, as he leaned over quietly and stared at the warm black mirror—him and his sensitive pedantic face, his ridiculous *pince-nez*, his delicacy of phrase, his languorous vanity.

Then she remembered him as she had last seen him: lying down on a brown cloak stretched upon the floor in the *serai* at Aqsu, his face shining with an ill-becoming sweat, his heavy eyelids closed, his *pince-nez* askew, his thin lips trembling—even then she had been repelled by him and his subdued, estranging ways. Near by stood Anthony Layeville, the diplomat, slender and haughty, staring into the distance with his hands folded across his chest; and young von Wald, the explorer, leaning over to lace his boots, his simple blossoming face hidden, only his blond curly hair visible; and Wildenbruch, the stiff, impersonal German, half scientist and half soldier, washing his sunburnt hands in the copper bowl; Serafimov, the exile, panting as he poured a glass of water over his shaggy head, so that it ran in rivulets down over his eyes, dripped from his chin, flowed over his huge black chest to which the shirt was already clinging transparently; and Goupillière, that detestable little Belgian whom her husband had

[364]

picked up in Saïgon, watching the rest with a stealthy, ironic leer, running his fingers through his hair. . . .

*

She heard footsteps at her side, and opened her eyes. It was Ling. He smiled at her, as if there were a secret between them.

"In five days," he murmured, "we shall be in Shanghai." There was something very odd in his voice. Immediately she began to distrust him, to feel a little bit frightened.

But only for a moment. Instantly she grew calm again. She could feel the red water caressing the hull of the boat as it flowed past, incessantly.

40

The Captive

SLOWLY THEY DREW CLOSER TO SHANGHAI. THE WATER was aflame, it seemed to Olivia; the shore was aflame. The foliage of the birches and the ashes on the hills glimmered like molten copper. The coolies wore only their loin cloths. Now and then they would leap into the muddy water and then emerge, hair streaming, mouth spluttering, their limbs like polished bronze.

They passed olive orchards on the hillocks, and pagodas clad in the foliage of arbor-vitæ. The steamers grew more frequent, as well as the filthy smoking barges. The huge gray oil-tanks of the Standard Oil Company and the Asia Oil Company appeared along the shore, like huddled prehistoric animals.

At night the crickets filled the air with their thin clamor.
Little boats lit by oil-lamps passed, selling tobacco, beer,
jellies, sausages, trinkets. Restaurant boats with colored
awnings floated by, and gambling boats, and gaily painted
brothel boats. In and out they wove, to and fro, upstream
and downstream.

Olivia lay on deck, her head on a hard square pillow,
and watched them. Her nerves quivered, the lights in the
river quivered too. Now and then a chill ran along her
arms, and a sudden coolness flowed past her temples.

And a moment later she would be hot again, and would
moisten her parched lips with her tongue and run her
fingers across her eyelids.

☆

The moon-faced merchant was dying.

He would sit there quietly in his big-brimmed hat, fanning himself and smoking his opium pipe until he fell
asleep.

He knew that he was dying.

He had given orders to the coolies to build a coffin for
him. He had only two or three days longer to live, he
whispered to them. When they stopped at Hanyang they
went and bought the necessary things.

And then he would sit there peacefully, watching the
coolies making his coffin and his costume and his paper
shoes, and the little cardboard houses out of silver-colored
straw, and the baskets of imitation silver coins, to be tossed
into the hungry jowls of the demons on his journey back
to the realm of ancestral phantoms. All these things would

[367]

stay with him after he died. He watched placidly. Everything was as it should be, his puffy eyes seemed to say, everything was appropriate.

Olivia thought of Lao-Tse's words, as she watched him toying gently with two walnuts in his right hand, rolling them about from finger to soft finger: "The tranquillity of the heart is the very crown of creation!"

✫

She grew weaker and weaker. She sat with a towel around her head now. Her face, when she raised her fingers to her forehead, felt insensate and crinkly, like taffeta.

She ate very little now. The food grew worse. No one any longer made any special effort for her. The rice was yellowish, the cabbage was discolored, everything was tasteless and undercooked. She took to eating tangerines. But of course, she had almost no money now, only a few coins, and had to be content with what they gave her. She gave up all hope of transferring to one of the steamers. After all, it didn't matter, it really didn't matter.

She was growing thinner, she noticed, and very weak. The food, the heat, and then, for another thing, she was bleeding almost constantly now. It never seemed to stop. It went on and on, a dark, trivial but incessant stream.

One day she looked at her face in the *laopan's* mirror. She caught her breath. She looked almost like a ghost, wasted with fever, her features looked incredibly delicate, her skin transparent, her eyes black and luminous. Never, she thought to herself with a thrill of delight, had she

[368]

looked so beautiful, so alluring! A certain enchantment
had crept across her features, a certain outlandish, bewitched look.

She spent her last coins that afternoon in Hankow on a
package of powder, a small tin of rouge, a flask of cheap
violet-scented perfume, and a lipstick.

That evening she lay back on her bamboo couch and
closed her eyes. A kind of despair, a really delicious kind
of despair, ran through her body. Her throat was aching,
her hands and feet felt cold. Everything was spinning
around, the lights along the shore, the stars overhead. The
singing of the mosquitoes sounded like a voluptuous song
in her ears.

Ling approached and sat down beside her. He was still
sweating, his bare chest was shining. He had something
cupped between his two hands.

Then he opened them, and laughed with pleasure.
"See!" It was a little pig, carved out of wood, with a tail
of braided strands of silk.

"It is beautiful! I have made it for you. . . ." There
was a mocking laughter in his sparkling eyes. "It is a symbol of unpretentiousness! Of modesty. . . ."

And he slipped it into her hand. At the touch of his
warm fingers upon hers a wave of calm, of serenity, ran
through her body. She felt very quiet. Nothing in the
world mattered. She closed her eyes.

A soft, intoxicating languour was stealing over her.
There was a smell of smoke, of incense, of distant flowers
in the air. She could hear the water gliding by, and, she
thought, the silken rustle of leaves on the silhouetted
shore.

Then she heard another sound, deep, deeper than anything, at the very bottom of the water and in the very core of her heart. The sound of the earth revolving on its axis, turning forever eastward. The sound of destiny, of her own unalterable destiny, of the fate of the whole world. The nocturnal currents of air and water slipped past like crystal arrows shot across the revolving earth.

All power was flowing away from her. She felt gently, sweetly victimized.

Then, through her lashes, she saw Ling's face. There was a single star hovering in the sky, right over his forehead; now it would rise, as the boat rocked gently to and fro, now it would fall and touch his hair.

The glow of a kerosene-lamp fell on his profile. The taut, Mongolian eyelids shone, the long black lashes cast shadows on his high cheek bones. Under his chin a black collar of shade fell obliquely across his neck, so curiously smooth for a man's, and across his powerful, broad shoulder. She began trembling, he looked so glistening, so powerful, so hard, so alert.

Alert, as if he too were listening to that subterranean sound, and to the silken rustling of the distant leaves. He was holding his hands poised in front of him, in a gesture of suspense. They looked incredibly powerful yet delicate, as hard as steel.

Then he turned and looked into her eyes. Hard as steel that gaze was. She felt him drawing closer, and closed her eyes once more.

Then she felt the touch of his fingers upon her arms, and her shoulder, and then below her shoulder. She could feel the warmth of his body beside hers, and the rhythm of his heart against her arm. And presently, the touch of his lips upon her neck, and his hard, steady fingers groping beneath her gown and caressing her skin.

She felt very calm. She could feel the black water gliding along beneath her.

☆

The tigerish landscape kept prowling past. They had passed Anking, and Nanking too. They were very close to Shanghai now. The river was as wide as a sea. She could scarcely see the opposite shore.

Everything seemed extraordinarily beautiful to her. "What law is it," she asked herself dreamily, "that ordains that our grasp on happiness, our delight in the symbols of life and the lasting joys of the senses, never appears till the signs of decay have already budded forth in our minds? It is at the very moment that we are no longer youthful, that youth begins to seem beautiful to us. When love has lost its freshness, we hanker for it. And then, well, little by little, we learn to resign ourselves." The sky was miraculously blue. Little silken strands were floating through the air, the signs of summer. Along the shore the locusts were screaming, and everywhere, through the quivering waves of air, she saw men leaning over, or stretched out, or pouring water over their foreheads. Wherever she looked she saw their brown, hard limbs, everywhere, even in the water, even in the cloud-besprinkled sky.

☆

She realized, one day, when she saw the *laopan* follow

her along the street in Hankow, that something was wrong.
She was being watched. They would not let her go. She
was sure of it now. She was a prisoner, in short; she had
deliberately allowed herself to be kidnapped.

But it mattered surprisingly little. It hardly even penetrated her mind, it remained on the surface. She wondered
hazily what would happen to her in Shanghai. What, she
asked herself, would they do with her there?

She had no wish to escape. She felt inexplicably passive
and serene. Whatever they did with her, that was her
destiny. Dimly the shapes of her past floated past her—the
gardener, the fisherboy, her husband, the Englishman
Layeville, Dr. Liu. Very far away, they all seemed, and
quite unreal.

She would see Ling smiling at her, and the piercing eyes
of the bald, brown *laopan* watching her with a preoccupied air. There was something incomprehensible to her in
that glance. It was almost a glance of hate, and yet abstract,
impersonal. She would close her eyes and feel very calm,
deliciously calm. She would feel the waters underneath
carrying her along toward Shanghai, and presently she
would fall asleep.

☆

Finally, one morning, the pink and copper and golden
colors of the Yang-tze faded. It grew vast, infinite. They
could no longer see the other shore. And in the distance
Shanghai appeared, on a tributary stream. It rose from its
flat and treeless banks, on a land of forgotten cemeteries.

That afternoon the *laopan* led her along a narrow street,

and bought her a new sheath-like dress of yellow brocade and a new pair of slippers, with very high heels. He looked at her carefully when she emerged, dressed in her new costume, her face heavily powdered and rouged. He nodded amiably. Then he pinned a paper flower on her dress, directly under her neck. And now she knew her destiny.

They stepped into a *ricksha* and passed through street after street. Ling had disappeared. He was nowhere to be seen. They were entering a disreputable section. She could recognize the brothels on each side, and the prostitutes, with their high heels and cheap jewelry.

The noises of the quarter melted into one. Like an everlasting song, pointless, yet forever nervous.

The flickering sunlight fell on the roofs, and the shopfronts, and the doorways, and the faces. Everything was alive and constantly moving. And yet over it all hung an extraordinary beauty and tranquillity.

She closed her eyes. A smile appeared on her lips.

"Shall I ever," she whispered to herself, "come closer to understanding than this? Shall I ever really change again? Will life henceforth be calm?"

BOOK SEVEN

De la Scaze

41

The Blue City

FOR SEVERAL MINUTES DE LA SCAZE SAT BESIDE THE table in his shabby little room, watching the wavering flame of the petroleum-lamp and beyond it the arch of blackness which trembled upon the yellow silken curtains.

Then he closed his book, turned down the wick and allowed the flame to die. He took off his *pince-nez* and looked toward the window. The curtains were still trembling. Trembling upon the warm and odorous airs of the great desert, which crept into Aqsu from the limitless southeast. Quite gradually, it seemed, the moonlight came gliding through the blinds, like a horde of tiny silvery moths, pausing for a moment in the darkness of the room as if seeking its accustomed path, then gently descending and unfurling on the carpet its glimmering battalion.

He felt the fever fluttering in his temples like the ripples in a pool. He had been here for ten days now. The fever had grown mild and steady, the chills and tremors had left him. He wondered, now and then, whether he should proceed eastward now and try to rejoin his wife. But then he would feel weary and indifferent, and all that would cease to matter. Unfamiliar and absorbing, yet not really unpleasant, this feeling of sickness. It sharpened the senses, made his nerves alert. So that now, sitting alone in his room and in fact totally alone in this city, he did not feel alone. He felt as if each scent and sound that floated into his room through the blinds were alive; intimate, and full of whispers intended for him alone.

Yet it wasn't only the fever that contrived this eloquence. It was more than that. Something else. He rose and walked slowly toward the window. As he touched the silk curtains he started; it was like the touch of a beloved woman, so deliberate and caressive. His heart beat more quickly. He opened the blinds and looked down the alley, breathing the nocturnal air of the street as if it were some cunning distillation not yet identified. But then suddenly it occurred to him that this new atmosphere which so enthralled him was indeed the atmosphere of love.

Cast upon the curtain of a window that faced him he saw two quick shadows, now distinct, now gone: lovers; the eager contours of their unclothed bodies, so briefly silhouetted, left him breathless. He leaned out and stared toward the end of the street. More shadows passing, visible one instant against the pale moonlit building and then gone. He felt both exultant and sad. A feeling of loss, of longing, knowing that such excitements, the tremors of passion in the dark city, were not for him.

Something was now tugging at him: something "evil," he suspected; something "dangerous." But he could not resist it, and quickly he slipped on his white jacket and hastened with beating heart down the stairway and out into the street.

★

He hurried through street after twining street, and presently found himself in the heart of the city.

Something in the place instantly struck him. He saw himself already as one of the inhabitants, a part of the city, and he knew that he was captive. Something would happen to him here, he felt certain. Indeed, as he looked around, he felt as if something had already happened to him; as if he had stepped into an entirely new world, full of strange symbolisms and secrets which already he was beginning to grasp. For it was as if he had been here before, long ago; the streets looked oddly familiar, the quiet faces shining in the lamplight he had surely seen at some earlier time; every street corner and dark alleyway was rich with ever so faintly recollected encounters, appraisals, solicitations.

Everything was slow, peaceful, and dreamy. Infinitely calm, this sea of twilit shapes. The people moved on bare feet or in soft slippers with only the softest of sounds. Very different from the panic of the great Chinese cities; different, in fact, from all other cities; there was about this place an utter seclusion, a secrecy, such as he had never seen before. The old bearded men were squatting beside the lanterns in little groups, whispering softly. When de la Scaze passed they scarcely raised their eyes; but he could see the added darkness of curiosity entering their eyes, and their voices pausing, then continuing softly. Gentle creatures, full of tact and subtlety, each gesture subdued and gracious, each contour of the voice so mellow and mature. Now and then two or three women passed quickly. Tall and slim they were, and though their faces were hidden he was convinced that they were very beautiful. He thought of his wife, Olivia. No, these were creatures of a different race from hers, utterly different. He could see the dark skin of their hands, soft as satin, glowing and perfect, and their eyes like the city itself, so dark, quiet, deep in shadow, and so eloquent with understanding, with more than understanding.

Gradually he became aware of the spirit of the city; and he recognized the echoing awareness of the city itself. Nothing passed unnoticed here, or uncomprehended. Things were seen all the more exactly for existing in the shade, so to speak.

He longed to fling himself into its warm and understanding embrace like a diver waiting to join the water, or a lover about to join his mistress.

*

He slept all of the following day until sunset. Then he rose and walked through the city again.

The Moslems were gathering for prayers in the twilit mulberry grove at the very edge of the city, beyond the *serai* in which he knew that Serafimov and Goupillière were still being held as hostages. Here one was sitting alone under an apricot tree beside the stream, reading aloud to himself from the Koran, and there a very old one was stooping over the sandy shore, going through the cleansing rites of Mohammed and slowly pouring water over his white head and shoulders, drop by inefficient drop. Some birds were sitting sleepily in the branches overhead, ruffling their feathers now and then, or fluttering their wings for an instant.

The bazaars of Aqsu were growing quiet. De la Scaze could see a few Turkis still smoking their waterpipes under the matted awnings. Now in the daylight he could see them more clearly. Almost all were afflicted by alarming skin diseases, venereal sores, infected eyes; some of them were leprous. But all, no matter how neglected of body, had an amiable smile, a glance full of humor and tolerance.

He passed the little walled gardens, the balconies, the old houses once pretentious but now squalid. In a niche at each street corner stood a little oil lamp, still unlit. "There are seventy streets in Aqsu," Layeville had told him. Though at first it seemed unlikely, he could believe it. Every few feet a little crooked alleyway darted off into shadow, hideous little paths no more than three or four feet wide. To pass through them he had to stumble over the shapes of the sick and the poor, begging, teasing, or fast asleep.

Dusk was gathering and a blue twilight was gliding like an incoming tide across the streets and over the faces. "The Blue City," the natives called it. Here and there still leapt, like a fish, a flash of the sun; a window pane aflame with the last red glow, or a laughing face ruddy with a momentary glimmer. Then it grew quite shadowy, they all seemed suddenly submerged in a blue sea, the voices became hushed, the faces sullen, the gestures deliberate. The street children still wandered, but more stealthily, back and forth between the various shadows of the bazaars and the blue alleys. Dressed in utter rags, with their brown skin showing through in a dozen places; yet still possessed of a certain purity and pride which they would lose in a few more years. Full of a boy's irony; wickedness was still to them a phrase for laughter rather than self-doubt, self-torment, and fear. They were enemies only of those who displeased them. Good and evil meant nothing to them. All these things could be seen in their faces, their smiling dirty brown faces, turning so easily upon their dirty necks; their white teeth, their flashing mischievous eyes gave to the streets whatever these possessed of happiness and freshness. The old men contributed to them their sly dignity and malicious wisdom. The old men, the old old men, seeking in philosophy their last consolations out of a shabby yet everlastingly fascinating existence.

The haughtiest ones were the young men of twenty or so. Their teeth had already begun to decay, their complexions had grown impure. Yet how much handsomer, thought de la Scaze, than the Europeans. Weary they seemed, eyelids heavy and lips parted, as if after a bout of love-making. But they were the ones who ruled in the one province that seemed to matter to them, that of love. All around them rose the terrible odors of the city, their garments were drenched with the negligences of many months, they were emaciated, they were utterly poor. Yet how haughtily they walked, he observed, how gracefully they wore their shabby tunics, how innocent and yet wicked they looked. But above all, he noticed, cruel: able to inflict pain, and aware of that brief power; sadists in short, aloof

but alert with that ultimate yet most primitive of per-
versions.

Beside them the passing women, incomparably lovelier,
seemed, though veiled, far less mysterious and far more
human. A hideous old creature was sitting under an arch-
way, tending a fire made of camel dung and boiling her
black tea. She looked up and smiled a toothless smile at
him. He felt queerly happy, and reflected how, after all,
it was always the glance of a woman and a woman's voice
that gave him comfort and confidence; never a man's.

Then suddenly it was dark. The lanterns began to
flicker softly in their niches at the corners, the old shadows
disappeared from the pavement and new ones, more eloquent and impenetrable, crept into their place.

He began to walk thoughtfully along the narrow street
back toward his house.

Suddenly he held his breath. For a moment he stared
into the darkness, sick at heart, not knowing what was
troubling him. Then he knew. Passing under a street lamp,
visible for one instant in the cold sharp light, shone a face:
the most beautiful he had ever seen; more than that, the
only utterly beautiful face, he realized breathlessly, that
he had ever seen. The swaying garments, the feminine
hand held quietly and delicately poised at the breast, the
silver light on the cheeks and the darkness, ever so faintly
insolent, under the long eyelashes, all scarcely seen yet
utterly magical. Now the shape was gone, without a sound.

He felt weak, he trembled and leaned against the wall.
He felt as if something had passed by, more than a mortal
shape, rather a symbol of a whole overwhelming world of
creatures and passions that he had never known. He experienced a stab of despair at having missed something,
something indeed to which his entire life had fruitlessly

[383]

been pointing; and likewise a feeling of enormous uncertainty regarding his own past ardors, the ideas which had guided his life—a longing, say, for recognition, loyalty and peace. Out of the torrent of darkness of many years he had seen emerging for less than a second a casual shape, revealed by the deceiving silver flash of a lantern, and he felt a heavy longing, a heavy hope, a heavy despair, a heavy happiness, all together, with an intense and utterly novel sort of thrill.

☆

He sat down in the darkness and waited for T'sing to bring in his tea. Nervously he tapped his fingers upon the silk coverlet.

He saw himself at certain times as a member of a dead clan, a dead aristocracy, a dead equipment of thoughts and intuitions. Wealth had brought him loneliness and disaster, not support. There existed no support for him; his reflections and sensibilities were now without a home, just as he himself was without a home. Both were frightening, equally so. How useless all the delicacies and profundities of this western way of thinking now were! What he wanted most was that some one should long for him and should put her arms around him. That was the way to escape, the only one.

He began to long for a woman, violently. For the feminine pressure on his hand, the feminine breath on his neck, the feminine flesh against his own; for the kiss, the ecstasy, the consolation. He had never felt desire so strongly before, even remotely. Never for his wife, certainly. It was a new thing; it intoxicated him like a perfume, a drug. He could not rid his mind of the shape of that lovely girl. Each detail—the delicate hand, the warm skin, the mocking flash of the eyes, the perfection of tread—all trembled before his eyes. He resolved to look for her, to search until he found her.

And simultaneously he began to feel, almost pleasurably, as if he had been captured. It was not a home he was entering so breathlessly, but a prison. He knew it. For a moment he saw very clearly. He saw clearly how sudden and unforeseen desires that can never be classified are the ones that seize the heart most frightfully; how unexpected are the outlets which the intensest of passions must seek; how then each single word, breath, object, instant of the day, are made into terrifying agents of desire, sentries of an inner darkness; and he glimpsed the vast desert that lay dried up in him, and yet more powerful the vast approaching lake that had lain dammed up within him, for so many quiet years.

Yes. There was something infinitely sweet awaiting him in these blue streets which shimmered and purred beyond the silken curtains.

He was overcome by an awareness of those vast territories outside the window, those incomparably vast stretches of sand and wilderness and rock and snow, and of slowly, slowly approaching hordes: the glittering tents, the flashing black hair, the cruel eyes, the thirst for blood. And the power, the power! All of it slowly and silently drawing closer, about to reveal a new kind of life to him!

T'sing brought in the tea and lit the lamp. "I am sorry, master. My sister is very sick. Therefore I was late. I am ashamed, master. . . ." He continued to murmur apologetically. But de la Scaze didn't hear him, and looked out of the window.

"Thank you, master." De la Scaze saw the amiable grinning face peering toward him out of the shadow, then vanishing. He remembered oddly the word "cholera" out of T'sing's disconnected chatter.

But then he forgot it again and, turning toward the window, forgot similarly all the warnings that this moment of clarity had murmured to him; he forgot that he wanted to go east to Shanghai, he forgot his wife, he forgot the four others who were also waiting in Aqsu—the Russian, the Belgian, the Austrian, the German. He leaned toward the warm feminine air that rose from the street, and opened his arms wide in a blind, passionate gesture of desire.

42

Hussein

THE NIGHTS WERE VERY GRADUALLY GROWING
cooler, but still every evening de la Scaze walked
out into the streets and wandered toward the
busier quarters of the city. His fever had subsided, but
still, he thought, he had better stay on awhile. In fact, he
presently discovered that he had secretly resigned himself
to staying in Aqsu all winter; it was growing cool, he
would reflect, and to try the trip now in his weakened con-
dition would be folly.

T'sing had brought him a long Chinese robe of green
silk one day, and this he now wore every night. It made a
great difference to him, actually, the wearing of this
Chinese robe. He was growing rather vain. He had given

up wearing his *pince-nez* when he found he could manage without it. He looked younger now, he decided, as he glanced at himself in the mirror. He smiled back at himself. He felt pleased. Yes, he was looking definitely younger.

He would get up from his bed in the late afternoon and climb down the narrow creaking stairway toward the little alley that led to the bazaars. Out of the shadows he would see the figures emerging. Many of the faces were familiar now and nodded smilingly in reply to his nod. The Chinese were the ones he first grew to know; partly because it was only the Chinese that could speak either French or English, for the most part, partly because they were so friendly, and then partly because of T'sing. T'sing, ever eager to give pleasure, soon learned to carry gossip to his master. Forever curious, this unimportant little man, constantly peering like a moth into windows at nightfall and deep into the secular mysteries of the city with his bright black eyes, gleefully running back and in his thin high voice relating a scandal or a calamity:

"Ling, the silk merchant, is blessed with twins; blessed Ling, who remains in ignorance of his wife's treachery!" or, with pretended commiseration, "Liu's mother has starved to death, Liu's little sister has gone into naughty ways, Liu's little brother is already a thief; soon they will go to Yarkand and you will see them no more. . . ."

Lovable in his way, was T'sing, and yet he went about his errands so bizarrely and mercilessly, that at last de la Scaze began to distrust him and dislike him. He began to think about finding a new servant.

His fever had left him many days ago, and now he took to walking for hours at a time. Or to sitting until long after midnight in a Turkish café, listening and slowly learning their words, guessing a few of their secrets. Little by little, sitting there in his green silken robe, he grew expert at detecting subtleties which previously he could not even have comprehended. By his gait, his gestures, his features, his voice, he learned to tell what a man had gone through; how much he had suffered or enjoyed; how much he respected himself, understood himself, loved himself; and above all, what he loved in others. The sensitive braggarts, the hesitant pretenders, the bleak philosophers, the bullies, the buffoons, the orators, the pensive ones, the cowards, the spies, those who took delight in the sorrows or the vices of others, those who cherished their own disasters as if they were precious ancestral satins: all of them he began to recognize and understand.

Late in the afternoon he would see the harvesters returning past the city walls; the old men who played incessant bird-like music on their bamboo flutes; the cripples, quite happy and alert, the dreamlike idiots, the pious ones, the watchers squatting along the wall in the brilliant sunlight, gazing at the clouds, and the people in shadow with eyes covered with sores and almost blind, slowly succumbing to the depravities of eavesdropping; the old women lost in a life of their own, simply one of recollections and of weird plans toward a coming sickness and decease; and the young women, leaning over the water, lovely in their traditional and dreaming contours, sweet and expectant as unplucked fruits, still totally free of any individuality or thought, still pure.

Then after dark he would watch the Moslems. Or passing down an unlit street he would come upon a group of Turkis, desperately drunk and all agog, noisily looking for a brothel. Once he passed the shabby black prison in the drabbest part of town, and wondered whether Wildenbruch and von Wald, the two young scientists, were still there; he thought of inquiring, but then forgot about it again. Once, in a deserted street long after midnight, he heard the shot of a pistol and then, in the unnatural quiet, the quick tripping of bare feet upon the wet pavement behind him. And once he saw, among the buildings that rose into the gray wilderness of approaching dawn, two pigtailed, long-robed silhouettes noiselessly dragging a third shape over the flagstones, out of darkness back into darkness.

At one place there was a madman. He sat there forever, in a corner near the door, incessantly muttering to the newcomers, now imperiously, now in a whisper. A ghastly creature to look at, inhuman as a plant, rigid and sessile. He seemed to grow slowly, breathe a strange nocturnal air, spread roots, change color. Dark, hairlike arteries seemed to be spreading all over his skin. His eyes were quite without expression or intensity, except for the vaguest suggestion of hatred.

He would tell of the past. "I know of a time when famines and floods covered all of China, all of unholy Russia. Women lay in the limbs of high trees at night, praying for their children. The old men burrowed through the wet earth like moles. . . ."

Or of the future. "I foretell a great fire. An age of fire. Great tongues of flame will sweep across Siberia, and up from the grasses of the Ganges and the Yellow River. All will be consumed. All. Except those who have been purged and made eternal by the fire of the spirit. By love."

"What sort of love?" some one would ask jokingly.

"By the love that destroys! Love without appeasement or end!" His voice was now full of bitterness.

☆

The Russians and scattered Europeans had their café too. This was in the most squalid quarter of all, significantly enough, not far from the ugly Russian church, very near the *serai* where he and his companions had stayed when they first arrived in Aqsu. One evening he peered curiously through a window into the *serai* itself. On the floor he saw a huge sleeping shape, and at a table near by, a small man reading an old newspaper. Serafimov, he felt sure, and Goupillière. But something about the atmosphere of the place disgusted him. He turned away quickly and never went back.

It was in the European café that he began to realize that an amazing and intricate underworld existed, layer after layer below the surface of the city's life. Now and then, after midnight, here in the café or in a neighboring passageway, he saw faces, both male and female, many of them beautiful, all but a few utterly depraved, every feature revealing their dedication to the thoughtful and elaborate vices of forgetfulness. There were a few, it is true, who looked pure and untouched. Lovely as flowers, the strangest of all. They were the ones whom no one understood, the flamelike ones, the truly ruinous, the truly evil.

Most of the Russians were those who had fled through Siberia after the revolution, and had finally reached Aqsu, the loneliest and least frequented of the larger cities of Sinkiang. Some were now engaged in habitual and ineffective conspiracies against the Soviets, preposterous little games, fatuous intrigues. Others entangled themselves in counter-conspiracies, so that finally the life among these people became a shimmering network of espionage. There was one, for example, who had killed his brother somewhere in the forests along the Yenisei, and had fled; one dealt in perfumes; one was the agent for an Egyptian millionaire, one had escaped from Aginskoë on a charge of treason. Some (not unlike himself, perhaps) were pathetic wisps of dissolute western Europe, left stranded here for the most casual of reasons and without the will or the power to return; there was one who had been deserted by his Danish friends, one who had fallen sick on an expedition, one who had been sent to Kashgar by a German company which subsequently went bankrupt, one who had stayed because of a tragic love affair but eventually convinced himself that this was the best climate for him. There was a prostitute in town, a middle-aged Russian woman named Tastin, with a moneyed and glamorous past; she too was caught here, like a fly in a spiderweb.

All these things de la Scaze discovered through T'sing's smiling chatter. Presently he noticed that the people were regarding him with increasing distrust. They were, naturally enough, so he thought at first, watching him in reply to his own watchfulness.

But not they alone. He was being watched by the Chinese as well. He had heard of the sudden and unexplained disappearance of certain men—"enemies of the government of Sinkiang." He was thoroughly convinced now that the officials were spying on him. Now and then he saw a quick hint of antagonism in a passing face, or yet more disturbing, a certain ironical leer of understanding. He knew how grave this danger might well be. And yet, he felt oddly indifferent toward it, or, if anything, began actually to feel stimulated by such a thought. The concept of flight and peril operated upon him like a mild drug.

Once or twice it occurred to him that he should leave Aqsu for some other place, any other place. But he had very little money left, for one thing; he had wired to Bombay for more, and would have to wait. Also, he was not sure that he felt strong enough to undertake another journey, even a short one.

And all the while he kept searching, searching. That lovely, elusive woman's shape still haunted him. She grew more and more real and exact. The sensuous insolence of her gaze, the perfume of her body, the rosiness of her breasts, the shadowy climax of her thighs, became so urgent, so precise, that he felt as if he had already known her. And as if, for that reason, he had some sort of right to her. He longed for her incessantly. He would imagine her lying at his side, her lips against him, her eyes full of mockery, her limbs inert.

And his brain would go reeling. Nothing else would matter. He would gladly have descended into eternal hell fire, at these moments, in return for one hour's possession of her body.

✪

One night on his way home, just at that instant before dawn when the buildings became eloquent and somewhat savage, he found that he had lost his way. He was in a street that seemed strange, no building or crossing alleyway appeared in the least familiar. It was very quiet, no

[393]

one on the street, no lights; it might as well have been a street of the dead.

Suddenly he grew afraid. Like a breeze passing over the dusty road, ever so softly, he heard a sound behind him. Hardly the sound of bare feet on distant stone, hardly even the sound of human breath.

Then he felt the touch of a warm hand upon his hand, and heard a soft voice beside him. "Sir," it murmured in halting French, "wait. Do not continue this way." The voice paused to recover its breath. "You are going the wrong way. You must not go further! Dangerous . . ." The little brown hand tugged at his hand and turned him around. "Let me lead you back."

He looked down and saw two black eyes shining at him through the twilight. The eyes of an old man. For a moment, in this whimsical confusion touched with danger on the one hand and shyness on the other, he felt a flash of understanding, a quick awareness of something not unkind; he felt moved. He allowed the hand to lead him back along the street and across to the bazaars.

Finally he turned to the little white figure that was leading him along. "Thank you. I can find my way now." The head nodded. He paused. "What is your name?"

"Hussein."

"Hussein." He hesitated a moment. "Come to my house tomorrow, Hussein, and I shall repay you."

The head nodded again, then was gone.

★

But when Hussein came on the following afternoon,

punctual to the moment when de la Scaze rose and drank
his coffee, the latter was rather surprised. For Hussein was
no old man; he could have been no more than fourteen.
But oddly sedate, he was. He sat and watched de la Scaze
quietly, answering his questions, smiling gently, anxious
to please.

"What do you do, Hussein?"

"Oh, many things; I find many things to do."

"Important things?"

Hussein smiled, rather embarrassed. He shook his head
and began to fumble shyly with his skullcap.

So de la Scaze dismissed T'sing, in spite of the latter's
threatening falsetto obscenities, and hired Hussein to be
his servant, and from that day on Hussein came early every
afternoon, prepared the coffee, swept the room, lit the
incense, brought out the drinks, laid away the clothes,
polished the brass on the handbags, wound the clock, re-
filled the lamps, emptied the ewers, ran the errands, arranged the flowers.

But he changed, rather curiously, from day to day. Even
his appearance changed. And the longer he stayed, the less
de la Scaze could understand him.

✫

For example, at moments he appeared innocent, imper-
ceptive, quite stupid. Yet at other times he saw through
people with an experienced and subtle brilliance that
seemed inspired. And there were other contradictions, too.

At first he behaved very quietly and modestly. He would

[395]

sit in a corner, watching his master with restrained subtle eyes, quite motionless. It wasn't until later that de la Scaze realized that he was perpetually acting. Forever changing his ways, adopting a new manner and attitude to suit the mood of his master; or, later, to suit the wishes of each visitor or passer-by or indeed his own lively caprice: there was no telling, ever, what he really thought, what he really wished, what he resembled.

He would accompany de la Scaze on his walks each evening, carefully adjusting his pace to his master's, respectfully walking a bit behind him, now and then taking him by the hand to lead him through a crowd or out through a dark and winding street. And back in the room he would amuse de la Scaze by telling tales, whimsical, cruel and pathetic, about the people they had passed. Strangely sophisticated certain of these anecdotes might have seemed to some, and de la Scaze would see him sitting in the corner, laughing silently with malice and delight, eyes sparkling. He always in turn listened carefully, almost painfully, to his master, trembling with curiosity and a wish to help, sending forth in reply little waves of humble affection and loyalty.

☆

But he changed. As winter arrived and de la Scaze began to see him more, he bit by bit became a different person entirely.

He lied, for one thing.

Sometimes it was amusing and unimportant. De la Scaze

[396]

might ask him, for example, about his family. "How many are there in your family, Hussein?"

"Oh," he sighed, "not very many. Four brothers, three sisters. But many cousins and uncles."

"And your father and mother?"

Hussein dropped his eyelids in pious sorrow. "They are both dead, sir! I am an orphan . . ."

De la Scaze mumbled sympathetically.

"They died many years ago. When I was only four years old. My uncle then took me. He was a cruel, cruel man. But he is dead too. Now I live with my brothers and sisters. I love them all, but sometimes they deserve it very little!"

"Indeed. How old are you, Hussein?"

"Nineteen years, sir."

That amazed de la Scaze.

"Yes," said Hussein, rather dejectedly. "I am already full of experiences. See," he said, approaching and showing the side of his brown cheek to de la Scaze, "soon I will be a bearded man!"

Several days later, de la Scaze asked, "How did you learn your French, Hussein? Is there anyone else here who speaks French?"

"I learned French in Tangier and Rabat." At first de la Scaze did not grasp the names; they were pronounced rather oddly. Then, for a moment, he appeared incredulous.

"Yes," announced Hussein demurely, "for three years I was there, with my father. That was three years ago. And then I learned French."

"Did your brothers and sisters go too?"

Hussein smiled rather patronizingly. "But sir, I have no

[397]

brothers and sisters!" And then, as if suddenly remembering something, he grinned at de la Scaze quite bashfully
yet wickedly, as if to say, "You must forgive me; life is,
after all, a most farcical and inexact affair!"

Once he came a bit later than usual, very downcast.

"You're late, Hussein."

"You are true, sir. I am sad. My mother has just died."
He walked slowly across the room and sat down in the
darkness, tugging at his ragged shirt. Something troubled
him and he did appear, in fact, quite miserable. De la
Scaze scarcely had the heart to remind him that, after all,
his mother had died many years ago and that it was most
disquieting that she should have died a second time. "I am
sad to hear that, Hussein."

It was two days later that he said, "Tell me, Hussein, is
your mother still living?"

Hussein brightened up for an instant. Then he grew
thoughtful. "No, sir," he said with reproachful dignity.
"She died two days ago, just as I told you. I do not tell lies
about my dead mother!"

"Oh. I supposed that your mother had died when you
were a little boy. So you told me once, if I remember
rightly."

Hussein appeared disgusted. "You must have remembered wrongly, sir. No, no; two days ago!" And he began
to moan gently.

De la Scaze began to think that Hussein's family were
all creatures purely of his imagination, invented out of
loneliness or possibly shame: for he seemed to live in an
iridescent and ever changing world of surprises, disap-
pointments, and rather gayly shattered illusions. He had
invented a world of his own, brilliant and touching, gal-
lant yet horrifying, all in his boy's mind. De la Scaze won-

dered whether he ever spoke the truth, whether he understood at all what truth was.

✫

Once he asked Hussein about his father. Hussein shifted nervously and lowered his eyes. "My father died in the plague. Ten years ago."

"Plague?"

"Yes. Cholera. My father was a stranger in this city, you see!"

De la Scaze was puzzled. He felt a bit uneasy. "A stranger?"

"Ah yes! You see, when the plague arrives in this city, all strangers die. Every one."

Again de la Scaze felt that sickening little spasm of fear: as if he were being watched, as if the whole city knew everything about him, were lying in wait, full of secrets, full of little plans, tender yet hostile.

"And so your father died too?" His voice was sick and weary.

"Yes, sir. . . . He was a beautiful and loving man, I think." Hussein's voice had grown very gentle.

43

Evenings in the City

JANUARY AND FEBRUARY PASSED, AND PRESENTLY
March too. De la Scaze felt less well, spells of weariness came over him after the slightest of efforts, and
the momentary fevers returned. The cold was still
intense in the streets. Nothing seemed to have changed.
Everything was in a state of quiet, of suspense, he thought,
of watchful expectation. Aqsu lay outside his window like
a sleeping animal, caught between desert and mountain.

He hardly ever ventured forth during these two months.
He took to wearing his *pince-nez* again, and would sit beside the brazier all day long, reading copies of Shanghai's
French newspaper which Hussein brought him from time
to time. They were a year old or more, but still, it was
better than nothing.

[400]

Hussein had of late been adopting a new personality. Careless, vague, simple and gentle, usually. But spells of puerile inanity and cunning as well. And once or twice he lost his temper for no apparent reason. He could be very nasty if he chose. He screamed at the top of his lungs, grew pale and wild-eyed, stormed down the stairway and out into the street. But the next day he would appear as always, meek and rather wearier than usual.

One day de la Scaze missed a few *taels* out of his pocket. He suspected Hussein instantly. So he decided to put him to the test.

A few days later, therefore, he left three paper *taels* carelessly lying on the table beside some books. He intentionally provided Hussein with every opportunity, walked out frequently, appeared absent-minded, and so on.

Then he realized that his tactics had been painfully and insultingly obvious. He felt rather ashamed. He put the money back in his pocket. The next morning it was missing.

Then he tried again. He placed two *taels* on a dark shelf in a corner of the room while Hussein was busy preparing the tea. These he covered with a book and on the book he placed some letters.

The next morning the *taels* were still there.

On the following morning he found that the *taels* had been slipped into the book.

On the third morning they were still in the book.

On the fourth morning they were gone.

And when he glanced at Hussein, Hussein smiled back, rather mockingly. The farce was over, he seemed to say; it had been, in any case, rather silly and transparent.

And oddly enough, de la Scaze felt no anger or disgust at all. Rather, a quaint curiosity, almost pleasure.

[401]

Several times after that he did the same thing. Each time, after several countermoves of a similar kind, the money disappeared. Even though he was really very hard up now (the money for which he had wired to Bombay had never arrived, of course) de la Scaze never tried to recover it. It began to play the rôle of a curious mutual understanding, a gentle if inane sort of ceremony, like a secret handshake.

In his loneliness he grew more and more dependent on Hussein. He began to see in Hussein a reflection of his own boyhood. Now and again an accent or a gesture would call back to mind his own young days—his inconstancies and hesitations. At other times Hussein seemed to spring across the dividing years himself, and revealed the shrewd and comprehending prejudice of an old man; the same airy and moralistic manner of condemning others, with all his ironical tolerance.

And then, little by little, de la Scaze began to feel toward him as if he were his own son. One night Hussein was sitting quietly beside the window when de la Scaze awoke from a dream. He saw the quiet little figure gazing absent-mindedly out into the street, and suddenly something seemed to burst in his head, his heart beat violently, and he rose and placed his hands on Hussein's shoulders. "My son, my child . . ." The words rose in a great breath of sympathy and hung on the edge of his lips; but actually he said nothing.

Hussein looked up at him and smiled. "Master?" he said, very faintly.

*

Sitting by the window, he could see far off the twilit hills, white and ice-ridden. All sorts of thoughts would go through his mind. He would wonder why the immediate past had slipped so totally away. What had happened to his wife? She seemed remote and unreal, bewilderingly so. And to the rest of them? To Layeville, for example? Staring at the far-away snow reminded him of Layeville. In China, both of them. Were they thinking of him? Did they remember him? And the others? The Russian, the Belgian, the two young geologists. Were they still in Aqsu? The wonder faded away; he didn't care. Shadows, only shadows.

But the hills grew more and more real. They understood and passed judgment upon everything. A terrific power he now could feel emerging from them, monstrous, anything but cold and indifferent. No longer rigid and cold as stone, but supple as flesh and veins, these hills were!

Gazing at them before the moment of sleep, he began to identify with them the power of sleep. Sleep grew more and more charming to him. He began to feel homesick for the picturesque territories of sleep more and more, day by day. And then, when sleep did arrive, he savored its descent upon his nerves as if it were a drug. Time vanished; time, and place as well. Hours, years, heaven, the seas, the planets; they became intimate, without visible meaning except as fragments of his past and of himself.

☆

He began to write each evening in a little diary which he had long ago abandoned.

[403]

At first, scraps of autobiography; bits about the places and the people he had recently been seeing. Then anything that came into his mind; fragments, sometimes isolated words, sometimes even meaningless patterns and scrawls, which it relieved him somehow to set upon paper.

One day he wrote the following:

"If one is both sensitive and thoughtful, life must naturally become tragic.

"One grows aware of the infinitely beautiful and the infinitely evil. There is no way of avoiding them. They belong, as a shadow belongs to each object on which the sun is shining, to our very flesh and bone as long as we live."

And then, a bit later:

"Evil. Four types.

"First, absence of awareness. That is to say, of 'good will guided by reason.' This type of evil consists of a blind obedience to impulse, indiscriminate energy. Animals. Soldiers. Men like that Russian Serafimov.

"Second, sterility. This is the sin of acedia, of laziness. An inability to perform good; an inability to counteract the encroachments of inertia. Sterility. Addicts to drugs, or daydreaming. Many women are like this. Layeville.

"Third, triviality. Materialism, that barrier of tangible details which exists between men and the truth, that is to say, the eternal; this dominates the spirit and results in a desire to do harm to all spiritual creations. It is contagious. Jealousy, etc. Athletes, merchants. Goupillière for example.

"Fourth, demoniac possession. This might be the result of a prolonged accumulation of unexpressed energy; inhibitions; e.g. religious mania. Paranoia."

And then, under this, in a subsequent and more violent hand:

"No. Evil is none of these. Evil cannot be explained in terms of human weakness."

And several days later:

"Pain sometimes brings lucidity but sometimes a sheer elaboration of illusion. We need illusion as we need bread, without it we die. I have learned one thing. As long as I live I shall struggle against seeing things too clearly! My life and eternal happiness depend on the success of this self-conscious deception."

*

One day Hussein asked, simply and evenly, "Why are you so sad, master?"

"I am not very sad, Hussein."

"Yes, you are. More and more you forget things. You grow careless and sleepy. You do not even notice one any more. Nothing interests you. Yes, master. Something has saddened you!"

"Nonsense, Hussein."

Hussein paused. "I do not love you this way, my master," he said, in a low and peculiar voice.

*

It was then that de la Scaze decided to renew his walks through the city. The cold was growing less and during the noonday hours the sunlight was warm in the open streets. And so, late one afternoon, he started off.

[405]

For the first few days he walked slowly and briefly. He would feel his body trembling with exhaustion on his return, and the temptation to slip back into a life within walls was strong. But he resisted it, and presently he found himself again walking through the blue streets at twilight, watching, listening, suspecting, longing.

And again the old excitements began to tug at him. Suddenly he remembered the shape of the girl whom he had seen on his second night in Aqsu. A great desire welled up in him again. His skin grew hot, his heart beat more quickly. He resolved to look for her again, to find her at all costs.

And so, every night now, he began to look for her in the streets of Aqsu.

★

One night in late March, some time after his nightly excursions had been renewed, he came home after midnight. Hussein prepared some tea and tended to the brazier. Then he said good-night.

"Good-night, Hussein."

Something in his own voice disturbed him; something new, and rather insidious.

He sat down in front of his mirror and gazed at the face he saw there. At first he saw only a mask, half in blackness, half aglow in the orange light from the brazier. Then, little by little, he could detect the actual features. Large glittering eyes stared back into his own, penetrating deep into his thoughts, full of understanding. The mouth was softer, the skin more lifeless than his own, it seemed to him. Experience had spread its almost invisible veins across his entire face. And yet it was an interesting face, magnetic, almost fascinating. Yes, there was a certain power in it, a flashing energy. And something else, too. A certain wickedness, perhaps? Something which he had also noticed in all those other faces, those sly and watchful hordes that lived their endless life in central Asia. His face had, after so many years, entered upon a new and singular sort of existence. Very strange. But he began to understand. He himself had changed. A new self had come into power.

44

Early Loves

ONE COLD AFTERNOON HE SAT BESIDE THE WINDOW, watching the empty and desolate street veined with frozen trickles of water. For the first time in his life de la Scaze was beginning to feel what it was like not to have enough money to live a free life. He was hard up at last. In fact, he could no longer afford to buy decent food. But he didn't mind, as yet.

He was less well than he should be, he knew. Chills and fevers began once more to creep over his limbs from time to time, and set him shaking and sweating. His skin was growing dry and wrinkled in an alarming fashion. And his hair was thick with dandruff and was beginning to fall. It was the food, for one thing. He ate too irregularly, and much of it disagreed with him. There was none of it he really enjoyed. He drank vast quantities of tea instead. And this in turn kept him from sleeping soundly.

He remembered, as he sat there, how he had lain beside a window many years ago, staring at the gray landscape of northern France outside, equally oppressed and bewildered. And as he looked out at the gray Oriental street, it occurred to him, how little really had happened since then; how, after all these years, he still was experiencing the very same longings and apprehensions that had troubled his childhood.

Some mystery fell like a shadow across his existence in this city; and across his existence before that too, he realized. What was it, what could it be?

One by one he conjured up before his mind the ardors of his earlier days: perhaps, he thought, the secret lies there!

With a hot sigh he let fall the curtains across the window, placed his hand upon his violently beating heart, and allowed his mind to wander once again among the subtle landscapes of his childhood.

✻

The ugly, melancholy château near Compiègne! How well he could remember it—rambling, arid, listless, though like an absent-minded old woman still pretending to dignity and performing the graceless and wavering posture out of sheer weariness, sheer inertia. The panes were missing from some of the windows, the grass was high and wild, and in every corner of the cellar, the garret and the stables, the smell of moisture and decaying wood lay curled like a snake.

And yet, the mere thought of it moved him almost to tears. The hours he had spent there, ill and sullen, tortured by boyish desires which he could never resist, harassed by every stray word and gesture, longing to hurt everyone else in return. And then the hours when he used to sit entranced in the declining arbor, reading, watching the green sunlight upon the ancient mossy façade, the emerging leaves, the butterflies, the spiders amid the grape vines, the white kitten playing on the gravel. He could even remember the old morocco-backed volumes—*Astrée, Alexandre, Le Grand Cyrus.* How the sonorous names and the immense passions had thrilled him, young though he was! Asia! Through the crisp ironic pages of *La Reine de Golconde* or *La Princesse de Babylone* would flash the cruel charms of that continent—the scintillation of garments, the gold and silver, the vast stretches spotted with magnificent tents and delicate oases, the seductive smiles, the ruinous perfumes, the fascinating tyrannies. And a bit later, when he read *Les Liaisons Dangereuses* and *Les Egarements*, already he felt as if he had experienced, in his thirteen sequestered years, all those intricate and disillusioning attachments which bewildered him and yet at the same time filled him with such longing.

For hours he would sit in the garden, watching the ducks on the pond below, and in the distance the hues of April hovering upon the forest, the hill, the comatose pasture lands. The apple tree was in bloom. Heavy, as if each twig were laden with snow; and when he entered the shadows underneath he felt as if he were entering another world, the continuous sound of the bees in the budding and honeyed silence, the intoxicating fragrance, the new

grass already deep and soft, the intruding sunlight upon
the trunk, everything so still, amorous and secret that
when he stepped out again he felt dizzy and sad, as if he
had just arisen from a blissful dream.

But overshadowing all other memories was the memory
of his mother. He could see her leaning over him, the
light of the lamp on her cheek, her smooth black hair,
violet scented, and her long green earrings; and her kind
and gentle face, distinguished by that extreme loveliness
which springs from a pure simplicity of mind and nobility
of heart; so accustomed to forget herself, she had been, and
so full of adoration, that the many acts of cruelty and
injustice performed toward her lost all weight in her mind
when balanced against the few gestures of affection that
came her way—an unexpected kiss, a dutiful tender word,
a hasty caress. All the humiliations, bitter moments of suspense and bewilderment and unrelieved anguish, had still
left her miraculously free of grievance. Perhaps because
she had always been so very modest, expecting nothing at
all and forever eager to give away out of the love that
filled her heart. And yet, since she never really dared
expect even the faintest gesture of love, she appeared at
times deceptively cold. And he could never guess at those
moments what she really thought of him, how much she
really loved him, or indeed how unhappy she was.

They would go painting together in the garden or the
meadow near by. She would spread out her water-colors
and design idyllic little scenes—a girl with a pink parasol
and a kitten in her arm, great big eyes, silky curls, and the
raindrops falling on the tight silk, each drop shining. They
looked to him like tears shed by the angels of heaven in
lamentation of the sad fate which awaits all little children.
And he in turn would draw a flower or a bird with his

[411]

pastels, and under it write "For my dear Mama." He would feel bewildered but flattered later to see that it was not her own picture, but his, so crude and simple by contrast, which she would place on the *écritoire* and command everyone to admire.

Suddenly filled with an intense longing to see her clearly, he strove to conjure forth the vision of her face. But in vain, of course; it was gone forever. The gray eyes, the soft brown hair—even they seemed faint and illusory: and actually all that he could see was the dim contours of a face neither lovely nor charming, and all that he could say about it was that it represented, everlastingly for him, love. The only thing that returned, that was real now, was his desperate love, suddenly and bewilderingly alive again, all the more poignant after the lonely, estranging hours and miles which intervened. He could remember her one summer afternoon, a vague black shape in taffeta, sitting in her room beside a jar of orchids and weeping. And when he entered shyly, she snatched him into her arms, hugged and kissed him with sudden violence, and then began to weep, her features distorted and horrifying. He too began to cry, moved by a new sort of love, moved by her womanly tenderness, perhaps, or by the lamplight on the silk, or by the faint perfume of the orchids in the black jar, or by terror. It wasn't until much later that he really understood this isolated and disturbing scene.

When he was a small child of very delicate health he used to have bad dreams, night after night. He would dream of the devil, for example, whom he always saw for some reason as an obsequious pallid creature wearing a blue shirt and carrying a cane. Or he would wake up, in the middle of the night, all of a sudden dreadfully afraid lest his mother should die. The name of his mother, music

[412]

upon his lips whenever he murmured it to himself, would
haunt him through the darkness. And he would leap out
of the feverish bed, run into her room where she seemed
already to be awaiting him, burst into tears upon her
breast while she caressed him. "Paul, Paul," she would
whisper, "my darling Paul." Three or four years later, he
would awaken, similarly frightened; he would arise, creep
softly to her door, pause, tremble, then return again and
lie awake in his bed, wondering unhappily what was
wrong.

It was three months after the scene in her room that
summer afternoon (which occurred when he was fourteen) that she died. She had for two painful years been
secretly and mortally sick, it now became clear. He heard
his aunt's footsteps climbing the stairway one evening in
September, and suddenly realizing everything in an instant of dazzling perception, had fled breathlessly. He sat
crouching in the garret, first still as a doll and then weeping wildly, with the utter, hopeless, unreasoning anguish
of childhood, when grief is less ravaging perhaps but even
more vast and imperious than later—for it descends, so to
speak, in all its majesty, no barriers have been erected, no
replies have been devised. It is as if the sun were to be
buried forever and existence were to become novel, dark,
and strange. That was how he had felt, seeing through the
crevices in the sloping roof and through that wilderness of
tears the gradually subsiding glitter of the sunlight upon
the rich green foliage in the garden.

Three days later he crept into her room one evening.
Her paintings, and his own silly little ones as well, were
hanging on the wall, on the little marble-topped table lay
an old album, a bowl of wilting flowers, and the *Médita-
tions* of Lamartine, and under her bed stood her pair of red

morocco boudoir slippers. He stared at them all with wide eyes, until suddenly the sight of the morocco slippers, like the edge of a knife twisting ever so slightly in the flesh, called forth the sting of his slumbering grief, and his tears began to flow wildly. He saw the pear tree glowing in the sunset outside. All shuddering with golden rain, it seemed to be. He saw now how she had loved him, and there was no one left to love him! How he too had loved her, and there was no one left for him to love ever again!

☆

After that he went to Nancy to live with his wealthy aunt. That too he could remember in detail. The iron balcony, where he stood at night, feeling himself to be a glamorous and passionate figure, like Robespierre perhaps, or Saint-Just, watching the huge gilded street lamp through the foliage, listening to the water trickling over the baroque angels into the huge gray scalloped sea shells. Below him, the ugly garden, the sylvan view, the statue of a nymph inexpressibly *gauche* and wistful; beyond, the tiny canal with its lily pads, the garden house, overgrown and dank, the rows of willows and maples so weirdly graceful; mellow and moribund as only the trees of northern France could be. And covering the landscape, like the shadow of a huge bird, the spirit of distrust.

And then his own room. The books scattered about on the floor: a huge illustrated Froissart, *Le Chevalier de Maison Rouge*, a translation of *Kenilworth*, and the poems of Verlaine which were already at that time exercising their intoxication on him. He could still remember the scenes on the wall paper, the temples, the enormous birds, the sheep, the stupid shepherds and shepherdesses with their hideously muscular legs; the bed with its lavender-scented coverlet bespangled with crimson flowers, on which he would lie in the late afternoon, watching the dusty rays of the sun falling on the carpet, yielding habitually to those images, mysteries of the flesh which he only faintly understood and which grew so sweet to him that they haunted, positively haunted, him all day long, and often suddenly in the middle of the night aroused him out of sleep; the ornate gilt clock, covered with a dome of glass, the paper-weight which displayed, as soon as it was shaken, a wintry village landscape in a snowstorm; the two bronze lions from Nemours, the heavy green curtains, the mirror into which he used to stare without interruption until suddenly his face seemed to become dangerous and alien, and he fled in terror.

He had understood his aunt with the cunning and word-less but complete subtlety of childhood. And yet, how he had despised her! "The boy must grow stronger," she used to say in her very low voice. "The boy must learn to *en-dure.*" She herself had endured too much; that was what so incurably ailed her, no doubt. She was not wicked or malicious by nature, but her life was now on a plane of incessant harshness and denial. Sorrow had done that; sorrow unqualified by such a sweet modesty as his mother's. So that the concepts of lenience, sympathy, comfort, under-standing, had deserted her for once and for all. Weakness in her eyes demanded punishment, and grief was a form of weakness. The expression engraved upon her masculine face had grown more and more bitter, her gaze was cold and hard as stone. And still, there was a certain stupid animal majesty about the manner in which she bore her bleak avaricious existence, so utterly unworth enduring.

The only thing that ever softened this gaze of stone was a glimpse of the misfortunes of others. When a piece of bad luck befell a neighbor of hers, or a relative, an expression of quiet joy, almost a certain ecstasy, would flow over her face. She would look kindly and pious at those moments. Once or twice when little Paul hurt himself or fell ill, a look of sweet contentment would glide across her eyes and her lips. He almost believed, then, that she loved him a little bit, after all, and his pain would thereupon almost give him pleasure.

She was half-mad, really. Only one thing could have saved her. Love. But of course all hope of that had vanished bitter years ago, and since she had to do without it she inevitably moved closer and closer to the cold cliff-like edge of solitude, and finally fell over quite noiselessly, like many another old woman, into the completely lonely but protected sea of madness—that province of the weak, the solitary, the utterly grief-stricken, the too old. All these things he had understood, even as a boy, or had, at least, suspected.

☆

His first love affair had come when he was eleven years old. A widowed cousin of his mother's, Madame de Serrano, had come to stay at Compiègne for a few days. He could remember nothing of it, except the scent of lilacs that flowed across his cheeks when Madame de Serrano leaned over to kiss him good-night one evening as he lay

in bed; and how in a sudden access of passion, remembering his mother, perhaps, he had put his arms around her
neck and held her head, for an instant, before relapsing
into the darkness of the coverlet and his shy boy's bewilderment. But for weeks, for months thereafter, he thought
of her as he lay in his bed at night, intoxicated by her
womanly sympathy, agonizingly jealous at the thought of
all the others who might at that very moment be speaking
to her, listening to her, touching her. . . .

And then, when he was fifteen, a distant relative,
Claudine Montpellier, came to visit his aunt. She stayed
for three weeks. He could scarcely remember her now. She
was several years older than he—twenty or twenty-one,
black-haired, black-eyed, large, languorous, with a slow
and sleepy manner, a dim and stagnant face. How it had
first happened he did not know; but he could recall very
vividly indeed the assignations, conveyed on bits of green
paper with all the secrecy and classic formality of a scene
in Crébillon; the meetings in the warm garden, amidst the
foliage beside the clumsy but suddenly evocative statue,
his wonder and delight to find her so maternally understanding of his ardors, so responsive, so resourceful. How
thrilled he had been to feel her breathing quickly beside
him, to recognize her own desire, to feel the incomparable
mystery of a woman's body slowly revealing itself for the
first time to his finger tips in the complete and leafy darkness. The thought of those curves preyed on his mind all
night, all day; he couldn't tear himself away from those
detailed recollections of the previous evening, the detailed
plans and conjectures for the night to come. And then, at
ten o'clock he would climb out of his window and would
find her waiting on the bench beneath the sycamore; and
finally they would lie down on the warm grass among the

heliotropes and he would reach a trembling hand underneath her black muslin dress, insatiably curious to understand more and more deeply the textures, the curves, the
rhythmical secrecies of that soft milk-white skin; while, to
his hot surprise, she plucked tenderly at his clothes, equally
ardent, equally curious it appeared to exhaust those puerile mysteries. How quickly they had learned! How mature
and unabashed their approach had become after three or
four nights, and how complete and elaborate had been
their abandonment!

She left, suddenly, after three weeks; he never understood why; his aunt was as always, brusque, unfathomable.

For months he had lain hot and panting at night, struggling to recapture each instant, each suave conquest of
delicate amorous territory, each new flutter of the heart
and ecstasy of the flesh. He had wept with longing. But
then he forgot her. Two years later, his aunt came into
the room one day and said, "Your cousin Claudine Montpellier has just died. I think you remember her, don't you?
She was tubercular, you know."

★

But at that time he had already entered upon what it
pleased him subsequently to call his "years of secrecy." He
could later remember almost nothing about them except
the constant feverish reading; how he had imagined himself to be now like Julien Sorel, now like Frédéric Moreau,
now like Hippolytus. And then the poets—Verlaine at
first, then a bout of adoration for Baudelaire, then Rim-
baud, and finally Mallarmé. He could not read without

trembling that poem about the sighing and silvery-nailed
enchantresses who pursued the lice in the little boy's hair;
in the sound of the September beeches he could hear the
very words of Verlaine,

> Les sanglots longs
> Des violons
> De l'automne
> Blessent mon coeur
> D'une langueur
> Monotone . . .

and about whom but himself could such a line have been
written as,

> J'ai plus de souvenirs que si j'avais mille ans,

which held inclosed in its brief compass, so he supposed,
all the incalculable and inescapable sorrow of the world?

Later he wrote poems himself, and these were subsequently (some years after the really brilliant success of his
two novels, *La Famille Quidinet* and *Le Forêt Sentimental*) published under the title of *Préludes*. But no one
bothered about them in the least; they went quite unnoticed. But it didn't matter, his aunt had died in the
meantime and had left him her entire fortune.

☆

Thus, in the fragrant privacy of his room overlooking
the Quai Voltaire, the world began to change for him.
Everything was reversed, in a sense. The sea no longer
seemed vast, but rather a small and tranquil isle of water;
death appeared as gentle, love as austere, loveliness as

insidious; winter as a time of spiritual riches and growth, summer as a time of majestic and loveless stagnation; and so on. His life, it seemed to him, was becoming a persuasive sort of poem.

But one day, in a sudden fit of disgust, he discovered that his chief emotion in writing a poem lay, simply, in the fact that he was indeed writing a poem. The world seemed far, far away, it was leaving him behind. He trembled with anxiety. He rose, walked out into the street, and went strolling along the Seine.

It is always odd, of course, how the most trivial thing can change a whole life—a stranger passing a window, a distant sail on a lake, a shape on a beach, losing one's way some evening in a foreign city, a girl's smiling face glimpsed in some southern village. But it is always like a finger casually pressed, to open the fascinating and fatal casket of our waiting impulses. On this same raw March evening in the Tuileries gardens he paused near the carrousel to tie a shoestring; and it was there he overheard, uttered haltingly in a young girl's voice, a rather foreign voice, Spanish perhaps, one single word: the Mediterranean.

The Mediterranean! It seemed incredible to him, then and there, under these bleak hazy clouds, that such a southern land could really exist as he imagined; such a caressing air, such blue lapping wavelets, such sun-drenched leaves. Perhaps it was out of the centuries of human contemplation that they arose, out of the poetry, the ornamentation and the longing which had surrounded for so long each glittering Ægean isle, each stone foaming with spray and shaded with arches of foliage, even the azure dome of the sky.

And, as his gaze fell unseeingly upon the darkening

statues and the leafless trees, he noticed that his whole body was trembling with excitement.

Four days later he found himself on the *Général Cambion*, bound for Mallorca.

☆

It was in Palma that he had met Olivia Barrios. Palma, with the rows of boats rocking in gentle unison under the starlight, the scarcely visible figure of an idler in ragged clothes or a dark-skinned girl standing provocatively by the black water; the walk in front of the cathedral which stared majestically across the sea, the fountains on each side of the great stairway hidden in foliage, filled with tentative murmurs and reclining figures; and on another night the bay full of scattered fishing-boats moving slowly across the sparkling water by torchlight, the oars, the net, the fisherman's dark body alert and extended, all fringed with the glaring light from the torches, and, as he watched, the silvery fish emerging in the meshes of the silvery net, the whole bay suddenly silver as a breeze fluttered across it and created ten thousand ripples, the sky inexplicably bright, everything flashing in a moment of glory as if it were about to melt away; everything demanding of him one thing—that he fall in love.

He would remember his mother. And with her, the everlasting sweetness of the womanly spirit, the truly womanly; so modest, so tender, yet so full of a fire far more enduring than that of all men but a very few, in its obsessions far more courageous, in its sufferings far more superb, in its fidelity far more forgiving. He would long, then, for a

[421]

woman's voice, a woman's shape to see and be near, perhaps to touch. He felt flushed with desire, all of a sudden.

And it was not long after that he discovered (one evening as she entered the dining-room of the Victoria; the musicians were playing Haydn's "Surprise") how incredibly beautiful Olivia Barrios was; the luminous tint in her cheeks, the ironic pout on her lips, the flash of her eyes which seemed so innocent and yet so wicked. She puzzled and excited him, and very shortly his conscience announced, "You are in love."

It was only after he married her, of course, that he discovered little by little what his wife was like. One night in particular—as he was leaning over to kiss her neck while she was sitting in front of the mirror arranging her hair— the window was open and they could hear the young boatmen singing on the Lake—she turned her beautiful black head away impatiently, and he suddenly saw her for what she really was: a selfish, heartless calculating woman with romantic yearnings; grasping, lascivious, languorous; without real affection, without a trace of solicitude or understanding. He sauntered alone down the street in Cernobbio that night, feeling a curious sort of relief, as if, since he already suspected that he did not love her, after all, he had now discovered a perfect and natural reason for his indifference.

So on their journey together through the Orient, he discovered at last some sort of calm, it seemed that the world after all possessed nothing that he could not bear to be without. He longed only to see more of the world, more and more, in a quiet way. He met the little Belgian, Goupillière, in Saïgon one day, and together the three of them flew by plane to Kashgar at the end of August, just when the heat was beginning to subside a bit.

In Kashgar he would sit and scribble away at his essays (collected later under the title *Apollon*)—notes on Claude, Piranesi, Bellini, Delacroix, discourses on Restif de la Bretonne, Marivaux, Delavigne, Stendhal; he felt only occasionally a twinge of longing or despair, at something never attained or forever lost, youth, say, and its self-forgetting and self-misunderstanding brightness. But not often.

Not, that is, until this new excitement began to blossom forth in him, and grow and grow, day by day. Those measureless spaces, dried-up rivers, monstrous precipices, anonymous tribes—little by little they crept into his mind, casting novel and disturbing shadows there.

And then, when he found that his money would not reach; when he began to suspect that he was being spied upon; when he fell in love with a passing shape and his flesh was constantly on the alert; when in a whisper here, an insinuation there, he learned of new dangers—of vast tempests, unendurable cold and heat, bestial hatreds, frightful epidemics—then his heart did begin to beat more quickly, and the future seemed full of excitements. Danger, danger: the thought of it was tremendously warming. Something deep inside him longed for it; for pain, for torture, for extremity. Captured, at last, by reality! Ensnared by the will of these hordes, these unpredictable Asiatic hordes, with their beautiful, shining limbs and their eyes flashing with obscene cruelties, all slowly approaching, about to take him to themselves, their ancient and consuming selves.

45

The Seventy Streets

AGAIN DE LA SCAZE DISCARDED HIS "PINCE-NEZ" AND again he learned to reverse his hours—to sleep by day and to walk and observe by night. He grew so familiar with the sceneries of night that each street corner by moonlight or in moonless darkness was known to him—places that by day, if he happened to pass them before sunset, still looked quite unfamiliar.

It occurred to him now that he might visit the *serai* again, and discover whether his little Belgian and the huge Russian were still there. But then, instantly, he was filled with a feeling of uneasiness, of disgust. The past, again. Better discard it altogether. The thought of his wife, of Dr. Liu, and all the rest of them, crossed his mind.

But a moment later he willfully dismissed all recollections of them, for once and for all.

The nights grew less chilly. They glowed like sapphires, and presently the universal odors of April arrived, and the breath from the scattered opening blossoms in the gardens slipped over the wall and filled the dark silent streets. Here and there the white branch of a fruit tree hung negligently over a wall and when a breeze passed its petals fell through the darkness, down perchance through the ray of a solitary lantern, and onto the black pavement.

Near by flowed the river, red and shallow. Through the poplars that lined the shore could be seen the yellow desolate hills and, on clear days, the remote peaks of the Tian Shan, the Mountains of Heaven, to the north.

The trade routes were now being opened again and from the south and west came the traders. A number of Russians had just arrived, coming by way of Andijan, two weeks to the west. These brought iron, oil and cheap manufactured objects from Russia, and in return took wool and sheepskins and woven things. All night they filled the city with their noisy and elementary drunkenness. From the south over Leh the Indians began to come, more delicate of face and dealing in more delicate objects—silks, rugs, perfumes, and such. Quiet men, these; they detested and despised the noisy Russians.

He grew to know Aqsu thoroughly. "The City of Seventy Streets," Layeville had called it. He came to know all of them, finally. Most of the dwellers were Turkis, a few were Mongols, almost all of the rest were Chinese. There were no more than fifty Russians, some of them White Russians, the rest agents of the Soviet who little by little through secret channels were gaining power over the city. They lived near the *serai*, most of them, in the shabby

[425]

foreigners' quarter. The Chinese quarter was the quietest part of town, and the cleanest. In the other sections the narrow winding streets and the wide bazaars were littered with the refuse of months, thick with intimate odors of one kind and another. North of the city wall stood a Chinese temple upon a hillock, nestling amidst the tamarisks and overlooking the gardens and houses of the officials. South of the city, outside the walls, lay the mulberry grove and the cemetery. Here among the stones sat the occasional mourners, absent-mindedly picking at their toes or biting their finger nails, now and then singing softly or muttering in a sudden access of devoutness. Near them prowled the shaggy mules and the scavenger dogs.

✫

He now preferred to walk alone. Through the city and out beyond the walls he would go, further and further until each little road and nettle-edged path into the hills or the desert was known to him. Best of all he liked to climb the low hill that overlooked the city and watch the black and silent labyrinth dotted with its feeble lanterns. He always had the feeling, on these nightly excursions, that he might find something—a revelation, a shape. Perhaps the shape of that lovely girl whom he could not dispel from his mind. Perhaps love, reality, life itself. For he was secretly quite sure, he *knew*, that all these things were quietly waiting for him in this city.

One night as he passed the cemetery where many of the beggars slept, on his way to the temple grove, he saw a white bundled figure lying beside the stream that followed the path. He stopped for a moment, and peered inquisitively. Then he saw that the man was not sleeping, but was staring at him with great frightened eyes.

He turned around and was about to walk on when a frail voice cried to him, "Sir, have pity!"

He paused and looked back at the recumbent shape. "Pity a poor old man who has suffered much," whined the old Mohammedan in a soft musical voice and raised his hand.

De la Scaze reached into his pocket and held out a paper *tael*.

"No, no," said the voice sadly, the head moving slowly from side to side. "You have misunderstood me— It is not money that the grief-stricken heart desires—"

De la Scaze was about to put the money back into his pocket when the dark little hand reached forth and quietly slipped the note out from between his fingers. "Sit beside me, kind stranger," said the Mohammedan, "and I shall tell you a tale."

So de la Scaze sat beside him, among the stones and little mounds and sleeping shapes, watching the brooklet at his feet flicker beneath the starlight. All the while, with a great show of despair, the old man recounted to him his losses.

"All of my life I have been terribly in love," he began after a moment's quiet. "She has been dead for twenty years. But I am still in love with her—" He folded his hands primly in his lap and gazed imploringly into de la Scaze's eyes. An odd face, he had. Peaked and remote, terribly wrinkled, yet suffused with energy. It was in his watery, lashless red eyes that this energy lay. For they seemed to be looking for something, to have been looking for something for many years, with a wild, inhuman intensity. It was an animal look, the look of a dying animal frantically searching for a last refuge.

"Your wife?" asked de la Scaze softly.

"Ah no. . . . My daughter." He lowered his eyes. "She died when she was fourteen. My only treasure. Eyes like a deer's, a voice tender as the murmur of this stream. Yes, she loved me as a daughter should love her father!" His voice grew proud and he smiled. "I was a great man then, with fire in my eyes; a lion; but with my gentle daughter I was like a little lamb."

He glanced at de la Scaze with sudden fretfulness, and then continued, in a quick and breathless way: "You think I am mad. Yes, I am mad. Love like this is a kind of madness. Madness begins when a man enters upon a secret path of his own through the wilderness. I have walked along my secret path for twenty years, but it is a path of love, full of warmth. Love is a lantern I carry by my side. It reaches its golden finger into the darkness and its warm breath rises and covers my old shoulders like a shawl. I live all alone, and I see others, their words and faces, as only waves in a lake, gray and watchful, without names, forever about to vanish.

"But the solitude of being an old and foolish man! Nothing to befriend me except my little lantern of tenderness. No one to speak to, no one to understand me— You think such a love is wicked and unnatural? Ah, the laws of nature are not the laws of man! Look around. On every side I see the most desperate of unnatural griefs, unnatural cruelties, unnatural fears, hatreds and desires, flourishing like weeds in this wild country. Nature. What is nature? All that nature really is, as far as I can see, is fickleness, inhumanity; and now and then, very rarely, she exhales a breath of sweet and delicate tenderness." His voice grew elated, his eyes glowed. "Yes, yes. Very rarely. But I have known her to be kind.

"Look around. Do you see these sleeping men?" He pointed a shaking bony finger toward the slope where the white stones and the white bodies lay, almost indistinguishable. "There lie the inhabitants of this world, sleeping, or half asleep, or freshly awakened out of a nightmare, or weeping quietly with self-pity, or praying. They are so still that you do not hear them, their faces are so gray that you do not see them. And yet, if you could hold a candle to a single one of those hearts, you could see all of life, the shape of history by this little red gleam, the horror of our isolation, the uncontrollable love of man. Do you see?" He leaned with a happy smile toward de la Scaze and touched him very lightly on the arm.

"Oh, stranger," he cried, in a soft little girl's voice, "I feel full of love! Full of happiness! I love those sleepers! I love you! I love everyone! I love this lovely world which I am about to leave forever!" Suddenly he turned away and buried his insane and passionate little face in his arms.

☆

Another night he sat down amongst the trees that girdled the tumbledown Chinese temple. Most of these were tamarisks, but one was a fruit tree in full blossom—an apricot tree perhaps; its petals hovered upon the edge of each twig like small butterflies, and underneath it existed a veritable maze of scents and gleams, little paths fluttering back and forth among the twigs and budding leaves. Here he sat down.

[429]

He was half asleep when he saw a great masculine shape lumbering up the path toward him, swaying unevenly, bubbling and belching as it paused to drink from a dark bottle that caught the flashing moonlight for an instant.

De la Scaze moved uneasily. Instantly the figure paused and stared. "Who is there?" a voice bellowed melodramatically, in Russian. "Friend or foe?" And the face peered into the shadow of the trees, full of suspicion.

"Friend," replied de la Scaze after a moment, in halting Russian.

The stranger seemed reassured. He came up to de la Scaze and stood beside him, glowering at him. Then he sat down without a word. De la Scaze could smell his violent breath. Presently he slapped de la Scaze on the back. Then he put his arm around his shoulder.

"My friend," he said bluntly, and paused, searching for words to express the geniality and eagerness that was so irresistibly welling up within him. "My name is Mihailov," he said finally, with relief and sudden positiveness. "Pavel Mihailov. . . ." He began to laugh gently. "And you?"

"I am French. Jean Barillot is my name. Barillot."

The Russian seemed mildly disconcerted. "French," he repeated, pensively. "From France, is that?"

De la Scaze nodded.

"Oh." The stranger seemed reassured. He paused, then raised the bottle to his lips again. "I am from Russia," he said rather soothingly.

"Russia is a great country," said Mihailov, as if in corroboration. "Greater," he added quite flatly and amiably, "than your France. Greater than England, even. Much greater," and his voice grew more assertive and hostile, "than Japan— Yes."

"Why is Russia so great?" asked de la Scaze with gravity. "The people? The land?"

The stranger was puzzled. "Russia," he replied with vagueness and dignity, "is full of new things. New music, new sports, new machines, new cinemas, new buildings and bridges, new railways. All very important! Everything shines with newness in Russia. Everyone is full of enthusiasm. The people embrace each other on the streets out of enthusiasm for their big new country; they laugh, they leap, they cry with joy."

"They do?" said de la Scaze, in an interested manner.

Mihailov looked at him suspiciously. "Everyone," he said, in a rather surly voice, "must love the new Russia, for it is the greatest country in the world!" He grew thoughtful. Suddenly he threw away the bottle into the clump of tamarisks and placed his chin upon his palm. "I am very homesick for Russia," he said in a hoarse whisper.

De la Scaze looked at him. He could see the young beard curling over the coarse skin and the long lashes covering the eyes. His face was round and red, like an apple. His teeth were black, his face was covered with pimples, and yet there was something so young, so potent, so full of spontaneous and indiscriminate love in his face that he seemed almost glowingly handsome. Two or three white petals were clinging to his matted black hair, rather bizarrely. "How old are you, Pavel Mihailov?" he asked.

"How many years, you mean?"

"Yes."

He hesitated. "Twenty-seven." De la Scaze suspected that he had invented this. Perhaps he didn't know precisely how old he was.

"Where were you born?"

"In Novosibirsk," announced Mihailov with pride. "It

[431]

was then a little village of log huts. Now it is a great and wonderful city, full of important new houses and new people." His voice grew melancholy.

"When I was a boy," he murmured, "my father took me hunting. We would go deep into the forest in spring and kill the bears. Or we would go trapping sables. Or in the winter we would pursue the wolves. On cold winter nights the wolves came to the edge of the village and watched us. Sometimes in the middle of the night they crept through the street, hungry and full of rage." His voice trembled softly with excitement; he looked into de la Scaze's eyes with eagerness, longing to convey what so moved him.

"Sometimes we went out in the winter night in a sleigh, to go to the church or visit a sick neighbor. We would see the wolves then, and kill them. Then we would come home, sit by the fire, drink, sing! I was a happy boy—" He brushed his fingers across his eyes, hardly able to speak.

"Are there no more churches in Siberia?"

Mihailov hesitated. Then his voice sank into a confidential whisper. "Yes. There are still churches in Siberia. The women still hang flowers upon the wayside ikons. The people still get drunk and dance to the music of the accordion. In some places nothing has changed. The people are weak from vodka and syphilis and malaria, all of them. . . . Yes, I too," and he pointed to himself. "Life changes slowly in the loneliest places of Siberia. The land is still wet in the spring with shining lakes, where the wild animals come to drink at sunset. The endless forests of larch and birch still hide many things."

He stretched his arms and groaned. "But here! It is terrible here! I tell you," and he leaned over and breathed heavily into de la Scaze's face, "everyone changes here, as if by magic. As if they had stepped into another life. I

[432]

have seen it many times. Everything that is secure vanishes. What you have learned is unlearned. You change; you do not become a different man, but a different self comes up in you. It makes you unhappy.

"But it makes you wise! I have learned that." He got to his feet, tugged clumsily at his breeches and, spreading his legs, looked out over the sleeping city. De la Scaze could see the thin glittering stream cutting like a needle down across the quiet dark night, and beyond, deep in the stillness, he could see the city, shadowy as the earth itself; it seemed incredible that there should still be life in that silent ocean-blue pattern of walls.

Mihailov turned around, tucking his big shirt back into place. "Everything in life must be seen before we die. Night as well as day, the frightening as well as the soothing. Yes. Don't you agree?" He sounded older suddenly, and for a moment his dark face, staring down at de la Scaze, looked like the face of a saintly old man. "Yes. The wicked as well as the good. That is the only way to understand things. That's what my grandmother always taught me."

*

Once or twice strange things happened. One evening as he walked through the bazaar, and the lights were being lit one by one, he stopped beside a curtained window. Through the red silk and the iron lattice-work the sound of a voice slipped, like the light from the flickering lamp inside the room, out into the street. Bewitching. The

[433]

voice of an old man, he thought one moment, and the next, the voice of a girl. Very faint, tremorous, dreamy.

And when he lowered his eyes to the pavement again, he saw another shadow lying there beside his own. For a moment he stared. Then it vanished. Behind him he heard a quick fluttering noise, like the wings of a bird or the rustling of a leaf across a path. When he turned around and looked, he saw no one.

This wasn't the only time. Several times he felt singularly as if he were not quite alone. Almost alone, but not quite. On walks through the alleys, through the bazaar, along the stream, across the cemetery—it happened in all of these places. A shadow, a noise of disappearing footsteps, a whisper behind a wall, a warm breath on his cheek, the touch of a woman's garment brushing against his own.

Some, of course, were bolder. After they had grown used to seeing him, day after day, some of them would come up to him, and tug at his sleeves and smile, now with an air of mockery and now with a pleading and intimate tenderness, imploring him to come with them. They would whisper in low voices, or laugh, showing their white teeth. But he never dared to go with them, perhaps because he was afraid that they might, after all, only be teasing him. And then, of course, he had no money left.

And then, too, there was this little terror in him. In those eyes, those voices, he could detect the endless centuries, the nameless hosts, and the caressing, destroying power which lurked within these. He would feel himself drawn on by an intense longing. And an instant later he would draw back uneasily.

☆

One night in May he walked into a café and sat down, feeling rather dizzy. He closed his eyes and listened to the monotonous music in the next room, trying to banish all thoughts from his mind. He felt weak; he hadn't really had enough to eat for several days.

When he opened his eyes he saw a stranger sitting opposite him, a European. Tall and slender, quite respectable-looking except for a certain expression on his face which disfigured him far more effectively than any rapier cut or scarring disease could have done.

As soon as he sat up and looked about, the stranger began to smile at him. "You are a newcomer to this city?" he said.

De la Scaze nodded, amazed that the man should have addressed him in French. "I have been here a short time. Not long."

"Several weeks?" The man spoke in a deep and precise way, sensitive and yet full of confidence. It was a good, comforting voice to listen to; de la Scaze hoped that he would go on talking.

"Yes."

"Several months, perhaps?"

"Since October." He was hardly aware of what he was saying, the man's voice was so magnetic and persuasive. He seemed to hover over de la Scaze's head, shading him, soothing him, so to speak, with the unguent of his voice.

"Ah. I have lived here eleven years. My name is Antonopoulos." He smiled. "I know the city well. And what is more, I understand it. . . . That is what counts. Not to be deceived. It is a rich city, full of amiable secrets. You would hardly have suspected that?"

De la Scaze smiled politely.

Presently Antonopoulos rose. De la Scaze was amazed to

[435]

see how tall he was. "Come," he said, lightly placing his hand on de la Scaze's shoulder. "Let me show you the room above. . . . This place," he said rather vaguely, as if an irrelevant idea had just occurred to him, "belongs to me. You must make yourself at ease. I am always happy to see Europeans."

A girl was dancing in the room upstairs. He sat down beside Antonopoulos and watched, suddenly breathless and alert. As fragile as a flower she was, her fingers and tiny feet moving as exquisitely as a petal swaying in a gentle breath of air, repetitious, monotonous, yet ever so full of the subtlest variations, a new curve hesitantly introduced, a new shadow serenely exploited. Her peach-colored child's body was fluid and lovely. But her face, framed in yellow brocade, was as stagnant as porcelain; totally expressionless except that in its complete stagnation a certain rather frightening knowingness, a depraved irony, was to be detected, like the nightmare glaze of a yellow rose in a jar which one has thought to be real, and, on leaning over to savor its fragrance, discovers to be of wax.

De la Scaze's hands began to tremble. At first he did not know why. A soft little delirium began to operate in his brain.

Then he understood. This was the girl. This was that entrancing and elusive shape he had glimpsed on his second night in Aqsu, and had been seeking ever since. Drops of sweat appeared on his forehead, his mouth opened, his lips quivered.

But then, before he knew it, she had vanished again. The music continued, but she was gone. For a minute or two her intoxicating body still danced before his eyes, insolent and beckoning. Then he ran his hand over his forehead and looked around.

The end of the room opened onto a tiny balcony, and the night air crept through the thick silk curtains that trembled gently over the doorway. The flames in the lanterns flickered ever so faintly, so that the faces of the watchers seemed to change in expression momentarily, as the flame moved to and fro.

On the balcony two boys were singing; rather gayly, rather carelessly, a quick throaty sound of laughter now and again breaking across the perfumed words. It was a song of love, full of subdued and traditional similes; but beneath those two voices de la Scaze felt a curious disturbance, not sorrow, rather a childlike despondency, a precocious weariness and disgust with the patterns of life. Presently the boys entered the room. Their faces were painted and they wore long embroidered garments. One was slightly older than the other. Both of them were smiling, and in looking at the face of the younger one de la Scaze felt an abrupt twinge of memory: the features were not unfamiliar. But he could not decide whether or where he had ever seen them before. "Those are her brothers," explained Antonopoulos.

While the two boys did a dance Antonopoulos talked to de la Scaze. "That man in the corner," he said, pointing to a gross middle-aged man in a brocaded robe; full of fleshy folds, eyelids dark and shimmering, but yet not without a certain echo in his eyes—understanding, resignation, some peculiar power or wisdom: "that man is Koumis. Have you ever heard of Koumis?"

De la Scaze shook his head. It made him unhappy to look at Koumis. He felt very weak, suddenly.

"He is a god in this city. Many years ago he resembled a god, too—strong as Vulcan, muscular as Mercury, regular as Apollo. Now he is the richest man in the province."

De la Scaze turned sideways. Antonopoulos was speaking

[437]

intently, with an urbane mingling of admiration and hostility.

"He trades in the white drug," he continued blandly. "Heroin. Have you ever taken heroin?"

De la Scaze shook his head absently, watching the slow symbolical gestures of longing, the ornate narrative postures of the dance.

"The drug comes across the desert from China, sent in small concentrated tins. It is sent out from this city to the Caspian, the Black Sea, the Indian Ocean, Istambul, and the Mediterranean. It is very complicated. Most of the clients are young men of twenty or so. Those two boys, for example, use heroin. Most of the boys in this city use heroin. It is neither expensive nor difficult to purchase here. . . ." He went on and on. De la Scaze wondered why he was being told all this. The dancers had left, everything was quiet.

The man leaned toward him and whispered, "You need money, perhaps?" De la Scaze could only bring himself to shake his head.

Suddenly sickened, he rose, nodded farewell, and walked quickly home through the silent winding streets, his heart beating violently and his mind still dizzy with the fragrant image of the dancing girl.

☆

When he arrived at his house, Hussein was waiting for him. He had apparently just arrived. He had a bit of news. One of the traders, a man from Khotan, had died three hours ago of cholera.

46

The Somnambulists

IN LESS THAN A DAY, IT SEEMED, TWO SHAPES ROSE
quietly out of the gutters and began to press their
fingers against the throat of the city—heat and pestilence.

For the first three days de la Scaze remained indoors. He
felt a bit frightened of going out, and then, he was feeling
rather unwell himself. All day he sat by the window and
watched.

It was unbelievable that heat, such intense heat, should
descend so quickly. It had the curious effect of making the
city seem suddenly full of life; full of some quivering atmosphere, as if a river had been turned from its course
and led through the streets of the city, and life were now

a life under water. The men looked strange; the atmosphere trembled with an unnatural clarity that almost resembled the silky air of night; sounds seemed distant and hushed, like the rustling of dead leaves in the wind.

The people sat naked in the shadows of the street, gently fanning themselves. Little eddies of dust flew up now and then as a horseman or an ox-cart passed very slowly beneath de la Scaze's window. Their bodies were covered with sweat, their eyes were wide open and bloodshot; they looked completely weary, limp, indifferent, yet vaguely alert, as if straining their ears to hear a distant sound—the violent coming of horsemen, the violent coming of storm, the coming of some omen of relief. In this quiet the city assumed a certain majesty, as if already it were preparing to pass out of existence into the noiseless dignity of the past.

So that, when the full power of the epidemic descended, it came quietly; like a phrase in music, so to speak, or like a passage in a dance, movement suspended, the gesture prolonged until it suddenly becomes unreal, the extended arms alive one moment ago become crystal, lifeless, and the breath is held.

☆

He saw, as he sat on his window sill, men actually falling in the street. The bodies were covered and laid close to the wall, so that others might pass by, loaded with the bodies of their own dead. The bodies of the women who had died indoors were brought out and laid beside these. For sev-

[440]

eral nights they remained here. Stains appeared in the gray felt which covered them; flies gathered; the air became vile. Finally they were carried outside the city walls.

The old men sat in the streets, very calmly talking of evil spirits and their incalculable but mighty ways. Now and then a woman would suddenly begin to wail, continuing for five minutes, ten minutes, then quickly subsiding; or a strong young boy would burst into hot tears, in bewilderment or fear perhaps as much as in grief. But there was little noise, little hysteria for several days. Only muttering and mumbling; and now and then a bonze or a Taoist monk hurrying past.

Buckets of excrement were carried through the street, dripping upon the pavement and defiling the air, and finally emptied beside the city wall. Once an old man, too weak, too mad to do better, proceeded, after waiting dumbly all day, to drag the naked body of his daughter by her two hands along the street by starlight. The crouching shapes in the street watched quietly until he disappeared. Many of the houses were so hot and fœtid that people took to sleeping in the alleyways.

*

On the fourth day de la Scaze walked out into the middle of the city toward sunset. Attracted more and more irresistibly toward the lives of the wretched, the unlovely and unlucky, he felt, as he stepped into the street again, that he was at last entering the warm, the bitter, the endless and exacting life of the city. The hot air, shimmering like oil in the long orange rays of the sun, embraced him, ran its fingers over his brow, surrounded him.

The appearance of the city had scarcely changed. The same old men sat chatting in the shade of the bazaars. They were the ones who seemed to have survived best. Perhaps their exposure to several epidemics in past years had made them immune. At any rate, there they sat as usual, senile, mindless, guided through the days only by their increasing madness and the thought of approaching death. They sat there like vultures, wrinkled and hideous, watching all day long. They still longed for power, they saw the warm-blooded smooth limbs of the young and longed to govern them, to distort with their birdlike hands and voices the lives of the strong and the beautiful. Talking, talking, making old men's plans with old men's slyness, forever waiting for a chance to perceive and proclaim the victories of the old and sterile, forever trying to drown in words the unbearable fact of their uselessness in life, their joylessness, their lovelessness.

And the beggars. They were there too. De la Scaze recognized them, one by one. They had grown quite indifferent to him; they knew he had no money left. They were still there, all of them. Full of the rotting diseases of love, covered with boiling sores and lice and the pale swellings of ticks. But they seemed to have grown rather fond of the horrors of the flesh. Adroitly gesturing, after years of habit, so as to display most vividly to the curiosity of the passer-by their varied ills—faces toothless, or eyeless, or noseless, or mouthless, with stumps instead of limbs, perhaps, with no expressions left at all that were capable of revealing or even simulating humanity. Many of them were insane; shadows who had at last flown free of the spirit, free of pain, longing and despair; and sat there, gesturing in an awful mechanical manner, thinking only of vice, and lice, and the wild intoxicating hope possibly, just possibly, of the spectacular luxury of a coffin.

What had most impressed de la Scaze in all of China was its lack of pity. All of China was engaged in an everlasting struggle for life. The most utter and inconceivable suffering awaited all who, little by little, began to give way in the struggle. But there was no room for pity in a place where almost all would require it; and where the shabbiness of human pity, its weakness and luxurious unreality, were so clearly revealed. All day the ulcerous beggars, stained with blood and spotted with pus, performed their horrible litanies. Everywhere and always they demanded their due—not pity, but clear-eyed contemplation and recognition. They themselves were pitiless. They had ceased long ago to pity even themselves. Long ago they had accepted their rôle as emblems of horror. Look at us, look at us, their fingerless hands seemed to say; that is all we ask. Their hideousness had become their only means of climbing out of the pit of incessant loneliness; and the revolted glance of a passing stranger had become, horribly, their only possible pleasure, a contact momentary but intense.

But the others, too, were resigned. Even to death. Even the youngest and strongest. When they saw death unmistakably approaching they gesticulated a bit, wept a tear or two perhaps, went through the familiar and mechanical postures of defiance; but it was only a manner of ceremony, as if death were a merchant and they instinctively went through the routine of barter even though they knew that, in the end, they would have to pay. It gave to death, and indeed to the whole long process of collective suffering, a gentle and dreamy touch. Lost in sleep, they seemed to be. Gentle somnambulists, one and all. The awareness and bitterness of reality were discarded. Reality was far too difficult, too incalculable, too piercing an atmosphere to be breathed. All life was spent in devising maneuvers to escape it. Everything they did was a sort of game—even the thing that to some mattered the most, namely money, seemed after all to be an unreal affair, a tangible and comforting hoax designed to cast a concealing shadow over the merciless shape of destiny.

And at the moment of death the device was still sustained. They lay back quietly and thought of their possessions, their families, little bickering promises of all sorts about the clothes they would be buried in or the sanctity of the place where they would be buried or the number of prayers that would keep them company on their cold journey or the matter of priority among the mourners; or perhaps of nothing at all. Merciful boundaries of the human understanding! To none of them did it quite simply and unmistakably occur that their life, their fragile glittering terrible adorable life, was about to cease forever.

★

The days moved past with incredible slowness, the incessant nights were filled with the shy sounds of despair and death; no clamor; only the stifled conversations, the rustle of clothes, the staggering footsteps, the soft hot loads dragged along the alleys. All rising out of this cistern of silence, the silence of the city waiting patiently, waiting and waiting, no one could have explained precisely for what.

✻

He could not tear himself away from these people. They grew closer to him, dearer and more magnetic—unnaturally so. He was quicker than ever to detect the accidental gleam of beauty in a passing face, the musical posture, the flowering gaze, the exquisite tread. This frightful susceptibility to beauty; this connoisseur's awareness of it, the expert's power to see and evaluate at a glance the loveliness of a lowered eyelid, the sun falling on a smooth cheek, an innocent but passionate feminine gesture, or the revealing yet timid contour of the lips, or the careless southern stance. He had reached that final state where it was the innocent above all, the simple and unaware of heart, who moved him. More and more constantly these haunted him. Now he was truly captured, he knew. He was being watched every minute; not by the spies of the government this time, but by the delicate little emissaries of his own spirit. Yet it was oddly pleasurable, this feeling of subtle yet complete imprisonment.

He too was sick and starving, it occurred to him. He attained the infinitely sweet sense of being one with the sufferers—the young and the old, the beautiful as well as the terribly ugly.

A wild excitement filled his heart. Life, life, life! Here, on the very brink of death, he was discovering it! Slowly but surely it was ensnaring him! Something was awaiting him, some sweet and awful consummation. Some final

[445]

revelation. A curtain would be parted, his fate would be visible at last, and clearly.

Lying on his couch at dusk, he would begin to tremble —now with excitement, now with horror, now with love. The hordes! The cruel, glittering hordes of Asia! He would see them marching past, through the shadows of his room, in their various attitudes—the mothers, the newly born, the harlots, the cripples, the soldiers, the degenerates, the hopeless addicts, the merchants, the spies, the very old ones. Most of them hideous, some of them incredibly beautiful. And he would sob with longing.

☆

The days and nights, by some celestial perversity, were more beautiful than ever. At noon the sun transformed the roofs mossy with fumes, the drenched walls and spotted streets, all into gold. Gold fell on the features and the exhalations of the dying, so that these too acquired an exquisite and tender loveliness. At night the stars shone coldly and serenely. The figures that passed along the hot streets with their naked burdens were covered with silver, and the whole pestilential town lay quiet and eternal under its silver labyrinth of roofs, the silver hills, the silver clouds that hung unstirringly and lovingly overhead.

47

The Dying Field

THE EPIDEMIC REACHED ITS PEAK ON THE SEVENTH day after de la Scaze's visit to the Greek's.

He walked through the streets every day now, fascinated, and out to the city walls. Outside the city walls he saw the real thing—the plague herself with the veils torn off.

A desiccated old woman was standing half-naked in the stream at dusk, stooped over some clothes, fumbling at them in the water, apparently trying to wash them. They were the clothes of a child. Tearlessly and mechanically she rubbed them against the stone. Finally, when it was growing dark, she sat down wearily and fell asleep, leaning her cheek upon her elbows. The clothes floated gently down the stream and disappeared.

[447]

Another woman walked along the walls, wailing. When she saw de la Scaze she came up to him and held out her hand. Then she muttered something. But he couldn't understand. Then she folded her arms in front of her breasts and moved them to and fro, as if she were rocking a child to sleep. He shook his head. Suddenly she burst into a frenzy, pointed her finger at him, shrieked hysterically. Then she calmed down again and walked away, shaking with rage. She stumbled and fell down but rose again clumsily. Her clothes were stained and torn with years of wear, her hair flew crazily in the breeze. She walked away from the city, clearly unaware of where she was going.

Others departed from the city likewise. After sunset, when the heat had grown less, a column of fugitives passed out of the city through the southern gate. Most of them didn't know where they were going, either. Rumors of cholera had reached them from the neighboring cities as well. So they walked slowly out into the empty land, sleeping perhaps in tents or out under the starlight for two or three nights. Then they came back again, since there was nowhere to go, and besides, they were homesick, and curious too, somewhat.

Again and again and again he saw how, when the most horrifying of moments arrives, moments so unspeakable that we must forget them instantly even when we glimpse them from afar—at those moments the eyes of the victims themselves, though still wide open and staring, are suddenly covered by a gentle and merciful film; a dream; a tender madness; they have entered their own world.

One woman had left the town leading her little son by the hand. De la Scaze had noticed those two before. They were a striking pair, for in the eyes of both of them was a vacuous yet intense expression of adoration such as he had never seen before. "They are mad, both of them," Hussein had explained.

Now she returned with the others, after three nights on the hillside, carrying him in her arms. Her face was wet and drawn with exertion, and she had to rest every few minutes. Finally, long after the others had entered the city she too approached the walls and walked through the gate. She looked very tired but quite peaceful, by no means unhappy. Love still shone in her black eyes.

Children sat upon the city walls, staring out at the dying and dead that lay scattered among the hot stones. With eyes singularly intent and lips half open they watched the gradual movements of those who had given up hope. And sometimes one might see a child walk out silently toward the slopes where the people went who wished to die quietly. The eyes of the children were by far the most melancholy of all. They hadn't yet learned how to look the other way.

People and animals who know that death is coming, instinctively walk to certain remote and quiet haunts which subconsciously, without thinking or understanding why, they have remembered and selected for retreat on some previous excursion. It may be a quiet corner of the forest or a quiet spot on a hill, a peaceful cavern or a protected niche among rocks: they recognize it when they see it, for they have saved it for this occasion without knowing it, quite unawares. When the time comes, they go and hide there, knowing that it is quiet and familiar and that they will be left alone. With human beings it is frequently a secret retreat, not in the landscape, but in the mind; an attitude; a vision of some kind, perhaps; but it does the same thing for them.

That was where many of these people were going, and that was why they went so calmly, many of them. Some walked out across the hill and disappeared, and others who carried their retreat within the spirit lay down quietly in the shadow of the city walls. One woman had brought a large piece of black felt with her, and this she placed over her body, covering it completely. There she continued to lie motionlessly.

Some of the men were curled up in curious poses. The disease appeared to affect the genital regions now and then, and the men would suffer inordinately.

De la Scaze saw a child dying, its eyes beseeching him like a little beggar boy asking for food—hand instinctively held out, still trusting perhaps that a gift from a passing stranger might bring relief.

Some maddened creatures had walked among the corpses and stripped many of them, and had performed terrible mutilations, both on the men and on the women. His heart now reached far out into provinces of existence never before touched, never suspected, never thought possible. There they lay, their spirits already uncoiling into a remote but very restful universe, their bodies for a few final moments flashing into a dazzling and inhuman beauty, voluptuous beyond words. Near by would sit one or two, watching—worshipers of the dead, and the indescribably lonely ones.

At twilight their perspiring faces grew pale and remote. They sat there quietly, in the Dying Field, some with their heads in their hands, others lying as if asleep, faces buried in their arms. Some lay naked on their backs with their eyes closed and only the briefest expression of pain fluttering across their glistening eyelids now and again. One or two moved spasmodically from side to side, no longer able to control themselves. But most of them sat there quietly, watching without curiosity and apparently without terror, with possibly only the faintest regret that they should be dying in rags; and without coffins and the ceremonial prayers of their children; destined, in short, for birds and dogs; and therefore with no chance of a peaceful and consoling journey into the provinces beyond.

The shadows beside the walls; the parade into the desert; the coming of the birds out of the mountains. But once, beside the stream, de la Scaze beheld a still more frightful Vision of Death. The dying sunlight lay like gold upon the black water, and beside the water lay a dying woman. Near by lay her dead child. But the child was scarcely recognizable, for a large half-starved scavenger dog was crouched over its dark and shimmering body, tearing it to pieces, the head already half-severed. She reached feebly toward the child, and the dog snarled viciously. Both had vast hungry eyes, the woman and the dog. There they were, staring insanely at one another from the very brink of death. The one with the sharper teeth won.

Overhead, the beauty of the sky shone more magically and more mercilessly than ever. Stillness and heat crept westward from the desert, and from the mountainous west, which was sending forth birds and more birds toward the stricken city, shone the brilliant snow, still faintly visible miles away. Desert, the growing heat, the empty red slopes: all this in the east. To the west and the north rose the icy and sacred summits of the Tian Shan. De la Scaze could see them, very faintly shining across the roofs and through the tangle of eaves and balconies as he walked back through the quiet streets each night.

48

The Dancing Girl

THE NEXT DAY WAS THE HOTTEST OF ALL. DE LA Scaze stepped into the street in the late afternoon; but instantly the odors and the stagnant heat set his temples beating and his eyes aching. He felt ill for a moment and leaned against the wall. Then he hurried up the stairway again and into his darkened room.

He lay down on the bed and closed his eyes. But what he saw then was not darkness, but light. A dazzling and iridescent wilderness of light. "Now I am sick," he thought. "I haven't had enough to eat. I am starving."

It occurred to him for one brief moment that he might flee from Aqsu. It was not yet too late, not yet. But he would have to hurry, hurry. . . . For a moment he felt alert and panic-stricken. But only for a moment. Then he felt limp again. "No, no," he whispered to himself. "I must stay. I belong here."

Hussein came up and stood beside him. "Master?"

De la Scaze saw his black eyes staring into his own. Earnestly and anxiously. Then another expression entered them. De la Scaze could not have said what it was; there was no word to describe it. A curious kind of pleasure, of delight.

"Hussein," he murmured, and then, as Hussein leaned over, he whispered something softly into his ear. Hussein left the room.

Half an hour later he returned. Carefully he unwrapped his little packet, placed the contents in the bowl of a long slender pipe, lit it, and gave it to de la Scaze.

☆

A curtain seemed to have been softly drawn aside in his brain, and he now gazed out, as it were, into a tremendous new world. Infinitely gentle, infinitely soothing. Everything was lovely, novel, amazing. He looked from side to side. He saw the familiar furniture in the room—the *chaise-longue*, the hanging lamp, the brazier, the mirror, the little ebony table. But they seemed to be glowing with a light of their own. Incredible, suddenly. The table shone with an astounding brilliance; the mirror shone like an infinite lake of quicksilver. Odd that he had never noticed it before. For the first time he really saw these objects. He was filled with excitement and wonder.

Then, unexpectedly, the room was filled with color.

[453]

The lamp; its colored glass glittered with a dazzling quality. Now at last he understood the true meaning of red, yellow, blue. Their richness, their power; their profound harmonies were now reflected in his own delighted mind. Strange shadows were revealed which he had never before suspected. In the bowl of the brazier; in the ornate carving of the ebony table; in the quiet folds of the curtain. Long, round, or angular: they flashed forth in numberless suggestive geometrical patterns. Now he understood the inchoate beauty of a straight line, the subtle perfection of a curve. In this crystalline world everything—shape, color, shadow—grew harmonious and exquisite, as if a waterfall were flowing through his dark room, casting light upon everything, creating a million new reflections and quivering shadows, giving fluency and life to each line, filling the room with music.

Music. Everything was now music. The lamp, the mirror, the long chair, the table—these no longer existed. They flowed away before his eyes and joined, as he lay there listening alertly, the waves of music that were now trembling upon the air. This was reality at last pierced to the core; time was caught on the wing, transfixed, space was captured like a butterfly in this network of music. As if it were a tremendous violin being played on the sandy shore beside an endless black ocean, he heard the sound of the whole world revolving on its axis, the planets wheeling in their predestined paths, the sun roaring across the organized infinities.

★

When he woke up again his sight was blurred. He sat
up in the bed. In the further corner of the room sat Hussein, fast asleep. De la Scaze looked down at the bed, at
the pillow.

He picked up a small mirror from the table and looked
at his face. Suddenly he saw what he really looked like.
Black hair delicate as silk, curling down his neck, curling
over his ears. It was quite long, but in spite of that it had
begun to recede from the forehead, quite unmistakably.
Also it had grown visibly thinner, and, yes, a few gray
hairs had at last made their appearance. Not yet bald by
any means; after all, he was only thirty-seven years old, he
kept saying to himself; but it all had begun to give to his
face a rather reflective, almost dedicated look. An "intellectual" look. "And yet," he thought, "I have always been
rather stupid. It is only that my tastes have been sharpened and refined. People have confused that with intelligence. But of course it isn't intelligence. For this reason:
that intelligence requires, above all, balance; clarity; confidence. These I do not possess."

He looked down again at his own face. Well, the skin
was too pale, too fine; the features were too delicate. He
no longer looked young. A hundred tiny wrinkles had furrowed their way into his skin; around the eyes, in the
forehead, around the mouth. Also, a curious peeling process had lately been taking place. Little flecks of dried-up
skin were breaking off all over his face, and on his body
too. He had frequently been deceived, as he sat in front of
the mirror, into suspecting that he was a handsome man;
or, perhaps, not precisely handsome; rather—though the
word was too flattering—magnetic. But he saw that he had
been quite wrong. He was really rather ugly. Or, to be
again more exact, unattractive. People disliked a face like

[455]

that. It lacked coarseness, humor. It was too secretive, for another thing. Emotion burned in those black eyes too purely, too untainted by the drag of the coarse and masculine body.

And those hands, clutching limply at the edge of the coverlet. Where had he seen those before? They were too frail by far. The hands of a sick person, fingers long and tapering; too graceful, too eloquent. He had noticed frequently that fragile and unprepossessing men were apt to have hands which they considered "distinguished" and "beautiful." His own were like that, alas. Except, unfortunately, that he had taken to biting his nails a good deal of late: the tips of his fingers looked pink and puffy, rather indecent.

And then his body. It gave him no pleasure at all to look at his own body. It was pallid, timorous, terribly thin. The ribs showed through alarmingly. It had been starved, in more ways than one. It had lived on itself, like a plant without water. It needed something else. The touch of another body, among other things. Reciprocity. Caresses. Love.

Love! He felt faint. It was as if a wild perfume had suddenly flooded the room.

"Hussein!" he called.

Hussein gave a start, and opened his eyes. "Master?"

De la Scaze beckoned to him and whispered something into his ear.

Hussein brushed his hand over his brow. Then he turned away and began, very softly and slyly, to smile. As he left the room the smile spread and deepened into a quiet laugh, musical, malicious.

About an hour later he returned. "She will be here in

a few minutes, master," he said, with great politeness and gravity.

☆

Breathtakingly beautiful, she was.

She had entered rather shyly. She hadn't liked him at first, he could see. Smiling rather timidly, glancing away, lips twisted faintly.

But only for a moment. Because suddenly he himself changed. Suddenly he felt a dizzy and desperate need of love. His body seemed to wake up, bewildered but eager; his finger tips became alive, his lips trembled.

Clumsily he drew her to him and tried to undo the thin silken buttons of her embroidered robe. She lay back and watched him, indifferent, sly, amused. His breath came unevenly, his heart beat wildly as he slipped off the yellow silk from her arms and her waist, and her body emerged, fresh, lovable, each hair carefully plucked out, flawless as a crystal. And suddenly full of far more than longing he buried his head in her body, kissed her everywhere, while she caressed him gently in a distant motherly way.

And later she lay on his bed, fast asleep. He could see her body glowing ruddily in the light that shone from the lamp. The body of a child, but so utterly desirable, so unerringly designed for love that its very childishness made it seem incredibly dissolute and lovely.

He rose from the *chaise-longue* and stood beside her. The innocent hands, carelessly curled like those of a child around some imaginary object, the finger nails like little sea shells, pink and shining; the skin, warm and rich like

[457]

an apricot hanging in the sunlight; each vein in her throat so tender, color of the evening sky, moving ever so faintly to the beat of the blood; the arched foot, the toes lined with silken blue veins and each one studded with a pearl; the flat downy ear, the puckered mouth, the trembling eyelids, the long black eyelashes. A child, mindless, serene, perfect.

He sat down again. Through the shadows of the room he could still see each detail of her body. It glowed like gold. It grew luminous, momentous: a symbol of goodness and security, and, yes, of a profound maternal solicitude, like a lamplight in the middle of a desperate and storm-ridden forest.

✿

That night he dreamt about the events of several months before. He saw the sand again, the clear empty landscape, and his six fellow Europeans—the aristocrat from England, the exile from Russia, the fugitive from Belgium, the German geologist and his young Austrian companion, and his own Spanish wife. Very clearly he saw each face: one cold, disdainful, Grecian; one powerful, bewildered, hopelessly lost; one inquisitive and truculent; one hard and fanatical; one blue-eyed and sunny; one soft, ripe, electrically languid.

There they stood, waiting in the courtyard of the *serai* for a trivial bit of information, in careless and temporary postures. But of course, what they were really waiting for was a decision neither from the Amban nor the consul-general nor even the Governor. Caught at a critical mo-

[458]

tionless instant, they were, between flight out of one world and flight into another, awaiting a reply to the little question which lurked hidden in their hearts, that inescapable question from which all thoughts and actions sprang. And their gestures were those of birds, each one of them poised on the edge of a flight into his own particular and fateful kind of refuge, some impelled by terror and some by love, so it seemed to him at this moment.

*

On the following evening he sat at the window again, chatting with Hussein.

Hussein was being very strange, he thought, but his brain was so full of thoughts and imaginings that he did not trouble to observe more closely.

"Any news of the city?" he asked lazily.

"The city is better. People are beginning to hope."

"Fewer deaths?"

"Fewer deaths."

They leaned out of the window together to listen to some distant music. Way at the end of the silent street they could see shapes passing slowly. And high above, the stars.

"Look at the stars, Hussein." They seemed very soft, very near by.

Hussein sat down again on his cushion without replying. His eyes were lowered, his lips were moving slowly.

"Hussein!"

Hussein raised his animal's eyes, pleading yet secretive.

"Hussein! What is the matter?"

Hussein hesitated. His face took on a look both ironic and sad. "Nothing, master. . . . My mother died yesterday."

"But, Hussein . . ." He paused, bewildered and somehow miserable.

"My mother was old and wicked. I am glad that she is dead. But my brother died too. He was young, and he loved me. I am full of grief for him." His black curls shone softly, his black eyes glittered feverishly: a child, a child of night, like his sister who had lain upon the bed yesterday.

His heart leapt. "And your sister?" he whispered.

A little smile appeared on Hussein's lips. "You love her, sir?" His voice was very beautiful, very musical, a nocturnal thing.

De la Scaze stared at him without a word.

"Ah, do not fear, sir! She will never be cruel to you. She is never cruel to strangers."

De la Scaze's heart grew warm with tenderness.

But the next moment he understood. He sat down again on the *chaise-longue* and stared silently out into the night, terribly afraid.

49

The Visitor

O N THE FOLLOWING AFTERNOON HUSSEIN FAILED
to appear.

De la Scaze sent out the boy from the house
next door to inquire. Presently he returned. De la Scaze
was lying on the bed in his silk robe.

"You have been at Hussein's house?"

The boy shook his head. "No one at Hussein's house."

"Why not?"

"All dead."

De la Scaze waited a moment. He glanced toward the
window. He could hear the sound of voices, very quiet,
very calm, emerging from the old gray walls along the
street. Then, "Hussein?"

"Hussein dead too. Hussein dead this morning."

And then, his voice failing, his heart half dead, "Hussein's sister?"

The boy lowered his eyes. He seemed to be blushing. He shook his head in an embarrassed way, then turned around and left the room.

De la Scaze lay back on the bed and closed his eyes. His temples were throbbing with fever.

☆

Again, slowly, the world grew crystal and musical. The furniture in the room—the brazier, the *chaise-longue*, the mirror—seen through that delicate spiral of smoke, again grew suggestive. His body seemed very gently to slide away, to slip through the air out past the frayed yellow curtains in the doorway. Only his ears and eyes, incredibly alert, remained; watching and listening.

Then, out of the texture of sounds one strand emerged. The sound of footsteps on the stairs. He knew instantly that it was the tread of an Occidental, not only by the clicking of the shoes, but by the self-imposed precision of each new step. Vaguely familiar, that tread. It came closer, and paused in front of the door. Then, after a moment, the sound of a knock on the door. Hesitant, yet firm. "Come in," he said. His voice was so airy, so suspended a whisper that he could not believe that the visitor had heard it.

However, the door opened and a man entered. He bowed and smiled. "Good afternoon, Monsieur de la Scaze!"

De la Scaze nodded his head mechanically. The stranger
looked at him in a very friendly way; rather aggressively
so, thought de la Scaze as he glanced at him again. That
smile was almost impudent.

"To what do I owe the pleasure of this——" he began.
But the stranger's manner was so controlled and precise
that he hesitated. Perhaps this man knew him, after all.
An old friend, possibly? His memory for faces had always
been bad. And indeed, now that he thought of it, the
man's voice and expression did seem familiar; and the
fussy manner in which he moved his hands; and the minc-
ing walk, and stooping posture. "Won't you be seated?"

"Thank you!" The man sat down, rather pompously,
on the *chaise-longue*. He crossed one leg on top of the
other and joined his fingers in front of his knees. De la
Scaze had once known a man, a distant relative of his,
who habitually sat in this manner. Rather affected and
graceless, it now seemed to him. He began to dislike the
visitor. Also, he now noticed that there was a rather unpleasant odor in the room. Of sulphur, perhaps. A vague
smell of disinfectant.

"I understand that you are not at all well," observed the
visitor, in a queerly alienating tone of voice. His accent too
was unpleasant. He spoke in a prim and self-conscious
way, like a certain unpleasant fellow he had once known,
a poet, who came from Bordeaux. "Yes," he said, leaning
toward de la Scaze. "You don't look well at all, really!"
His voice grew very anxious and caressing. It became clear
to de la Scaze that the man for some reason or other was
trying to make a good impression. That antagonized him
yet more. But it gave him confidence.

"I haven't been well," he said dryly. "I have been rather
slow recovering. The climate ——"

[463]

"Ah yes, the climate," rejoined the stranger with energy; "dreadful. . . . You should never," he added brightly, "have come here. It's notoriously bad! You haven't been recovering at all, you know! You've been losing ground, actually ——"

Very tactless, that was. De la Scaze's eyes hardened. "Yes?"

"And then, of course," he went on briskly, "this business of not having enough money . . ."

It occurred to de la Scaze that the man might have come on some financial mission; to lend him money, perhaps. . . .

"Don't misunderstand," said the stranger hastily, with an awkward smile, "perhaps I shouldn't have said that. However . . ." He paused. It was very embarrassing. None, thought de la Scaze, are so unattractive as those of "æsthetic" inclinations who have risen from the lower bourgeoisie, who affect a taste, say, in literature, who wish to appear worldly, who attempt, most infelicitously, to speak with a false ease; as a rule they impress one either as singularly conceited or as monstrously servile. Very apt to be men like this one—pallid, nervous, spinsterish. And with it all, oddly furtive and indecent.

Slowly the stranger gained confidence. He began playing with his ivory-handled cane, which he kept spinning around between his knees. He talked on and on. De la Scaze hardly listened to what he was saying. He did observe, however, that the topics were growing increasingly informal. Most of the time he stared coldly toward the window. Occasionally he stole a look at the intruder. A very vulgar man, to be sure; and yet, so disarmingly inept and withal so very eager to be friendly. His hostility began to fade.

[464]

"Of course," the stranger was saying, with a shrug of the shoulders, "the fact of the matter is, you have really been very unwise—I'm not blaming you in the least, you understand. You were trapped, so to speak. (I use the word without insinuation, I assure you, monsieur!) After all, what could you do? Still . . ."

He smiled. His teeth were very bad. Then de la Scaze noticed that he was wearing a sky-blue shirt. Also, there was something very peculiar about his hair. A bit bald, he was, and the thin silken strands had a reddish, dyed look about them. It struck de la Scaze as curiously farcical and hideous. Suddenly, for some mad reason, he wanted to laugh, almost hysterically. "The devil!" he wanted to cry out. "Why, you are the devil, the devil himself, in person!" But then he collected himself. "Absurd," he whispered to himself; "absurd, of course . . . I must really be more polite. After all, he is my guest, unwelcome perhaps, but still, a guest . . ."

The stranger caught his eye and smiled coyly. He raised his hand to his collar, in a rather angular, spinsterish gesture. "Yes. Like Robespierre, I affect light blue. . . . Robespierre's is a highly underrated character. A very great man! And St. Just similarly. Those two have been my romantic ideals, so to speak, since childhood. St. Just and Robespierre!" He simpered. Very unpleasant that simper was.

De la Scaze felt that he should deport himself more severely. But he felt very dizzy. And a curious ache was spreading beneath his ribs. "Please," he began.

But the stranger interrupted him. "My friends have always considered me rather *dix-neuvième siècle*. Well, perhaps I am. . . ." He lowered his eyes demurely. "My tastes are what you might call reactionary. Would you believe it, I still," and he simpered again, "read Marivaux and Madame de Staël. Let alone George Sand, whom I genuinely adore!" He whisked his handkerchief out of his pocket and ran it across his forehead. Then he whisked it back again, with a flourish. "This heat," he murmured, rather smugly.

"But I am boring you, monsieur?" he said, in a tone of suave self-reproach, his eyes imploring. "He who talks of himself, as La Bruyère has said— But I bore you. Forgive me. What I wish to say is this, quite simply. You must prepare yourself, monsieur." He pursed his lips and began to tap his knee gently with his finger tips. The furtive, indecent quality of the man was now acquiring something a bit menacing; something toad-like, really frightening.

De la Scaze waited for him to go on.

"Prepare yourself. You see, if I may put it crudely, I know rather a good deal about you." His voice grew hesitant and tense, his fingers shook with nervousness. "And I regret to say that your health will not allow—your sojourn on this most wretched planet—to be prolonged—in short, late this afternoon you must expect your spirit to join—" It was almost humorous, this ill-bred yet macabre circumlocution.

"You mean I shall die this evening?" de la Scaze asked blandly. He was growing exasperated again. This ludicrous tact, this poisonous false gentility. A madman, a lunatic.

"Ah, you put it rather bluntly!" The man's hands fluttered in pretended confusion. Suddenly those fingers, those eyes, that voice, seemed to de la Scaze unspeakably evil. It was as if abruptly a lid had been removed and he had been allowed now to peer for an instant straight into the pit.

"But I see that you have grasped my point," the intruder continued. His eyes narrowed and glittered like those of a

ferret. "May I remind you, apropos of this—coming event
—of one or two points?" He leaned back, suddenly pious
and pontifical. "First of all. The problem of evil." He
cleared his throat and pressed his long fingers together
professionally. "You have pondered on that before, I am
aware. But may I make one or two suggestions? For example, love. What do you think of love? Think, for example,
of that episode—last night was it? Doesn't it seem, after
all, now that you look back on it, highly sordid? I don't
mean merely *post coitum tristis* and all that. No. More
than that. Consider . . ."

The vision of Hussein's sister, exquisitely lovely, returned instantly to de la Scaze. He was amazed at the thrilling exactitude and sensual detail with which he was able
so abruptly to conjure this scene into being; her hair, her
lips, her closed eyes, the curve of the cheek bone, the warm
apricot skin.

"Regarded quite rationally," the man continued silkily,
"hadn't love best be regarded as a type of insanity? Doesn't
it, after all, convert power into danger, desire into obsession, weakness into utter frustration, solitude into mania,
and so on? Doesn't it lead one's energies into unhealthy
channels? Into a *cul-de-sac*, so to speak? Especially," and
he looked meaningly at de la Scaze, "in a case like yours?
That is," and he coughed, far too obviously, "in the case
of a person so secluded and, shall we say, reflective?

"And then. As I was saying. This matter of evil. Has it
ever occurred to you that perhaps we have all been wrong,
all these years? That perhaps those very things we prefer
to hide, whose existence we most arduously strive to forget, called evil—the desire for blood, those nightly terrors
half-recognized, the longing for pain and slavery and hu-
miliation, scarcely remembered glimpses that defiled our

[467]

earliest childhood, and so on: perhaps these things, called
evil, when so enchained in darkness by general consent,
so-called propriety, gnaw at something in us that is far
more important? That is, our soul? Perhaps they should
be recognized, released into action, nourished even—" His
voice faded away. He gazed absent-mindedly out of the
window.

"And then this third matter," he said suddenly, glancing with great earnestness back at de la Scaze. Rather the
glance of a reformer, thought de la Scaze, of a missionary;
serious, sanctimonious, and a bit silly. "This third matter.
Death. Well, a rather frightening word. And a frightening
thought to most of us. One might as well admit it. But
why? Quite plainly, why?" His voice assumed a sweet rea-
sonableness. After all, thought de la Scaze, he spoke rather
well, there was no denying it. All the proper *nuances*, the
sententiousness, the beguiling catchwords.

"Death. The end. We know it. Everything can be vul-
garized, made unreal and pompous, except death. It will
never change. Nothing can assault its profound dignity.
Whatever happens to men, whatever collective degrada-
tions they may endure, whatever self-forgetfulness more
loathsome than any disease, this one thing will remain.
We meet it alone. And when we meet it we become, even
if only for a moment, truly ourselves. For a moment we
attain an actual nobility. Do you see? Yes, death is a peak
that rises high above this mortal wilderness! All life is an
instinctive preparation for death, really. A process of
strengthening one's mind, of very slowly annihilating fear,
of very gradually acquiring a dignity which will be summoned to our side at the moment of death.

"Do you really understand? Think about it. Oh," and
suddenly the voice changed, a greenish shadow crossed

[468]

over the figure and made it seem larger than it actually was; "oh, salvation is a strange and merciful thing. At the very lowest moments we suddenly find it. It is in the deepest despair, quite unexpectedly, that we suddenly experience the lovely and familiar touch, the sweet security. Our hearts beat with happiness, we are at last saved. . . .

"Yes. Saved. You may think"—and his voice grew soft again; his face was, de la Scaze observed through the haziness of pain, now covered completely with shadow; only his eyes shone, his teeth gleamed, and his hair stood up rather eerily, on either side of his head—"you may think that I am hardly the man to go discoursing about salvation. But, call me whatever you wish, I know more about it than you might suppose. It is one of my hobbies, so to speak. . . ." He tittered. Then he rose; slim, noiseless, graceful; like an animal. Suddenly a peculiar acid smell filled the room, more intense than before. And this was followed by a quick surreptitious little sound, like a rat scurrying across the floor.

De la Scaze felt very dizzy, very feverish. He closed his eyes in a sudden spasm of pain. When he opened them again the stranger was gone. He had, thought de la Scaze with a terrifying irrelevance, forgotten even to ask his name.

But then he noticed that the visitor had left a card. It was lying on the chair where he had sat. He rose and crept across the room. He hesitated for a moment. Then he picked up the card and read the name: *Paul de la Scaze,* printed on vellum in fine italics; not engraved, not even in very good taste.

De la Scaze began to tremble. Then he grew calm again. "I must have left it there myself," he murmured. "Of

EPILOGUE

50

Epilogue: The Encounter in Shanghai

AFTER HE HAD WAVED GOOD-BY TO HUGO AND HAD
watched the boat slowly moving away into darkness until he could no longer recognize his face,
Joachim strolled slowly back through the lamplit square
and into the tangle of Shanghai's unlovely streets. Once
more, as he turned back toward the water, he glimpsed
the jungle of boats glimmering silently upon the water—
the giant hulls, the caravels, the barges, the junks, the
paddle-boats, the sampans.

The boats looked terribly human to him, full of longing to be away, to go sailing across the water. "Oh, Hugo,"
he thought, suddenly stabbed with affection and solitude,

"what will become of you? Good-by, good-by, for I'll never
see you again!"

☆

The first street that he passed was lined with gambling-
houses. A radio was blaring dissonantly in one of them;
the sound of Negro jazz reflected bleakly the nervous,
reckless, centrifugal air of the city. Through a window he
saw a group of Mexicans playing roulette. This was the
street of the smugglers; of the conspirators, the agitators,
the spies, the addicts, the procurers, the slaves. Over one
door he read the sign *Black Peacock*; out through the
doorway two young Korean sailors came tottering drunkenly.

The next street was the street of the brothels. Slender
women strolled by in very high heels, dressed in sheath-
like gowns, paper flowers pinned on their shoulders. Their
faces were quite pale and expressionless, quite melancholy,
quite lovely. Most of them were Chinese. But there were
darker ones, Hindus and Latins, and some with blond hair
and gray-blue eyes.

It was growing very late. The figures were growing
fewer. Far away, through a narrow alleyway, Joachim
could still see the water of the harbor and the starry sky
trembling in its black arms. A group of students went
sauntering past—some of them Chinese, others Russian,
some curious and observant, others arguing and gesticulating, still others lost in thought.

He sat down in front of a café. No one bothered about
him, no one spoke to him. A yellowing French newspaper,

several months old, lay crumpled under the table. He picked it up, unfolded it, glanced over it absent-mindedly. A clash in Manchuria, trouble in Japan, bloodshed in Ethiopia, cholera in Sinkiang. In one small corner he read that word had just reached the British consul in Shanghai of the death of a British explorer, several months ago, in Tibet. The name looked familiar to Joachim; he began to wonder; he placed his chin in the palm of his hand and closed his eyes sleepily. Behind the door he could hear the clinking of the *mah jong* pieces and the soft tinkling of the players' voices.

☆

Presently he woke up again and saw a door opening across the street, and two figures emerging—a man and a woman. The woman was black-haired, beautifully shaped —at first he thought she was Chinese; then he saw that she wasn't. South American, she looked, or Spanish. She was pale and expressionless, like all the others. A little red flower hung from the collar of her yellow brocaded dress. For a moment she stood whispering to the man, holding his arm, caressing his hand. He was gazing vaguely down the street. Finally she leaned over from the stairway on which she was standing and kissed his great bearded face. Then she vanished behind the door again.

For a moment the man stood hesitantly at the bottom of the stairway. He was swaying slightly. Joachim could see that he was drunk. Then he came limping across the street in Joachim's direction and sat down with a deep alcoholic groan at the little green table which stood near Joachim's.

Joachim turned and watched him. He was dressed very shabbily, in filthy gray trousers and a tattered purple sweater. A heavy black beard hid the lower half of his face. There was a deep scar in the middle of the man's forehead. A huge man he was, and something in his posture as he sat there, stooping over like a bear, stirred Joachim's memory.

Then the man sat up and looked over at Joachim blearily, unseeingly. Now Joachim saw his eyes—beautiful blue eyes, the eyes of a child, half sad, half mad. Then Joachim knew who he was. He felt deeply excited now.

He smiled drunkenly at Joachim. "You speak French?" he said, haltingly, in a tremorous, hoarse voice.

Joachim nodded. "But not well." He was surprised to see how nervous his own voice was.

The man nodded his head in reply. Then he ran his huge, filthy fingers through his beard. He looked very earnest, very thoughtful. But Joachim knew that he was drunk; a tenuous pearl of saliva was trickling down his beard.

"My friend," he murmured, in his trembling, resonant voice, "I was like you once. Yes! A young man. A newcomer to the world, eager, observant. But times change, times change. . . ." For several minutes he sat silently. Then his voice grew gentle and reminiscent. "Go through a wonderful or terrible experience, my friend, but what you learn is nothing that can be put into words. Nothing becomes clearer. The world keeps on growing more and more baffling. . . ."

He stared with his limpid, unseeing eyes into Joachim's. "How old are you?"

"Twenty-three."

"Ah. . . . I was twenty-three once. Everyone is twenty-three once"—his voice rose querulously—"and you will be twenty-four one day! And then twenty-five. And then, some day, you will die. . . ." He worked his fingers clumsily around the bottom of an empty glass that was standing on the table. Then he stared down the street thoughtfully.

"My friend," he said, and his voice was new and strange, "I once had a vision. Life was changed for me after that. Is it possible, I began to wonder, that in this life man is after all not the hunter but the game? That he must give up his innocence, and then his youth, and his eagerness, and his love, and his faith in his fellow men, and his power, all for nothing? Without any real reward, except a final willingness to leave this world? He will stand quietly and contemplate what he has lost forever—all that is glorious in existence. He closes his eyes. He resigns himself. Perhaps he sees something to console him. But it is a phrase, a shadow, a device, an illusion; there is nothing to reassure him, life is not like that and never can be. . . . I have been wicked, my friend, I have done evil beyond words; I have played the traitor and the destroyer, out of fear, out of revenge. But life is over for me now. . . ." He paused, and belched noisily. "Listen. There is only one victory possible for a man—that of having lost with a certain dignity of heart, at least, and nobility of spirit. That is all, that is all, and it will always be all!"

Joachim felt profoundly excited. His hands were trembling. For a moment he felt dizzy, and the Russian's face grew blurred and remote.

"But," and the Russian leaned over; his voice now trembled with an inner joy, an exultation; "but listen to me! I have been saved! Do you hear? I," and he pounded his chest with his hairy fist, "have won the only possible victory!" Joachim now saw that tears were flowing from his eyes—one from each eye, tremorously climbing down his deeply lined cheeks. Tears of drunkenness, perhaps; tears of delight, too.

"Do you want to know a secret?" he whispered. His face had grown savage and beautiful; the face, thought Joachim, of a ruined hero. "Do you want to know something? Listen. I am a murderer. Yes. . . ." He paused again. His fingers twitched nervously at the bottom of the empty glass. "They can come. They can get me. I'm not afraid. It won't matter. Wherever they put me, they can find no smaller room than I have always lived in, the food can be no worse than what I have already had, they can make me no more lonely than I have always been." He closed his eyes.

"Well," he muttered presently, "I'm rambling on. . . . I'm drunk. And do you know what I'm really drunk with? Life! That's it. Life. . . . The world, the world!" Again he stared at Joachim. Then he shook his head slowly and looked away again, in a wild, inarticulate grief.

"One last thing," he murmured gently. "Everything, remember, is forgivable. Everything, everything. For it all springs from love, however it may appear. . . . Man is eternally imperfect, the mercy of God is boundless. There is nothing that cannot be forgiven."

The stranger rose. "Good-night," he muttered, in a weary tone, and limped away. Joachim heard him coughing and mumbling to himself as he disappeared down the street.

★

Now the street was empty. He watched his cigarette smoldering on the pavement. Only one small lamp was flickering in the shabby doorway near by. He noticed a small child lying on the stairway opposite, fast asleep. Fast asleep on the endless sea of history.

He ground the dying cigarette under his heel and walked slowly down the street. He could see the turrets of Shanghai as he strolled along, and the big, watchful clock-tower silhouetted against the gray sky, suddenly miraculous. The stars had faded. His heart began to ache with longing. Something had happened to him; something in him had changed, had grown, had suddenly begun to blossom. He was a part of the world now. The hot, sleeping city looked inexpressibly touching and beautiful to him, lovable beyond words.

THE END

THE SEVEN WHO FLED

SET IN LINOTYPE BASKERVILLE

FORMAT BY A. W. RUSHMORE

MANUFACTURED BY THE HADDON CRAFTSMEN

PUBLISHED BY

HARPER & BROTHERS

MCMXXXVII

The

Harper Prize Novel

Contest

Its History and Terms

THE
HARPER PRIZE NOVEL
CONTEST

The Harper Prize Novel Contest is held every other year. The purpose of the Contest is to give prominence and success to a writer whose real quality has not hitherto found a wide audience. Any author is eligible for the Prize who is an American citizen and who has not published a novel in book form prior to a certain specified date (announced at the beginning of each contest), and only unpublished works may be submitted. The judges of the 1937 Contest are:

Louis Bromfield   Sinclair Lewis
Thornton Wilder

Other eminent writers and critics who have served as judges for these contests include:

Harry Hansen	Dorothy Canfield
John Erskine	Carl Van Doren
Ellen Glasgow	Henry Seidel Canby
Stuart P. Sherman	Grant Overton
Jesse Lynch Williams	Bliss Perry

The first Harper Prize was awarded in 1922 to Margaret Wilson's *The Able McLaughlins*, which also received the Pulitzer Prize. The second winner was Anne Parrish's *The Perennial Bachelor*. The third was *The Grandmothers*, by Glenway Wescott, the fourth Julian Green's *The Dark Journey*, the fifth Robert Raynold's *Brothers in the West*, and the sixth Paul Horgan's *The Fault of Angels*. The seventh award went to H. L. Davis's *Honey in the Horn,* which also won the Pulitzer Prize. To this distinguished list is now added *The Seven Who Fled,* by Frederic Prokosch.

Comments of Noted Writers and Critics on the
HARPER PRIZE NOVEL CONTEST

"It seems to me to have been awarded consistently to novels of the highest merit."—*Sinclair Lewis.*

"The Harper Prize has had a singularly distinguished record . . . reflects the best that is being done in contemporary literature."—*Louis Bromfield.*

"All interested in contemporary literature should be grateful to Harper & Brothers for establishing a literary prize of such value."—*William Lyon Phelps.*

"I have come to look forward with eagerness to the announcement of the Harper Prize award."—*Harry Hansen.*